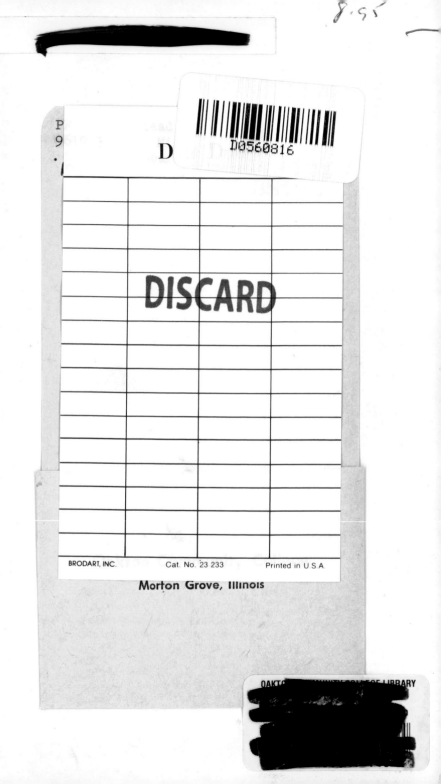

MISS HERBERT

Miss Herbert

(The Suburban Wife)

·

Christina Stead

RANDOM HOUSE

NEW YORK

Library of Congress Cataloging in Publication Data
Stead, Christina, 1902–
Miss Herbert (the suburban wife).
I. Title.
PZ3.S7986Mi [PR9619.3.S75] 823 75–40561
ISBN 0–394–40517–X

Manufactured in the United States of America
9 8 7 6 5 4 3 2

For my friend
Cyrilly Abels

1

*Playtime,
Maytime*

DR. LINDA MACK had brought the five girls down to her Devon cottage in the car: it was June and the weather was fair. The cottage lay under fields and between two wooded spurs on a slope that ran steeply to the hidden sea. It was a stone cottage with a barn, the trees were very old; above, the high Atlantic sky streamed west.

They were five friends and a stranger. These five friends were old girls of Miss Appleyard's school on the south coast; the stranger had gone to a high school in the North. Dr. Mack was thirty-two and the others about twenty-five. This was a farewell party. Dr. Mack had taken a post in the Pacific Islands; Eleanor Brent, a handsome, athletic blonde, was leaving for a pleasure trip round the world. Dr. Mack saw that each one needed help. The stranger, a dark-haired, thin-faced girl named Janet Jackson, had given up science teaching and had become a typist in London "so that she could take a job on the stage at any time." But though she struggled she was unlucky: she had unfortunate relations with people. Linda Mack was small and fair; at first sight, rather like china, brittle with a flat surface, but she shone when she argued, with little white teeth, and clear blue eyes behind flashing spectacles. Vina de Saiter, with a thick pale braid round her oval head, looked like an abbess and had a commanding drawl; she had been for many years in a wheelchair, a result of infantile paralysis, and had already at the age of twenty-seven given up medicine and law for want of funds and become a teacher in private schools. She intended to become a Labour M.P. Vicky Ingle, a tall dark woman with a soft bosom and rounded hips but long thin arms, and an old-maidish look, was a sociologist, who had just finished a study of workers' nutrition; her special grant had run out and she was looking for a job. Mary Bird was a lively little woman with a small high solid bust and shoulders like an old-fashioned doll, was reddish with auburn hair; she looked determined, had a loud, clear voice and seemed steady enough in her profession, a secretary to women's organizations. She lived alone with her mother who had been a great fighter, a suffragette and free thinker, "a Darwinian," she said. The mother had married late, had one child, was deserted by her husband and had gradually become confused. Mentally now, she led an up-and-down existence between truths of the New Testament and progressive truths. "Mary will never get away," the others said; "I am sure Mary will get away," said Dr. Mack.

In the holidays, in all their years since Miss Appleyard's school, these girls, with others, had walked, camped and talked together, slept in hostels, tents and old inns, in houseboats and sleeping bags, in fields, woods, by riverbanks and on the sea beaches. They had belonged to the same societies as students, and all the time with intense interest and energy "pulled to pieces" (as they said) their own puzzles, women's worries, mankind's problems. They were happy together, like children who have grown up together; they had "wrestled and lain down together." The group was smaller now: some had married and become housewives—those seemed faded. When they had children, they took on a new sort of life. These girls were getting older and one of the things they discussed, naïvely, earnestly and rather sadly, was their hope of marriage. They felt their own strengths kept them together, and their clear understanding of their fate; but what was their future? They were aimful, yet their future seemed vague, dubious: they were "neither happy nor unhappy."

Eleanor Brent was different. A nobly built beauty, playing-fields champion, excellent student, loved at home, admired at school and by men, she had been happy and confident always. Her future was planned, too; she was "an engaged girl." But with all this, she was unsettled; she was only quite happy with women friends. She had attended plenty of discussion and study groups, and meetings, with men. There she said what she thought correct, depending on her textbooks, afraid to accept any idea she had no authority for. She sat, swinging her beautiful legs, saying things in a loud gallant voice or a small thoughtful sweet one; she smoked and laughed. She wanted to be taken seriously; her beauty did not save her from sharp comment and even sarcasm; so she tried to be as correct as possible. But with the women she was at ease: she could say the simple things that came into her head. And then, because she was much the handsomest of all, she was happy with them: she did not have to think of her beauty; it was just a natural thing, like the calm broad ocean, a sunny morning, a happy life.

That Saturday, after morning mists, they had the sun all day. They had been for a swim at the beach which lay down the valley. Now they sat in the kitchen, which looked seaward, and sang sea chanteys. Five women sat on wooden chairs in a horseshoe from the fireplace and around the table, and on the table Eleanor lay, like a starfish, and waving her arms and legs in time, singing in a clear, trained voice. "O, Shenandoah, I love your daughter—" Her pretty hands floated about in the air; her ring flashed. She sighed, put her arms under her head and shook her hair loose; it flowed over the edge of the table, long and fair.

"Still wet," she said in an ordinary voice, then sang out: "I had a glorious swim, and oh, darlings, I feel so perfect; don't think about eating yet, my pets—I'm staying here, relaxing." They sang again, then she said, "Oh, to think that in four days from now I'll be on the sea!"

"Do you think it's right to leave your fiancé?" said Mary Bird. Someone, half ashamed, muttered that she might lose him.

"I couldn't lose Robert: it's all agreed upon," Eleanor said negligently. "I told him if he made me wait, I was within my rights to look about me. And he agreed. You see, we've got the future all planned. And it is so lovely to look forward and know what life is going to be." She stretched dreamily.

"Did you hear about Tom Dickon marrying that nurse?" Vicky Ingle asked her.

"Yes, poor Tom!" said Eleanor, "it's queer to think I wore his ring. Our views were too dissimilar; it was just as well it all came out in the noisy exhibitionist way it did."

"What happened?" someone asked.

"Oh, Tom was just about the most eligible man in first year and Eleanor hooked him—"

"We got on so well together on the dance floor," murmured Eleanor, "and I thought his ideas were just half-baked student's socialism. I took no notice." She laughed indulgently. "And so they were. But of course when they got him into a May Day march and there was a brawl with the police, the Senate couldn't overlook it; and I expect Tom didn't want them to. He had a will to fail. I suppose he felt that later on he wouldn't have the guts"—she bit into the word—"the guts to stand up to the real challenges of life."

"I think he meant it, though I don't agree with him," Dr. Mack said. "Tom thought we were learning nothing about real people, real life. I agreed, but argued that school is a necessary discipline. He felt he'd go through his classes and come out a stuffed shirt at the other end."

"Yes, that was it; he knew in his guts that his socialism wasn't so," Eleanor said indifferently.

"I'm sure I saw you once," suddenly said Janet Jackson, like a direct thrust, "you were Lady Teazle; a friend, a girl friend, took me to see the dramatic society's show."

Eleanor turned her head, sat up and looked for the first time at Janet. "That was the night I became engaged to Tom Dickon." She laughed.

"The nurse is seven years older than Tom," said Vicky Ingle. The girls agreed that the nurse must have been too strong for his weak nature and so had used her influence over him. They discussed the wrongs and rights of it; a woman had no right to marry a younger man, "a woman always ages first . . . it's a sort of mother-and-son relation . . ." But what induced Tom Dickon to yield? "He couldn't possibly love her."

"Tom's just weak," said Eleanor. "He has good impulses."

They ended by supposing that he felt some obligation or gratitude towards the nurse.

"I heard they lived together several months first," said Mary Bird. That explained it.

"But I don't see that," Eleanor objected. "If a man lives with a woman first, he can't respect her. That wouldn't explain it; just the opposite."

"You might say it's a kind of punishment: a poetic revenge for throwing up his career, the university and Eleanor," Vicky Ingle said.

"My dear, I returned his ring to him as soon as he came out of prison," Eleanor said.

Most of them agreed there was nothing else for her to do; "He must have expected it."

"I think a girl ought to stand by her fiancé in trouble," said Vina de Saiter.

"When he goes to jail?" they asked in horror.

"Dear little Vina, our gallant little extremist," said Eleanor.

"Once he's broken the law, he's outside the pale," someone remarked.

"But suppose he did it for what he thought right?" said Mary Bird. "My mother was in jail as a suffragette."

"Oh, let's play Truth for a change," said Vicky Ingle. "Ell, what was your first sexual experience? I mean, the very first inkling you had. Of course, none of us has real sexual experience, but nowadays they call all kinds of vague embryonic stirrings sexual experiences."

Eleanor gave a silvery laugh, stretching her swan's-neck arms high above her head in the tangles of her hair. "Let Linda Mack begin."

This was a joke, because Linda Mack had always denied that there were any sexual feelings; it was part of her severely chaste, rational system. She had a delightful voice, delicate but clear, each beautifully uttered word separate, tones like the ringing of many fine wine glasses. She said cheerfully, "Well, until a few months ago I said that there were no sexual feelings—at any rate I had had none—and I felt we were allowing ourselves to be imposed upon. I thought the poets had invented it all; and then parents—for the sake of marrying us off and getting us out of the way. Though my dear parents did no such thing. You know my mother married again, and my stepfather already had a son. Last February my stepbrother Charles sailed to start life in Canada, and on the boat just when the bell was ringing I kissed him; tears came into my eyes and I had a feeling which must be what you mean by a sexual feeling."

"Eleanor now."

"No, Eleanor last."

But Eleanor now hugged her knees in her arms, and blowing out her red unpainted lips she pushed the words with dainty elegance between her teeth. "When I was just twelve, some boys took me into the bushes and played with me. When I told Mumsy, she explained to me that my body was a temple that no one must ever touch till I married. She told me my husband would have a golden key to unlock the door." She laughed good-naturedly. "I believed that literally and for years it was linked in my mind with the Taj Mahal. Mother always thought it a beautiful tribute to a wife. I used to dream about seeing it. There was a picture in the back of our geography book. I imagined a woman's body lying inside all those marble screens, wrapped round and round in white muslin."

[8]

"She wasn't wrong; there are two sides to sex. The Taj Mahal —and the boys in the bushes," Mary Bird said. She continued with her experience. "Two beetles were joined; I pulled them apart and it gave me a horrid but hot feeling."

Janet Jackson said at the age of three she had suffered jealousy because Dickie, a neighbor's boy, aged four, had preferred Joan, her two-year-old cousin. "I remember the pain inside me to this day." She continued by telling them that on her brother's third birthday, several little cousins had gathered for a party. Led by a pale, thin-faced, boyish girl of eleven, assisted by a beautiful boy of twelve, they had played an infamous, sadistic game called Butcher's Shop. She had been selected for the first carcass. She lay on her belly and the boy pulled up her shirt and down her drawers. The others were customers and called for what they had heard their mothers order: "Some lamb chops—a leg of lamb—" and the boy butcher with a stick carved the joint in her flesh, while the customer pretended to receive the meat. An aunt walked in; the little girl was level with her buttoned boots. The aunt's bluff roundnesses continued up to her brown puffed-out hair where she stood against the sun. "I never could stand well-developed women and perhaps it was since then. Yet I am sure she was graceful; I have a distinct impression of her small belt. The truth is, I never did care much for women of any sort."

The cold rude words made them all change attitude; they stopped their game and got up.

But Eleanor cried, "Oh, I think we've had a jolly good down-to-earth understanding talk and that's what is so good about Linda's weekends. We get our teeth into things; we dissect too much perhaps, but we do get into the blood and guts of life, don't we!"

The girls went out onto the verandah, where, led by Eleanor, they sat whistling, singing and hallooing with shrieks of laughter, to occasional foot-travelers seen between the high hedges or on the path along the stream. Bent, bony old laborers and a tall, doll-faced, straw-headed youth with a horse, they shouted at. They rushed down to the gate to see a herd of cows tramp by, one cow heavy with calf swinging slowly along last of all. They discussed animals' labor, the things they had seen and then strung back, pushing together through the high weeds, Eleanor frolicking round them, embracing one and another. She missed her footing in a hidden rut and fell in the grass. When she got back to the house she complained of nettle stings, and they went into the kitchen again while she pulled open and then pulled off her loose, neat clothing. First she stood, with her blouse open showing them a red rash under her breasts. "Look, the nettle ran right into my blouse. Have you got anything for it, Linda?"

"I always let it alone," said Mary Bird. "It's true that ointment may spread the poison."

"But look," said Eleanor, rolling up her sleeves to the shoulders. Then she began to undress, taking off her things, with measured graceful movements, as she looked at little spots of red on her arms, back, waist, thighs. She undressed completely, in case it was not nettle rash but some insect, and stood with the women round her, looking at her skin, unselfconscious, quietly sparkling, when they took (all but Janet) the attitude of maids-in-waiting. Janet, ashamed of this nakedness, went out to the verandah. Inside, Venus, in her young maturity, was examining her breasts, and comparing them with the breasts of the others; and in a low tone, she was asking them their advice. The advertisements offered creams, massage, types of garments to develop the breasts. "Men like a developed figure." What should she do? she asked Dr. Mack.

"But there's nothing wrong with you," said the doctor, puzzled.

She dressed again in fresh clothes, standing, just as calm, in the middle of them, and the discussions went on, about what men liked in a woman, what they detested.

"Oh, your breasts will be bigger someday," one of the girls said, laughing. Eleanor blushed. They went on talking with the frankness of the swimming bath and gymnasium. Dr. Mack with sweet reasonableness declared the Venus ideal was a sensual male's dream but the full-blown figure of Venus a handicap to a woman in active life. She herself had a love of great distances: she felt thousands of miles of air and mountain and plain in her body. She wanted to conquer space with her own limbs. "I like to be a woman, but I think I'm lucky to be so small a woman; my needs are less." For years she had studied her own economy, practiced fasting, nightwatching, endurance. She had studied nutrition and made inquiries of health experts and faddists. "How medieval our eating paraphernalia is," she said now. "Tureens, fish knives, pots and pans, dishes, the variety of glasses and spoons. All we need is a dried pill the size of a grain of yeast—perhaps a grain of yeast would do!" During the years she and these girls had gone walking together they had witnessed her experiments and seen her calculations. How far could she walk on a piece of chocolate, a banana, a "handful of dates," a bowl of rice, a walnut, a hard-boiled egg? She knew now. "We eat as the sot drinks, anything and everything, wastefully and coarsely." She had reduced her traveling rig to a few pieces of thin silk and wool, which, with the concentrated foods she had decided upon, would all fit into a small rucksack. At home, in her comfortable middle-class home, where she was trusted, admired, treated with the greatest consideration, she had carried out other experiments in austerity.

This was their last meeting, when all would be together. Dr. Mack had established herself in practice with money left by a grandfather. She belonged to a well-to-do Whig family, generous, proud, with a severe, altruistic cult of personality. She had begun saving money at once for her double life aim. She was a passionate patriot. Her first aim was to work in every part of the British Commonwealth, "so that my opinion will be honestly my own, based on my own knowledge." The second aim was to see every part of the world, "so that I won't use a name like Popocatepetl," she said laughing, "without knowing exactly what it means." And yet, she would not remain away too long: "the country belongs to those who spend their lives living in it." She was a champion of many liberal causes, of free trade, minority rights, social services, nationalization of industry. She wanted to burn up her life in services; but she had, they knew, another hope: to find some greater cause, the best of all, and bind her life to it, as a living body is bound to a stake. This aspiration in her lively, gold-shining little body, expressed with her dry sweetness, made Dr. Mack their leader: they allowed her to question and teach them.

And now, to Eleanor, she said that her weakness was that she had no aim. Eleanor's voice rang out and her pretty hand, balanced like a group of small living bodies at the end of her white arm, made a stage gesture. "I have no aim? But my pet! I want to marry and have my own home and have my children and then I want to be a person in my own right! I'm going to write, Linda darling! I don't want to swim rivers and root out fever from native villages, perhaps, like you; but I do have my own projects among the cities of the plain."

"But those are not your projects," said Dr. Mack smiling. "Society gave them to you and you meekly accepted them."

"You and I, Linda darling, are very different people. Society grows fat on your studying tropical diseases and on me being a simpler kind of woman, happily normal, Linda darling. And oh, I do feel that it ought all to be plain sailing. I know what I want and it's all planned; I believe I'm going to be happy. And I hope all you dear ones are, too. Why not? Society wants us to be happy, doesn't it? And it's our natural right. So why shouldn't it all chime in together? 'In harmony, in heavenly harmony, this universal frame began,' " she sang. "I think if we follow our instincts, we and society too will be best served."

The next week the same group and many others, were at the wharf for Dr. Mack, who was leaving for her post in the Pacific Islands. And then, later, one or two of them lost in a great crowd of relatives and suburban people to farewell Eleanor. Charming, tall, satin-limbed girl, in soft yellow silk with a satin belt of braided ribbons, at the moment when a thousand paper ribbons were still frail bridges between herself and the land, Eleanor looked around and found a stranger, an agreeable man, beside her. They smiled and spoke; in their comradeship as travelers they were already closer than they were to the wharf people.

"So it began and so it went on," Eleanor wrote. "From the very first it was all barriers down." She sat at the captain's table and by the second night was going everywhere with the agreeable dark-faced stranger. At Panama she sent a cable to Robert Ware, her fiancé, breaking her engagement; and to her parents she cabled that she was to be married as soon as she returned. But she broke this engagement at Hong Kong for the sake of a gay young commercial attaché, with whom she thought she might be in love; and "after India," she had the curious thrilling experience of midnight cabin parties, "much more adult than the bed-game we played in the dramatic society," with a clever, vicious, middle-aged Indian civil servant with the bronze, the small mustache, neat head and clothes of a certain trademarked Englishman of class. And when the ship reached England again, she did not go up by train but by car—thus avoiding her parents' welcome—with a young colonial businessman; and she lived with him for a month in a London flat, telling her parents she had got a job *au pair* as companion-secretary with a wealthy Mrs. Whitney. She went to see them several times and casually lied and put them off, not much caring whether they saw through her lies or not. But she felt too active and intelligent for the idle mistress life and began taking correspondence lessons in writing with a Mr. Beresford Banes who ran a Fleet Street literary agency. She enjoyed the night-clubbing and dancing, though she did not dance well with her new companion and she needed new clothes. Suddenly, she made a scene in a Piccadilly hotel, and went home to her parents, by the last suburban train. She found they were surprised to see her and thought she should not have thrown up her job. They did not think her world cruise had improved her.

"You got engaged to a man without letting your mother see him; and then dropped him in a few weeks! That isn't like you."

She was restless at home, and the only things she enjoyed were the literary lessons which she worked at all day. She refused to go back to work in her father's office.

"Daddy, I adored working for you, but I must strike out for myself. It's high time, my pet."

"Perhaps it is," he said with a tired friendly smile. He was a tall, fair, good-looking man, with a loose graceful stride; they had always been friends—he called her "mate" and "pal." Her mother, a middle-sized, pretty, fair woman, a former Miss Herbert, lady-like, decisively petty, had always said, "Ell and I are like sisters." In the few months she had been abroad, her parents seemed to have made lives for themselves; Eleanor felt left out. For the first time, she realized that she had quite grown up. "Waiting for marriage is an eater-up of girls' time," she said.

"Two broken engagements in ten months!" said her mother looking at her bitterly. "People are talking in the family. I never thought I'd have any trouble with you. I was always so proud of you. You've got the Herbert looks. A lady keeps her word. You'll get a bad reputation—men will think you're not to be taken seriously, women will say you can't hold a man."

"Oh, Mumsy, I can get married anytime. I want to be sure of happiness—Robert was a youthful mistake, now I want to be careful."

"The trouble with you is you never know where you're going! Robert was the right man for you. I liked Robert. And he was a gentleman too: in all the weekends we had him here with us, I never saw him treat you with familiarity. I could trust him. I don't like the sound of those men on the boat."

Her mother of course knew how to wound her. The suggestion that she was aimless offended her and she scrutinized her mother's face, seeing it as it was now. She was "a Herbert"; she was like Eleanor's plain sister, though she had been pretty and her features were neat. She had frizzled fair hair which had bleached and silvered but was lively still. She had, like Eleanor, an oval head, a squared forehead with rather deep-set eyes under swallows'-wing brows. But the eyes were pale blue and tired; the face also looked flat and totally without imagination. Imagination (Eleanor thought) was that interesting but unexpected quality of hers which disconcerted some men, but she was glad of it, she meant to make her living by it.

"I wish you had come along with me on the boat ride, Mumsy, my pet," she said gently. "You would have had the time of your life and seen what lovely innocent fun it all was. And I feel so much better equipped for life."

She was restless, and when July came she told her parents she was going to take a long walking trip around England, Wales and perhaps Scotland, with Vicky and Mary. "We'll take rucksacks and thumb rides and hike and sleep in hostels; I'll get wholesomely tired and try to see myself in perspective and then, darlings, I'll come back and settle down for good. Only one thing! I must get a little attic room to myself and concentrate on writing. That's the only way to do it, that's the classic way."

Her mother begged her to take a room in a students' hostel run by the religious society she belonged to. Eleanor promised to look into it, but thought she would be better "without pervasive influences."

But before she left for the walking tour, her mother had written a letter to Dr. Robert Ware, who was working in a northern hospital. He got leave, came to London and stayed at their home. Eleanor and he had walks and talks together; one evening they arrived home long after supper was finished. Because she saw no reason not to and she dearly loved accord, Eleanor had once more become engaged to Robert. He was a small, tight-faced man with a fine Roman nose, soft straight eyes and brows, long irregular lips and a long scar on his cheek. He looked very determined; this look and his scar had aroused her admiration and loving pity long ago. Except for a brief time, after Panama, she had worn his ring, a large square-cut emerald in platinum which was much admired. When Robert left for the north, she went to see him off, kissed him with tears in her eyes; and within a few hours had herself taken a train north, to work in a big hotel near the station in a northern city. She was now said to be on her walking tour. She had made up her mind it was necessary for her to see "the underdogs' life" so that she could write from first hand. Because she was strong, she worked fairly hard, but she would also throw herself on one of the beds, made or unmade, and laugh to herself, thinking of her picaresque life. She was the real thing; she had guts; she was delighted too at her unlooked-for success with all the men, the squalid corridor and bedroom hugs, tussling and slapping. She turned her inviting eyes on every new male: she felt free, in her rights, happy and brave. In a gay, healthy riot, she tried her powers on the kitchen men, the waiters, the travelers, on the manager, on the men in the delivery vans; they laughed (some did), they looked sideways, but they came to her. She was at the height of her powers; no man could resist her, she felt. In her off-hours, she would walk to the station or along a side street where travelers took hasty meals in fish bars after the station restaurant and coffee shop shut; she got what she called "the signaling sign of sex" from many. At other times, in the kitchen, sitting round with the staff, hearing scandal, laughing over smut for which she had a new liking, hearing herself teased and talked about, and "understanding" their troubles, she lived in a romantic dream, full of ardent hopes and guilty foolishness. She learned to see men better, she thought. There were men who kissed and fondled her: kitchen hands who tried to go for walks with her in their best clothing, pathetic jackets and trousers which didn't match, their greasy, floury hair combed; porters, strong-backed men with broken feet and iron-tired faces—A long time, she thought gleefully, since they had a chance at a ripe peach like me. There were young, gliding, angular and poor-looking waiters; she didn't like them but she felt obliged to induce them to move towards her in all the mirrors of the dining room. She handled heavy bundles of dirty linen and clean linen and had "one grand riot of beastliness, so that I will know the whiff of it all my life. And my goodness, how it's going to pay me back in good crisp poundnotes for my back-breaks and the times I've been near to vomit."

At the end of six weeks she was discharged "because of the cook's jealousy," she told her friends. "They had taken me off the rough work and put me into the housekeeper's room to do fine mending: it was necessary work and they had no one so the manager tried me out and found me good." She twinkled. "But one of the cooks, a little squab, with the figure of a gray dumpling, got her knife into me because she thought the manager was her cup of tea."

To please her mother, Eleanor now took a room in the student hostel. The hostel room was a cubicle at the end of a narrow corridor with wooden walls. It was divided by a thin plank partition from the next cubicle, in which lived a man of twenty-five named Mr. Bede, so the little maid said. She could hear his pen scratching, she could hear him groan in nightmares, his cot bumped the wall against which her narrow cot was placed—every movement in both beds was recorded by the thin wire mattresses. A window looked out on a bus thoroughfare. There was a mantelpiece on which stood her alarm clock and a photograph of her fiancé, Robert Ware, in a silver frame. There was a small table near the door with an ink-stained red and white cloth, and on this was her portable typewriter, with a directory and a dictionary. In the folder were some routine articles she was doing for the Banes Literary Agency on general themes—child care, tree pruning, jam making, English weather, difficulties of Continental travel for the English, street improvement. She copied the text out of encyclopedias, newspapers and out-of-date magazines which she picked up in Charing Cross Road, and then rewrote it a little. These articles were often sold as the original work of needy people of title and rank who were on the books of the Agency. They sold their names for various sums, from half a guinea to three guineas.

Early one morning, Rita, the "funny little maid," had brought her a letter forwarded from home. It was Robert's answer to her letter giving her change of address. The long years of study and overwork were changing him, it seemed to Eleanor—she had merely glanced with boredom through the pages, written closely with a fine pen in a slanting hand with uneven spaces between the words and a hideous tail to his *g*'s, a repellent handwriting it was to her now.

Dear Eleanor,

You have drawn heavily on my indulgence, but let that pass: it is in the past, you promised. But all things considered, on no account must you live alone in London in a boarding house or room. The idea of my future wife living in squalor in a free and easy way in a house where anyone is free to come and go, is distasteful to me. It is quite impossible for me to give my consent. Your best plan, if you cannot stay with your parents and must pursue this fantasy, is to go and see my aunt, Mrs. Adelaide Gideon, who runs an agency of the highest reputation for governesses, teachers and home-help. You have a good degree and she will certainly find something for you. You will be able to earn your living, perhaps not in a very brilliant nor satisfying way; but you may acquire some notions of household management and child care, which will, doubtless, be of use to us later on. I don't doubt your good intentions, but appearances must also be in our favor.

Your decision was a surprise and a shock to me; but I am doing my best to be perfectly fair . . .

Please follow my advice . . .

I cannot even begin to express my self-reproach . . . at leaving you alone . . .

You will realize that anxiety about you is bad for my work . . .

Yours affectionately,
Robert

She cried in the end. He did not appreciate her. Her present work was hard grubbing, raking the dust of long-accepted mediocrity, and she was worn with the legwork. There was no honor in it, low pay; she did not sign her own name to her articles. She ate little, slept badly, and could not get up a new idea after hours or days of struggle. She had had so many ideas at school and college, it seemed; now there seemed nothing there inside her head. She idled, read snatches, lay on her bed, looked out at the street—"A street itself is a subject." She worked at her articles in the morning, but there were all sorts of interruptions.

About half past nine every morning, Rita the maid would dart in for the first time. She would run in and out, depending on the whereabouts of the housekeeper and the houseman, her husband.

"Your fingers go very fast, why don't you go in for one of those speed competitions? You get good prizes for them . . . a friend of mine has her B.A. and now she is working in a factory: that's the ups and downs of fortune for you . . . There's a black man upstairs—do you understand, black—from Jamaica." She thought this terribly funny. "He's so cold: He can't get warm. He asked me for more blankets. Oh, look what I found under your pillow! A flea! Ha-ha! Do you believe I found a flea under your pillow? It's a dead flea! I put it under people's pillows just to give them a fright. But you weren't frightened, were you? Some people are frightened of fleas. They think it's—something else. Something else, never mind . . . I have been in places, mind you, where you can wake up and find yourself covered with flea bites, covered, literally. You have to put on two pairs of stockings. Although, I, unfortunately, haven't got two pairs of stockings, not whole stockings but stockings in holes . . . You would make a good nurse, do you know that? You look like a nurse I had in hospital . . ."

Next door the clock was ticking; Eleanor heard Mr. Bede breathing. Last night he had had friends in. They talked freely, and once or twice they had mentioned her in an appreciative suggestive way that made her blush and laugh with pleasure. Why didn't they ask her in? She would have liked to bounce in and say, "I'm here, talk just as frankly as if I weren't here! I know what you think of me. I'm a good piece of work. Ha-ha. Why don't you kiss me? Gather ye rosebuds, you know." Oh, the slow young man. She lay on her cot and took part in their talks, unseen, unheard.

When Rita came in to clean the room, prettily, holding her duster and broom, she would eagerly begin on the hotel gossip, and then, touchingly: "It's interesting what I tell you, isn't it? Believe me, you see life when you work in a hotel, you see everything. My girl friend and I often talk about what we see. If I could write, I could write a book that would take a whole day to write, about what my girl friend and I see. The blackamoor," she said in a low mysterious voice, beginning to laugh, with her eyes wide open and bending over, as if to make her voice softer, "the blackamoor sleeps in a striped shirt, and he piles blankets over him, and the sheet is quite white; my girl friend thought the black would come off, but it doesn't. You see them in bed, asleep, sometimes; you know all about them—they can't hide anything from me, that's the fun of it."

"Do they kiss you sometimes?" said Eleanor.

"Ah," sighed the maid, not hearing, "but I am sure one of them stole my lunch on Tuesday. I used to cook it downstairs; then Mrs. wouldn't let me do it, they eat there. And I started to bring it in a billycan; my uncle used to cook it for me, but then I had nowhere to heat it, so I started to buy some rolls, and I put it down near the staircase and it disappeared. Who would you say took it? I have a live flea, too: if I find who took it, I'll put it in his bed, and then," she said, beginning to laugh, "when he gets up, he'll be bitten, just as if he'd had a hypo."

"Don't they kiss you?" said Eleanor in a dreamy, oily voice.

"Oh, kiss! Students are muggy kissers and huggers," replied Rita, "just mug and hug; I take no notice. You see life, though," she ended seriously. "My girl friend and I often talk it all over, all about life."

Eleanor would listen patiently, and when Rita went she would begin to type furiously, feeling she had been interrupted. She worked hard rewriting and retyping a little story she had written, entitled "In the Morning," in which a beautiful girl, at the gate of the tennis court, sees the setting sun on her dark-complexioned lover, a Greek (or Italian, or Spaniard). He is much more demonstrative than her English fiancé. She thinks, Theo (or Arturo or Carlos) seems gracious, passionate, responsible, but how would he fit into my pure English background? Children of the sun are unpredictable. Do I want children with black eyes and brows? Theo kisses her with more ardor than respect, though she sees adoration in his face. She gently pushes him aside. She sees respect in his face; his desire ebbs; he is ashamed, and ready to fall at her feet. Yes, she could manage him; but she has the future of others unborn to think of. In the morning of a perfect day she returns to the arms of Peter, the curly-headed Cambridge man.

This story, she was confident, conformed as she had written it, to the set of rules she had extracted from various books on writing and from Mr. Beresford Banes's writing course. A well-typed list of these rules hung above her table and read as follows:

> *Short sentences.*
> *Short paragraphs.*
> *The simple, not the involved.*
> *The concrete for the abstract.*
> *The everyday for the strange.*
> *The direct for the roundabout.*
> *'Ware adjectives!*
> *Pare your prose to the bone.*
> *No editorialising: no crotchets, no politics.*
> *No slogans, no cant, no journalese.*
> *No pluperfects.*
> *Write about what you know.*
> *Time, place, person, all clear.*
> *Simple relations.*
> *Start at the moment of crisis.*
> *Write for your market.*
> *Polish, polish, polish.*

Under this, written in her clear office-hand, between two lines, were the words: SUM TOTAL—S U C C E S S!

Gazing at this card whenever she sat down at her table, Eleanor recaptured her confidence; and she would break off to write to her father, "I am getting my teeth really into it," or, to Robert, "I am settling down to real hard work and feel like a million." She meant it. She had already rewritten the story "In the Morning" twenty-three times, arranging it differently for each "market" and repolishing it according to her rules. It grew simpler, clearer, more barren each time. She was unable to understand why she had no success with it, but she plodded sturdily on. She said to herself, I follow the rules, I am bound to win; and she had business sense. She began to hang about the fringes of literary society, pertinaciously kept up contacts and kept a literary diary. She visited editors, with her charming smiles, her fresh beauty and wearing some furs her mother had given her. She joined a couple of committees where she was sure to meet writers, publishers and people with a name. She was very happy with the great, addressing them, coaxing them with servile unction. She met Mrs. Blanding-Forest, a gay little artist of very small talent who did society portraits; and Mrs. Mallow Bounce, a poetess, a shabby white-haired pudding in upholstery prints, well-to-do, of good family related to the liberal intelligentsia. With Mrs. Blanding-Forest Eleanor was religious and nice, with Mrs. Bounce, a radical—all for love of harmony. She soon found out that these women were enemies; she never mentioned one to the other; but by schoolgirl adulation and an enthusiastic display of ladylike manners, got herself counted a humble friend of each. They were both very small women; each liked to add a young Juno to her train, and for both she did free secretarial work: "It would lead to something." But it was all hard work.

She had a place where she could go to ask advice, where she could stay overnight and find companionship, when this struggle was too much. Eleanor was very fond of Mrs. Appleyard, the sister-in-law of the headmistress of her old school on the south coast, and there she met some members of her old set of friends.

Mrs. Appleyard had got a degree at a time when degrees were rare with women; she was a rationalist. She was now gray-haired, broad and heavy, and spent most of her time indoors, in a deep-seated farm kitchen chair with a wooden back as high as the mantelpiece. The charming house, looking on a private square, was polished and sparkling, furnished with familiar antiques and curios. Old Appleyard girls met there, gossiped, stayed the night. If they were broke they could get a meal there; they could tell their private troubles and get help. There was Diana Cruse, Mrs. Appleyard's adopted daughter, who was managing a small theater; Vina de Saiter, invalid writer; Beryl Bourne, a physician; Georgia, a girl who taught some art subject at Dartington Hall.

At present Diana was at work, and Eleanor, who had been working for three weeks, was chatting with Mrs. Appleyard.

"I am tired, pleasantly lazily tired. At the hotel, Apple, I had a good bout of physical work; now I've been at work in earnest, intellectual work, real slogging, and I feel I've earned a week off, Apple dear," said Eleanor, who had cuddled down into a reclining chair and was swinging her arms and legs about, drawing out the strands of her hair, looking at the ends in the light, smiling and letting the coaxing words ooze in a sugary fashion out of her puffed lips. "I was worn out every evening, and glad to sleep like a farm hand. A farm hand has to pitchfork muck and so had I. I felt justified, though. Real life, no paper shifting, I said to myself. Let me tell you one thing, Apple, never hesitate to give a tip to workers in hotels: they need it and they earn it. You learn that every single thing has a price, a low price, and you expect to be paid, however low the price, and they expect to pay, so it's a bargain. I'm not made to sit on my bottom, Apple, I've got muscles and I like to use them. At least at first I used to revel in the dirty work. I got a kick out of knowing what goes on. One scamp, can you believe it?"—she laughed and then pulled a straight disgusted face and sat up— "did his business in the middle of the floor. Oh, that's not so uncommon. I once knew a girl who said you find out about people in hotels. True. Some of the hotel workers I knew were misanthropes, soured on people—dirty beasts all, they said. But I don't mind anything. I can take anything. I don't mind the hallway hugs and mugs and the whiskery kisses, the spit and polish, not always your spit, but always your polish, the sweet and sour, and the bedrooms after they've been slept in. Better than the tame cats in Mother's New Religious Society. Robert and I used to be tame cats! Oh, Apple, I guess I'm a Wife of Bath, or a Merry Wife of Windsor, I don't mind Falstaff and the buck basket. Oh-ho! You know, I'll never get rid of the gentility you Appleyards taught me at Ladybridge, though—I feel it. I feel that no matter what I'll do, I'm irreversibly a lady and it's a wonderful feeling, Apple dear, for it gives me leave to do anything; it gives me a standard, a set of weights and measures, isn't that so, dear? Anyone who has ever been to a school like Ladybridge is safe for life. But still, look at the fun most of us miss! Oh, what a good time a real gorgeous country Phyllis, big and buxom with skin like a sun-ripened peach, what a good time she has with the ploughboy! She would have been married or at least bedded years ago and had her quiverful already! Look at me! Nearly twenty-six and I haven't had any real good time yet, exercised my rights. For," she said earnestly, turning and looking Mrs. Appleyard in the face, "we do have rights, don't we? Each human being has his rights as a human being! I loved my girlhood; I worked hard, played hard, Apple, I shirked absolutely jolly well nothing. And now I've made up my mind to enjoy my adult rights to the full. Am I right, Mrs. Appleyard? Don't you agree? Oh, I am full of plans and longings. Do you think Robert is right to have made this agreement with me? You know we have agreed to wait till we are thirty to marry, and to be faithful to each other now just as if we had married. Of course, that is lovely, isn't it?"

Mrs. Appleyard's blue eyes roved in her broad biscuit-colored face and she looked through the windows, and at the old china, the polished copper, the vase saying *Rapee,* the blue rug, at the small figures on a balcony in the distance, the birds.

Eleanor coaxed, "We made a promise to each other and we

must keep it to the letter, mustn't we, darling?"

"Of course, a promise is sacred; a promise of that sort does not even bear discussion with a third person."

"But, Apple, my pet, don't you feel women have rights of their own? I know you believed in women's rights."

"I do still believe in them."

"Yes, I know. So do I," cried Eleanor, springing up. "Women's rights. Yes, why not! Life to the full. When I talk things over with you," she continued, her beautiful, rosy face taking on an unpleasant chubby look, "everything falls into place, I see straight and think straight." In a merry, childish tone she began to run over all the things she would do, what she would tell her parents, whether Apple would receive letters for her here till she got settled. "There's no question of a double life, Apple, it's just that I simply must find myself. And a single girl must lead a double life!" She laughed gaily.

"What do you mean?"

Eleanor gave her a cross look; she thought this hypocritical. "Well, you've heard of James von Ulse, the count who's in so many of the New Religious Society's activities?"

"A little, I just know the name."

"Well, he's asked me to go to the country with him for the weekend. And I'm going, Apple. He's taking me in his sports car to a smart country hotel, and he's going to register me as the countess. He isn't married, in any case."

"What about Robert?"

"But it's not that kind of thing," she protested. "It's just off the record. I won't wear his ring; and I feel it's my right to have this experience. The only thing that worries me is men don't like inexperienced women; I'm worried about that. But I suppose it will be all right once he gets me there." She looked searchingly at Mrs. Appleyard.

Mrs. Appleyard thought she should return Robert's ring to him, but Eleanor was surprised and protested: "But this is just according to your principles, your own dear high principles, don't you see? Freedom of women—it isn't free love, which I know you don't approve of, but just the right of every individual to taste life. Don't you think I too have my right to my own little scrap of happiness? And besides I have a right: do you know the Count has taken at least half a dozen girls from the Society to the country. Everyone knows it, no one bothers about it. In fact, I have been too much in my shell. Although my parents never dream of such things, the fact is, they do go on and that is real life, and I have been torn between wanting to keep the dear things in their pretty little dream world and living my own life. And women are like medlars, as Shakespeare says."

"Ell, why don't you go back to your job for the Banes Agency? That's what you're suited for. What about that ghosting job for the botanist who was writing his memoirs?"

"Oh, Apple, things did not turn out quite as I expected with Mr. Toblet, the botanist. I used to get there every day at nine, work till one, then they brought me lunch and at two I went to work again till five. The man opened the door, the maid brought the lunch; but the housekeeper was his sister, a dark, fleshy, suspicious woman I disliked at first sight. You know what a worker I am, Apple. She used to come in every so often but she always saw me with my files and my chapter schemes, writing away. When we were working together, she would come in and sit there for a while. She had some other name, a half-sister perhaps: and I wonder if she was a sister after all. Now, that is. You know I am rather naïve: while I was there, I treated her as his sister. I hinted to him once or twice about my staying there, for that had been part of the bargain, but he was evasive. I simply did my work and left. At the beginning, Apple, the first interview which we had in a room at the agency, he promised me all kinds of things, by word and hint, too. When I left, I felt like a servant dismissed in disgrace; and in fact, I hadn't a reference, had I? I wasn't mentioned on the title page. No one would know. That's the devil of these ghosting jobs. It makes me mad when I read about Mr. Toblet's style, his research work. In the Foreword he says, 'My thanks are due to so-and-so and Blank and Smith and Miss Eleanor Brent who arranged the bibliography.' " She laughed and threw herself down on the carpet near Mrs. Appleyard's feet. "Oh, I don't really mind, Apple darling. It's all experience in the long run; but the devil of it is the cheating."

"You mean using your work?"

"No, no! Why," she cried, sitting up and getting rosy, "he told me I was the finest-looking girl he'd ever seen and that we'd get along like a house on fire; and that I wasn't to pay room rent, I was to stay with him, he had a housekeeper who would look after me like his own sister. He took me out to dinner, we danced and he gave me a handbag from Mappin and Webb's to seal the bargain."

"Why don't you go back to regular work with the agency, if you're afraid of the contacts you get ghosting?"

"I don't know, dear," said Eleanor, stretching herself out like Gemini in the Zodiac, "I am so sorry for the poor dears, though some of them try their airs and graces on me. Sometimes the titles on file, as we call them, live so wretchedly—one dusty room, teacups, plates, a basin. Some are stiff and embarrassed, some chatty and embarrassed, some just greedy-needy. Some," she said idly, looking at the ceiling, and teasing out the strands of her hair, "are pigs. I've had to sit half an hour or more in some stuffy sitting room because Madam is at tea: and I wasn't even offered a cup. But she was obliged to see me in the end, though I was an inky journalist, for it was my article and she had to give her signature."

"What shabby souls!"

"And shabby clothes, too, Apple," said Eleanor, sitting up. "Oh, I don't mind the absurd dears, it's all experience; but I don't, no, I won't be snubbed that way. I'll go to Mrs. Gideon's Agency, Robert's Aunt Adelaide, you know. Robert wants me to governess, I'll give it a try. Fortunes have been made governessing."

"I never heard that," said Mrs. Appleyard, laughing. "I've been a governess and I liked it, though in the end I had to give it up, for the children simply exhausted me. First, I encouraged their young minds to limber up and then I was half dead from their crawling all over my mind, sucking out the knowledge. Everything was new to them, root, branch and leaf! It's exciting; and you're young and very strong. And very lovely. I think children should look at beautiful adults. They look so closely at you, you can see their remembering, considering cat's-eyes. Sometimes I'd feel ashamed, but you need not. You have a beautiful face, Eleanor, my dear girl, don't be foolish. Men can't help looking at you; don't let it make you reckless."

"Ah, dear, I know the fine line dividing a good time from libertinism. Don't worry about me. I'll never do anything you wouldn't approve of, my sweet."

"But, then, what about Count von Ulse? Do you love him?"

"I don't know," she said coyly, "but I should find out, shouldn't I?"

"Well, then you have decided to go away with him?"

"I must find out if he is sincere, mustn't I? If he will really call me his Countess, at a hotel, that is quite serious, isn't it? Of course, I intend to go no farther; we'll stay in different rooms, of course. You see, it's a rule with men, to keep them in doubt, isn't it?"

"But then you are fooling the Count."

"Oh, I doubt very much that any woman could fool the Count; waste no tears on him, my pet. Of course, my parents don't know and Mother would probably die of horror if she heard it, for the Count is her beau ideal, she's sweet on him herself—always in innocence, dear Apple, of course, you know what a perfect sweet Mummy is. But you must know that there is a secret society in the New Society consisting of all the girls the Count has taken to the country or to his town flat—don't be horrified, darling, you yourself believe in women's freedom, now—and they call themselves the Harem of the Count. They won't let me in! I have to qualify. So I am meeting the Count with his sports car right in front of the Baker Street Meeting Rooms and some of the girls will be there to check up. They have a secret grip, and a brooch they wear. That's why I want to go."

"I can't make you out, Eleanor—you simply have no morals."

"What do you mean?" she sang out querulously. "You yourself don't believe in morals, Mrs. Appleyard. You always said domestic women were treated as cattle, they should be free. They used to be sold like slaves in England till the middle of the nineteenth century, isn't that so? Well, I'm striking a blow for freedom. The so-called moral system is just imposed on women by men, isn't it? Well, I'm asserting my rights and my freedom."

Eleanor was very heated, for Mrs. Appleyard had become stern.

"You are a wanton, Ell."

"Apple, that's hypocritical."

Eleanor loved this kind of debate. She soon cooled down and assumed flattering poses and tones of voice, for she was very fond of Mrs. Appleyard and all she stood for. At night Eleanor fought the battle over again, seeing her own points clearer, and she was so puzzled by what she called "Apple's dual attitude" that she tackled her about it the next day.

"But, Apple, it's no secret that your Diana goes to bed with Thomas."

"Diana and Thomas are in love: they are not philandering."

"But there's no difference; in physical fact, in reality, it's the same. Words don't decide these things, but facts."

"Everyone knows the difference."

"There is no difference at all. If Diana is clean and sweet, so am I."

She argued about it to the last minute before going to the country with James von Ulse. When she returned she hurried to ask her old friend's advice.

"I hope you enjoyed yourself," said Mrs. Appleyard.

"It very nearly was a flop. Of course I told James I was a virgin; it's no business of his and I thought it wiser. But oh, Apple, it's funny, things go by opposites; the first night he merely amused himself with me and disappointed me terribly, and when I asked why, he said because I was a virgin. Naturally, I saw to it that the second night I earned the right to join the Harem. I didn't feel I could merely pretend. Besides, it was my right, wasn't it? But even the second night, oh, heigh-ho, such is life, wasn't worth a penny: he did nothing for me. He fooled me. I told him he was a sham Lothario, I was so angry."

Mrs. Appleyard was so angry with her that she turned pale; Eleanor was in a querulous mood. "I'm cheated and you scold me; Diana does just as she pleases and she's living under your very roof. You can't have it both ways, Apple, my pet. You just capriciously call one 'love' and the other 'carnal pleasure.' But carnal pleasure isn't love; you oughtn't to give it that name. The physical thing is the thing. You can't say the same sexual act is black one time and white another. Either it's wrong or it's right. Where's your logic, Apple? Love is respect and sex is lust."

"You're drifting, Ell, my darling girl, don't you see it?" And Mrs. Appleyard gave her a good talking-to. Eleanor listened with gentle pleasure, went and washed her hair and in the afternoon had her photographs taken in the nude by a photographer who took all the girls in the Count's Harem.

She wanted to see the Count again and other men as well. She was restricted at the hostel, so she moved out and found a room in town. She had made good contacts through the Banes Agency and thought, in spite of initial troubles, she would soon know her way about in literature. She had got tired of the posting out of her own original story; the agency legwork seemed easier.

Her room was a pleasant back room in a lodging house in Camden Town. She did casual work for Banes's Agency, deviling articles out of an old encyclopedia and correcting students' work for the correspondence course in writing. She soon made up her mind to begin her own correspondence course, tired of the low pay and boredom of deviling; and she liked the fun of reading new and amateur MSS. She could stay at home when she pleased, write when she pleased, and save on fares, food and clothes. Saving on food would be good for her figure, which was getting larger; walking to save fares was healthy.

Her trouble was clothes. Sometimes, now, she had to refuse invitations because she had not the right clothes and she could no longer be bothered to sew for herself as she and her mother had always done, thinking handmade clothes "nicer than shop clothes." She had to have a couple of evening dresses and a cloak because she went out three afternoons or evenings a week to work as professional partner in a dancing studio. She might go to dinner and the theater several times with the same man. In the end, though, it became cheaper and more convenient to go to the movies, where it was dark and she could wear a plain dress; or to let the men call upon her. She had a couple of presentable Chinese gowns and some Indian scarves.

She got up late but would go into town several times a week to carry the students' corrected work back to the office and to pick up new work. She learned several little tricks for saving money. If a suitable man spoke to her in the bus, she would strike up a conversation with him, a gay, friendly chat, with a very ladylike air; and so she sometimes had her bus fare paid and might be taken out to lunch or afternoon tea. Occasionally she allowed some of these men to call upon her, just to see how they behaved themselves. But she preferred the men who were sent to her with introductory letters, or even just her address in a notebook, by old student friends now in the provinces or abroad. She had had an affair with a Swiss student of economics who always sent his younger friends to visit her now. She preferred such men. They belonged to her class and sort; she could use old university phrases with them; she felt there was no harm in making love, if they could first refer to Bertrand Russell, Bosanquet, Whitehead. It gave her confidence in herself: she felt she was still moving in intellectual circles and was respected for her opinions. She kept a few of her old textbooks in a little trunk, and sometimes, after the man had gone, she would sit dreaming for a while of the fine dialogue that had taken place and she would open the old textbooks and glance through them, nodding her head at old underlined phrases, saying words to herself. She felt these momentary affairs were serious, a credit to her; and when it came to the men she met outside, in the street or bus, a gay twinkle would come into her eyes, she would look out the window with a grin, say to herself: I work hard, I have a right to my little fling: you have to have experience of men and manners to write.

She usually felt proud of the number of men she attracted, but sometimes, without knowing why—perhaps when she passed one of the other lodgers on the stairs—she would feel a little shamed: might they think her disreputable? But then she would think of her family, her attainments, the compliments she had received, her engagement ring and the fine impression she made wherever she went. I am just celibating a little, she would say to herself. She had never done anything inexcusable or bad.

The people living in this house were very poor single people or families living in one room apiece, with a gas stove and wash-bowl—night workers and day workers, parents and their children trying to live decently in their one room. Eleanor liked the people and became a friendly neighbor to all of them, to the nightwatchman on the floor below, living in a mere cell with only a locked door between himself and the married couple next door, to the Polish dressmaker on her floor who had a similar room, to the German family next to her. Her room, like the other small ones, was only separated from their room by a locked door and a ward-robe placed against it. The German woman worked in the daytime at some stamping machine; at night they had parties which seemed like political meetings. If their little girl was ill or waked in the night, if the mother wept with shame at their way of living, *"Pfui! Eine Schande!"* Eleanor heard it all, she waked with them and waked when they slept, listening to their breathing.

She wrote to her mother, "When you see how nice they are, how decent, how responsive to friendship, how they struggle to assimilate and send their children to decent schools to be one of us, and how really good and patient, not discontented at all and so hard-working, you come to have a sort of affection for them. And of course, you can tell brother George, from me, Mummy dear, that I am closer to the people than he is, and here is proof that the agitators are all wrong, for these people do not want anything better; they know how to make the best of it and their lives are a pattern of uncomplaining self-help. As for me, darling, it is a great lesson in shift-for-yourself and make-do. I get a power of fun out of it."

Her mother, who would once have worried about her poverty and foreign neighbors, now did not reply to her letters for weeks. She had declined into a despair which was illness. She had lost faith in her Society.

Robert still wrote to Eleanor at intervals. She sometimes read his letters, skipping the details of his work and disappointments; sometimes she tossed them into the drawer unopened.

Several letters coming together made her curious. He was insisting upon an answer to his question. What question? He had fallen in love, or, as Eleanor said, "got into a romantic involvement," with a convalescent patient. In the pile of letters she found his agonies of hesitation, tragic confession, a series of abrupt decisions and remorse.

I don't know if I am in love now, or ever was, or if I loved you. I know nothing any more. I only know that our long engagement was a terrible mistake; we should have married years ago; and I would never have been faced with a decision which is tearing my mind in two. Please answer me. I know how horrified, disgusted, astonished you must be: but don't answer me with this reproachful silence. Virtue is much easier to women than to men; that is their strength. It is wonderful. If only I had it! Oh, the despair of having got to a place from which there is no return. I don't know what is the matter with me. I must be distorted somehow. I make up my mind that it is all done with and again I tell Cathy I love her and the rest follows: and again I long to be innocent. But I cannot be a boy again and at times my heart beats so horribly that I feel life is not worth living. What is all this leading to? And I know it is spoiled between us, too. You don't want to help me and you don't understand a man's difficulties.

Eleanor at first read this with surprise, then with a bored smile; suddenly, she became very angry. The wretch had deceived her; after all his holiness talk and making her wait and wait, he had simply gone ahead with affairs behind her back. She wrote him letters and dropped them in the wastepaper basket; and this went on for days, her excitement growing. In the end she wrote a brief note breaking their engagement and asking if he wanted the ring back. But he wrote at once, a long letter full of tears, saying that she might have helped him but was too narrow to do so; at any rate, she must keep the ring. "Good thing!" said Eleanor, for the ring was in pawn. Afterwards, she sat by the window and looked into the garden. Some children were playing in the garden, rushing up and down in Red Indian feathers, and howling. Tears came into her eyes: she turned to her writing table, put her fine fair head down and began to cry.

She heard a tapping at the door. She opened and there saw Miss Edelbaum, the dressmaker, who stood there in her strange homemade outdoor clothes with an eager smile.

"Someone has come to see you. I thought it was for me, but it is a young man, a new student," said Miss Edelbaum. "I think he is new, for he didn't know where you lived."

"Thank you," said Eleanor, running down the stairs. A middle-sized young man with red hair stood there; he had jutting brows, a furrowed forehead, bright blue eyes.

"My name is Sompnour, Arch Sompnour, my brother sent me along, you know—"

"Yes," said Eleanor, "please come up. I can just fit you in, if you can come about this time in the evening once a week."

The young man looked, a comical question in his face.

Miss Edelbaum was moving about the landing upstairs.

"Yes, you see," said Eleanor, in a loud voice, "I have a good many pupils and I am helping one of our elder statesmen with his memoirs, but I might be able to fit you in—"

"Oh, I see," said Arch Sompnour, following her upstairs.

Nodding and smiling in friendly excitement, Miss Edelbaum stood on the stairs. "Just going to get some water for tea, to the bathroom, you see—I have no water in my room," she explained to the young man.

Young Mr. Sompnour stood for a moment with his back to the shut door in Eleanor's room, the liveliest merriment in his little red-gold face. He peered out, shut the door again, hung up his coat and came forward holding out his hands. "A perfect Ghirlandaio. And she gives lessons! My brothers ought to be kicked all around Green Park. Come, my dear, kiss me; I had no idea you were like this, I thought you were just another pretty girl wanton—"

"I like you better than your brothers, but you do know your way about, don't you?" said Eleanor. "I'm not sure I like that."

"Come, try me—if I know more than you, I'll teach you."

"I didn't mean that way." But in saying the prim words, she smiled and held out her lips. "I am glad you came, you can console me. I had bad news today, about my fiancé—"

"About your fiancé—" he said, laughing all the time.

"Yes, I have just written and broken it off and had his reply. And of course he blames me." And she gave her visitor the letter.

"Ah, the meowing tomcat! I'm not like him," he said, tapping the paper with his fingernail. "Let's forget him, he's not worthy of you."

"I am willing to forget him; let's try," said she, with a smile.

But later he told her that he had been checking up on William, the family chauffeur. "William has been getting away with murder," and he had forced William to tell how he had used so much petrol. "It seems he took you down to the country with brother Laurence. Well, I don't blame him. Now, let's see, you said you could give me a lesson once a week."

"Oh, I'm free much more than that: that was for neighbors' ears."

"Then you don't have many pupils?"

"A few," she said, smiling with a pretty knowing look.

"Fair one," he said energetically, "you're wasting your beauty and youth. You could shine in society."

"Yes, I know I could."

"Why don't you try to get a duke?"

They laughed.

"I like to be myself, I am quite happy as myself, and you see I want to write; but of course if a duke falls into my lap—"

"Ah, you worry me. Why is a girl like you living like this?"

"Ah, dear Lady Poverty! You know, I believe there is something of the nun in me."

"There is in every woman, and other things, too!"

For some time she had a very lively affair with Arch Sompnour, who promised her that she would not suffer through him. "I don't promise to marry, I don't say I love you and I always fix up my girls with another man before I leave them." This is what he did.

Mrs. Brent died. Immediately afterwards, the widower went to live at his son George's farm, once called Sunnytop, renamed by George, Commonwealth. For the last time, Eleanor went through her memories of her mother, shed a few tears; and then, it seemed, she forgot her. But for a few months following, she dressed strangely, like an old woman, with a gray felt hood on her untidy hair and in an unbecoming dingy black dress, long and weighted with frills, tucks and floating panels, and an old-fashioned overcoat in gray broadcloth, belted and with wide box pleats. These she had got secondhand in the Kentish Town Road. Coming up the stairs, looking older, she would stop and pant as she had heard her mother do; and for some time she quarreled with the men she now called her pupils and used language Mrs. Brent had used in the house: ". . . and getting no thanks for it . . . if I had known what I know now . . . a man who takes advantage of a woman."

Her mother was buried according to the rites of the New Religious Society. At the funeral Eleanor had met many old friends, and was now close to the Society again, as they put it. Although it was some time since her adventure with Count von Ulse, the secret club of the Count's Harem still flourished among the young women in the Society.

Soon afterwards she received an invitation from Manilla, one of the Harem, who lived with three or four others in a flat in St. John's Wood, a cold, windy, dirty maisonette, which they camped in.

"Our Count James is getting married to Zuleika," said the note. "The do's in Paris and James is paying all expenses for Rita, Joan, Hannah and Margot. Little bird says we're ALL going to get invitations: that means wedding presents. We're broke, aren't you? Come, stay the night, we've got a bed in the east wing, let's make plans. James is turning Catholic to marry Zuleika, so that's the end of him."

Eleanor went, loafed pleasantly around, imitated her girlhood, but could not help crying at night; their lives seemed wayward, they had had many disappointments; again she had been living alone so long that she suffered from every malicious innuendo. However, she helped draw up the list of presents they would give, and agreed to share a room at a small hotel in the Latin Quarter. The girls were lending each other things to wear, but she was too tall and too large—she could not borrow.

"Do you remember when you used to write to advertisers for bust developers?" one of the girls asked her. "Wasn't that painting the lily?"

"I always knew you'd break it off with that Ware chap."

"Your trouble is you have no discrimination: you just feel you have to say yes—you're slipping."

It had seemed at one time an exciting barbaric feast, the league of free women, an orgy of lies, confidences, the Truth Game, sensuality; but when she got home, Eleanor felt stale, old and sad. "Arch Sompnour says I do not play my cards right. I'm too timid. I don't take chances; I'm so damn petty-bourgeois. But Manilla and the rest were pretty daring, devils in their time, and where are they? Where did I go wrong? Do you have to marry young to keep your faith in things? But I've got to have my share of living. Oh, the men, the men; why can't I keep a man? Other women get married; I just haven't got the knack." She pouted, her face trembled, and she blubbered, crouched on the edge of the bed, her face in her pillow. "Others get away with it: they have a good time and then they marry. Men don't care these days. What's the matter with me? I've got all the looks you need."

But presently she turned over and lay on her back. She began to think about her parties with Arch Sompnour; he was a wise spender, he spent but he got value. Last week she had been to the movies with a curious old man from the dancing class who had frayed cuffs and collar. He had given her a box of chocolates and expected "the works" in return. Another old man had given her a Tom Thumb sunshade: "Ladies like sunshades," he said, smiling. She noticed the roots of his black hair were white. There was the pleasant, healthy big man she had danced with at a "Social Club" she had been taken to. She had seen him in uniform in a police car outside the house a few days later. What was that private house with the laurels and holly, up near Swiss Cottage? A girl in black tights had run out the night of the fire, when Eleanor was walking home. It must be easy, pleasant and safe, in many ways, in a house. Women had married well from houses. It all lay in your own character: with character you could never be downed. Some of the men she met had such strange ways. They wanted her to do certain things, but she was a straight, clean, ladylike girl: she would do nothing but what was natural. It suddenly crossed her mind that once she had thought, How could I ever face a man again if I had been to bed with him? Why, it was "a sweet secret"; or else she didn't think of it at all. She had been a shy girl. In the old days when she and her university friends had been talking about marriage, they had all agreed that a wife should never sleep in the same room as her husband; and unless she had a perfect figure, she should never let him see her naked. Pondering and puzzling, Eleanor forgot her troubles. She gave a great sigh and thought: All beginnings are difficult and I've almost won through. I can't turn my back on London now. And you can't write in ideal surroundings; you have to be in the hurly-burly. My trouble is, I suspect, that I can't accept formulas: I have to find out for myself. I love human beings. I take them as they are. I'm not conventional, I'm human, all too human. Besides, I have a right to my youth.

Some minutes later it struck her that she was thirty years old. She jumped off the bed, seized a woman's magazine and read the first story she turned to. The plot was a classic: a woman's hesitation on her wedding eve when an old lover reappears. The first lover, who had fascinated, seduced her as a naïve girl and then "let her down badly," now had lost his charm for her. The better life planned with her bridegroom had already changed her. All doubt quashed, she becomes a happy bride; the past is buried. How true, thought Eleanor, there is humble truth under these banalities; it had meaning for romantic women like herself who had been tempted by their own good looks. She extracted the outline and rewrote the story a little. It seemed wonderfully good when she had carefully repolished it to suit the requirements of another magazine. She sent it out confidently, thinking, If it sells, it will mean I've struck oil and I'll get married this year.

She had been promised it. Arch Sompnour believed in marrying off his girls, he said. He had already married off four of them. "I respect women, but I only like to go out with girls who have good faces and good legs. It's a weakness, but it makes it easy to get them married. You'll be easy too, but you want to step out a bit more, take a chance."

"Me take a chance!" she cried, very much surprised. "You don't know me, Arch!"

He eventually placed her with an attractive, well-dressed man who was one of the partners in a celebrated firm of jewelers. He began by taking her into the shop to buy her a pair of earrings. A clerk went upstairs and presently the partner came down, looked and came forward with a respectful and gracious air. He took her out a few times to dinner and the theater, to exhibit some of his new designs; she wore a simple dress selected by him and a jewel or two, which she gave back. In this way, she met a man she had heard about, "a famous man, Joe is, he has an office down in Hatton Garden, everyone knows Joe." One day she was sitting in Joe's office when he said he would take her uptown to meet a friend of his, Lord Exitt. He called a taxi, went downstairs with her, she entered the car, and the door was closed upon her; it was not a taxi but a private car, and in the private car, the owner, a heavy-faced man with a ring of gray hair. They had got as far as Kensington Palace Gardens when she determinedly opened the door of the car and jumped out. She had suddenly become frightened of the future. Floating, dreaming, taking what came in trafficked districts and poor rooms, was just innocent pleasure, all off the record; but what was this? What life was she letting herself in for? She would no longer be free and belong to herself.

For the wedding weekend, Eleanor was invited to stay with Marky, an old school friend who was living with a foreign journalist named Ivo in Paris. He was a correspondent for the Eastern press. They were at the Gare du Nord to meet her; but she did not want to introduce them to her London friends and so avoided them, found a taxi and awaited them on the doorstep of their home in the rue de la Contrescarpe, a poor, populous street.

"Oh, you dear, dear people," said Eleanor, throwing herself into the arms of this couple and hugging and kissing them; to Ivo, a short, handsome man, she gave an extra kiss. "I'm getting short-sighted, you know, I looked wildly everywhere, and then thought, in this strange Paris, who knows what may happen to a girl, so I took a taxi. I scribbled the address with lipstick on my mirror, not trusting my French," and she burst out laughing.

She knew no French and had been brought up in that British tradition which thinks French taste trashy, French food fanciful, French dress frill and French men lechers; it was with Germans she felt safe. When the taxi driver rushed her across Paris, across the Seine and to the venerable but dingy street on the Montagne-

Ste.-Geneviève, she had had a tremor: perhaps he was conveying her to a brothel. When he set her down at the right address, she was gaily excited, giggled in his face and handed him her tiny gratuity with a flourish. "For you, you're an honest man," she cried in English. He looked at the tip, at her, at her little grip, and drove away.

Ivo went out to get some wine. Eleanor followed her friend Marky into the long narrow kitchen, which overlooked the playground of the Lycée Henri IV. Little boys in black tunics were running about and two looked up for a moment at the young women. Marky was middle-sized, twenty-eight, sober, very pretty, with curly chestnut hair, a small voluptuous figure, and taste and color in dress. She was a commercial artist.

At lunch the guest had a glass of wine and got into high spirits, telling them all about the Count's Harem, which had shifted to Paris for the wedding, and about certain of her adventures that she thought would please them. For instance, about Karel, who was a student at the London School, a Social-Democrat from Vienna; she and he "had ding-dong battles over economic theory." Jahng was a close friend from Switzerland, studying banking and writing a report on the English class system. "But he will never understand that we do not view it the way he does, he will never get really inside us. I keep telling him we do not mind being middle-class, for instance; it is a way and a very good way of thinking, living, breathing. To be born middle-class and pretend to be anything else would be affectedly snobbish, even if you pretend to be working-class. In England the best people are completely without affectation because they know where they are."

Her voice became drunken, although she had not yet finished the glass of wine. "Oh, my dear ones! And you, my dear ones, could never be so happy, shine and beam with happiness as you do, you darlings, in England, for in Paris these things are quite normal, but in dear old fusty England, people must be married. And even here, I suppose you are not received in society?"

They looked at her and laughed good-naturedly. "Have some

more wine," said Marky, who was sitting in her usual tense quiet, opposite. "It will settle the first."

"Oh, my dears," said Eleanor loudly, "but you do miss good company, it is a pity. On the train over, I met Mrs. Blanding-Forest, an artist. She did the whole Royal Family and she was most curious when I said I was going to stay with an artist in Paris. I said a woman artist, of course—only it was on the tip of my tongue to tell her where I was staying, but I thought it better not, in your situation! She makes friends so quickly, she has so much good faith, I felt it would not be quite fair to her and I should have felt a perfect fool, putting her wise."

The next day Marky went out with her to buy gloves and walked with her as far as the Church of the Madeleine, where the wedding was to be celebrated at four in the afternoon, and on the way they met the Harem.

This day Eleanor was at her best: her noble beauty bloomed and there was an Oriental look in her eyes, but her walk was athletic. The five handsome girls—all healthy, warm-cheeked, and in their best—excited interest and admiration as they walked slowly along the boulevard from the Opéra, stopping every now and then to look into the shop windows and argue about shoes and blouses. On the pavement below the church, they met a group of Londoners, New Society people who were praising the bride.

Eleanor turned away impatiently to climb the steps. Now they were talking about a friend of the Count's, Edwin Thieme, a man she did not know but who seemed quite popular, perhaps because he sold fine wines. Eleanor imagined a short, cherry-faced man smelling rather like a stave soaked in port wine. As she turned to the steps she heard "There's Edwin now," turned her head, noticed a man of thirty-three or four, walking quickly, lightly, with chest-nut curls, his coat flying open, tall, of football build. He greeted them from down below, then started rapidly up the steps, came opposite to Eleanor, glanced, and startled, looked again, once more, twice; and went on. But he had looked at her and she at him with the same intensity and knowledge that an animal has, when it looks straight into the eyes of a human, a meaningless but profound and moving look. Eleanor, who had looked into many men's eyes, had never seen it before. At the same time, she felt a slight bruise on the left side of her heart and it seemed a shadow wheeled across her. She thought, That's like death. But she had never thought about death. She also thought, He knows me—no one else knows, but he knows. At the church door someone introduced them. They forced themselves to look at each other. She saw an empty darkness, an empty stage, the veils falling, falling: those were his eyes. She could not smile, but turned away. She reached her seat and saw him sitting already, two rows in front. He turned round.

I suppose this is love, it must be, she said to herself; but I feel nothing. I don't know him: how could it be? I'm not going to waste my time and be made ridiculous. But she might have been floating, she scarcely felt anything touching her.

She did not care for the style of the church, nor what she could see of the Catholic furniture; and from where she was seated, she would not see much of the ceremony. All round her, at short distances, were men she knew too, and women friends of the bride's, beauties the Count had known well. A silver blonde was sitting between two empty places, drooping, with uncolored lips, in an ivory coat, with mournful eyes like an ousted hanger-on; an orange blonde without a hat, young and pink, looked as if she were full of cake; a dainty, respectable little woman, with hair dyed fair, a severe profile and long narrow slippers, was passing chocolates to her fiancé. Eleanor turned and saw two rows behind her five girls sitting together, one of them an Indian beauty with a rosy caste-mark on her forehead and a blue and gold sari, a younger Indian all in white, alongside them three Indian men in European dress. In her own row, Eleanor saw a striking Negro woman, who looked in this half-light like a polished carving; she wore a dark blue blouse with a skirt of spongy white material heavily embroidered in red, yellow, black and blue. With her was a European girl, dumpy, very young, with a faint fair mustache and wearing an expensive, ugly fawn silk dress, much pleated; and beside her, an impudent boyish little woman with high milky breasts and a lime-colored blouse that looked like a scarf lightly thrown over them; a heavy-faced brunette, a suntanned blonde—

It really is a harem, thought Eleanor, at last, settling back into her furs with satisfaction and assuming an expression of indifference. Meanwhile she kept thinking, as if stung, "What a beauty! What a beauty!" She meant the man.

She saw the scarf, the big curly head in front, and once more she felt a threat, like a premonition of disease. I can't stand him: I'm tired of these affairs. I'm only waiting and waiting to marry; I'll marry Robert anyhow, I think. I want to be settled for life. I can't take the punishment. This is a terrible affair. It might not happen in a hundred years, with a hundred men. But it has happened. He'll ruin my future: I can't face it.

He was with a girl about twenty, a brunette dyed red, pretty but with her fat-cheeked coarse middle age already showing; she would be plain. Eleanor assumed that Thieme and this girl were lovers and she looked her over carefully: She's young, greedy, without style; he won't marry her. She was conscious that time had no pace and no divisions: people were very still, or made slow, gracious movements; some were unusually shabby, some so beautiful that she stared, could not turn her gaze away. There were people there in street clothes; others with gold embroidery. It was all very strange. The people were not very clear in the dark interior. She might have been asleep hearing a dream symphony, the people and church swirled round her in a stately circle. Thoughts went through her mind that had never been part of her before: There are side booths, confessionals, I suppose, thousands of lives have been lived before me. People have gone through whole lives of suffering: even now they are here going through some part of their lives. Aren't there a lot of us on earth at present? But more dead: where have they all got to? Just streaming out into what's faraway. And those to come—a cataract of light! Ages and ages of people. It's funny they won't have heard about me: nor anyone here. But then he is in the same boat. If I allowed it and our lives were to begin to circle round each other from now on—what a thought! On and on. I couldn't do it. I'm happy now. Perhaps someone in this church will die tomorrow, even tonight. Perhaps he will or I will. Oh, no, no!

These stray ideas were as fragrant and delightful to her as patches of low-growing flowers on a forest floor: are they there yet, or only spring shadows? They are there every year, but new now. A great quiet wind blowing round and round her on which the church and audience were dim paintings from past time, carried before her eyes, recollections, images and breaths of passion, like sprays of flowers. She had never lived so intensely, except perhaps one night long ago, when, on the stage at the university, she had appeared as Lady Teazle and a dark-eyed poet came down the hall and had stood looking at her, over the footlights.

She knew by the whispering that the Count had arrived and was standing there. She peered through the church twilight, and then, a wonderful bustle, a thrilling sensation and the crowd of beautiful anonymous women seated round her at the back surged, half rose and craned—their glorious rival, Zuleika, a small, fleshy brunette with heavy, voluptuous features, and dressed in white brocade, old lace and seed pearls, had come in on the arm of her half-French brother, her dark eyes straight ahead, holding up her bow-back nose, wearing an alert expression. Her dark eyes roved once to right and left, she straightened her neck and marched on, with a slight scowl of triumph. Thieme looked her up and down for a moment, turned round and gave Eleanor a sweet, bold smile. With her heart in her mouth, she smiled back. If he were the groom! Oh, if she were the bride! It could be.

She sat through the tedious ceremony in great elation, thinking, Oh, joy, joy! Zuleika is tied up but I have met my man. Presently the bridal party came down the church, and Eleanor was astonished to see that they leaned on each other's arm, they bent towards each other, and gave only shy vague glances to each side. But is it serious? Can they be serious? At the sight, all the Members of the Harem felt an unpleasant shock, for they had counted on there being no love in the marriage; some wept quietly and regretted their flirtations; others had darker feelings. But Eleanor, looking at the Count, said between her teeth, "Playboy! I can do better than that." She turned and smiled significantly at the people nearest to her. "They suit each other so well, don't they? And as they are both such new Catholics, I don't suppose the little mistakes mattered! Well, I am glad the Count made an honest woman of her; it clears the air. And I suppose it is really fitting that it should be in the Madeleine Church!" Her neighbor gave her an indignant look; Eleanor grinned.

She turned, and there at the end of her row stood Mr. Thieme. She moved towards him, acknowledging friends, in the crowd.

Walking out of the church, settling her furs, she waved graciously, spoke vaguely, found herself walking with Thieme on the footpath below the steps; and he was continuing a conversation: "And that's the Princess, she's a friend of Count von Ulse; over there, that's the bride's father, Monsieur Asfanigo, he's talking to the Marquis, I forget his name; and there's the Duc de Bonbonne, who's always in the gossip columns, he comes from the Dordogne, also a friend of James von Ulse."

"Do you know them?" she asked, forcing herself to look at his face for the first time. She felt her face dropping into folds and dewlaps; his cheeks thickened and fell, he looked the hopeless melancholy of a bloodhound. He looked sulky. She glanced away, and putting up both hands, smoothed her cheeks.

Some were to take taxis across the Seine; some said they would walk across the Place de la Concorde to the Left Bank. Thieme and Eleanor separated and a party began walking quickly towards the river.

"What is he?" said Eleanor to Mrs. Foxe, a lady she had seen speaking to him.

Mrs. Foxe bent daintily towards her. "He's written a little book on wine; he sells wine."

"What is he? He's not English!"

Mrs. Foxe caught her breath. "Oh, yes, he is!" A pause, then she said quickly, "A German grandfather, I believe."

"Yes, I was sure some other blood—"

"Oh, Edwin is very English."

"But the wine," said Eleanor, laughing, "where does he get his interest in wine from?"

"Well, all his customers are English, or nearly all—he not only sells to the Count but is a very close friend of the Count."

Eleanor tittered. "I didn't know James von Ulse made friends of tradesmen."

This shocked Mrs. Foxe. She murmured again rapidly, "Oh, no one considers Edwin a tradesman, though, of course, he brings out the most wonderful little books about where to dine, and guides to the Continent. He is quite artistic and literary."

Eleanor laughed aloud. "Oh, my dear, a wine salesman artistic and literary!"

"He doesn't stand behind a counter."

"Does he go round with a van delivering bottles?" cried Eleanor sportively. "Surely a man who looks like that could find something better to do!"

Mrs. Foxe looked at her, not knowing what to say.

Meanwhile, Mr. Thieme said to the man at his side, "Who is *she?*"

"I knew her mother, a charming woman; she died recently. Her father inherited a woolen business in London and has sold it out and retired now to live with his son in the country, her brother George. I know them well. The mother was a friend of the Count."

"A friend?"

"A very religious, genteel body, a sweet but sawdust woman."

"The daughter is not like that!" said Mr. Thieme. "She is a beauty, of course, but what coloring and how she walks, what a natural unaffected manner! She has a sweet voice too; it rings in an undertone. There are lovely girls here, but none compare with her."

The other man, a man of forty, looked about him nonchalantly. "Yes, there were some pretty girls at the church, weren't there? What do you think of the bride?"

"The bride!" He thought for a moment. "Oh, yes!"

"She's considered very beautiful."

"Oh, but this one! The fair hair that shines in the sun with a faint purple blush, there's nothing like that; and eyes like that, long and brilliant, and that face, small and dainty set on the broad throat, that's an extraordinary type of beauty; and she looks unconscious of it."

"No pretty young woman is unconscious of the smallest detail of her looks, my dear Edwin."

Thieme said, "And you can see she is a modern woman, her face is alive with intelligence."

"Intelligence, oh yes!" said his friend, laughing. He left him at Eleanor's side.

Crossing the great white square of the Concorde, Thieme walked rapidly and Eleanor kept pace with him.

"The scaffold was just about there; of course that's the Arc de Triomphe! These are the 'Elysian Fields,' there is the Tuileries with the Louvre beyond. Glorious, isn't it? More splendid than Rome, more elegant. This is a famous view, the Seine: that's the Orangerie and there is the National Assembly. Notre Dame, eh, like a great medieval ark in a ditch, but what beauty and what glory! I am not a tourist, I know it well, I went to school here," said Thieme. "These are the banks of the Seine you have seen in a thousand pictures, perhaps. Down there beyond Notre Dame are the quays where they unload the wine: the wine market is there too. See the water! Today it's like satin, isn't it? Samite. I used to think of samite like that, bluish-white. Did you? Do you know that in the Madeleine I happened to turn round and saw you—"

He stopped talking and looked at her. She smiled, almost winking, and a pretty, strange lecherous look moved around the corners of her mouth. There was a pause. Then he continued in a dreamy tone: "Your hair and face, in the half-dark, floating like a goblet on a polished table in a dark room, a windflower, a night moth—but real flesh and blood."

Eleanor bent over the parapet and looked down. "To me it's too pale. All colors in Paris are too pale; and I don't like their style of architecture, it's faddish, not good taste. I don't know why they paint these quays so much: they're not very interesting. I like the green English countryside. The French countryside is so bare. During my university days, I tramped with some girls through Holland and Germany; the villages and the people were so charming. They are so sweetly human, you feel so much at home with them. I don't feel happy with the French, I feel they're carping."

"You don't know them," he said as they began to walk again, "and I do, so at present we can't agree. If you are tired, we'll take a taxi."

"Me tired! I'm never tired," cried Eleanor.

"Take my arm crossing the street." When they got to the other side, he said, "Is it true that you know you are a beauty?"

Eleanor laughed.

He took her hand, palm to palm and his face became again serious, almost mournful. He had an athlete's head.

"Don't do that," said Eleanor. "I feel faint. The morning was too long and I had no breakfast; my friends, where I stay, had only coffee and pastry and I can't eat pastry for breakfast. I hope they give us something to eat. Are you a good trencherman? I suppose not, selling wines; wines are bad for the appetite, aren't they? But I suppose, like vinegar, it's good for the figure. Do you know where we are going?"

"It's really not far at all now," he said. "The wedding breakfast is rue de la Chaise—a chaise is good if you are tired."

"Oh, I am used to it. I work for a literary agency and have to stump up and down dusty stairs and walk miles to save bus fares." He was silent; and looking curiously at him, she saw he had an embarrassed, sulky look. She smiled. "I am not an heiress, like the bride. I sweat out every penny. Perhaps, if I had been like

Zuleika, rich, the Count would have married me instead."

"Why do you say that?"

"He asked me once."

"And you refused?"

"I just let it drift; I like to take my time."

"Do you regret it?"

She had a mysterious smile; she said demurely, "I like to take my time. I want most of all to be myself . . . Besides," she said in a sudden brisk tone, "I was engaged to a friend of the Count; and I am still, and I like to keep my word."

They were not far from the rue de la Chaise when she showed him her engagement ring. "We met when we were very young and I think it has gone on too long. It seems to have lost all its meaning —but this! And this is beautiful."

When they ate they did not sit at the same table. Eleanor was radiant; every man at her table thought he had interested her. The girls at the table gradually drooped. She stayed late, enjoying her triumph, but noticed the guests were going; it had become cold.

She had promised to wait for Mr. Thieme, but when another man said "Are you coming?" she hastily got her things and went out with him; and when once they were out, she got him to call a taxi and send her to the rue de la Contrescarpe, where Marky and Ivo lived. In the taxi she said to herself, "Escaped, escaped! No, never! He is trouble. The hand of fate! I don't want to see it."

Though it was nearly nine, they had not dined, but were waiting for her, and had some glasses and a bottle of vermouth on the table.

"Oh, dear you, so hospitable always," said Eleanor, sinking down on the narrow couch in the front room, "but if you knew what I have put away already! I have done nothing but stuff all the evening."

"How was the wedding?" asked Ivo, pouring her a glass.

"A very grand wedding, of course, all the known and unknown friends of bride and groom. And very smart. The bride looked lovely. And there is plenty of money. So, happiness ever after! Although, I know through you, my dears, that happiness can exist without marriage."

"Was it the bride or the groom who was your friend?" said Marky, in her nervous way. "Is that couch comfortable? That is where you are sleeping tonight, I'm afraid. Wouldn't you rather sit in this armchair?"

"I'm quite comfortable lounging, darling," cried Eleanor, "after all those hours sitting, watching Zuleika being made an honest woman of. I knew Zuleika, we all did, she was one of us, we were all friends; but Count James was a friend of poor Mumsy, and for her sake, I wanted to be there. She would have been so happy for his sake, for we were always wondering whom the Count *would* marry, and Mother thought no one good enough for him— except perhaps me," Eleanor said with a frank laugh.

"Yes, Ell, you should have a grand wedding," said Ivo, laughing. "A movie wedding is your style: I can see you a pillar of white satin by day and a pillar of gauze by night."

"Well," said Eleanor gallantly, "and I want to be there when you make Marky an honest woman, though I don't suppose she will wear white—what do brides wear who are—h'm—"

"Are not white enough?" said Marky, with a sparkling laugh but looking annoyed.

Eleanor smiled charitably. "But I suppose you'll keep it quiet, if the day does come? My pets, I keep your little secret and I have told no one I am staying with you. It would seem very strange, wouldn't it, anyway, for a wedding guest?" She burst out laughing. "Yes, things do go by contraries, don't they? But I forgot! I brought you a wedding present. Yes, my precious ones, to me it's the same as if you were married! I scraped together some money for the Count's gift, and then Daddy and George knew I was broke and they came through with a small check, and I thought, I'm hanged if I'm going to give it all to those people who have everything and don't need it; so I halved it, half for the official wedding and half for the unofficial, for it's just the same to me and I know it's just the same to you!"

Marky looked at her blushing; the sulks fading and her face lighting up, she smiled. "You are a dear, Ell, that's kind."

"Eleanor is the best of friends, the dear silly-billy," cried Ivo, getting up and hugging her.

Then Eleanor brought the parcel, some linen.

"And may it bring happy dreams to a real marriage bed, for I know you two know what happiness is," cried Eleanor excitedly.

They looked at the linen, and Eleanor bent over it with them, spreading it out. Suddenly she said impatiently, "I must hurry things up myself. I've waited too long. Do you think I'm right to wait so long for Robert? My life's passing. A woman has a right to happiness when she's young. I must look round for another man. Robert can't bring me happiness, when he puts everything else first, don't you agree?"

When Marky went to dish up the dinner, Eleanor sat at the table with Ivo leaning on her elbow and talking into his face, urgently: "Women do get overripe, don't they? I've a good mind to look round and marry the first man who asks me. There are plenty of men round who know the short cut to a woman's thighs. Do you think Robert imagines other men don't want me? Ivo," she said, nestling closer, "you and Marky are happy without being married, aren't you? Would you recommend me to make a try with some other man? One can always marry afterwards, can't one? And if you've made a mistake, no bones broken, eh? The door's open, you walk out, together or apart. Or someone else walks in. The Count and Zuleika are a case in point. The Count had a harem, you know. Zuleika was just one of many, but she came out with the official stamp on her, in the end. Oh," she said, putting her little white teeth together angrily, and flushed, "I won't be cheated, Ivo. I will have what the others had. Ivo, you and Marky are happy, aren't you? Why shouldn't I go to bed, too? I will find someone to marry me in the end. Why," she said, beginning to laugh and look with shining eyes at him, "I never thought Marky would have the courage to live in sin; surely I have as much courage as Marky? Dear Marky: I always thought of her as such a dear child, and I am two years older; and what always seemed so funny to me, Ivo dear, was that I was always the romantic one and she was the serious rational one, with no nonsense about her. No one at school would ever have imagined Marky as a scarlet woman, she seemed so cool, so sure of herself, not the sort of person who goes in for illicit passion!"

All this Eleanor mouthed, in a languishing confidence, smiling, leaning back in her chair, then coming forward again, to put her head on her hand and look trustingly into Ivo's face. "I suppose that there is a fate waiting for each of us, that has nothing to do with our natures. Ah, Ivo, I long to meet my fate. Marky," she said, jumping up to help take a tray from her, "I have been discussing it all with Ivo. I have got to look elsewhere for a man. I must have a man. I won't wait any more, the altar calls."

They took a walk about the quarter, but at night she tossed about, kept awake by the solemn tones of old church bells, by voices in the street, by an owl, a jingling horse, a cat, the moon, a cough, a whistle, by anything and by the wedding fever, by something knocking on the wall, creaking furniture, students on the stairs going up to the attic, and Mademoiselle Jacqueline, the old woman who lived in an attic room coming down early to wash the stairs. Hungry for warm life, real love, she pressed her ear against the wall; she heard low talking—Marky laughed. Eleanor tossed. "I'm a donkey! Robert ruined me. I'm too honest. Even Marky knows how to hook and hold a man. And I know dozens of men. In the morning I begin a new life."

Even today a new man had been attracted to her; she could say the same almost every day. Streets, subways, shops, stairs, night, day—eyes, eyes, secret smiles, hands laid on, kisses; and here she was tossing alone and obliged to console herself with pictures from the past. With them, she fell asleep late, and slept late in the shuttered room. When she got up, they were ready to go out and had laid breakfast for her in the kitchen.

She ran out to them, her thin white nightdress flying round her body. "Good morning, my sweets, did I keep you awake? I was up till two, reading and thinking." The high morning light flushed her; her cheeks and lips were red with strong life; her long pale hair fell over one shoulder. She said irritably, "I made up my mind, I must get a man who knows his way to the center of gravity! A man who belongs to me, not to his career. I have got to have a plan and stick to it! I am too much of a dreamer. Ivo," she said, throwing herself on his breast and kissing his face, "Marky and I are so much alike, if she can do it, I can, isn't that true? I haven't the courage to take the plunge. Oh, dear Marky," she said, turning and looking at her schoolmate, "Marky, you and I were brought up ladies, but I have let it spoil life for me." She stood up and looked at them both. "You are quite right, both of you. Good for you! Is this my breakfast? Bless you, my children, for feeding the hungry and housing the roofless. Now, where do I put the key? And when do you expect me?"

"Can you be here by six? There's a friend of Ivo's, Danilo, a Rumanian, who wants to meet you," said Marky.

Ivo, ready to go out, in a raincoat, his hair neatly brushed, with a bundle of notes for his article in his overcoat pocket, plunged into a description of his friend, a rich man brought up in the Balkans in troubled times, very poor once and still dickering with revolution; at any rate, he still had some rebel friends, the milder sort. "We told him one of Marky's friends was coming, a real beauty. 'I don't believe she's as good as you say,' Danilo said, and he's coming along to check up. I only want to be here when he sees you," said Ivo.

"Does he take you out?" said Eleanor.

"And in," said Ivo.

"He's a ladies' man," said Marky.

"Is he a revolutionary?" asked Eleanor, hesitating.

"Just like you," they said.

"Bless you, you never lose your sense of humor. One of my friends, Jahng," she said, making a sour face, "did nothing but lecture me. You can't convert people that way. It's like Hitlerism. He used to make me cry. He always left me feeling blue; but when I asked him to explain, I could see he didn't understand the most elementary economics. I couldn't make him see the simplest things like supply and demand. Besides, I said to him, 'You say this is going to happen; well, test your belief by waiting to see if it will. If people want it, it will come!' " She suddenly smiled. "Eat, drink and be merry."

Presently they had both gone out and she telephoned her London friends to meet her in a little restaurant in the Place du Panthéon, not far from where she was. Some of the girls said they knew French. They knew very little but instead had met some French students who spoke English and who were informative, gay and flattering. Berenice, a sulky girl, tall, very plump, dark and handsome, sat throughout the meal with an offended expression, staring at the corner of the dingy ceiling. She felt that the students, the waiter and the owner were insulting her by too much familiarity; besides, she resented James's marriage and she wanted to be in London with the young man she hoped to marry. Manilla had "other fish to fry" and left them after lunch. Bobby, a music student, a very pretty, dainty girl with little curls on her forehead, wanted to go into the Luxembourg Gardens, but in the end Bobby and Eleanor, escorted by two students, went to the Place de l'Opéra and began to walk along the boulevard towards the Madeleine Church. They were having a lively time and about to go to a café when Eleanor's heart jumped into her mouth as she saw before seeing Edwin Thieme coming down the steps of the church. He wore no scarf or overcoat. He's just a wine merchant, said Eleanor to herself.

"I thought I might find you somewhere around here. I've been looking for you," he said. "Are you engaged? Eleanor, come with me."

Bobby instantly said she had to go back to the hotel. They put her in a taxi and were left alone.

"It seems to me so strange I met you: I was only at the wedding yesterday by chance. I am here on my way south to meet someone who is coming from Egypt. I was told to buy a wedding dress and I thought I should look round here on the way down. If you like, we could walk to the shops together and look. I don't want anything very expensive—just one, simple and pretty, for a family wedding at a country church. In Paris they specialize in that particular look of young girl's innocence."

"A woman always loves to look for a wedding dress—why not? Is it for your sister?"

"I have no sister; it is for my cousin."

"I don't think I'd let anyone else choose my wedding dress. And isn't it odd to let a man pick it?" She laughed. "Perhaps it's a good idea, but I have a feeling it's wrong—or is that superstition?"

She scarcely seemed to know what she was saying or doing. He led her. She kept suppressing a smile which played round her lips. While they talked of something or other, she was saying to herself, What a beauty he is! and her unnatural excitement seemed to come from his beauty.

"You had better tell me what she is like," said Eleanor.

His cousin was of middle height, a bit taller than she looked, but not as tall as Eleanor, and she bent over a little as she walked, bent her head and shoulders as if thinking or even as if limping.

"And it has a queer effect on you, you feel touched by it," he remarked. "You might even say she walks a little sideways, and it's pretty the way her curly hair hangs over her shoulder. She gets ahead quite quickly, of course—I don't mean she's lame; and she takes a big step. It may be that one shoulder is a little higher than the other, and it's as if she carried a bundle or jar on her shoulder. She sits bent over too, sometimes with her arms folded under her breasts and her hair falling over both shoulders. It's appealing if you're a kind-hearted man; and I am. And she keeps her eyes thoughtfully towards the pavement. You feel she's lonely, interesting, personal. When she begins to talk, she's quite different: girlish, affectionate but very observant. I'm afraid she knows very little about the world: the family have always wrapped themselves round her. She had some illness as a little girl. Sometimes she reads, but she has so much mental and moral resource that she can spend whole days in the country sitting in a chair or on a wooden seat outside just looking at the trees and birds and clouds." After a pause, he said, "You see, a dress too ceremonial wouldn't do."

"What's her name?"

"Harriet."

"You're very fond of her, aren't you?" Eleanor asked gently.

In the meantime they had been to several shops; and this explanation had become necessary. The saleswomen had supposed, at first, that the wedding dress was for Eleanor.

Thieme bent his head. "I'm going to marry her. I'm going down to Marseilles to meet them coming from Egypt."

"Why in the world did you let me look for a wedding dress for her? You've made a fool of me!"

There was a long silence. They had left the rue St.-Honoré, where they had been visiting dress shops and had come up the rue des Pyramides, for Eleanor had to meet her friends at this corner of the Louvre. They had reached the tiny half-circle where stands the gilded statue of Joan of Arc. Thieme put his hand on her arm; she shook it off and darted across the road towards the railed-off statue. He ran after her, seeing the full head of traffic coming, took her arm, and a bus turned right upon them as she, still running, struck him in the face with her open hand. The bus driver turned pale and pulled up sharp; people on the pavement gathered and started to call, "What is it? What's the matter?"

Eleanor, without looking, darted across the other side of the half-circle and began to walk swiftly down the rue de Rivoli. She caught sight of herself in a jeweler's window: she was red. She walked very fast. At the next street she hesitated, stood thinking for a while, turned down towards the rue St.-Honoré and came right up to the rue des Pyramides again before she calmed down. For some minutes a man had been walking at her elbow; it pleased her and calmed her—she began to saunter. She stopped to look in a window, a display of women's goods, to see the man's silhouette, but even before she had stopped, the idea of Thieme's thoughtless, insulting behavior, taking advantage of her, fired her imagination again and she strode on, shook the man off. At the corner near the Tuileries she looked round and saw Thieme.

"Go away, I don't want you."

"I saw the traffic coming—that was all. You nearly killed us both," he said with a mournful smile.

"I'm not in a dying mood."

"Listen to me."

He touched her arm; she turned quickly, looked at him and changed altogether.

"I'm a bloody fool, I flare up. But," she said, her lip trembling, "don't you ever dare try it on with me again."

"I don't understand. Come with me and sit down."

They entered the Tuileries and sat down. He told her that he was thirty years old. He had always believed he would meet the right woman. "*A woman waits for me.* I thought that was a beautiful verse of Walt Whitman. I was afraid to get involved with the wrong girl: I didn't want to cheat any woman, I didn't want to cheat myself."

Eleanor looked at the people passing on the sandy path. She felt uneasy: this was the meaning of his veiled and empty eyes.

"Harriet's father abandoned my Aunt Edith soon after Harriet was born and my parents shared their home with my Aunt Edith and her baby. To tell the truth, she was a kind of servant, but I didn't know it. I loved Aunt Edith and I loved Harriet. She's thirteen years younger than myself: she's only seventeen now. I was fond of her; everyone was always fond of her. I never heard any unkind word about her from anyone. She was always very much attached to me. When about fourteen she had a long illness and I went to see her and after a few days I noticed she was in love with

[58]

me; but I thought it was just a first attachment. The next year her father died and left her some property; and seeing I wasn't married, the family suggested a marriage. I allowed myself to agree, as I had begun to think I was becoming too much the bachelor, and if there was a woman, perhaps she was in another generation, or none at all—at any rate, for me too late. Well, I would never live that way again. It seemed very honest; now it seems shabby, stubborn. I'd never go back to that. They were able to take Harriet to Egypt last winter for her health, and then they wrote to me to arrange the marriage: she was willing. She will be at Marseilles tomorrow with the others. I am already late."

"You can get a wedding dress in Marseilles."

"I am simply telling you all this because, since yesterday, I am sure that it's a great mistake and that no matter what pain it causes us both, I should not marry my cousin."

"Why?"

"I want to marry you. You are the woman."

"I'm engaged, also," said Eleanor, hesitating. "I'm not in love either. Well, that word has a lot of meanings. It's threadbare, it has no meaning. I've generally heard the reverse. Men say cruel things to a woman; 'I'm not in love with you, but you've got me twisted'; or, 'I don't know what love is, I've never been in love, but I'm mad about you'; or else, 'You expect me to be in love with you, I suppose, women like you want a man to grovel to them.' Why do they say that to me? Why do they insult me? They say the word 'love,' but use it to insult. Why does it make them insult me? I don't ask them to love me."

"They all were in love with you, probably, but plenty of men hate to lay down their arms and say they're beaten. They don't like to say, 'Take me, Paphian.' "

"But I've been quite happy in my own way up till now," she said. "I've wanted my rights, that's all, my home and children, and I thought everything was all right when I got engaged to Robert. But it went on so long. He had to qualify, then to specialize, now for a couple of years, going from one hospital to another, he's been no better than a sort of medical tramp; and now he's a registrar. When will it end? Do you think I ought to be bound by my promise? Don't you think it's unfair to me?"

"You never had a passionate love affair? You don't think of that?"

She answered in her cold china voice, with a singsong: "I'm a romantic woman, and I feel society, I mean nature, owes me a happy life. I like things in their place, I like beauty in things and tranquillity, decency; I like things to be pleasant and I think the right kind of living gives us that, don't you?"

"But not passionate love?"

"I don't know what you mean," she said petulantly. "Love is all the same, isn't it? You love, kiss, live with a man—when you're married. I don't know what else is meant," and she sounded tearful.

"Venus unknown to Venus," he said, with a slight smile, looking at her face and sparkling eyes, which slid about from side to side uneasily. Eleanor flushed. "Look at me!" he said. She looked at him and then, feeling his influence more and more, looked away.

She said, "But I'm not happy this way, I don't like trouble. It gives me a disorderly feeling. I believe in fair dealing and self-control. This is just deviation. You can't get married with that feeling. I don't believe in that kind of love. I never have."

She started to frown. He took her hands from her lap, kissed them, kissed the end of her hair, loose from the neck-knot, kissed her mouth. "I am so happy, I feel as if I'm drunk on wine divine," he said.

She laughed, crushing his face as if she would crush all the juice from the fruit. "You're a great lover, I don't mind spending the day with you if you like—I like you, I think we do hit it off, don't you think we should find out? This is Paris, isn't it? And it isn't quite too late to find out if we made a mistake!" She laughed gaily. "Oh, let's not sit here: let's walk. Paris is Paris: the advertisements don't lie."

"It's too soon," said Thieme. "We've found each other, but

haven't found ourselves yet. You're really only a girl."

"Let's go, let's go, let's eat. It's a gorgeous day, just the day for some fun. I didn't sleep much last night—you know girls don't sleep on a wedding night, and the others looked pretty fagged out, but I don't, do I? The air is like wine, love is like wine, let us have some wine divine. Will we?"

"Are you going to love me, dear?"

"Oh, yes. Give in to every passing fancy, that's what I like. It makes life gay."

He was puzzled. "You don't think it's a passing fancy?"

"I'd rather think that," she said energetically and quite seriously. "You make my head go round, you unbalance me. Fun is fun, we oughtn't to take it for something else."

"Why, you're the most unawakened woman I ever met."

She continued loudly: "You don't want to spoil our lives and make your poor cousin ill, just for a passing fancy. After all, you don't know, do you?"

However, she enjoyed this new kind of courtship. She drank one glass of wine at lunch and, as before, became quite drunk, lolling back and laughing genially, the sunlight from the window slipping over her like golden water, all her fine natural colors enriched, and when her lover asked her if she was enjoying herself, she swung her knees towards him and waved her long white arm.

"I'm enjoying myself and so are you. Now I see you can enjoy yourself all right, in spite of those big eyes you make, grandmother. I thought you were sexless, Edwin Thieme, I know those love tunes, Edwin Thieme, I know all love tunes, Edwin Thieme. Speech is silver but practice is golden. I know you. You're in love with me, aren't you? And I know what love is; I know what passion is, too. But I wouldn't marry you, Mr. Thieme, because you don't mean it. If you mean it, you've got to make good. You can't play fast and loose with me. A c-c-celibate! I've known a few celibating young men, just a few." She leaned forward, resting her chin on her hand and said in a lower tone, sweetly, reasonably, "But you know, I think we ought to find out. I believe in trial marriage.

You're going to be very unhappy with that little girl, Edwin. She doesn't know anything about life and love. You're old-fashioned, but the proof of the pudding is in the eating. We're not neuter gender, none of us is neuter gender. We have to think it over. Everyone has rights. We have the right to have fun; but we haven't the right to make people miserable. Have we, Mr. Edwin Thieme? We must all stick to the rules and regulations. But," she said with a beautiful leer, "there is plenty of room, between the rules and regulations, to write in our little bit of romance and serenading."

"You aren't used to wine, are you?" he said, smiling.

"Never," she stuttered. "I come from a very respectable, religious family, a very good old family, landed gentry. We're related to the Herberts, that's what I am, a Herbert. Look in the picture gallery at Gosling Park and there you'll see Caroline Advisa Herbert. I'm her dead image, she's my dead image, because she's dead. But we have our responsibilities, Mr. Thieme: not breaking up homes and abandoning fiancées on the sandy shore; remember matrimony is holy, Edwin."

He asked her where she was staying, thinking he would take her home. "You didn't sleep last night and the wine has been too much for you, and me, perhaps—you were worried and this has all upset you."

She looked coolly around and wouldn't tell him the address. "They're bohemians, they love life, they're not for an engaged man with a fiancée to meet in Marseilles: I'm afraid I couldn't introduce you, though you could hobnob about wine together."

They walked along the quays, but presently Eleanor told him he bored her and she wanted to see Paris for herself and then go home. "I'm sorry I didn't go off with the other four musketeers," she said with a giggle; and then she insisted upon leaving him standing on the pavement by the Quai d'Orsay station, where he had got her a taxi. "Rue de la Contrescarpe—*plus tard, plus tard, le numéro!*"

"*Bien, madame!*"

"Good-bye, good-bye, Mr. Thieme," she called, waving her

hand gracefully, the fingertips curled and tinted like the petals of a giant white camellia, a gesture she had learned in dramatics at school. "Till we meet again! You've been perfect. You've shown me the real Paris and you're the soul of courtesy, every gesture shows instinctive courtesy. God bless you! Till we meet again!" The taxi driver, laughing, drove off.

Thieme followed along in haste and was astonished to see the cab stop at the next bridge. Eleanor leaned out of the cab and spoke to a sailor with a pompon; and after some discussion between the three the sailor entered the cab. Before Thieme could catch them, they drove off, up the rue des Saints-Pères.

The sailor and the chauffeur had some rapid conversation. Then the taxi stopped at a small café with tables in front, and Eleanor, laughing, got out and went in to the café *terrasse* with the sailor. The waiter brought them two cups of black coffee. After two or three cups of black coffee Eleanor felt very reasonable, though she had a slight headache. Meantime the sailor in his few words of English said he had been in London, and at Great Yarmouth; and presently he asked her where she lived.

She told him, "But you are not taking me home!" He called a taxi, and to her surprise he did not get in, merely gave the chauffeur the address. When she got out in the rue de la Contre-scarpe, she saw someone standing at the window in the white wall, which was Marky's window—a bright-eyed, sweet-lipped man with a bald head.

"Who's that? Who's that?" His bold clear bright eyes were fastened on her, he bent over the window sill to study her, and smiled with wonderful sweetness.

The hall door opened into a lobby. The door was opened before she reached it, the same man standing there, his head thrown back, his arms out. "Eleanor! They were right, they were right, by Jove, I didn't believe, couldn't believe—forgive me! I'm Danilo, call me Danny—give me your things!" He snatched her handbag from her, eyeing it. "Very pretty handbag," he muttered without confidence, looking from it to her modest skirt and blouse and walking shoes. "You are very English," he said suddenly with a humorous look, then his smile flashed.

Holding her by one hand he danced into the next room, where Marky and Ivo were, crying, "You were right! By James, Ivo, I underrated you!" He punched Ivo lightly on the chest and moving away danced a light step. "A beauty! Where did you find her? Oh, yes, you're Marky's schoolmate. Didn't know—Marky very lovely girl, very nice—er—ankles," he said hastily. He burst into a delightful merry laugh. "Never fear, Ivo, never fear. Marky, I say! Never fear! Lovely woman merits respect, I know. Don't worry about me." He rushed to Marky, who was carrying round a plate of snacks. "Can't eat now! One last bite!" But he changed his mind, brushed his lips with his handkerchief, looked round, starched correct, twinkling. He was of gorilla build, handsome in the Macedonian style, with very willful mannerisms. "Beautiful girl," he murmured to Eleanor, passing her.

"Now, Danilo," said Ivo smiling, "remember she's a lady; she's not one of your houris. She's a hard-working girl, she's engaged to a doctor, she's respectable. She won't fall for your tricks."

"We'll see," he said with immense self-reliance. He took a step forward, stood between the three, with a bright expression. "Trust me! Trust me! Know women, Marky. Never make a false step. Not often, that is."

"Yes, you must go straight this time," said Marky.

When Eleanor went off to the kitchen with Marky to ask questions about Danilo, Danilo turned to Ivo with a radiant face. "We'll see, we'll see, my boy! You're wrong, my boy. She's no schoolgirl. At the very first glance, in the street, I saw an experienced woman."

"You are absolutely dead wrong," Ivo declared. "You're corrupted with too many libertines: Eleanor's a nice girl."

"She's a nice girl, oh, boy, yes! But not what you mean." He gave a shout of laughter, hit Ivo on the shoulder. "We'll see, we'll see."

In the kitchen Eleanor was saying in a sweet, low voice, "He is very nice, your Danny. Foreigners have such adorable flattering manners, don't they? But tell me, sweet, who is he? Does he live in Paris? Is he married? Is he married?"

"Yes, but living apart."

"She won't divorce?"

"She's his insurance policy, he says. Besides, she's rich, and richer when her father dies."

"Too bad! I think we hit it off."

"Yes, you did. But watch Danny! He's dangerous."

"He's an overwhelmingly fast worker, isn't he? Oh, I shall watch my step! But I do like him. I see no harm in a dinner and dance. Would that be safe?"

Danilo had an appointment and left them at eight.

She was very tired and went to bed early. The others retired to the kitchen and murmured to each other. They were very happy that Eleanor had scored with Danilo, a connoisseur. "What a pity Danilo's married to that iceberg," said Ivo. "Danilo is tremendously impressed. What a magnificent girl, is what he said to me. I said, 'You can look but you can't touch.' Eleanor's the kind of simple, wholesome girl might make a good wife for Danilo and settle him."

Eleanor, in the dark, was not asleep. She was to meet Thieme at the Gare du Nord, just before nine, in time for the London train. But during the evening, in a corner, Danilo had asked her if she danced, and whether she wouldn't like to "step out" the next evening and go to some night clubs.

"We won't say anything to these nice little lovebirds," he whispered. "They don't like night life—once in a while, birthday —respect them, respect principles, just you and me, we'll get together—think we'll hit it off, eh? Have you brought along a nice dancing dress, eh?"

When she objected that she expected to leave for home the next morning, he had said, "Sleep in, you need it; go the next day. Do it for me. For my sake, make a little concession. My sake.

Lovely girl, beautiful—h'm—ankles. Want to ask your advice. Don't get on too well with my wife, not her fault, not my fault. Just fate. Fate, I met you tonight. Do you believe in fate? Let's go dancing—see if we hit it off? Make a little concession for my sake. Sweetest woman I ever met"—and a sugary kiss, an expert kiss.

She laughed to herself, I'd be a fool to miss it. Hugging a pillow, elated at her success in Paris, Eleanor fell asleep, slept well, but wakened early. She opened the shutters that looked into the old pale-walled street; morning flushed the roofs, people passing. Seeing them looking, she put on her fur coat and sat with her hair hanging over her shoulder. A taxi drove up and a man getting out looked up, anxiously.

"Oh, the pesky man," she muttered between her teeth. Thieme paid off the driver and stood under the window.

"Lazy girl! I've been up for hours. I didn't sleep. How do you feel today? It's a glorious day! Come on! Are you dressed, darling? Come and have breakfast and I'll take you to the station. I'm coming with you to London. I've telegraphed Harriet. Come down quickly. I'll tell you everything. I'll wait."

Licking her lips with a darting red tongue, Eleanor shut the window and moved slowly about, picking up and dropping things. At last she dressed quickly, ran downstairs and gave him a kiss. "Let's go and talk. I'm starved and those lovebirds aren't up yet," said she.

In the café opposite the gates of the Luxembourg where they breakfasted, she told him that she was staying another day in Paris, and that in any case she thought they should see more of each other, to see if they hit it off.

"We don't really know each other yet," she said naïvely. "Yesterday you weren't prepared to go all the way, were you?" She looked at him resentfully. "You let me go; you might have let me go for good."

"I'll do anything you like today to make up for it. I am yours now, even if you're not quite sure. The family will never forgive me.

But it would be madness to let you go: I'd regret this day for the rest of my life."

"Well," she said gaily, "let's see Paris. We won't talk about anything serious now. Let's experiment with each other first."

He was so full of enthusiasm that he wore her out. When he brought her home in the afternoon, he said, "Why won't you let me meet your friends? You don't want to commit yourself? Or you're ashamed of what I've done? Do they know your fiancé?"

But she put him off, saying she and Marky had to have a talk; they hadn't seen each other since school, she had to hear all about Marky's love affair and so forth, "And you know normal life must go on. I owe them something; they are my hosts." Tomorrow, she said, they would really discuss everything. In the meantime he would have had an answer from his fiancée and her family. Till then, "We are better apart."

She hardly knew what she was saying, trusting to habit to get rid of him. She flew upstairs to find out if there was a message from Danilo. There was: he would call for her at six. What a relief Danilo was. Thieme upset her. At times she felt he was touching on some great instability in her, a cold inky well in which the self she enjoyed would be lost. Why all the drama? she thought. It all leads the same way; I'm gay and romantic, and I'm a practical person, too." She forgot all about him as she flew about getting ready, except for the healthy feeling that she had a choice of different men.

"Lovely, lovely!" murmured Danilo, on the stairs, going down to the taxi. "We're going to get on."

They had dinner in his hotel, the old Chatham. Pojarski cutlets with cream, and vodka, to begin with: a small, dainty, rather dry meal. Then they drove to a well-known mediocre nightclub in Montmartre, with handsome Russian hostesses, the sword dance, roast meat on spits, the usual program, but to Eleanor new and elaborate. After that, to the Moulin Rouge, where there was a ballet of young, strange beauties, naked in fishnet; and here, after running his eye over her face, with a businesslike expression, Danilo handed across the table a gift wrapped in tissue paper: an evening handbag from a jeweler, Avenue de l'Opéra, black and nicely fitted. Eleanor flushed, sparkled and smiled.

Danilo leaned back in his chair, eyeing the ballet and Eleanor at the same time. "You like it? Is it to your taste? That's good, for you're to my taste. We suit each other, perfectly, eh, we understand each other! I knew the moment I laid eyes on you," he said, leaning forward. "Sympathy, can't miss it. Eleanor," he murmured, and a very sweet expression came into his face, which, though at times stern, even somber, even cunning, expressed also gaiety, tenderness. As he leaned forward, his eye roved and he started. "There's Roddy!" He sat up quickly and sized up a neighboring table. There were three or four men there, one of them a tall fair Northern type, thin-cheeked, very sleek, personable, about thirty-five. "Man in my business," muttered Danilo. "American, didn't know he was in town. Do you mind"—he leaned forward—" if I ask him over? He'd like to meet you, English beauty. Nothing like an English beauty, fresh, rose-leaf—"

He leaned far back in his chair, looked firmly at Roddy. Roddy, half collapsed on the table, warned by others, turned, waved a hand, smiled fishily, and seeing Danilo's urgent gesture, got up and staggered over to their table. Danilo introduced them, pulled out a chair. "Sit down, sit down!"

"Champagne," said Roddy.

"Had enough!" declared Danilo. "Evening's young yet! Wait awhile!"

But Roddy called a waiter and named a champagne, then sat silent, smiling, smiling at Eleanor. Suddenly, he recited:

> " 'The *Graces* naked danced about the Place,
> The *Winds* and *Trees* amaz'd
> With Silence on her gaz'd,
> The Flowers did smile, like those upon her Face,
> And as their Aspine Stalkes those Fingers band,

(That Shee might read my Case)
A Hyacinth I wisht mee in her Hand.'

"English as the madrigals, and like them, fresh with frank conceits, naïve and intricate, isn't that so? Am I right? I am so fond of old English poetry, exquisite rhythm, natural music."

Danilo began twisting his head, trying to attract the attention of both at the same time, briskly murmuring compliments and "Eh? Roddy, eh?"

Roddy, slopped forward, seized Eleanor's hand and put it to his lips. "Persuade her, persuade her!" cried Danilo, dancing in his chair. "Stay a few days more and we'll show you the town, eh, Roddy!"

"I majored in English literature, I'm a devotee of English genius," said Roddy, "and now I realize that old story about peaches and cream is true."

"Persuade her, persuade," said Danilo, hurried. "Roddy, let's shift."

"I'm quite satisfied," said Roddy, once more lipping Eleanor's fingers. "Aren't we quite satisfied here, Beauty's Queen?

'Shall I come, sweet Love, to thee,
When the ev'ning beames are set?'

"Yes, let's go. Let's go to my flat; we'll get Martha, a friend of mine, nice girl, she's very unhappy, a fellow let her down—she needs cheering up, we'll cheer her up."

Danilo frowned. "Eleanor has her friends, she can't stay up all night. Very nice friends, friends of mine, they entrusted her to me, they said, 'No whoopee, nice young Englishwoman, first time in Paris.' "

Roddy paid no attention to this gibberish but insisted upon going off and telephoning Martha.

They got a taxi and started off for Roddy's flat. They made a few calls on the way, looking into night clubs, and Danilo became impatient. "It's getting too late for this young lady. I have to shepherd her home."

Roddy became querulous. "I know what's on your mind, watch out for this wolf, Eleanor. Listen, Eleanor, don't waste your time on him. Come with me to New York. Introduce you to society! You'll make a hit. You'll marry the first rich man you meet who isn't married, even if he is. You'll be a great success, howling success; what do you say, Beauty's Queen? Come with me? I'm sailing on Tuesday week, I mean it. I'd be only too proud to be your sponsor. I know New York. You'd make a hit. Shakespearean type, 'Of hand, of foote, of lip, of eye, of brow.' Say yes, eh? Ay! *It stinted and said, Ay! Wilt thou not, Jule!*" He quoted, lolling about, resting his uneasy head a moment on the cushions, very unsteady and queasy now. He became angry at his sickness, pounced around, grabbed her hand roughly and said, "Don't be stupid, girl, I'm offering you the world! What's England got to offer; what's this Bosnian got to offer? Do you want to waste your time, waste your life, waste your looks on petty cash? Are you engaged? I see you are! To whom? Some two-by-four accountant, some petty-cash lawyer's clerk, I guarantee." He flung her hand on her lap and said grouchily, "A world to gain and she's temporizing."

Eleanor went with them and did not return to the flat in the rue de la Contrescarpe till late dawn. She slept till midday, and was awakened by Marky, to say a man wanted to speak to her on the telephone. She got up yawning. "Oh, Roddy, is that you?" It was Thieme. She had a long, tedious conversation with him and wanted to meet him for tea, but he had news for her. His cousin and her family were on their way to Paris—now what should they do? Fly to London and get married at once, to present them with a *fait accompli,* "cruel but decisive," said he—or wait and face the music. "While we are not married, they never will believe that I am so dishonorable. The best thing is for us to catch the four o'clock train to London. Can you make it?"

She promised at last.

It was Saturday. Her friends were both at home, and over

lunch she told them in her own way what had happened. "Roddy has offered to take me to New York, on Tuesday week, and coming home in the cab, your friend Danilo, who is practical, made me an offer for this evening, but I don't know what it entails," she chimed naïvely.

"My God," said Ivo, "if Roddy means it, I agree with him. You are lost in that English swamp; what will you get out of a life in the suburbs?"

"But I like the suburbs, I want my home and children and that's all," Eleanor said, "and I want my own career, in writing. I don't think I should like America."

"But I'm sure Roddy de Kuyper can do what he says; why don't you take a chance?"

"Oh," cried Eleanor, throwing herself about amiably, "what advice! You two are safe in the harbor of happy dreams and believe in love; and you advise me to marry for money! Now make two and two of that if you can!" Leaning back to the wall against some dusty, faded tapestry, she stretched her arms against it and laughed softly. "Ah, but, darlings, you're right too, it's lovely to be wanted again. It seems wicked wishing to want to be safe and married; and yet it's the fate of women, isn't it? If you're sure, really sure, like you and Ivo, it doesn't matter dispensing with the little matter of legal permission! But I'm romantic, my precious, I want everything, the white wedding, the friends, the table silver, the new Jacobean; I even want modern walls. Tell me," she said, sitting up, "of course you don't regret the step you've taken, for, of course, law doesn't mean much to you, does it? But don't you feel rubbed the wrong way, when you are left out of things? Oh, I want all life, I don't want to be left out. That's it. But then you have love, of course, real love," she crooned, "that's so different. Oh, no, I don't think I could strike that sort of bargain. I want the real thing, signed, sealed and delivered, I'm old fashioned. Let me sell you America, Roddy said last night; but I'm afraid I'm not buying. I want nothing but the good old ways, smelling of lavender and musk. Yes, darlings, I was tempted—last night I was very much tempted, but I've made up my mind I'll hold out, hold out for respectability. It's settled," she cried, jumping off the couch, "till someone comes up, like poor Robert did, with a straight proposal. I'll tell him thus far and no farther"—she drew an imaginary line with her toe—"and I must have love, too, so America is out."

She would not let them come to the station. She set off with her little bag and went to the Chatham. She waited in the lobby. Presently Danilo came in, grabbed her case, gave it to a boy and went up with her in the lift. In the evening they went to the Tour d'Argent and he found her a room in a large old-fashioned hotel in the rue des Pyramides.

"My wife, you know, my wife; otherwise, you know—" he muttered.

During the next few days, they met frequently. He took her out every night and once bought her a blouse with the finest embroidery. She sent a postcard to her father at Commonwealth Farm in Essex. She said, "Paris is all they say: dream city. Wonderfully cheap by our standards! I was able to stretch my money and stay a few more days for the museums—and shops!"

Danilo was busy, did not take her to the train, but promised to telephone her when he got to London.

Three weeks later, in London, she received a printed announcement of Edwin Thieme's wedding to Harriet. She put it in a drawer with theater programs and restaurant menus. "I was right: it was just an episode." She told some of her friends that she had had a proposal in Paris, "but the man had foreign blood. I didn't feel at home with him."

Danilo came to London and took Eleanor out several times; she also went out with Roddy. Then she became ill and had to take a holiday at her brother's farm. There, for a change, she was warm and had regular meals; she dozed and the days passed quickly at first. Her brother and father were sympathetic when she told them about the difficulties of the literary life in London. She began to realize, as she talked, how much of her time she had filled in with trashy reading, detective stories and women's magazines, "to get a line on the publishers' viewpoint." She had worked quite honestly as well. She tossed in bed; early in the morning she got up to look at the blackness outside. It was winter; the idea of returning to London was cheerless, but she must. She walked about impatiently. "Work, work," she muttered, "dear work, it is my lifeblood." She sat on the edge of her bed. "I must think this out. Yes, I am a woman first, a real female. I must have the experience of love, marriage, children. The lust for life has been my trouble; I have avoided the easy paths. I must marry and then life will be an open book, not chewed-over stories from magazines." She became nervous, bit her lip. "I must be waiting for Mr. Right like every woman who can't marry. Should I have taken Thieme? But I want fresh air in my marriage, not passion, love, the hand of fate. I can't be all-in-all to a man. I'm a modern woman. I'm thirty. No closed world, but society, neighbors, friends, the stream of time. A man with a profession is best." She went downstairs, drank some black coffee, smelled the thin morning coming, walked about outside till it came, breathed heartily, opened her arms to it. "Oh, lovely world —and let me come to my work!" George coming up from the barn saw her, smiled queerly. She sang out, "George, I must go back to town. Work calls."

But now she had a distaste for all sorts of experiences. She thought she must shut herself in and concentrate. She decided to go to a hostel for women only, run by her mother's Society in Regent's Park Road; she would pay less, there was cheap catering and some room service. Her family advanced her some money and she was able to take it easy for a while. She soon made friends and lived the life of the hostel, feeling almost like a schoolgirl again.

They were all women there, some retired, some lazy, some Indian Civil Service widows, some at work. She visited them, exchanging commonplaces and gossip, hearing their stories, bringing biscuits when she had tea with them. She enjoyed the food in the restaurant but rarely spent money there. In spite of everything, she put on weight. Her clothes never quite fitted; they became dingy, they wore out. She saved money on cleaning, on light, on baths and heat. She stayed in bed when it was cold. She got up late, roamed out at nightfall, sometimes dined with the men who called on her. Men visitors were freely allowed. She still had one evening dress and she made herself another in black, "of simple elegance," following Marky's instructions. She received men upstairs in the afternoons sometimes, but she had retreated a little and preferred the older students or men from the Society; they looked respectable. She had one of the smallest rooms, with a cot, a pine table, a chair, a gas ring, but no basin. "The inky way is rough," she would say to visitors smiling. The ladies were kind to her in her poverty. She began to adopt their tone, to harmonize with them, and when Paula, one of them, said roughly, "Get out of here before it swallows you alive," she hardly knew what she meant, though she went about repeating this remark plaintively. Paula had a certain interest for her. She was a big-boned, rough, dark woman who was a schoolteacher and suffered from backaches from long standing.

Paula was thirty-eight. She went to a physiotherapist twice a week; he was her lover on these visits. She paid him his fees regularly. "But don't you think she's paying him for being her lover?" Eleanor would say to the other people in the hostel. She even remonstrated with Paula, the woman herself.

Paula said, "It's love, it's passion, it doesn't matter what you do when you're in love. If you've ever been in love, you'd know that ordinary conventions just don't apply."

"But aren't you ashamed to pay him, and isn't he ashamed to take the money?" asked Eleanor earnestly.

Paula had a pretty little room looking over the back garden. In the garden was a giant elm, ash trees, some apples and laburnums.

"I've always been unhappy, but I will have had something," said Paula. She had rosy chintz curtains, copper and pewter, framed drawings. "I'm an art teacher, but I never saw the beauty of anything; I just saw conventional things and all I saw down there was rough grass. That was what I saw for years and I felt sick with aimlessness. Then I went to see this man, and when I felt what he was for me, I made up my mind, so I don't care what it looks like to anyone, not even to him."

"But," said Eleanor in a gentle, reasonable voice, "he has a wife, Paula."

"She comes in to see me in the waiting room. She talks to me. She knows all about it."

"And aren't you ashamed—don't you feel a bit fidgety?"

"Why should I? I pay them; they need the money. They're poor."

The Hostel for Ladies was a place full of lugubrious love affairs. Eleanor began to think of moving under the wing of the Society. It seemed very cozy and earnest. She felt at ease in their discussions of philosophy, spiritualism, love and social problems. Ladies could help society and things might improve. Could politicians heal the wounds of one bereaved mother? Was matter itself spiritual, or vice versa?

One morning she answered a ring at the front door while coming from breakfast, and found there a young man, dark, white-skinned, neatly dressed, with a belted raincoat and holding new fawn gloves. It was a spring morning. The front hall had just been painted white; the trees opposite had come out early; the sun shone on the porch.

"Miss Brent, please," said the young man.

"Miss Brent is not in now," said Eleanor. "She goes to work early. Perhaps this afternoon, about four—I couldn't say for certain—and then you might ring three times."

The young man looked at her earnestly, rang the bell three times, said, "Oh, I beg your pardon—well, I will try again," and with other polite remarks, he went down the steps, but paused at the gateway, looked back and hesitated before he went away.

What a sweet boy, I like those frank eyes! said Eleanor to herself, going back upstairs. I could manage him.

It was too early in the morning: she was not ready for visitors. Besides, a month before, an ill-dressed inquisitive man had come and asked for her. Paula had answered for her and described him, "an ex-flatfoot!" thus making her very uneasy. Once she had received a sinister, begging letter which sounded threatening. She had difficulties and unpleasant experiences which she carefully concealed.

Two or three years before, she had been in a hotel room late at night with a foreign embassy official, about fifty years old, called Rocky. He was large, tall, fair, sanguine, rather lethargic at times, otherwise a fluent talker, good-natured, considerate. He treated Eleanor as if they were playing a delightful society game. He drank too much brandy. Eleanor had been to different hotels with him, but on this occasion they went to his own hotel, because, he said, they were old friends now and he was feeling tired. "And you are a quiet girl, Ell, you're better for a tired man."

A little later, in the dark, she became cold with fear: she thought the man had died. She had to push away the dead weight of his body; then she quickly dressed and went out in her stockinged feet, shutting the door quietly, and locking it. It was very late; she reached the next floor, put on her shoes and went out of the hotel without being seen, the desk, too, being deserted. She rubbed the key with her handkerchief and dropped it inside railings near the hotel. She had never heard anything of him again and did not know whether he was alive or dead. She carried very little with her always and did not think she had left anything behind her in the hotel.

By now she had quite forgotten it, except when something like this happened. Then she would think uneasily, I have nothing to worry about. Is there something I should worry about? What was that nasty thing—oh, Rocky! But no, I dreamed that. That was a dream. Perhaps someone told me. But what had it to do with me? He must have had heart disease. She had become prudent in the meantime.

The ill-dressed man had handed her a summons from the "Chief of Police" for some trouble over an insufficient bus fare. The ridiculously portentous heading of the summons had given her a great fright, but she had telephoned the family lawyer and explained, "I was daydreaming and went past my stop." She had been cautioned and excused, but since, she had become more careful.

During the day Eleanor thought about the genteel young man and ran downstairs to open the door when he rang in the evening. Her room was tidy and the window was open on the view she had of green backyards with old trees and vines. Next door was an aviary, flowers, a pool. Heinrich Charles was merely on a recruiting visit for the Society. He had a full-time job with them as organizer.

He was of middle size, youthful, dark and slim, with a long head and rounded jawbone, a full face with a hollow and dimple in the cheeks, a short nose; his eyes were dark on white of the perfect shape and color of model eyes in an optician's shopwindow; his mouth, too, was long, sweetly laid open, eyebrows, mustache, dark and slender, and tufts of hair showing under his black homburg. There was a wonderful appealing gleam as he smiled; the peculiar eyes, swimming in their whites, turned up with an appeal that turned her bowels to water.

He seemed astonished to find that she was the woman of the morning, and frowned a little, turning his head to the window for a moment and pursing his lips thoughtfully; but then he turned back, laughed charmingly and said he quite understood her motive. She agreed that it was better to be careful with strangers and they talked about the convenience of the hostel for lonely women. Then without embarrassment, between laughter and apology, he began to talk about himself, in a most beguiling way. His name was foreign because he was foreign. The Society had many branches abroad and his family had joined in Switzerland, where he was born.

"But I am not Swiss. The Swiss visit un-Swissness upon the fathers and the sons. Though my mother was born in Lucerne, my father is foreign—German—and so I too am foreign in Switzerland; I am seriously thinking of becoming British. I admire the British very much indeed. The Society employs me here and I like it here." He spoke three or four languages.

They sat on either side of the window for several hours, talking like old friends. He had known her mother and Count von Ulse; he disagreed with the Count for his many deviations and thought his conversion to Catholicism showed how false his views were. "But surely it was merely for the marriage," said Eleanor.

"Every act betrays us and reveals us," said he. "This was very significant and a final proof of his mundanity."

"I was at the wedding in Paris," murmured Eleanor.

"So was I, and so we might have met a long time ago!"

"But our acts did not betray us to it," she said.

She promised to go to a nearby Society Center on Sunday; there were refresher courses in the week, also. He offered to come to escort her, the next Sunday. She bought a little pamphlet on world peace; they talked about the Oxford Movement. He had visited the community at Glion, the cliff village above Montreux. Heinrich Charles said a moral revival was necessary in good times to combat materialism; in bad times, socialism.

On his next visit he talked about her wonderful eyes, called her a "woman of the world" and said he preferred English manners to all others.

In a little while they became engaged. Shortly after, they had a long conversation, which Eleanor called "an utterly frank talk," and Heinz "making confession." It had begun with Count von Ulse's wedding.

"And there I nearly met my fate; I met a man who said I was his fate," Eleanor said, and they discussed Mr. Thieme, whom Heinz knew slightly. "We have such a lot of friends in common; it is like coming home," said Eleanor. "Heinz, I have been thinking over my past, as they used to call it. I'd like to wipe the slate clean and start all over again. The affair with Mr. Thieme was quite innocent and rather tragic. He met the family in Paris, they came here and married immediately. I received a wedding announcement, but no other word . . . But everything was not so innocent." She opened a drawer in her writing desk and from under loose papers brought out some cabinet photographs of herself, naked, in various poses. "There's no real harm in it, when you're young and have a good figure." She gave a little laugh. "We middle-class girls have so many inhibitions: it takes years of struggle to become normal, healthy, hearty women. If I had been a working girl I should have been married and a mother years ago. Of course, I probably should have been very restless and unfulfilled intellectually, and I'm not sure I should have liked to be matey with the milkman and dustman"—and she mimicked a Cockney woman— "It's 'ot todie, dear!" She was a good mimic.

Heinz said that he understood Thieme in a way. At first, he, too, had had high ideals and believed that chastity led to pure thinking, but he was soon tempted and he yielded. "Two or three older women became rather fond of me," he said demurely. "They thought they were in love with me and I felt I was doing something to make them happy."

A few days later he said during a visit, "You are really a Herbert, aren't you? It would help me socially to say my wife was a Herbert. Is it the same family?"

Eleanor smiled. "Mother would not say she was, but she said, 'We come from the same county; and there is a portrait in the Long Gallery at the seat which is wonderfully like you, Eleanor.' "

"I think that is rather good evidence," Heinz said. "I shall say you're a Herbert and leave it at that. And the Brents? Are they a good family? Should I mention them? You see, I am still a foreigner, and I want to get my values right."

He seemed very pleased when he went away, saying, "You are going to be a great help to me. My family is very pleased."

However, a few days later, Heinz was overcast. He sat looking at her and out of the window, and at length said, "In that other house you lived in, in Camden Town, there were foreigners, Poles, a Hungarian cook you said, and," he added in a lower tone, "a Jewess, you said? Did you like them? Did you feel anything, that is to say, in reference to your own scale of values, did you feel they had a totally different, a minor set of values, apart from being poor? I know you're of pure racial origin and you're very broad, but I ought to ask you."

Naturally, said Eleanor, although she liked them and wanted to help, one could hardly feel that they were the same—in fact, they did not acknowledge the same values. What had been right and nice about them, what showed they were reaching out and up, was that they sent their children to the best private schools they could; she had once been prejudiced, but now she saw there was something lovely and touching about a coalheaver spending his money on a fine school uniform and paying fees and seeing his son win prizes for Latin and Divinity. "Once I thought it very bogus, a raw joke, like a sideshow, but live and learn."

There was a pause, and Heinz said, "I've been to see a genealogist, and he seemed to think it would be easy to prove your connection with the—other Herberts: a quite close cousinage, he thought, was sure, and he has promised to look up some manor house or hall that belonged to that family to which you might have some claim."

Eleanor laughed aloud and kissed him on the cheek. "That's sweet, my pet, but I don't want to sail under false colors; it's not my style. Hatton Garden Joe wanted me to pretend I was a White Russian; he said I was the type, and if I could cultivate a Russian drawl"—and here she imitated it—"he could do a lot for me. I can sing and recite a bit and I can learn anything. But I said, 'I'm me, Joe.' Mother has always felt she was one of those others, but darling Mummy was so keen on kinship; I don't think I care. I'm very democratic, Heinz."

After another pause Heinrich said, "We must be absolutely above suspicion, you see."

Eleanor exclaimed at this. He then said, "I have a confession to make. My blood is not absolutely pure. One of my grandfathers made a mistake"—he laughed—"I don't mind, I'm rather proud of it. He was an official in a middle-sized town and fell in love with a beautiful Jewess. The family was wealthy, cultivated, they loved music, had salons, and my grandfather stood firm; he married her. So my grandfather was of pure race, but my mother was half-Jewish. I don't have the name."

"I suppose I should have known," said Eleanor after a slight hesitation. "You are so very dark, aren't you?"

Heinrich said impatiently he was not of *that* swarthiness, he was merely a brunette, an old European type, an Armenoid. "My grandmother was as fair as you are, a beautiful gold-haired Russian girl."

"I don't think it matters, Heinrich," said Eleanor, very practically. "This is England, you know, and we need not mention it, though I am quite proud of it. They say a little admixture improves a race." She looked at him carefully and laughed. "To think of your being partly Jewish! What fun."

This new flavor in Heinrich excited Eleanor; she thought how romantic her life was. Heinrich had confessed that he was very ambitious—he had great hopes in England: "The English are a sensible people, they admit foreigners, they admit anyone. They have very little caste feeling. You would know, if you had lived in Switzerland, it's a snobocracy full of intrigue. Here your old pattern of *laissez-aller* works in my favor. A foreigner has a chance at a knighthood; he has merely to obey the rules. I'm thirty, I know where I'm going. I'll have an English wife and children. Who's to say, with my way of going to work, that I won't end up in the House of Lords?" Eleanor burst out laughing, but she was charmed.

"Oh, Heinrich, the best thing is we know what we want, and life is so simple when you know that!"

She was in a hurry to shed her old life, and she went round the town visiting small flats and arranging new furniture in them in her mind's eye. "I'm afraid I'm born to be a good wife," she kept saying, and she was already very impatient when she was called Eleanor Brent—let the day come when she would be Mrs. Charles. "Sir Henry and Lady Charles!" "Oh, Heinz, you've awakened all my sleeping lust for life. I was like this when I was a girl. When

I'm married I'll be at peace. I shall simply throw away all my *excess baggage.*"

Eleanor in her confessions had mentioned only two or three wealthy lovers, including James von Ulse. Heinz had seemed very much impressed. However, a few days after the last questions, about the Herberts, he seemed perturbed, and after sitting for some time in silence, he said, "Eleanor, I think that what you granted those others, your—lovers, you should grant me before we marry. It is only fair. Otherwise, you put me on a lower level."

Eleanor refused, and then said she must think it over: she must weigh the for and against. They were not like those others, they were setting out for a life partnership. She wanted it all to be above board. He was to come back in three days for her decision.

She thought it over for some hours and then went to consult several of her friends. She did not speak of it in the hostel because of Heinz's position in the Society. All her friends were against Heinz. "He sounds tricky to me: he doesn't ask for it for love, but so that he won't be cheated."

"Oh, but, darling, this isn't a question of love but of equity. I see his viewpoint but I'm very worried whether it is right. If it's right, I'll do it; if it isn't, I won't."

Another said, "Don't be weak, for he's weak."

Diana Cruse said, "Don't give in, I see his character: if those are his words, then he won't marry you after you make the concession. He seems to be quite a quibbler. And you're a wobbler. Hold tight."

"Do you think I'm a wobbler?" Eleanor asked, in surprise. "Oh, no, I have a very strong will. Mother always said that what I wanted I'd get. But I will hold out!"

The engagement drifted along. Heinz had to make various arrangements: he had to make trips abroad for the Society; and he wanted to buy a house before he married, but could not get his family to agree to lend him the money. Meantime Eleanor lived in her usual way, seeing no reason to change till she was sure to marry. She did not worry about buying clothing and gave up looking for flats; but she gradually gave up going down to Fleet Street, contenting herself with the thought that when things were settled, she'd begin a book—without a book to her name, she'd always be on the fringe of literary work. Editors only respected writers with a name made. She also met a few men in the same way, for she was not very interested in Heinz as a man, although she liked him well enough; and she thought, If something better comes along, I'll return the ring. He looked at it often, admiring it for the price he had paid, and saying, "This is really an investment. The price of diamonds has risen since I bought it." But she didn't mind; she smiled. She was indifferent to his character; if they married, things would go along in the usual way and she would be glad to be usual. It is true that sometimes she got very impatient.

Heinz told her of an affair he had had with two sisters, both older than himself: a most difficult entanglement. Eleanor was not at all pleased. That week she ran wild with her men, resentful and jealous: a fury burned in her; for a moment she wanted to go to the devil, roister, never marry—her heart burned. She would never marry the wretch. But they already had the habit of their engagement. Heinz apologized, he had tears in his eyes. "Don't let me go. I was just beginning to have confidence in myself."

Eleanor went to Switzerland, to Lausanne, to stay with Heinz's parents for a month before her marriage. She was to call her mother-in-law Leni—she called her "Leni darling"; her father-in-law was "Volodya." Leni was a fine, big woman with sandy hair, boastful, jolly, lazy but house-proud; she had a slavey from the mountains whom she drove half to death. Volodya was a talkative, able, small man with graying dark hair. They "fell in love" with Eleanor and declared that she was exactly the girl they had always hoped Heinrich would marry.

"He was a very naughty boy, he could not make up his mind," said Leni.

"Why should we think about it now when he has brought home such a fine girl?" asked Volodya in a hinting tone of voice, and twinkling with men's mysteries.

Eleanor said, "I'm putting myself entirely into your hands, Leni darling. I know the very least possible about housework, I have always been so busy outside; and you must simply teach me how to cook the things that Heinz likes, for I want to know the straight way to his heart."

Leni was delighted with her: "Oh, we are very simple people really, and we like very simple dishes—potatoes, and red cabbage and apples and big pancakes—do you like that? It is all very good, though, and *very economical,*" she said, with a merry smile and a wink. She had a well-organized kitchen full of dishes, all very clean; but it was the slavey who did the work. Sometimes they would bake a cake together and sit in the kitchen praising themselves and it, and call Volodya in to decorate it. "He can't do everything but he can ice a cake." Then Leni would good-naturedly correct and scold him. Afterwards, they would make coffee and eat the same cake. Leni was shocked to find that Eleanor had no trousseau, "But then your poor Mummy is dead." She gave her a quantity of goods, and they bought some underclothes in Lausanne; it was all to go with a vase and a clock or two, in a sealed package, as bride's trousseau.

During this month Eleanor came into her own. She adapted herself completely to the Charleses and went home in a fine glow.

She told Heinz that she had learned to make him all his home dishes, "Apple and red cabbage, Heinz, bacon-and-egg pancake."

"I left home to avoid Mother's cooking," said Heinz with a smiling grimace. "Can't we have some rabbit pie or toad-in-the-hole? Bad as they may be, they can't be as bad as Mother's."

But Eleanor had formed a friendship with her mother-in-law and decided to follow her advice. Leni and Volodya were an ideal couple. And then they were so very economical. For among other conveniences, Eleanor suddenly saw in marriage an ideal system for saving money and growing comfortable. The man brought home the money; the wife saved it; so they lived happily ever after.

The Charleses had meanwhile agreed to finance a house in London which was to pay for itself: they were to let all but one floor in single rooms. The house was to belong to Vladimir and Lena Charles, though they hinted that with the first child or a little later, it might be handed over to Eleanor and Heinrich.

Busy with these plans and with some clothes for her new life, Eleanor would sit up late and sleep well. She looked fresh and gay, innocent, girlish. One clear morning in April, some weeks before her wedding, while she was still in Switzerland, she was awakened by a blackbird which had begun to sing on the eaves and had a pure voice and a musical sense; the separate rounded tones dropped down past the window into the orchards that sloped to the lake. It was not quite dawn. Wide-awake, Eleanor lay and smiled. Her heart started and she thought with a sharp pain, I don't love him. She lay and tried to piece their history together to excuse their marrying: "There is sentiment in it and sense too; we are two adult clear-eyed people." But her heart ached that day, and the cozy domestic routine, Leni's ways, seemed dull—there was a smell of mold. I am to marry a man I don't love. When she thought it, she flushed. How had it happened? Surely, she thought anxiously, there are other chances; I might love, but, of course, nowadays you can easily get a divorce! But she didn't want to marry a man she could divorce. Oh, if only I could talk it all over with someone.

She spent the last days of her visit obediently smiling, acting a perfect accord, but she was glad when she sat in the train and the train started. Now I must think this thing through before it is too late.

In London she was unhappy. Heinz had been at the train, of course; he began talking about the plumbing in the house. Is it possible to have children with a man you don't love? Will I love those children? She was flustered and anxious, as if about to walk with a meek willing crowd into a prison: She had made a fatal promise in a dream and was only now waking up. She had no sooner got home to the hostel than she went to visit her friends there, and had several long conversations with them about her marriage.

"But, Paula dear, I don't love him. Should I marry him?"

Contrary to her expectations, each of her friends said, "Yes, marry him, you must marry."

She went to see some of her married friends, and in an earnest low voice asked them the same question. "But is it right to marry a man you don't love? I always thought you married for love. You married for love, didn't you? Would you have married just for companionship?" All said they had married for love, but some said they would have married without. "At a certain age we must marry."

"Yes," she said, "I have let so many chances slip by, but, oh, I wasn't ready. I should have married Robert; I was ready then. Oh, perhaps I should marry blind and let what will come."

But the doubt, even a slight horror, woke up in her each morning. I should be waking up with joy. Only six days to my wedding.

The morning came. Heinz arrived with a white flower, a bouquet and white gloves for her, and together in the hostel sitting room they waited for their two witnesses. Heinz had forgotten nothing: he was an exemplary bridegroom.

Oh, I'm doing it, I'm going through with it: millions have done it, she said to herself, smiling. Those were just the jitters. And she said, "Would you believe it, Heinzl, my pet, I had the jitters."

"Well, I hadn't; I'd made up my mind and that was enough for me. And, Ell, I've changed my name legally to Henry. Please call me Henry from now on."

She found she was very nervous and stupid; she could hardly attend to what he was saying. "Henry?"

"Yes, to get rid of that stupid joke."

He was exquisitely turned out, a gem of a man; beside him, Eleanor tall and plump, in a dark blue frock with too many frills, looked dowdy; she wore a dowdy hat, but her flushed and slightly shadowed face, oval, bound in her smooth fair hair, was perfectly charming.

"I regret one thing only," said Heinz, now Henry, "and that

is that we're not having an Anglican ceremony. It would look better. As soon as I can, I intend to join the Established Church officially: but, of course, the Society is a kind of International I would be foolish to give up. I have friends everywhere through it. We might manage by having you become an Anglican. I certainly want my children to be proper Englishmen. We must all be absolutely on the up-and-up."

"But why?" said Eleanor, amused.

"A man has to plan every step in his career or else marry money, if he is to succeed. The advantage of England is that there are plenty of loopholes for you to climb into the top drawer."

Eleanor laughed. "Oh, Heinz, I'm in love with our future and I do mean to help you—to begin with, I'll unscramble your metaphors."

He gave her a proud, fiery look. She laughed. But when they came to the Society's rooms, she began to rustle and arch her neck and delightfully acted the bride. She was carrying a new handbag, from the Goldsmiths' & Silversmiths', which had been sent by Danilo. She had written not only to Robert, her ex-fiancé, but to some of her old lovers to announce her coming marriage; out of consideration she had written only to the wealthy ones and had received two or three small gifts. She was surprised and hurt that the gifts were so mean; she had imagined that Danilo would send her at least a coffee set. "He gives that to every cigarette girl," she said. Another had sent an inexpensive modern bedside lamp, and another six pairs of gloves. "I expected more from them," she complained, looking sulkily at these gifts. "They have cartloads of it; it could have come out of office expenses!" She did not explain to Henry who these donors were. He read the cards, and without comment, went on with their private discussions. But once in their home, he disparaged these particular gifts, with a quiet constant irritability. It gave her pleasure at first; then she became more serious and tender towards him, and in good time they were lost to sight.

*   *   *

Eleanor revisited the hostel once more to get a small trunk of old clothes and papers she had been keeping in Paula's room. They had tea. "This is my past," she said to Paula, looking at the little trunk, the chintz-covered room and Paula herself, "the dear past. The present for me is just this one day when I bury all this for the sake of Heinz—or, rather, Henry—and the children. Henry is doing the same."

"So you've decided about the children," said Paula. "Good luck to you and them."

"You see, dear, we will have my father-in-law's house, we have room. We have picked out a day and night nursery, a work-room for me, a sitting room and kitchen-dinette room in the basement. I am sorry you cannot come and see me, Paula, when we are settled in, but we are going to start off just with our own kind, you know; and that means I have to put all my dear bohemians in the attic of my private life and lock the door and throw away the key. Oh, my dear, I am going to live in full daylight, at least no more groping and hoping, no snatched kisses, no halfway affairs, but real love and life. Nothing shabby, mean or furtive: the good life. How I wish you could do the same!"

She and Heinz discussed ways of dismissing her old bohemian friends kindly. "I've loved them and I still love them, but they just won't fit in," she agreed. Heinz detested them by mere description; he feared too that they had witnessed all her errors of taste and known of the rich lovers.

"My private life has been my private life," she said crisply, "and they are the souls of discretion—in fact, they have to be: their lives are so muddled, poor dears."

They made out a list. Some names were stricken off at once; some were to receive wedding announcements for business or personal reasons. Eleanor would write a personal note to some from whom wedding presents could be accepted, and to certain others, too, she must write, explaining that she was severing relations. They put their heads together and had an amusing, a pleasant evening; but sometimes Eleanor would say, "Oh, it doesn't seem nice, I can't cut her off!" She could not cut Marky off. "Why, Heinz? I'll never be visiting Paris."

"Well, we'll let it fade away."

She could not cut Diana Cruse off: "Mrs. Appleyard would never excuse it. Besides, I'm not sure Diana ever had anything to do physically with her Thomas; she is quite refined, and aesthetic, even a little bric-a-brac: you can't lift a china petticoat!"

For a single moment of silent embarrassment, Eleanor wondered why she lied so about Diana and Thomas, whose love affair was of seven years' date. She flushed. "I'm afraid Thomas will never marry her, poor dear," she said.

A week after the wedding Diana invited her to lunch in the Strand and brought her a gift. Eleanor, dressed in the navy blue silk and fox furs in which she had married, talked sweetly about their new home, two fine high-ceilinged rooms furnished in brown and green, which they were to occupy till the house was got ready.

"We'll have only men lodgers, I made that a proviso," said Eleanor. "Henry and I agreed that girls are not so dependable: they are forever washing out things and making a mess, and then there is, of course," she murmured, "the question of men visitors—we don't want anything like that. It's not that we're such prudes, but it gives the house a poor look. And we will make it very clear to the men—no girls! This house is our investment; it's our hostage to fortune; we have got to get the right class of people."

"It is lucky you and I found easygoing landlords," said Diana, "for in a sea of millions like London, you have to let queer fish swim."

Eleanor said primly, "I think, Diana, when you marry, you will find that there are reasons for the accepted code. Looked at from the inside, marriage is much more like a sound business proposition than a picaresque tale."

They were sitting in a "palm court." The filtered light from above shone faintly on Diana's fair curls, lacquered hat-cherries, her teeth and a locket.

"You look very nice," continued Eleanor, "quaint and dear—

you are fitted for a cottage with curds and strawberries; oh, don't we waste our lives in London, eating our dreams! Though it's lovely to have that in one's background too, struggle and dreams and youth. I want you to come and see us very soon. I told Henry I must keep one or two friends from my schoolgirl past. Thomas must come, too. It will be all right! I'll only invite you when I have a dinner party of ten or so, and nobody will know you are together —there'll be no slip-up, or scandal."

"What on earth do you mean? What scandal?"

"Well, dear," said Eleanor very softly, "it has been said that you and Thomas are a little too intimate. But you can count on me to play the perfect hostess; there will always be others there to cover you. Henry is rather old-fashioned. That is the German side of him."

Diana looked at the wrapped gift parcel beside Eleanor's plate, at the sunlight coming through the milky glass roof, at the palms; and then said, "I never liked this place but it's really quite pleasant."

"Oh, yes, isn't it, Di? I think when I come into town for shopping I'll lunch here always. They have such nice girls, and how demure they look in those silly little caps. If we do get a little maid, I think I'll dispense with the white trimmings altogether."

She told Henry that she had felt "relaxed and happy" and that they had got over the sticky places beautifully, that Diana had at once seen what she meant about Thomas and that of course there was no reality in it: it was just a bachelor girl's dream. But when Diana refused her dinner invitation, she was pleased at that too.

2
·
Home and Children

IN PRINCESS STREET, a short spur street of terraced houses, running downhill off Finchley Road, Henry Charles's parents had bought a house for letting for about three thousand pounds, and had repaired the worst parts of the rotted flooring, put in some new pipes, painted the front doors and windows, bought a vanload of secondhand mats, chairs and divans; and handed the house to their newly married son for renting. Eleanor and Henry paid a low rent for the ground floor, which had the back garden, a small triangle. There were two upper floors with, in all, one large and six small rooms, disposed about the short staircase, with two landings and cupboards under the pitched roof. In the back attic, too small for a bedroom, they put an old gas stove so that tenants could cook. The walls had been painted a deep cream and had not been touched for many years. The house, all but the ground floor, was furnished in London lodging-house style, with thin brown curtains, brownish mats, and mended and re-painted furniture. The divans and upholstered chairs had a broken spring or so. But Eleanor had not wanted the rooms to be too depressing, and so they had put in a few pictures, ashtrays and mantelpiece ornaments. Her own quarters were furnished in blue and off-white, with a cheerful secondhand rug and two large blue vases.

The house was like many other lodging houses, better than some; it was near a station on the tube, not too far from London University, quite convenient for students. If they wished, they could register with London University, as suitable landlords. The question at once came up about foreign students: dark-skinned foreign students would perhaps pay more and ask less than local students. There were other lodging houses in the same street which made a good profit merely by renting to them. But Henry Charles refused absolutely to have to do with them, and Eleanor said, "Why raise unpleasant questions?" They further restricted the kinds of tenants they would accept: no workmen or laborers, or factory hands; just quiet, respectable people, clerks, schoolteachers, people in government employ, students. Nothing could be easier than the mere letting of rooms; almost any room of any sort in any street can be let. Millions of people, and families, have found out how to live their entire lives in one room in big cities. "But, of course, no families either," Eleanor said. They did not want their house to be classed as a slum.

Eleanor managed the house well: it began at once to be profitable.

"I'm encha-ahnted with the idea of running a whole house," declared Eleanor in the evening, stretching herself back in an easy chair of plain blue and kicking off her shoes. "We'll go over it inch by inch, fix it up gradually and we'll be able to get better rents and a better class of student. Some of those foreign students, especially the postgraduates from Germany, Holland and Switzerland—well, like yourself, Henry—get quite good allowances from their families, or even work here in banks and such. I've drawn up a schedule which we'll keep to strictly, over the whole year, say, or longer if you like; and it will be a delightful hobby, as well as good solid hard work, while we're waiting for the children."

She was now very busy, happy, pricing paints, wallpaper, tools and furnishings; she started to go to streetmarkets and "loved the bargaining." She intended gradually to clear out the poorest of the secondhand furniture on the ground floor and make an up-to-date home. She "haunted auctions," bought some "very good-looking stuff" very cheap, and made it ready for Henry to mend in the weekends.

"Oh, this is fun," cried Eleanor, and when Henry came home from work on Saturdays, she had a program for him. She had ordered wood for shelving and cupboards; doors and windows were to be rehung, made flush, puttied, painted. There were to be new fastenings, the hastily mended floors improved. One of the upstairs rooms could be partitioned off with hardboard to make two separate lets.

"Volodya," she said, referring to her father-in-law, "will find he has a property in prime condition. And, of course, Heinzl, my pet, we are building better than we know: I assume the house is for the grandchildren!"

When gay she could not resist teasing him with his "Heinz." It seemed so funny to her to call him Henry. She continued: "We'll raise the rents half a crown, they can hardly complain when we've improved the place, a pot of paint will do wonders; and we'll make Volodya open his eyes when the year's accounts are in. The shilling-in-the-slot meters will pay for a few new meters. I have a natural talent for budgeting: you'll find me in all the nooks and crannies with my notebook in my hand."

At night, after washing the dishes, which they did together, they discussed certain problems. A very gentlemanly applicant for one of the bigger rooms turned out to be only a painter and decorator, but he had his own small shop. She thought they should accept him: he might do inside work for them cheap, as a consideration for a low rent, for he absolutely insisted on her taking off two and sixpence . . . The garden needed digging, there was woodworm in the fence posts, some trees had to be cut down, they needed a shed, some new back steps, eventually the whole back hall should have new wood in it. She had mapped out a program for Henry and herself: they would work all through the weekends and this year give up their holiday. "Why should we pay a penny out to professionals when we can do it all?"

She went about the place all day singing, in a plain dress, her hair in a knot. She bloomed; and if she sat down by the hearth for a while to read a woman's magazine, she saw in it hundreds of hints, articles and stories which helped her, or alluded to her home and her life. Only sometimes—at night it might be—when she woke up suddenly, it was as if blackness yawned in her mind or heart: was this awful dullness, were these hours of looking blandly into each other's alien faces, marriage? She was happy in her silence; but should they not have "cozy chats"?

Henry was unhandy, tired after his week's work, running around town or on the Continent arguing, lecturing, persuading. He would have liked to spend his time with books, music and intellectual friends. Eleanor had done this in her youth and "packed it away." She was glowing with the "real work ahead." She said, "I'm completely earthbound, Henry, flesh-and-blood happy; I've got down to bedrock, I feel real life all round me, we've dug in; bless us!" Their part of the house within a year looked, mostly owing to herself, fresh, modern, spacious. They were saving money for themselves and making money for the parents.

Henry was a little tired. He was not nearly as strong as Eleanor, though he had a fresh, youthful look and soon seemed a little plumper. He and Eleanor followed a strict diet to keep their figures and for economy's sake. "We like simple things, your kind of home-style dish, plain and satisfying, Leni darling," Eleanor wrote to her mother-in-law. "Our digestions are good and our waistlines and bills are down." Eleanor worked out her weekly menus on Sunday nights. For breakfast she prepared something very indigestible, a happy idea of Henry's. He had boiled oats, two hard-boiled eggs and chicory "to give him ballast"; and so ballasted, he was sometimes able to get through to the evening without eating.

At other times she prepared a pile of large pancakes, with bacon, in the German and Swiss style, cold and heavy at eating; and another pancake, too, kept you from hungering—flour, egg powder, milk and raisins fried in hot fat and served with honey. This recipe she got from her mother-in-law. At night they might have codfish with boiled potatoes and mustard sauce; with custard and jam. No wine or beer ever came into the house, few condiments, no sauces or spices. They felt a moral pride in eating the "budget" cuts of meat and the kitchen grease with smallest fat content. They had a "real hearty meal" on Sundays and then followed the usual routine of cold meat served with a black sauce as in Germany, fritters or meat balls, shepherd's pie, an "all-vegetable day" and so forth. Eleanor called it her "streamline budgeting" and was very conscientious, very proud and happy.

The house was never finished, but she did not mind that, she liked it. As soon as a tenant left, she would be up in his room, cleaning, puttying, painting the window sill, fixing up a raffia lampshade. She still bought cheap women's magazines, but she now also bought monthlies for the "handyman" and "the practical mechanic." At night she would be eager to tell Henry the dozen details of her improving work. He was pleasant, polite, even gay; but she could see he was already planning the work he would do after dinner, at his desk, under his student's reading lamp. She had got used to that, too; she said to herself, It is a happy picture. She knew Henry aimed at the position in the Society Count von Ulse had held and she urged him on. She grinned maliciously to herself; she would, after all, be married to a Society head. She had joined the Society before her marriage, but she did not care much about it and Henry did not urge her to take part in its activities. Several times, when she hinted that she might do so, he said almost irritably, "There's plenty of time, you've got other work to do, leave that to others," and once he said frankly, "I'm not so sure the Society is going to claim me all my days. The Established Church is a better label socially. Leave it to me, Ell, please, when the time comes."

Eleanor began to foresee a time when they might be able to

take over the house next door. She could easily manage two, with a charwoman to help.

"I wish," she said once, "that we had a house with a big dining room, I could serve breakfasts. At ten shillings per, I could make a good bit on each tenant; we could buy groceries in big quantities and get a ten percent reduction. Students are hungry; the quality of tea, bacon, marg and baked beans doesn't bother them. I know all about it. I've had my belly-pinching years and no harm came of it." But this was going too far, for Henry: he wanted her to go up, not down.

"We don't need money as badly as that," he said. "I married you to make people look at me; I didn't marry a hashhouse cook."

"You have no imagination," said Eleanor, in a temper: "I'm a splendid manager: we'd be able to buy a house to let as a furnished private house in five years."

They had words about it.

"Don't you see," Eleanor cried, "that when we've got that far, I'll be free to write." The old ambition burned in her when she was in a temper, like an old wound. "I've got to write," she would burst out. "I'm not going to let marriage clip my pinions. You've got your books and outside contacts."

But usually their evenings were placid, sweet. They never ate in town, nor went to a theater, unless they got free tickets. They might go to Society lectures or other functions. Otherwise they were satisfied with their home. After dinner they now piled the dishes for the char, and then Henry would sit at his table surrounded by books of philosophy and current periodicals in various languages, while Eleanor with a pile of magazines beside her would read through and make marginal notes upon every kind of article and story. She felt an "editorial position in a woman's magazine" would suit her best. She had the critical faculty well developed and was, she could say, "a tiptop finishing-hand."

Every Saturday she spent the afternoon alone in her workroom, going over the week's accounts. At that time, Henry made her an ample household allowance but kept several pounds back for himself; and "the house" paid for his season tickets and all clothing: Eleanor bought no clothing, thinking that at any time they might have to prepare for their first child.

Henry had two weeks' holiday: the first week he went away alone to a seaside hotel owned by the New Society, while Eleanor kept an eye on the house; and the second week Eleanor went to the same hotel while Henry kept house. Over a long weekend they might hike, sleeping in country inns or farmhouses, or, in fine weather, in their sleeping bags. They divided their packs equally; yet for Henry it was too much. He was beginning to show town pallor, a shortness of breath and poor appetite. But he remained cheerful and patient; they had real common interests, in the doings of the Society, and in the children they hoped for and often spoke about. Where would they put them? What names would they have? Would they have a quite different view of the world? Does morality change? They even had slight disagreements about the children's education.

Every quarter, every year, Eleanor made up a balance sheet. One of her chief complaints was that though she worked so hard and made money, in English law the money belonged to her husband, and she had no commercial standing. What of the future when she had a position in the literary world? "I think I'll have a bank account then in the name of Herbert," said she. He never answered this.

In two years the house was in order, they had raised the rents, they owed nothing; but life was very quiet.

"Oh, if only Volodya would buy the house next door, then I would get up every morning full of beans," said Eleanor yawning one evening. They sat in the back room. A white carpet lay on the black floor; they had green curtains, orange, red and blue pictures and china ornaments, a black leopard, a blue fish, a zebra. They had a bronze vase and a fluorescent lamp for Henry's work. Eleanor was sometimes alone now, for Henry had begun his course of lectures. "Everything is in order now, Heinz," continued Eleanor briskly. "We must think seriously about the children."

"It was our idea from the beginning, wasn't it?" he said, not looking up from his writing.

"Of course. And now we must be businesslike and scientific about it," said his wife. "I have read all I can lay my hands on, and boiling it down to two points, we have: first, that we ought to be quite systematic about trying; and secondly, that we ought to try shock, change of air, change of diet, some complete change in our lives, for that very often brings it on." She was privately anxious, wondering if certain chemicals she had used in her old free days had made it difficult for her to conceive. Furthermore, she had been an athlete, and she had heard that athletes had children with difficulty.

They followed Eleanor's plans, and within the next three years had two children—Deborah, a dark-haired, small-boned girl, and Russell, a fair, affectionate boy with blue eyes and broad face. They had to take another room in the house, losing the rent; to change the plumbing; and with the second child they had to dislodge the tenant from a small room on the third floor for the Dutch girl who came to them *au pair* to learn English. She was a university graduate, knew English, and the arrangement worked out as poorly as usual.

The Dutch girl had naïvely expected to be treated as "a lady and one of the family, joining us and our guests in the evening," according to Eleanor's letter; and Eleanor, in a cozy fantasy, had seen them all happily industrious or meditative in the evening, Henry working, she and Corrie, like two old college friends, talking about life. But every day Corrie had rough housework to do that she had never touched at home; she had days off and evenings out like any other servant; she could not make free use of the telephone; her rights and position were always in doubt; and being *au pair* as "a friend, a lady and an equal," she was not paid for her work, receiving merely a trifle called pocket money. At mealtimes, she was expected to speak German, which she knew well, to improve their German. There was no nursemaid; the work for the two small children alone—endless, unpleasant and regulated to the smallest detail—exhausted her. Eleanor was a conscientious mother, but seemed to Corrie censorious, petty, rigid, ridiculous. The Dutch girl, highly educated in the arts, religious, conservative, healthy and not unlike Eleanor, had not even the smallest scientific knowledge.

When Eleanor first mentioned "germs," Corrie looked at her appalled; germs to her were a "superstition." It took Henry a whole evening to make her even willing to reconsider her notions. Gradually she became quite credulous when Henry spoke.

Eleanor was unhappy. Her mother had always said, "I get along so well with servants," and Eleanor had said the same. "Why does she object to the work?" said Eleanor in tears one evening, when Corrie after washing the dishes in a terribly stormy silence had gone up to bed, without a word. "She sees me working like a carthorse; it isn't as if I were lazy. It's share and share alike. Mother always said, 'The mistress of the house must do her share,' and I do more than mine. The trouble is, she doesn't like children; she lacks imagination. A college education desiccates some girls. And then at table, she always wants to talk to you. I can never get a word in. Her table manners are very poor."

At first, however, Corrie was quite happy, for she had heard that the English were poor cooks, instead of which she found a household which provided the food she was used to, though too little of it.

Now Eleanor spent more time wrestling with the accounts. She had two babies and three adults to provide for, out of what Henry could allow her. If she cut down on her own food, though it was good for her figure, it yet did not yield enough to feed Corrie.

"There is only one way out of it," she said to Henry, "and that is for you to hand your salary over to me, as I am the household economist, and let me give you your fare money and a bit for lunch."

This seemed a good plan to them both. "This way, I must save, and I can't be tempted by bookshops and restaurants," said Henry.

"And I really must discipline myself and get down to some

writing for profit," remarked Eleanor. "We agreed we should both have a career, as well as children, and I simply must start now. After all, that is what Corrie is here for, leaving out the frills and how d'ye do—she is here to let me work."

They then calculated how little Henry needed for town each day; and Eleanor again wondered whether she could not take breakfasts up to the lodgers.

"My wife is not going to carry breakfasts to students," said Henry, and the whole discussion and worry caused some irritation. "This is all a little dreary," said Henry. "We already have a houseful of strangers and one in the home itself—we're never alone."

"A home is a partnership," said Eleanor, sitting at the table and tapping her pencil on her writing pad. "I've got everything figured down to a halfpenny, Henry, and if I could only cut myself down on the accounts, as I have cut you, we should get along like a house on fire."

"Well, I suppose we'll be through the worst soon—when do you think we can get rid of Corrie? When she goes, you'll have one less to feed."

"No, the solution is for me to earn money, too. Why don't I start a correspondence course in writing like old Banes in Fleet Street?"

"Advertise my home in the papers? Certainly not."

"What am I to do with you, Henry, with your pride? Well, I must just set my teeth and go through the bills again. Something has got to come out."

Eleanor had so much to do, and did it so well, that at the end of each day she slept well. She began every morning at six, and by eight in the evening was ready to read magazines. She disciplined herself and sat down at the typewriter every afternoon at two, when the babies were supposed to sleep. She had a quantity of magazines about child care and managed to turn out two or three articles, spiced with her own experiences and hospital and neighborhood anecdotes, which she at first sent in to the Banes Agency. When Banes turned them down, she sent them round herself. But her old articles had been placed because of the fine names attached; by herself she could do nothing. The cost of this unsold work appeared in red in her accounts.

At first she had liked Corrie, a tall, pleasing girl, with smooth fair hair. They had been almost like sisters, laughing a lot and exchanging college experiences. She had written to Corrie's family and had letters from her mother and a sister. But now an almost unbearable strain had begun. Eleanor shed tears. For instance, Henry, who, like most Swiss people, knew three or four languages, thought that he would improve his position in the New Society by learning Dutch, for the New Society had temples, offices and a large following in Holland, with headquarters in The Hague. This required much study from the busy young man, and to acquire Dutch without tears he began to do the evening work with Corrie, helping to put the babies to bed, repeating little rhymes after her, setting the table with her, asking her the names of dishes. They began to have jokes in Dutch; they would burst out laughing at language-book quibbles. Henry dried the dishes, too, while Corrie washed. Before this, Corrie had not been anxious to wash the dishes, but now she liked to do it, laughed a good deal and would sit with them by the fireside afterwards, instead of going to her room with a polite good-night. Henry had taken to smiling gaily when he saw Corrie. She was eight years younger than his wife and himself. He began to explain his ideas in philosophy to her, and she was most interested and would talk with him by the hour about them.

Eleanor at first tried to master her jealousy; later she found herself with a political opinion, too, different from theirs. She was mild-hearted, afraid of clashes; she felt that if the course of history was flowing in any direction, even towards socialism, it would be useless for her to try to dam it. "Action in personal affairs may be right, if you feel right is on your side," she expostulated, "but surely it is wrong to try to turn history to suit your prejudices?"

"The other side believes in action; the socialists are ruthless and force us to action," said Henry.

"Why, Mrs. Charles, what does the word 'power' mean?" exclaimed the girl. "What does it imply? Not simply sitting on the beach and letting the ocean sweep us away, surely? We study the ocean, sail it, control it and fly over it and we might even jellify it. You have a thinker, J.B.S. Haldane—have you heard of him?—he said that for a joke, but it is not entirely a joke. It is human to control, only a jellyfish allows itself to be carried along; and even then—"

Eleanor felt a despairing frenzy: the words "Where am I to turn?" came to her. She forced a society smile and left the room with a pleasant good-night. She threw herself on their large double bed, struggling with her feelings, and tried to read.

At this time her dress was very plain for economy's sake, and she thought there was something mean and tawdry in a married woman's coquetry. She and Henry were embarked on a great, time-honored business, founding and rearing a family. What had soulful confidences and beauty hints to do with that —they were for unmarried girls. Eleanor now often succeeded in looking commonplace. All the commonplaces of her present life were delicious to her—even the fatigues, which sometimes made her cry—for this was real, common life, "down-to-earthness." This was what she had been looking for when she worked in the hotel as a maid, what she looked for when she was free with men, and what she had enjoyed in the lodging house, "life in the raw, real life," wholesome and sacred. In the home her function was real, wholesome and sacred. She was full-blown woman, wife, mother, neighbor, shopper; the magazines, hospitals and other women spoke of her, spoke to her. She did coarse work and enjoyed it; she loved the work that drew all her strength from her. She had always thought, I'm not afraid to starve, I can always go out charring. She would daydream for a moment about the ticklish strangeness, the mystery of a woman like herself washing floors for others—a masquerade with a queer quaint meaning. And I'd be a prime char, too! Ow, I feels me back todie, Lidy Florence; it's this parky wind. She sank her worries in these daily pleasures.

But an irritation gradually rose to the surface. One night she made a jealous scene, when she saw Henry and Corrie once more sitting close together on the hearth talking about "the need for a positive philosophy to wean the working classes from materialism," and laughing about something. She heard Corrie: "Oh, no, Heinzl, they couldn't understand it; can you imagine English workers conceptualizing?"

"Or English anyone?"

Corrie said, "How would you explain it, that without being able to think, they became so powerful? It's the water barrier, isn't it? We land powers have no true frontiers. Tell me, Heinzl—"

Eleanor strode into the room, rosy with anger. She shouted, "Don't flirt with my husband; you've got men of your own. I'm fed to the teeth with this highbrow talk and these language lessons; they're a pretext. Just coming here, itself, was a pretext. You speak English as damn well as I do. I'm on to your methods, Miss Ruysbroeck. Do you think, Heinz, I haven't noticed— Oh, you've done this to Corrie. She's flattered because you talk to her while I'm struggling to make ends meet or trying to earn some extra money to keep Corrie here. It's just not fair." She looked at Corrie. "Don't you sit there flattering yourself you're better than the English."

Henry sneered. "Where is your poise? Are you jealous of our maid?"

Eleanor flushed deeply, but Corrie jumped to her feet, saying, "I am not your maid"; and began saying she had been told to come as a friend and she had had to do all the dirty things that others would not touch. "What would my father and mother say if they knew I scrubbed floors? I'm a university graduate. I've been so humiliated all the time, but I said nothing, I wanted to stick it out."

"You'll have to wash floors when you marry," said Eleanor.

"Your husband does not love you," said the girl suddenly. "He likes me better than you, because I can talk with him. We understand each other." She burst into tears. "We saved each other from feeling lonely. You know nothing about it." She gave notice and went upstairs to bed.

When she was still on the stairs, Eleanor said in loud crisp tones, "These foreigners will never do: they're troublemakers."

"It's you who are the troublemaker," answered Henry; "you should gain her respect by dignified behavior. You behaved like a fishwife."

"I'm behaving like a wife, that's all." But Eleanor sat down and burst out crying. "Do you realize you've taken her side against me; she made insinuations about something between you. You insulted me when she was there. Henry, you should never have done that. Don't you love me?"

But Henry regained his good temper. "I am sorry," he said kindly. "I am very, very tired. I have taken on a new round-table discussion group with the Society, you know. I shouldn't have done it. But it means more money and more influence, and I was practically forced to do it. Perhaps you're right, Ell; I can't learn Dutch as well. Corrie laughs at me time and again. I get it mixed with German and make silly blunders. Can we manage without a maid? Let's try and be alone, Eleanor."

They decided, however, that Corrie should finish out her month, for they could not pay her till then; and before this month was out, Corrie announced her engagement to a young Dutchman in business in London. It was for his sake she had come. Corrie and Eleanor, now restored to social equality, finished the month pleasantly. Eleanor gave her some things for her trousseau, and felt a great joy, pride and dignity when the young girl asked for information about married life. She ran in gaily to Henry. "Imagine, Corrie thought children began complete but very tiny, like a small mustard seed!"

She gave a frugal party for the engaged couple before the end of Corrie's month, with innocent delight arranging everything according to the modest magazines she read. A bottle of sherry, a bottle of wine, a meat recipe she had seen colorfully illustrated, cheese and coffee—this was a spread for the young Charleses.

Cornelis, Corrie's fiancé, came with another bottle of sherry, which she whisked away into her kitchen cupboard. Everything went well. Henry, Corrie, Cornelis—"the Continentals"—amused themselves as Continentals know well how to do. She was wearing a homemade "dual-purpose dress, suitable for afternoon or evening occasions," from a pattern she had sent for from a magazine, and her shining hair was simply wound round her oval head. She had put on "a touch of lipstick" and her fair cheeks were naturally rosy. She happily watched them drinking and eating the hors d'oeuvres "cleverly contrived" from modest ingredients. She never drank now, "because of the waist," she would say, indicating her figure, and refused tidbits, too. But Henry asked for more tidbits and she was flustered and annoyed, because her plan did not allow for that; and when she saw Henry preparing to pour out another round of drinks and look with pleasant inquiry at her, and waggle the bottle which was nearly empty, she became silent, sat on a chair in the background, and her face fell as if she was going to cry. Over and over again she had read that "before dinner just one cocktail or one glass of sherry, according to your guests' fancy and pleasure, is correct; nothing more is needed to give them that pleasant anticipatory glow." She had written it herself. "More leads to raised voices and flushed faces." Now, mortified, in her mind accusing the immoderate habits of Continentals, she went away ("slipped away" she thought to herself) and put on the dinner; Henry should not have the second bottle of sherry. He came and got it; and she set her lips and her forehead blazed broad and white. But as she prepared the dinner her self-confidence returned and she anticipated her guests' enjoyment and praise. With intense glee, she was making something she had never tried her hand at before, economical but unusual, a combination of white cabbage, field mushrooms and baked sausage. She had imagined Corrie and herself gaily at work, preparing the meal between them. And now she ran and invited Corrie to the kitchen to help her.

They were very lively upstairs, the four guests and Henry speaking German and Dutch, Henry speaking with affectionate intimacy, it seemed, to the other girl, a German member of the New Society, named Hilde. Eleanor's cheeks flushed, her lips puffed with anger, and with a determined step she went up to them. The girl saw her, but being tipsy, only went on smiling. Henry, with his back to Eleanor, was saying, "I hope Corrie doesn't take my wife seriously. She's a real English cook—spring greens, suet pudding, and brown gravy, rhubarb and custard, with a few of my mother's worst thrown in."

Eleanor said in clear, cold tones, "Henry, please come and help me with the sauerkraut!" These little words chimed in the room and everyone burst out laughing.

Henry turned pale, his eyes took on a shine, he made a military right-about and left the room, Eleanor, without any word to her guests, following.

"If you ever speak to me again like that, I shall leave you," Henry said quietly, as soon as they were inside the kitchen door. His face was bloodless. She knew his cold furies, but because he was thin and she was fleshy, she had no fear of him.

She said, "Henry, this is my home; kindly reserve your philandering for the Society—there it brings you a profit."

Henry went on preparing the vegetables; he was a good cook. She noticed how his hands were shaking, and smiled to herself.

At the meal everyone was most ceremonious; they manufactured an agreeable gaiety and warmth, and congratulated Eleanor on the meal. She began to warm up, her eyes to sparkle; and when they had gone, she gathered up the glasses and plates, saying with a smile, "I think it all went off very well, don't you? In spite of the" —she paused, and gave him a wise smile—"the little excesses before dinner, the raised voices and flushed faces. But, lumping it all together—"

Henry came up to within two feet of her, looked at her, once more began to turn pale, and said, "You had better know that I will never forgive you."

Eleanor said calmly, "Oh, you will get over it, I expect, Henry."

But in the night she woke up, and began going through these unpleasant scenes over and over again, justifying herself. Indeed, she had been entirely in the right; why then, had she to suffer? She worried for a few days, and though she knew marriage has its ups and downs, her confidence was impaired, for she had innocently thought that Henry greatly admired her country and all that was English in her. She had felt he was grateful for the gift of herself, her beauty, intelligence and nationality. Again and again she struggled through these sufferings, and she suffered, too, as the mean thoughts, the recriminations streamed through her mind. It's all so petty, it's not us.

Eleanor decided, with a certain amount of good-humored scorn, to pass over Henry's pets and ingratitude, saying to herself:

> "All kinds of things and weather,
> Must be taken in together,
> To make up a year, and a sphere."

Always working to plan, she looked after Henry properly, but felt more at ease and more really herself when, at the correct minute, they kissed good-bye and she closed the door after him in the morning. She would then turn round, survey the clean little entry and clean short hall; her chest would heave with pleasant prospect of a "long, well-planned busy day." She enjoyed the small interruptions, telephone rings, callers, accidents to neighbors; "she had reserves of energy," and coped with everything.

After Corrie went, she decided she could organize things so as to do all the work without a maid, Henry helping. Early in the morning, even before six, she was up and about, in sandals, slacks, a sweater, with her hair hastily twisted up, cleaning, dressing, feeding the children, and putting Russell in his pram outside the privet hedge in the street where the morning sun struck, or, in wind and weather, in the entry with the door open. Meantime she would greet or talk to neighbors going to work, get an extra half-pint from the milkman, even exchange a few words with Mrs. Mac F. (as she called her), the woman opposite who went out cleaning, or say good morning to her own tenants. All this harmless and friendly activity irritated Henry. Pale with suppressed resentment, he saw "My wife dressed like Huckleberry Finn, gossiping with a charwoman; and my children, with flies on their faces sprawling in the gutter."

Eleanor's good reasons did not count, he could not understand them; "Surely simple dignity is a first consideration." His wife called him prim, unneighborly and out-of-date. He replied: "These are not my neighbors but yours. I should never speak to one of them." Eleanor laughed. "Oh, you, Henry, would never speak to your tenants either, but someone in this family has to be a coarse materialist and acknowledge the right of others to live." After saying this, she smiled, felt happy: she knew she was right. She put Henry's fussiness together with his insults and threats at the party: the unfortunate side of his nature. She was no idolater —her children had unfortunate traits, too. Deborah, about four, dark, restless, alert, sarcastic, was a stranger in the house. To Eleanor, Deborah had Henry's "unrealistic, carping nature." Eleanor thought to herself, Now, I open my arms to life, I embrace reality; these two are dreamers; and dreamers are cantankerous. Russell, her fair-haired, affectionate boy, was two years old. They had meant to have only one child, but both had felt the sadness of their "suitable partnership" and the second child was agreed upon.

Eleanor's early anxieties had disappeared when Russell was born. Henry would never desert a son. Russell was timid, always hiding behind her legs, putting his head in her lap, getting in her way. She was a busy woman. Russell, sweet, pretty and gentle, was "more like a girl than a boy"; he giggled deliciously, had gay sidelong glances. He was fond of a rag doll in a wool skirt, terrified of dogs.

Thus Henry, Deborah, Russell, all had their "amiable weaknesses." Eleanor, having discovered them, allowed for them as best she could, and went on with her own logic.

She worked hard, making clothes for the children, washing,

ironing, mending, writing detailed instructions for Henry and her mother-in-law, Leni darling, who was coming to stay for that week.

As she worked she became wrapped in herself, spoke automatically to the children, and, to her confusion, indignant phrases repeated themselves in her mind while she recalled scenes which had left her sore—even though she had always been considerate, sensible, humane and "exercised her saving sense of humor." Fiery, a complaint: "Leni comes to help Henry; no one comes to help me." A scene. In the original: "Henry, what you call self-reliance and self-control, I call plain self. If you would discuss our differences of opinion, you might find yourself in the wrong, so you retire into this self-sufficiency, to humiliate me. I won't be humiliated." This mental record ran quickly through, and she edited as it ran, till it then took on its enduring form: "Henry dear, let us just sit down awhile and thrash this thing out. A little frank speaking and soul-searching will do this family a world of good. You and I have had love and a deep sense of togetherness, and now we have our own futures and the future of our children; we have everything. It's perfect, what we have. So just let's pull out the mote each from his own eye, and see this thing clearly." Henry then ideally replied, "I admit I am too self-sufficient; and I grant that there is a grain of selfishness in self-sufficiency. You have a better form of it, self-reliance. A mother is closer to the human race." "Oh, but you, too, Henry, have the human touch—" But this rainbow interchange was coarsely interrupted by fierce words hurtling across her mind: "He gets the best end of the stick and leaves me all the dirty work. He's a brute, the cold little climbing devil." She went on ironing and biting her lips, tears came into her eyes: she was hurt by his cruel view of all she liked best. If she wanted to be a literary figure, he said she was trying to outshine him and had no right to the name of wife and mother—she was not a woman but an anomaly. She was neighborly. She would get up early in the morning to wash clothes for a sick mother across the street. He had caught her running across with a thermos flask of tea and an enamel basin of wet clothes, washed and wrung out. He was going to work, faultlessly dressed; she was dressed like an urchin—sandals, washed-out denims, soiled blue shirt, wispy hair. Her sleeves were rolled up. Deborah, in her pajamas, had run out into the street, asking questions about "the sick lady." Eleanor stopped in the middle of the street to tell Deborah to go inside. At the same moment, an aged woman who lived across the street, and who went mad in the hot nights, came out roaring to Deborah: "What you need is a good smack bottom." The old woman's fifty-year-old daughter, ready for work in her poor old gray costume and battered hat, went quickly up the street, her alert blue eyes looking into every face, searching for comment, criticism. She looked at Henry and went on.

"Tsha!" said Henry, "she shouldn't be here, but in a home. Her place isn't here."

"Oh, I wouldn't wish any poor old thing in a madhouse," said Eleanor.

"Tsha!" said Henry. "What a street. We must get out of it."

"The people are very decent folk," said Eleanor.

"I daresay it's bohemian enough for you," said Henry angrily, with a swish of his cane.

"Good-bye, darling," called Eleanor. There was no reply. "Good-bye, Heinz dear!" she caroled in angry mischief.

"Hold your tongue!" said Henry bitterly.

In the evening he entered with a rapid step, greeted them all coldly, pushed away the children, said nothing at dinner; but as soon as she began to clear away, he said crisply, "Deborah, take the things out for Mother. Eleanor, let Deborah take the things out. I have to speak to you. This state of things can't go on."

"I am very anxious to speak to you," said Eleanor. "Family life must have dignity."

"You have very few rights over the children, the house or even your own conduct, while you are my wife," Henry began; and a terrible scene followed, in which they fully expressed their opposed views of neighborly and human relations, and of husband and wife. Eleanor went out to the kitchen in the middle of one of Henry's sentences. She sent the sniffling little girl upstairs, and when she had finished, went up herself to kiss the children good-night. Russell was asleep, but Deborah was sitting on her bed stonily. She went to bed without a word and refused to kiss her mother or say good-night. Eleanor sat by her bed, talking to her softly, trying to explain her parents' quarrel in a natural way, but Deborah said, "Don't sit in the light like that, don't, don't look like that, go away. Put out the light. I don't want you."

"Do you want Daddy?"

"No, nobody."

Eleanor went downstairs and told Henry of this scene. "Nothing should count against the children's peace of mind!"

"A man doesn't live for little children," said Henry. "That's your department; you run it. I must have peace of mind."

Were they happy or unhappy, Eleanor asked herself that night, trying to dispel the horror she felt. Perhaps it was a necessary process of adjustment? They had had it out; she supposed it had "cleared the air and let out bad blood." She had always read in the problems department of women's magazines that it was better not to bottle things up.

Shortly afterwards, he took his one week's holiday at Torquay and she longed for him to be back. Her heart throbbed with the fear that they were "drifting apart"; she felt she loved him. During the week that she spent at the Torquay Hotel, she behaved sedately, sat with the middle-aged women, talked about the children, servants and costs, and some evenings was happy when three little girls from eight to ten sat with her and played "Racing Demon." The last two evenings she danced with a handsome, hollow-cheeked, silky blond, an air pilot. The music became sensual, the lights golden, the dancers floated; dreamily she recalled her long youth, a splendid carnal riot, but of classic innocence, it seemed now, formal as a Grecian urn. When the pilot said, "Come to bed with me!" she replied with sedate archness, "There was a song once:

> *'It isn't that I couldn't, it isn't that I wouldn't*
> *It isn't that I shouldn't, but I'm just the*
> *nicest girl in town.'*

"Although the word isn't nicest, but laziest. But the trouble is I'm not lazy, and I am nice."

She laughed to herself all the way upstairs; in her bed she laughed; on her way home she smiled. "Mother's holiday—but at least I know I am still in the running!"

Henry was not anxious to be alienated from her. However, when she returned he said a thing which startled her and made her more confused than before. He said he was afraid that they had drifted a little; a new courtship was necessary—he would like to share with her the love play she had learned from her wealthy lovers.

"Men like that," he remarked, "who have lived in the Orient, and sampled Paris and London, too, must have been amusing; and there's no harm in a wife telling her husband. Part of our trouble, Ell, is dullness; here we are, two intelligent, well-educated, experienced human beings shut up with two young animals who can't even speak our language yet."

"I'm quite happy with the babies," said Eleanor at once. "We have our own world."

But when he, with a pleased smile, kept asking her for the information, she was troubled and said she did not know, she could not tell him, she had always refused anything but the simplest form of love, she had never meant anything but a kiss, and somehow, once or twice she had been led further. Weeping, she said she thought it very wrong to bring such ideas into their home when everything was going all right; their interest was the children, and they had agreed to bury their past. She thought all these matters, Corrie and his indelicate curiosity, were satisfactorily closed when one morning soon after, she found a handwritten page on his desk between his piles of books. It startled her at first, then she drew a pleasant deduction; last of all, she could not help thinking that the page had been planted there for her to read. It ran:

CLASS: MODERN TRENDS *Class Discussion*

Manners and Morals are diverse: are our ways the only ways suitable to modern man?
Monogamy seems to succeed polygamy, although polygamous peoples have achieved great cultures: consider the Chinese, Arabs; in the U.S.A. the Latterday Saints.
But monogamy seems consistent with *plurality*. Pure monogamy, that is, an indissoluble union between one man and one woman, seems to be passing away.
Further, for the man the indissoluble bond, intended to protect woman and children and estate, there were always allowances made and illicit unions either passed over in silence, or actually regulated by law; e.g., in Belgium it was laid down that a man could have sexual relations with others, but not with maids in his own household. This was to release the man from a perhaps unbearable restriction; and at the same time to protect the family.
Naturally, no child born out of wedlock could inherit.
The object of all marriage laws was to protect family, for which alone marriage exists.
Discuss aspects of the above. Essays on one aspect of above.
NEXT DISCUSSION: All aspects of Plurality. Essays on any one aspect.

Eleanor read this through and through, saw it was for his course, but copied it out, to study it. I must keep pace with his students, especially the women, she thought to herself with a smile; and a moment later she sat down at her dressing table and combed her hair. It was drab; it had not the "grape-blush." She washed it, and when it was dry, gave it a hundred strokes of the brush; but she could not bring back its luster at once.

A few days later she found another sheet of paper, drawn up like the last, under Henry's desk.

CLASS: MODERN TRENDS *Class Discussion*

Personal Difficulties: question of chastity and transient unions.
In our society we sanctify marriage but it is no longer indissoluble. Even the Catholic Church sometimes allows dissolution.
Divorce and remarriage results in a sequent polygamy or plurality.
Ought we to see monogamy as the best state for the women and children? It is also cheaper for the man.
If extramural that is technically illicit unions protect the marriage, are they desirable?
Men at least are supposed to have knowledge of women before marriage; and in most western societies nowadays free sexual behaviour is not condemned as before; even though the law allows it as a cause for divorce.
This disturbs the family life as never before? For in the indissoluble marriage the women had to condone and accept; now, not only are the women and children thrown on their own moral resources, but the man is heavily penalized by having to keep the rejected family.

Does this mean that women are not equal
before the law?
Consider all aspects of this; and write an
essay on one aspect.
NEXT DISCUSSION: The position of women in marriage and in free unions.

To this was attached another page with a note in Henry's writing.
It read:

Modern society promotes monogamy as the
best system; but is not monogamy merely a legal situation, not an ethical one?
Does a man do his best for his dear ones if he
makes every effort not to break up the marriage? Even if this means that he is, in order
not to cause pain, secretly unchaste? Is
this then monogamy, as it has always been for
the man?
Query. Is my own situation unusual, or the
lot of the unfulfilled married man?

Eleanor did not replace this second sheet on the desk, but put
it in her handbag, ready to discuss this problem from all angles if
Henry should complain of a lost paper. But he did not, and so
Eleanor said nothing. They seemed happy. Occasionally they had
people to dinner who might help Henry in the Society, and Eleanor, having no help, had to prepare the dinner and entertain as
well; and occasionally they had friends, and these evenings went
off very cheerily. However, the strain was too great and they had
few dinners.

"I suppose this is just a marriage growing up," said Eleanor
to Henry one evening, when they had sat for some time in silence.

He was scratching away at his notes behind his barricade of
books. He lifted his head at once and smiled at her. "What is?"

Eleanor had wanted to bring the conversation to his "personal difficulties," but looking at his bland face, she could not. "This quiet," she said, waving her hand. "I suppose a marriage grows like a tree, four seasons, some difficulties, but branches"—she smiled —"and roots, and annual rings, and it gets taller and stouter."

"A pleasant thought," he said, "I must note it for my course. I have introduced the personal note into my courses lately and I find they go better, they get more response. One of these days I will be the popular Henry Charles and my books on marriage problems will sell like hot cakes, and then *our* difficulties will be over."

Eleanor rarely used the dictionaries, which were ranged on Henry's work table, but one morning, after a rather rancorous discussion the evening before about the meaning of the word "cursive" (for cursory), she went to the dictionary, and in going through the letter *C,* found another of his papers.

PERSONAL DIFFICULTIES

A man of honor cannot go back on his word.
He is responsible mentally, morally, physically, spiritually, for the lives he has created.
If he defaults, they may be twisted for life.
The woman is in an inferior position, legally, socially and should have every consideration, even when she is unsuitable.
In divorce, all parties deteriorate; it cannot be considered.
A man is not allowed to take alimony off his income tax.
Solutions: Each to "go his own way."
        Impossible.

Divorce.
        Ruins careers, social standing.

Thrash out differences.
        Ends in smoke.

```
Marriage counselor.
              What does a stranger know?
Resolution: To remain true to the woman se-
              lected by a man, adult, intel-
              ligent, healthy and in his
              right mind, for this is what is
              required of the woman; and the
              unfairness of the law must be
              made good by the man's gift of
              himself.
Those who cannot conform to this high moral-
ity?
```

Taking this as a sort of compliment to the family life she in her person represented, and as a sort of insurance, Eleanor secreted it also in her handbag. From now on, for some time, she would look at Henry with a suppressed smile of pity, and once she said to him, "Heinz, true marriage is a sleeping beauty; we have to win through the brambles first."

"A very pretty thought," said Henry, "and it may be true."

Henry began to go to the Continent frequently, to Switzerland, where he was opening a small branch of the Society in Lausanne, and to The Hague, where he gave a series of five lectures in philosophy; he stayed with his parents in Lausanne, and with Society members in Holland. Eleanor missed him and was overjoyed to see him back, asking him with wifely passion how he had got on, if he had been comfortable, ill, lonely; and telling him how the children had liked his postcards, how their health had been, what they had said. Deborah had said, "Russ is always good, and Mummy is good, but I am bad, aren't I?" Russ had learned to replace electric bulbs, Deb could operate a string puppet. Several times, when he returned, Henry looked at the dark front room they were sitting in and complained of London's dinginess and the freaks of architecture: "damp and drafts everywhere, the smell of garbage soaring outside our front windows, no heating, the coal chute in front of the front step, so that if the man leaves the cover off, you can quietly break your neck; waste pipes pouring dirty water down the necks of passers-by."

One time he came back and told her he had discussed their problem with his father: it would be better for them to put in a working housekeeper in one room, and let all the others that he and she and the family now occupied. He was away so much that Eleanor might as well go and stay with her family at the farm; he would come to visit them there and, of course, support them.

It was now that Henry began to take her out, to New Society meetings and socials. "You don't get about enough, on the Continent a woman like you would know how to receive people, help her husband in his career."

She flushed. "How can I be a society hostess when I am chief cook and bottlewasher and children's nurse? Can I cook the dinner, hand round drinks, make light conversation, and wash up afterwards?"

"Times are changing," he said. "A sophisticated woman would—a woman with your looks, on the Continent, would run a salon."

"I can receive as well as anyone," she said.

He talked earnestly with her about career. "Don't you agree that a man is justified in doing anything to succeed? There are hundreds of millions of nonentities, nameless. A man ought to try to leave a name after him; he must try to foresee the people who are going to win, and throw in his lot with them. To fail willfully is suicide. A man's duty to society is to do his best for himself, belong to the winners, make as much money as he can, get his name known. To follow that, he must cut himself off from whatever fails. I have a horror of failure, and to me success is a sort of awe-inspiring godhead, life itself. Cling to it, drink from its fountain: there is something in me that says that to me. I can't be wrong, can I? A failure is like a man who doesn't wash and goes in dirty rags on the public street. He could be better, but he is a cur and cynic, he would rather offend humanity. We are surrounded by those human strains that survived, by success. The law of survival insists that we survive. This is a great overriding law, and this is exactly what makes people religious, for they think they are throwing in their lot with the Great Power, with Fate itself, don't you agree? Rebels are madmen; they prefer to be stood up against a bloody wall and add their blood. A victim is a criminal in this sense, that he is contributing to the defeat of himself, his strain, hence the race. Don't you agree with me, Ell?"

"I don't know what you are leading up to," she said.

"I am speaking of general principles; the air is full of direction if you listen. Listen to what the world whispers and you can't go wrong. Eleanor, the town air is not good for us. There are guiding principles abroad, and we have to concur with the general will, for what is willed is what takes place. I am keenly sentient, I feel myself becoming more so, I am going to succeed. I don't want to think of you and the children living in this lodging house; I want to think of you living in perfect conditions—it would make me happier if you were in the country with your father and brother. I am going to have so many visits to the Continent that it will not be fair to you, and you will have time to think of your own career and not have to worry about a husband."

They had a great many discussions about it; and Eleanor, who always did her best to follow an argument, was baffled by all Henry's reasoning. She could not seize whether he wanted the family to live alone, or not. He was so subtle, so sweet, so affection- ate, that while at times she would begin to suffocate, thinking he was deserting her and their children, whenever she faced him, with his goodness, reason, sweetness and affection, she could only accuse herself: I am petty, mean, suspicious. I must think for us all, I must consider Henry's point of view. But every time they "cleared the air," she became more disturbed and understood less.

So (it seemed in later years) she was whirled by his curious confusion into a separation. With her children she went to the farm; Henry took a room in a Society hostel, and went straightaway to the Continent on Society business; and their house, her father-in-law's house, was sold to the Society. Thus she once more became a woman alone.

3

·

*Break-up
of the Home*

THE FURNITURE VANS had left and the cleaner was finishing up.

Eleanor stood in the front window of the first floor of the empty house and looked into the little street, taking in what she had often seen before. It was March, the privet hedges still looked thin. A house was empty, dingy; most of the others had recently been painted and each, like her own, had its nine white pillars, white gable upstairs and the white stones in the red brick. A silly little street, but warm and quiet. The woman opposite, a red chestnut, was cleaning her blue window frames and white window sills, with brush, knife, rag; through the open windows Eleanor could see her pure white curtains tied with white ribbon and her oval pier glass. The mad old woman was struggling back with her shopping; the Chinese student was coming back with his bread; the poet's bicycle still leaned against the lamppost as it had always leaned, summer and winter, night and morning.

"What if this street and these people will have seen all there is to see of my married life?" The sun was shining on her, the house was clean, the children were talking gaily—why did she think of this?

The Greens, friends of her brother, came for her in their car after midday. Mr. Green was a square-built man with a big face; Mrs. Green was beautiful and dark with a jagged profile and a languid boarding-school style of speech. They were both very friendly, but Eleanor thought it patronizing and she kept a sweet reserve. While she listened and spoke to the children, sentences passed through her mind: I've never been so jostled and rushed in my life. We've had the roof sold over our heads. Henry simply threw out his wife and children like old rags and bottles. But Henry himself said, "There's nothing wrong between us, Ell. I am quite satisfied with you and the children. But—we're too poor, life's too mean. We'll deteriorate. My wife making beds for students, my children screaming with others in the gutter—I never bargained for that. For a while, till I get my bearings, you can live with your people and then we'll get a house at Harrow or Surbiton, good suburbs. But I am soon going to take the children out of your hands, and you'll have time for a career."

Eleanor felt frightened. The more she argued, the more he confused her by running round in intricate figures, purposely forgetting, transforming, misinterpreting. Lying? She could never "have it out." She had begun to stay awake at night, her heart beating hard and terrible fears coming into her mind in the small house. Even now, in the car, with this calendar of disorder, months, weeks, days of discomfort and insecurity, doubt and anxiety, she felt the great astonishment coming over her again: Why had he done it? Was he trying to leave her? Had he a mistress? Who was she?

The children had seen cows and geese, now they were passing through a village. "We will soon be home, darlings, in our lovely new home. Uncle George has geese and cows—but watch out! and, oh, we're going to have such a lovely time while Daddy is very busy looking for a new house for us all to live in." As she said this she saw Henry's withdrawal as a plot.

"Am I a good boy, Mummy? Am I a good boy now?" Russell murmured plaintively. Whenever she was silent, anxious or even asleep, the sensitive little boy would imagine she was offended. She started, and put her hand on the fair round head that was rubbing itself against her leg.

"Yes, you're a good boy, Russ." I'm afraid he's not going to be independent, she thought to herself. And one day he may have to be the man of the family. What frightening thoughts! She knew she was very tired after the long struggle with Henry, a fight in the dark. She would rest for a few days and then see how things looked. Perhaps Henry was just as he had always been.

Mr. Green was droning along: "I think very highly of your brother, very highly, a trained technician, a thoroughly modern farmer, a real patriotic Englishman; and Marge is a"—his voice dropped doubtfully—"a very fine little woman. Joan and I are still very fond of her. It seems a pity. Pity to break up. They're very well suited."

His wife said, "Well, Matt, they're intelligent people; I suppose they know their own business best."

"Very great pity," said Matt, "don't you agree, Mrs. Charles?"

Eleanor was startled, "Broken up? Oh, but they're such good friends, and they were so radiantly happy. Dear Marge was always an independent little woman, but George was her oak. You see, they took me into their confidence long before—well, you know there was a divorce to allow Marge to marry?"

"Oh, yes, yes, yes," said Mr. Green hastily, "and that's why it seems such a pity."

"Well, 'the falling out of faithful friends, renewing is of love,'" Eleanor said cheerfully.

They came out of the concealed drive rising suddenly onto a plateau with a long two-story farmhouse on the other side. Beyond it was a swelling hill spur tractor-plowed and divided by a line of poplars. Marge herself ran out, small, dark, shining like a blackberry, all her little white teeth smiling through a veil of curly hair that the wind blew.

"Hello, hello all!"

When they had had tea and were walking toward the barn to see what the yield of eggs was, Marge took Eleanor's arm and said, "I'll just take Ell for a little walk, and bring her up to date on us."

"Yes, yes, yes, yes." Mr. Green ducked his great head with embarrassment and then was hidden by the barnside.

They walked down past two modern plantations of orange pippins to a high-grown patch just being turned up. Marge waved her hand toward the valley which turned round them and the skyline and said, "This is your new horizon, Eleanor. You see, Ell, in brief, George and I are very fond of each other still and perfectly good friends; but I have fallen in love with a young man who loves me and I have gone to live in my own cottage in the village, with Andrew; and for me it's all I could ask for. I don't want to lose George, I'm frank. I could live quite well with two men; and perhaps I'll get them to, at last. The house runs itself and you need have no troubles about expenses; I'm taking no money from George and you'll make your own keep. I've been running in twice a week to lend a hand and help Mrs. Burrows, but now I need not. I'm always so busy in the village. Now if you need me, I'll come up any time. And come and see Andrew—he's a dear."

Eleanor lowered her voice, though they were far from anyone. "Who is he, Marge dear?"

Marge began talking rapidly and excitedly. They had met quite by accident in the post office; he held the door open for her and she dropped a parcel. Then again, by accident, under a monkey-puzzle tree, her hair had caught in it and he was carrying a bunch of pink carnations wrapped in paper for his sister but gave them instead to her. He was young, slight and fair; his eyes were large and clear, a hooked Scots nose with sweet red lips "like sugar, like soft bees' honey." She confided eagerly to Eleanor: "His kiss is irresistible and he laughs sweetly with teasing fun like a child, and like a child he leans against you or kneels between your thighs. He lies there and says I need you, help me."

"Is that what he does?" said Eleanor in surprise. "Well, I can't imagine George doing that. And so you couldn't resist him?"

"I should die if I lost him," said Marge.

"But do you think you're likely to lose him?"

"You are likely to lose anyone, and so I'm on the qui vive."

"That seems very humiliating," said Eleanor. "Surely it's better to live out your life with a man who gives you peace, security, respect."

"I don't care about that." She tossed back her lively black hair. She held close to Eleanor, saying, "We'll be friends now. You must come and see us often. I don't often say that; we want to live for each other."

"And I'm sure that must be very lovely," said Eleanor. "Bless you, my dears, and may your dream last to the rainbow's end."

Marge looked up quickly, burst out laughing and then said, "Oh, it's no harm to be sentimental; I am, too. And now, Ell, darling, listen, I hear you're great shakes at this writing trick. I want you to teach me how to write; I want to write all about George and Andrew and me—and other things too. I want to write a novel, a play, something for the B.B.C. You see, Andrew admires writers, so I must be a writer. You're with me, aren't you? You're not angry for George's sake?"

"All this," said Eleanor, looking away, and with a rich tone, "is out of my world, you see; I've been very staid and routine. The golden mean was what I thought the golden rule. And then my experience is just a housewife's experience. I can't judge for you, dear. Henry and I were in love, we married for love and we have been radiantly happy. I think women remain the age they marry at, don't you? That is, if they don't change partners! That's aging by my method, isn't it? The years pass as if by enchantment"—and she said this word in a wonderful way, drawing it out and deepening it so that it sounded magical—"and I've just let the world of men go by. I've become short-sighted, I don't see beyond Henry."

"Tell me," said Marge, in a quick dry manner, "you and Henry haven't separated then?"

Eleanor bit her lip. She looked down at Marge's face. "This is just a wayside station in our plan, Marge. We laid down a design for living and we are building from that blueprint, Marge dear, and part of it is that our children shall be brought up in a gracious and serene setting so that they can have confidence and trust. To have faith in your background, to find out by putting it to the test of daily life that your background is real and good and fine, is the best foundation for a character and a career. Of course, you, Marge, with no offspring, can follow your own sweet whims, but Henry and I have grave responsibilities. We could not separate even if we wanted to, and we don't want to."

"Well, I am glad things are all right with you," Marge said vivaciously. "We just wondered when we had that funny letter from Henry—well, his two funny letters."

"What did he write?" Eleanor asked.

"I'll show it to you when they're gone. They've only come for farm food; they'll be gone soon. I told Andrew that I had to make you welcome."

Eleanor had to wait till the guests had had tea and until the end of a discussion started by her father and Mr. Green, with the thesis that England would be richer as a republic, that a monarchy, caste and privilege were a drag on industry and altogether uneconomic.

"Is that why you renamed it Commonwealth Farm?" said Eleanor, laughing. "Don't tell me you're starting a republic here!" She began teasing her brother and father. Her father had always disturbed her mother's peace of mind by saying that England would age as an empire, just like Rome and Spain, her colonies would drop off and then her only chance would be to renew herself as a republic and form trade treaties with nearby countries. "The analogies of youth and age are false," said Eleanor. "England has survived by a wise and benevolent colonial government." At one time, her father, Lindsay Brent, had attended Socialist meetings, with workingmen, but his wife had been so horrified that he had never mentioned them at home. After a few years of marriage he gave up going and began his book, on the English republic.

Eleanor had heard plenty of talk "all round the compass," but was inclined to laugh now, hearing that each root, each seed had been set, each branch pruned, each clod broken by George with a theory in mind.

"There have been gardeners since Adam without materialistic theory! Why is it necessary for you nowadays to drag politics into everything? Wasn't Mother a good gardener, Daddy, without a speck of theory? Politics are well enough in their place, but why, oh why, make the plowland a battlefront? It's the plague of the day."

No one agreed with her. Even Marge took sides in some question of Michurin and Mendel.

"You are such dogmatists," Eleanor cried nervously.

George admitted that he did not know very much, he needed time for proper tests; he had to run a farm. "My ideas are based on too few results in too few years." England, with its dead weight of monarchy, nobility and privilege, Eleanor pointed out laughing, still managed to produce thoroughly modern men like her father and George.

"But she is not changing fast enough," they said.

"Change comes of itself, by natural laws," Eleanor explained. "Scientists, philosophers, economists and legislators make changes as they become necessary; for rash rank outsiders like us to mix in, is only asking for trouble. We're upsetting the natural processes of society. You foment trouble and you don't know how to cope with it; you meet disturbance with violence and then you repress, and that's a step backward. This is a perfectly free society—let it grow up naturally."

Then they argued that it was not a perfectly free society, that covert understandings had repressed thoughts and thoughts had dwindled and died.

"Good manners aren't social cement, and putting a cross on a ballot paper isn't the sum total of civic duty," said George. "Intelligent revolt is also a civic duty."

"Everything has always been done for us, including revolt and bloodshed, by our servants in the colonies," said Lindsay Brent: "and we're sick of uselessness. If they ever want to put the iron choker on us, we won't be strong enough to rebel."

"Oh, dear Daddy," said Eleanor, smiling, "such a gentle firebrand! I agree with you all, up to a point. Things are not perfect and it needs energy to get things done, but the thing is to get them done orderly and constitutionally, so that no one can reasonably object. And as Henry says, our real civic duty is to succeed in our own society, not to languish after utopias and blue moons. If we don't get on in our own society, how do we know we'd get on in any other?"

"Well, in short, grin and bear it," said her brother, laughing.

"Do you prefer tear gas and baton charges and blood running in the streets, like the French have?" Eleanor asked angrily.

"A little might go a long way as a tonic," said her father.

Eleanor threw back her head and laughed. "Oh, Daddy, the idea of your spilling blood is too delicious, and I know not one of your parlor pinks would hurt a fly."

They went on talking, but Eleanor paid little attention; she hoped the conversation would stop and the Greens would go. The children had run out and now were back again, looking cold; she took them into the kitchen to get warm. The Greens got up, and presently she and Marge were free to go upstairs. Marge ran into her husband's room and fished in a little box. "Here it is."

The letter looked false. Henry wrote all his letters in a letter book first, then carefully copied the text out, with a neat space between each word. She read:

Dear Father-in-law and Brother-in-law,

If it will be convenient for you, I will send my wife and two children to Sunnytop Farm for a stay of several months, while I make necessary plans. Her present surroundings are having a deteriorating effect upon my wife, who is reverting to the bohemian ways she had when I met her; she was living in a squalid lodging house with people of the lowest class. I cannot have my wife running in and out of lodgers' bedrooms at all hours and appearing on the street in men's clothing. I have sold my house to a profit and I intend to offer my wife proper housing and other conditions as soon as I can find a house that suits *me*. She is free to accept it or reject it. If she prefers to live apart in her own way, I will take steps to provide for my children in another way. I have many business preoccupations and my work takes me abroad. I cannot keep an eye on my domestic affairs. I am always anxious, knowing that my children are running about wild in the streets and making undesirable friends. I have seen this process with alarm for some years and I am now determined to stop it. *I will take any steps.* But it seemed best to me first to send the mother away with her children to a healthier setting, as Eleanor will take on any coloring and she may at once improve. My life has been very difficult with no home, nothing but a sort of tavern or stall, to express in one word the lack of refinement I have had to contend with. I have endured hardship. A bargain should be kept; but it is nullified by the first party who breaks it. We have had many talks and I have been very patient, but I have never been able to make Eleanor see my point of view: she has a sort of greed for low life: and is on very questionable terms even with the male lodgers in the house.

This letter went on in the same strain for four pages, and for Eleanor, was the beginning of a long series of strange letters which were strung out through her years in the country, the divorce time and long after. They were accusing, deploring, threatening, mystifying texts, and every one of them had the power to make her unhappy and restless; she longed to unravel them and find some pure and simple thing at the heart of them, but by his perverse mystery, Henry had a terrible hold on her and caused her to worry, weep. She had never known self-doubt till she knew him; now every year that passed made her more timorous.

"Why does he call it Sunnytop still?" asked Marge. "He knows it's Commonwealth."

"Because he's a damned climber," said Eleanor between her teeth and flushing with rage. "A commonwealth would give him too much competition! The New Society gave him his chance and now he's joined the Established Church and the Tory Party. He's taking the children from me to put them in snob schools, and the next step will be to try for a title. Well, I'm good enough to be her Ladyship too—he's not shoving me aside."

"What does he mean by that letter?" Marge asked with foreboding.

But Eleanor had recovered herself. "This is the kind of gloomy fumbling evasiveness and changeableness I've had to deal firmly with all my married life. Henry is not above lying. His point of view is that it's the truth if he says it. Because Henry is above everything; he makes truth and lies. This letter, taken sanely, is nothing but a mess of lies and half-lies. I like to help and Henry feels he's being soiled if I take a basin of soup to a sick mother. We should be holy touch-me-nots and they should be dirty untouchables! That's his idea of society! What is wrong with me, Marge, is I'm not a rich old woman to make a pet of him; I'm a flesh-and-blood woman with duties toward myself, my family and society. As for "his" house, that's typical. I've been slaving for years, repairing, puttying, painting, beating old carpets, washing curtains, haunting auctions, mending sheets, to turn a shoddy little terrace house eighty years old into a desirable property. I'll admit I had a glorious time doing it: I love work. Give me work and I'm happy. But now my work is vulgar and not on a higher plane. The Charleses sold it without consulting me. Oh, this is a backward country, Marge! My work and my money belong to a stranger I married. I was better off as a literary devil working for Beresford

Banes. That's what he secretly means, the little beast. At first I had the purse strings and my fine Henry was as meek as a lamb, but recently I took an allowance and let him have the rest. The feeling of shame and indignation nearly throttled me. I often would have walked out if not for the children. Oh, it hasn't been easy. Yes, I have been sloppy and a gossip—yes, I have run downhill." Her eyes sparkled. "I chose to forget my position. I knew a clever wife can mold her husband, but I did it by sacrificing myself utterly. I stripped myself. I had the same tweed suit for years. I had really nothing. I was frightened to think of the day when I'd have to buy something for myself. Henry had to have well-tailored suits for his business with the New Society. I took to sweaters and jeans and sandals, and very comfortable I found them. And as for the rest, oh, Marge, I like people, I like helping, I like being a friend. Who but Henry would find it a fault? Oh, but poor Henry! I do understand him, too. I've shielded him and sheltered him so; it was like a child! He picks quarrels; things offend his sense of dignity, challenge his very being you'd think—a bicycle stood against our gatepost, a boy yodeling. Imagine Henry going to work, delicate and neat, in his homburg, shining shoes, morning dress, gloves and stick, with his mustache and his clean red lips, bravely, poor dear, scolding the dustmen, a savage crew they are on our street. Jack, that's the driver—the street rings to their cries, 'Right-o, Jack!' 'Step on it, Jack'—simply drove the huge cart at Henry as if he were going to run up on the pavement after him. 'You must bring a broom and sweep up,' Henry cried out undaunted, 'or I'll report you to the Town Hall!' Jack came growling off his seat and they crowded my poor Henry to the fence. Three of the men in their dusty workcoats and mucky shoes walked in on him, while he retreated step by step arguing and waving his stick. 'I'll sue every one of you,' he said. I came running out in my jeans and Deb came running out in her jeans and I called out, 'Never mind the cabbage leaves, Henry, I'll sweep them up—never mind, boys,' and Henry icily, 'You are not a street cleaner!' It was just a sham dogfight, all so silly, but Henry was all set for the Privy Council. He touched one of the men on his arm with the stick; the man turned round snarling, shook Henry's stick off and raised his fist. 'I'm going to get you thrown off the job,' said Henry. 'I'm your employer, you're my servant—' 'Don't make a fool of yourself,' I said. The men moved back like a flock of birds, twittering at him. 'Oh, for Pete's sake, leave the man alone, let's all get back to our jobs,' I said to the dustmen, and the other men moved away, but Jack stood there glowering, a broad, hefty man in washed-out clothes. They were both ridiculous. I took Henry's arm and started to walk him up the street, saying, 'I want to talk to you about Slipstone, the third-floor tenant,' and turning extraordinarily pale, Henry marched up to the turning, without a word. At last he managed to squeak—it was just a squeak—'How dare you humiliate me before those workmen,' saying 'workmen' as if it meant 'dirty dogs.' When he came home in the evening I insisted upon having it out. I told him English people were democratic and couldn't be got to work with a whip and an insult; I told him people in our position had to live and let live; that he behaved like the autocrat of all the Russias. Poor Henry. He would so love perfection, but the little life we led in a little house in a little street was nothing but compromise."

Marge was sitting on George's bed looking at her with serious sympathetic expressions; "You do need a holiday."

"Oh," said Eleanor cheerfully, "now that I've talked my heart out, I feel better already and I'll soon be glad to go back and take up the daily round, the common chore. A really happy marriage without contrasts would be too dull, wouldn't it? And I have love and we have the children: that's the good life, isn't it?"

Marge left about nine, asking Eleanor to come down and see them in her cottage. "We'll talk about everything, worry things out and abuse Henry and laugh at him, and you'll tell me all about his good side; and in two or three months you'll have your new home and serene days."

"Oh, I'm sure of that, dear," concluded Eleanor. "You see what we have is very real."

*   *   *

After breakfast each morning Eleanor ran up the stairs two at a time, locked herself in, but could not settle down at once, thinking over what Mrs. Barrow, the daily help, had said, perhaps, or other matters. Then she would take up a magazine or a detective story, thinking, What I will do is to take this plot, whatever it is, and build my story on it, just the story line without clues, murders and police. She would begin to read intently. So the morning, afternoon and a number of days passed. At last, she said at lunch, which she shared with her father, brother and Mrs. Barrow, that she ought to do work round the farm. This would give her new ideas, characters, settings. But George turned this down.

"The farm work's completely organized" (one of his favorite expressions); "there's nothing for you to do, unless you want to help me with the accounts. Haven't you a deadline? I thought writers always did."

"But I'm finding it very difficult," she complained. "Maybe I'm like my milkman who, when I told him I was going to the country, said, 'I couldn't live out of sight of chimney pots.' The only time I felt full of beans was when I got that letter from Henry and got good and angry. I wrote three or four furious pages, tore them up—when it comes to scolding Henry, then I can write."

"Why not write a story in which you are scolding Henry? That's simple. The story of the ill-treated wife. That's popular. Aren't you supposed to write about what you know?" Her father teased her pertinaciously about her writing.

"Write a story about a farm as if it were a character," suggested her brother. "I could give you the details, though I have no idea how to do it."

The next time she had a letter from Henry she did not notice the check but flushed angrily and bit her lip when she read: "I am sorry that I cannot fix a date for coming out to see you and I see no value in your coming in here for the day. I am busy and going to be busier, indications are." She threw down her napkin and said, "I'm simply so angry with Henry, Daddy, that I'm going straight upstairs to write the story of the injustice of a marriage, of a deserted family and a flibbertigibbet. Perhaps I'll write it out of my system. In any case I'll see where I stand. Our marriage could stand some analysis."

On the stairs she heard George saying, "Perhaps that wasn't a wise suggestion? I don't know what Ell's relations with Henry are, but I want the marriage to go on, if it can. Perhaps you'd better go and talk it over with her."

She was listening at the head of the stairs. Her father remarked: "I don't care whether she remains with him or not; it's for her to do what she judges best. Ell's my daughter and I have to be on her side whatever happens. Besides, I like Ell—she's a good girl. You can let her have her head. That wasn't the way with you. You didn't ask advice, you didn't air opinions: you had too much to think out. And you're still that way. And I'm still saying nothing."

However, when George had gone out, the father went upstairs and tapped on her locked door. She opened it.

"Ell, I didn't mean you to take my advice so literally."

"It was good advice!" She was glowing. "Come in, Daddy, my pet. I took your advice, but it worked upside down. I am getting on like a house on fire, and I am sure, sure, this time I have struck oil. It's sheer inspiration, my dear, automatic writing; I haven't felt like this since I sat for my finals. Just sit down and I'll inflict Chapter One on you."

She settled him on the old couch facing the two windows, and in her sweet clear voice she read:

DEB and RUSS at SUNNYTOP FARM

Mummy looked at her wristwatch and gasped. "Precious babies, the car will be here in an hour." But there was the dear old nursery to say good-bye to, and the kitten from next door and the wonderful old rowan tree with boughs like saddles upon which the children had many a time gone riding away to the land of enchantment, especially the old rowan tree. There was a tiny top leaf always glistening like a star, catching the sun until the first real star did

appear. Then there was the robins' nest in the woodshed and Mr.
John the Milkman who had come up that little street punctually at
ten every morning but Sunday for eight years and had seen them
before they could walk; and yes, there was Daddy, too. They had to
say good-bye to darling Daddy too. For darling Daddy was going on
a trip to find gold: that is what Russ said. And when he did come
home he was going to buy them a splendid new house. "Will it be
a castle?" said Russ. "No, only a house, fathead," said Deb, who was
five and eleven months. "Darlings, don't call each other names,"
said Mother.

The house they had lived in was a dear little red and white
house with a blue door. It was only a little house, but by some
miracle they had managed to squeeze so much love and laughter and
smiling tears into it, so many parties and stories and lovely quiet
talks and birthdays and Christmases and fireside evenings, that it
wasn't just a little house any more, that they were leaving behind,
but a great house, a splendid house, more than a villa, almost like
a fairytale castle, full of jewels: the jewels of happiness, love and joy
and little children's laughter.

And now there was Daddy with a big smile waving to them that
the car was there and they all tumbled out forgetting to remember
whether they had left anything behind. Russ had his woolly donkey
and Deborah had her new blue sunshade spotted with golden stars,
which Daddy had bought her only yesterday. But what had
Mummy? So Mummy made an excuse and ran back and searched
everywhere for some little forgotten thing, saying to herself, "This
little forgotten thing, when I find it, will be my memento." It was
like a treasure hunt. She looked into every corner and cupboard and
nook and cranny, and there under the kitchen window sill, where it
had fallen long ago, was a little silver ring with a green stone that
had come from a Christmas cracker. It was tarnished now and bent,
but it just fitted her little finger and she came out showing it to them
and said: "This is my keepsake from the little house. I will keep it
forever."

As she read on there ran through Eleanor's mind many vivid pictures of their real departure; real tears came into her eyes. She saw Russell jumping up and down in his new blue coat with its brass buttons and, underneath, his new corduroy trousers "for the farm"; and then she saw Henry, affectionate, natty, glad to be off, as he had been that morning. He had been so pleasant, kissing them, laughing, saying, "We'll all soon be together again; you are having your holiday a bit early this year"; and a fixed puzzlement grew up in her mind, clouding all these pictures, as if she had missed something that had been said or done. For it was all all right, wasn't it? But it was unusual; and she had done all the most usual things possible, knowing that was a recipe for happiness. Henry had kissed her on the lips and both cheeks in his foreign way and said, "Thank you for doing this for me; you'll see I'm right."

Eleanor had since, often, thought about it when she was alone, trying to see their lives with strangers' eyes so that she could understand things Henry said. "We must make a great change." Sometimes she was comforted by this, sometimes made more anxious, but what could he conceivably have against her? She had been more than text-perfect: she had been a thoughtful wife, "reasoned into all the corners."

She had stopped reading. Her father was speaking. "That's a lot for one go; you'll do more, won't you? I like it very much. I'm sure it's what mothers will like. You make the children so simple and natural, not little perverse monsters; you have a nice touch. I'm glad to have a picture of what it was like when you left." He was struggling for compliments.

She said thoughtfully: "Thanks, Daddy, but I'm not sure it was exactly like that, but I intend this one for the littlest ones. Adult truth would be monstrous for them."

"Ell," continued her father, "when you have time I'd be glad if you'd look over my little one, *The Republic of England,* and give it a professional touch. I think the grammar's all right, but I'd like it to be popular. I want to convert people. Just sit down when you're absolutely free and give me your honest opinion. I don't want truth with a veil on—I like naked ladies naked."

"Well," she said briskly, "I'll see you have a whole ballet of naked women if you like; I've had quite a bit of general experience at the unfledged manuscript; and a raw truth is much better than a streamlined finish. I don't know what hope you have of selling. It's not a very popular line, is it?"

She was disappointed that her father had been thinking about his work instead of appraising her own. He was glowing now, behaving like a youth. He said, "If I could put in a pretty girl and a tall good-looking boy into *The Republic of England* it would have a chance, eh?"

"Why not? Make it a Utopia."

"Oh, no, it isn't a Utopia."

She sat there alone afterwards, regretting her home. She and Henry used the same words, they belonged to the same world. She looked at her MS. with regret too. She longed to say to someone, "But it wasn't like that! I did find a trumpery ring and threw it in the rubbish bin. But what I did was to pick up a poker and smash a bit of plaster off the wall. Once Russell ran his tricycle into that bit of wall and the plaster fell off, showing the moldering laths. A symbol of my home, a trashy thing. Oh, it's been a mean struggle. Life isn't for that. Or what is life?" She sat thinking bitterly. They took it very calmly, George and her father. Her marriage might be on the rocks, but they pretended to notice nothing. She had no one to talk to. When they married, at Henry's wish she had cut off all her bohemian friends—that meant all her poor friends, that meant all her friends. I'm a coward, she said to herself.

She picked up the file in which she kept Henry's letters and leafed them through; but they were comfortless, worse together than separate—he seemed a stranger to her, living in a mental world of cold sterile confusion, and yet that world had the air of being carefully built up. He's hiding nothing, it's to give himself importance, she said to herself impatiently, slamming the file into the drawer.

Now Henry was writing that he was *"unhappy about many*

things; we have been blown off course." Suddenly, he would put in something glaring, concrete enough, but a lie, or a topsy-turvy deduction. *"You are happier than I; you always preferred your father and brother to me!"* he wrote, and nothing else in the letter referred to this; he simply put it in and let it lie. They're just pebbles to ripple the millpond, thought Eleanor. I despise his tactics. In another letter, *"While I was being tortured by your penny-pinching, I had to see large."* Then he would change his tune and accuse her of neglecting the children for her "creative work."

Henry now wrote that he had a Society post of great importance. However, he would be *"moving about and their home must be postponed. But you will be getting a larger check from now on. Our future looks bright."*

As the weeks passed she got used to taking the check from the envelope and keeping the letter till afterwards, to "riddle it out." Upstairs, she would pore over the letter, profoundly searching for something concrete, or a clear promise. A house seen, an address, a salary, a date—such things hardly existed. He wore her out; sometimes she would leave the letter there, all but unread for days. Then would come his senseless accusations, and after that, a business letter, an itinerary, or even some kind remarks. Henry had always had a morbid streak, Eleanor knew; he said bachelorhood was bad for him. Once she wrote a loving letter. His response to this caused her the great surprise of her life: it was a telegram from Lausanne, worded thus:

I PREFER DIVORCE TO SEPARATION AND WILL MAKE ALL NECESSARY ARRANGEMENTS AND FAIR FINANCIAL CONDITIONS STOP WRITING

HENRY

Eleanor looked at the signature several times, thinking she must have got the wrong telegram. Suddenly she became very angry—What kind of a trick is this? and she cabled back:

There presently arrived one of his characteristic letters, longer and more confusing than ever, in which were the phrases: *"Not sleeping for weeks because of moral problems and I should have liked your advice but morality is not for and against, red and black, and your mind runs on accountancy lines, so involved with banking money that you never allowed for flesh and blood, there being a weakness at least as regards others in being too robust and trying to get butter on both sides . . . righteous conformity and the lion's share that you intended to go with it . . . at item in an account book, the largest on Friday and the smallest on Monday . . . such people must have a fait accompli, well it is done . . ."*

What was the letter about? Who were the people mentioned in it? It was not written in terms she could understand at all, and she wrote and asked for an explanation "in plain language, a translation of your gibberish." She felt very firm; "I don't propose to have my life upset at this precise moment." So she wrote him a cheerful, sensible letter to show she was made of sounder stuff: she put the blame on his lonely wandering life. "The answer is, Henry, to get our home together as we planned."

She tried to work hard as before. She began work on a short story, but of course she was anxious and irritated. She would walk about the farm, go down to the bottom of the new orchard George was making and strange thoughts would enter her head. She had never thought about infidelity because she felt they were all happy, secure; dark ideas might actually bring misfortune. Besides, she intended to ignore all these things. She would not indulge Henry, whose weakness was that he tried to make himself important with talk of "problems." When she looked at these problems, they straightened themselves out of their tangles with a snap; these problems did not exist, they were merely a love of misery, imbroglio, failure.

Henry's answer was so unlike himself that she knew someone

else had suggested the words. He wrote briefly, "Please understand that I love another woman and I want a divorce. I am sorry to put it bluntly but your superficial attitude to life makes it necessary. However, I will be fair to you—you may count on that. Henry."

Eleanor had not been able to read his other letters and had completely misunderstood the last one, so that this came as a tremendous blow. She thought, I must conceal this any way I can, until I can deal with it. It was as much as she could do to fold up the letter calmly (they were having their evening meal, it was sundown), say a few words and get up to her room. She locked herself in and read these few words again and again, waiting for some solution to force itself through the words. She knew what the words meant: it was the immediate satisfactory solution she was looking for. She was overcome by a feeling of incredulity—nothing had led up to this, nothing accounted for it. Suddenly she flew into a great rage. How dared he, the weakling, the slippery liar? She hurried to her typewriter and began a furiously angry letter to him —thousands of angry words, reproaches and insults; all kinds of forgotten things came to her. She wrote how she had struggled, been patient, done without, hoped—she wrote on and on—the children came to say good-night, she kissed them and burst into tears, pushed them out of the room, and locked herself in. She put her head on her typewriter and cried, "Who have I? I have no friend! Oh, after all our plans!" She thought of their love affair, what he had said to her. She had been a beautiful, desirable girl— many men had seen that; she had abandoned them all for him. "You devil! I'll fix you!" she muttered. She put other words into this endless letter she was writing him; wicked accusations, coarse words, insults and orders poured through her fingers onto the paper. Great formless feelings rushed healthily through her mind giving her release and power, but she did not know what these feelings were because she had never had them before in connection with Henry. "Who would have thought the wretch had so much blood in his veins?" she said aloud to herself, with a contemptuous smile.

But suddenly she was tired, and when she looked at the masses of text, she knew that was no letter. I must write him a cool, calm, firm letter that will show him I am quite unimpressed; business as usual, Henry, will be the tone. I won't let Henry upset our whole lives, all the beautiful things ahead for the four of us, because for a moment some woman has found out how criminally irresolute he is. Yes, but what shall I do? I need an answer. I won't let him think he bowled me over. The truth is that at bottom, he only wants to impress me. It's the recalcitrant who wants love and is perverse because it hasn't got enough." The answer was to write an affectionate letter, showing how all-enduring her love was; she would be more like a friend or a dear sister. "Nothing can happen to us to hurt us. It's all been too perfect. Bless us all, we knew, both of us (the dear babies don't know yet, thank heaven), that life is not whipped cream and roses and that *'all kinds of things and weather must be taken in together to make up a year and a sphere.'* Wives, husbands, parents are no longer themselves, they think in terms of 'years and spheres,' they must overlook many things for the sake of life itself, for life is their duty and their happiness. I am simply forgetting your letter, dear . . . for you can't be so illogical and foolish as to build so much upon the lower animal functions. I'm a natural woman and a fair one. We loved, but we married for marriage and a family and I'm sticking to my plans. If there really is someone else in your life, I am certain this is only an infatuation, a sort of physical necessity, like eating or something even humbler than that, that comes from loneliness. I am going to get over to you somehow, and when you see me and think of the children you will blush for some hole-and-corner petting which is unworthy of us."

Eleanor believed that this letter would finish off the affair. She had to be complete, sound, confident; she could not face breakdown. Eleanor still was an unusually beautiful woman, with the kind of coloring and charm that continues into old age; she had only to look in the mirror to see the face that had made men fall in love.

She was courageous and told no one of the battles she was

fighting; but she kept his letters and copies of hers, thinking that one day long after it was all over, when Henry was gone (for unconsciously, she thought of surviving him), she would tell her children about how she had fought for them when they were helpless. She lay awake at night and spared herself nothing. Things she had not noticed at the time came into her mind now. She saw herself saving on everything, making clothes for herself and the children (she was good at it, she had an eye for style and color), calculating and recalculating for the children's parties and Christmas, sketching out her menus for the week, studying food values, with nothing for herself or Henry, nothing for the private life, leading an exemplary life, because it was for their future. She had always seen them going on together getting to be more than life-size, in a life that was not little, because they were so richly a part of their society; they were symbols too, good citizens, a happy family, the foundations of all decent civilization. For Henry to smash this was simply monstrous: it was unbelievable. Why? The more she thought of it the more inexplicable it became.

She would talk to herself, "You see, Henry, you can't build up a case because my memory is too good, I remember too well." She saw a scene just before her second child had come. She was sitting in the long kitchen divided by an arch from the dining room. There were four white chairs upholstered in red, a bar chair and a little bench in red. A nickel rail ran behind this and a red trellis which she had made herself, and indoor vines growing up it. She was ready, waiting for the baby. Everything had been made fresh, sterilized, re-covered; presents had come and Henry's mother had come to stay with them. On this afternoon they were all sitting in the dining part just before Deborah had her meal and they were having coffee—they all called it *Kaffeetisch,* in the family. Deborah was two. She was pettish, spoiled, running about the kitchen and making them all talk about her. She had thrown her doll out of the window, lost a monkey wrench in the backyard grass, turned the gas on in the stove, and stood on half a pound of butter. Everyone was smiling contentedly as they talked about these things almost in mutters, with long pauses between, because they were not thinking about Deb but about the one that was coming. They were embarrassed but happy, and Eleanor felt that she was the center of all this life. Leni and Henry were almost strangers, she and Leni had nothing in common, Deb was a little private world, yet they were all (but Deb) intensely happy, at ease with each other. Henry said, "Now there is nothing wrong, I have nothing to wish for— here we all are together," and Leni laughed and said, "Yes, and in another month we shall all be here." This comfort and peace went on for years. Surely Henry was really a good moral man. Eleanor knew every fiber of his being, she knew he did not want to run wild. He simply could not fight off the temptations of the traveler. She wrote Henry many letters telling him what she thought during these night hours. Henry would reply with letters that berated her, accused her.

This warfare went on for months, and then for years. Henry even changed his women, and his behavior seemed to Eleanor more and more vulgar, irresponsible and unlike anything she had ever seen in him. "He'll get no divorce! Let him buzz from flower to flower," she said in a burst of exasperated laughter.

On Saturday mornings she would go into the village and call upon her sister-in-law, Marge. The first time Marge came to the door in a sun hat, pink apron and pink gardening gloves.

"Oh, good," she cried, kissing Eleanor. "Come and I'll bake a cake; Andrew's at the airfield. They're busy, far too busy for comfort, he says. I want you to meet him. I'm in love with him, Ell!" she said, laughing and kissing. "Don't you fall for him, too. Women do. Oh, I don't mind if you do." She showed the house, six rooms round a corridor leading to a glassed-in back porch; beyond, a well-kept garden. She showed the roses, the rock plants and a vegetable garden in a field they had just bought next door. Marge's house was named Mayfield. "Plenty of work for willing hands," said Marge.

"And is gardening Andrew's hobby?"

"Oh, smoking's his hobby," said Marge. "Over a hundred

pounds a year go up in smoke, and his hands as well as his locks are yellow. So I took up smoking too. And so I am cleaning all day long. Come and help me cook. Jake and Lilian, that's Dr. and Mrs. Waterhouse, are coming tonight; they're old friends of George and myself. How is George? Lilian told me he looks tired. I am just too busy to get up the hill; I telephoned, but George was in the orchard."

Eleanor felt lively. She did not know what to say first. She asked in a mysterious insinuating tone: "Tell me, don't you feel any remorse, any twinges of conscience? But perhaps you're too happy? Of course, he isn't a married man and so you're doing no harm— to him, that is—but how does he feel about what he's doing? Or doesn't it bother you two happy creatures at all? Tell me"—she hugged Marge—"is it real happiness? Or are you sometimes worried because there's no real tie, and this question of age. I know he's younger. Though you don't look old, Marge, but young, so young. That's happiness, of course. I suppose happiness can exist outside the marriage tie. What would the old-fashioned Grundys say to that? Or aren't there any Grundys in this blessed village? Has England changed so much?" Then she would hasten to apologize, "You must forgive me, darling Marge, I have lived such a narrow life between four walls and I had to see that a houseful of tenants had clean morals, for our sakes and the children's. Such things haven't come my way, though I don't doubt they're happening every day. We have let down the barriers, haven't we? I've never even wondered how lives like yours and Andrew's are led, though led they are and to the full, I know. Only, what I should like to know," she said, lowering her voice, "is how you feel, how one feels about it. Do you feel clean and good? Or do you just feel you must, come what may? Don't you feel a little shy when you meet one of your old friends in the street, or someone who was at your wedding, with George? Do you smile at them just the same? Haven't you had any difficulties?" She laughed. "Oh, it would be too bad for us prosy old wives who've trudged the strait and narrow, if you have the best of all possible worlds!" She threw back her head and laughed full-throatedly. "My dear Marge, I believe I envy you! Yes, you have peace, love in a cottage, your dear, dear Andrew, a very understanding husband, friends everywhere. How lucky you are!"

Marge had taken off her gardening gloves and they were in the kitchen, where Marge was "knocking together a cake" for tea. She worked rapidly and had been discussing perfect pastry: need it be made in a cool place, whether there was "magic" in it. "Andrew is very fond of my cakes," she said. She now said, "Oh, a few of my friends pretend not to see me, Ell, and I assure you I don't want to see them. They're saying, 'Andrew or us,' and I say, Andrew. Why I'd die for Andrew gladly. How silly and fussy they seem." She added with a little malice, "But, of course, you feel that way about Henry, or once did!"

Eleanor answered, "I'm afraid, darling, that that kind of—feeling and the one we regular old married women have are two different things."

"I have been married twice already," said Marge demurely.

"Yes, but you gave no hostage to fortune. Do you feel you were wise, perhaps?"

Later they went into the garden to get a bouquet for Eleanor. "I've just finished planting out my tulips and borders, but you can have a sheaf of camellias."

"Fancy an armful of camellias!" cried Eleanor. "How wonderful!"

"And is Mrs. Barrow doing a lot for you? She's a sweet woman, Ell; she's not a servant, she's one of us. She would do anything for George—she's a love."

"I'm afraid I don't find her quite so satisfactory," Eleanor replied, "but she does her best. She half follows George round, when he's in the house. Whatever he mentions gets done first—that's rather inconvenient for us others."

"Oh, Jeanie is in love with George, I'm afraid, poor girl, and George hasn't a clue—he's trying to give her ideas on agronomy. It seems Descartes taught his valet algebra. George says, without a microscope people usually can't see the difference between any two fleas or any two men and women; ergo, we can also study agronomy. I believe that," concluded Marge earnestly.

"I'm afraid George has not got very far with Mrs. Barrow!" said Eleanor coldly. "The other day she asked me what cross-fertilization was, and I had to give her quite a little lesson in botany. I found out that she had no idea there were two sexes in the plant world. Do you think it quite wise of George to tell his ideas to a person who is going to garble them and may give rise to rumors in the village? I passed a dreary-looking kind of girl selling the *Daily Worker*. You have a very rabid little village, haven't you? I had no idea village life was such a cross-section."

Marge had very decided ideas on all kinds of things, but Andrew was just a kind man, she said—his answer to every question was the kindest to be found. "He used to be political, but I think he's too frail for it. He used to go chalking slogans in the streets at ten years old. He's a depressed-area child. I still can hardly get him to take anything but tea and bread and tomatoes." She gave a bubbling laugh. "And he says, 'I love tea and bread and breathing.' "

In the bedroom while Marge was changing her dress, Eleanor plumped down in an armchair exclaiming, "I do love a great deep cozy armchair—it makes me feel the whole world's my friend. Your hair's quite natural, isn't it, dear? And I look better with a simple bun on the neck. We're the lucky ones!" She added in a mysterious tone, "And where does the boy sleep?"

"What boy?"

"Why, your young Andrew."

"Here, of course."

"In a double bed! And why not? You're quite right to have the courage of your convictions. You are proud of your happiness, aren't you? You want to shout it from the housetops? There is such a thing as lovely naughtiness!" She sighed.

Marge laughed. "How can George have such an old-fashioned

sister? He told me you were very modern. You sound like Elinor Glyn."

"What was old-fashioned about her, ha-ha?" cried Eleanor. "Mummy used to read her in secret and kept the book hidden behind the sheets in the linen closet, and when she went out visiting I sampled all the forbidden fruit; and I listened greedily when the ladies at Mother's at-homes, thinking I did not understand, talked in low, measured respectable words about women's rights—and very queer rights they were, my dear!" Eleanor flung up her legs and bounced out of the chair. "They were all so silly and so delicious, poor dears. Mummy was horrified by sex! She told me how coarse Daddy was and without consideration: he woke her twice on her very wedding night!" Eleanor looked seriously at Marge. "She never wanted to have George and she thought he wasn't coming. To her, George was a mistake. She never understood the ordinary male; she fell for the utterly refined gentleman type, men who kept their sex life discreetly hidden if they had any —like Count James von Ulse. A German Junker, a great gentleman, who—was a little in love with me, I think. But he was very spiritual, a great spiritual leader, and I—I'm afraid I'm not spiritual, I'm of the earth earthy. You see, dear, he and Mother, too, belonged to a society which frowned upon the physical side of marriage—that's what made Mother so happy. But I was a young girl then, lusty and ready for the marriage bed. Oh, I was just as shy of intimacy as anyone else, but I had read books—I *knew;* and I wanted my babies, and I wanted a man who wanted babies. Somehow," she continued, laughing, "Count James von Ulse didn't quite fit into the picture."

Marge said, "Andrew would like to be here. He adores what he calls silly trifling talk—that man can sit where you are and talk three hours by the clock and each day's work to him is a regular Odyssey. I am teaching him to knit, because he only wears hand-knitted socks and he's going to be a very good knitter like I am. He sits there and gossips and knits; I rush round, stuff rabbits and

[151]

bake potatoes. We do the house together and then we garden together. We're so happy that I keep touching wood; I'm afraid something will happen."

"Isn't that only a sense of guilt? It's quite unnecessary; George doesn't blame you," said Eleanor.

"There, this cake is always a success. But I am lucky with cakes."

"And you are lucky with many things, Marge darling."

After a cup of tea, "because of the waistline, my pet," Eleanor hurried away, saying she had to make a call on behalf of a literary friend, a German exile.

"It looks as though we have a friend in common in this very village and that makes two good friends in Market Square."

In parting they kissed and called each other "sister, not sister-in-law" and Eleanor accepted an invitation to luncheon one Saturday, with Andrew. "To inspect your glamour boy," she said in a whisper, with a loving smile. "Bless you both, you two babes in the wood."

Opposite Marge's cottage was a five-sided green, the road on one side, the others made by old brick orchard walls over which boughs hung. Two lovers' walks opened between these walls, one with a turnstile, and through this turnstile Eleanor went with swift and lilting step. The lanes went into a short main street and out of this she turned to a side street uphill, old, ugly, with small brick houses in the shadow of several warehouses and factories. Flora Dawson had been at school with her, though two years ahead; she had become Dr. Vent, and Eleanor had lost her at her marriage. Now she found her again settled down as a village doctor, married to an elderly man who owned one of the factories opposite. They had been athletic schoolgirls and were now middle-aged women with big bosoms, but they embraced warmly, Eleanor with a graceful strong winding and Dr. Vent "as she now was" lending herself to it with the reserve of a headmistress. She was a short, thickset but soft-bodied woman, wearing a navy-blue coat and skirt and white blouse with her graying dark hair in a floppy bob. At school Eleanor had disliked and mocked her because of her measured dry speech which covered a speech defect; this had developed into a thoughtful hesitation with a sympathetic undertone.

She had a cold front waiting room with a long polished table, stacks of old magazines and starched white and dusty green curtains and a number of large canvases on the walls, scenes of forest glades, placid rivers, and two portraits of herself as a graduate and in a velvet hat and gown. Behind this, looking on the quiet back garden under high walls, was her surgery. On the walls were photographs of her three children, two girls with a boy between them.

"How on earth did you manage all those and this too," cried Eleanor, hugging and kissing Flora again in her joy.

"I married before I was qualified," Flora explained, "had Joan as soon as I got out of the hospitals; and in the meantime, Johnnie had gone into the manufacture of plastics and so it has continued. He keeps up his painting and has had two shows."

"Oh, what a full, glorious life, what all-round people you are," cried Eleanor rejoicing. "That is the way to live."

"Why, don't you live that way?" Flora asked in her pleasant starched way.

"Yes, but I've been a landlady, a char, as well as doing my writing and bringing up two children. It isn't quite as honorific, I'm rather ashamed of that part. So in the end Henry decided to make a big change, and we have come to live at my brother's until we can get proper accommodation."

She began to tell the details. "I have been visiting someone in Market Square," Eleanor ventured presently. "Do you happen to know my brother's wife, Margery Brent—it seems funny to call her that, but that's her name, after all?"

The doctor's face stiffened professionally; it was as if a fine white veil fell over it, but her eyes softened and smiled. "She is one of my patients and so is your brother."

"And so is Andrew?" Eleanor laughed.

"Andrew?"

"Andrew, the—her friend, how shall I put it? Her 'paramour' is the old-fashioned word."

"The friend she lives with," said Dr. Vent, looking down. "Ye-es!" Her voice softened and drawled, "He-e ha-as qui-ite a co-ough, poo-or ma-an."

"A cough? You mean he's—?"

"A chronic cough—he smokes too much."

"I suppose these cravings mean some unfulfillment," observed Eleanor, "or nervous tension. I am not a puritan; I only think, shall we say, domestic experiment and shocking the natives must make one very nervous—I couldn't bear it. Perhaps I am lazy emotionally or perhaps I think life is more serious—and sweeter. Do you suppose the village minds very much? Do they have that burden to bear? It is so very brave to rebel against convention; most people are so unimaginative."

"I see people here one by one and I see them in their homes, intimately"—very slowly she said "intimately" as if drawing a picture with it—"but I don't know much about the village as an en-ti-ty. I don't know what it thinks. It is rather a drawback."

At this moment a middle-aged woman with soft hair and a silky muslin housedress came to the door and asked the doctor if she was ready for patients' messages.

While she sat there the doorbell rang, she heard the voice of the servant-secretary, she heard Dr. Vent on the phone, and then a boy, excessively shy, came into the room, carrying a doctor's instrument case. She recognized Dr. Vent's son, now a medical student. He greeted her and went to the end of the table to cut himself some bread. The evening sun slanted over the fence; she heard the factory workers' voices in the street. A cat ran across the grass. Presently Dr. Vent came in with a straight face. She had to go out. Eleanor said good-bye at the car door and went leisurely up-road toward her home hill.

It seemed strange that the dull swot Flora Dawson had organized this rich independent life; it seemed as if it must have consumed many more years than Eleanor had had. Eleanor felt close to her, yet she was somehow a little frightened. She began to walk quickly; rebellious thoughts came disorderly. What an odd thing I never thought of medicine! I would have made a good doctor! It's too late now. Dr. Vent's satisfied calm, her free entry into privacies, the portraits, the devoted husband with a profitable business, her early marriage—was it envy Eleanor felt? "No, I'm captain of my soul and master of my fate," she said aloud, striding up the hidden driveway. At the top she saw the long two-storied farmhouse with the declining but still-high sun on one end and slanting through a doorway. To her left the troughed landscape fell away and rose in fogged greens and grays in the early spring. "It's spring—*I like to breathe.*" She stood expanding her lungs. The sun fell on some large glossy leaves nearby, she heard scuffling in the bushes, but she cared very little about these dim hidden lives. My desk, my work, she said to herself. I have an infinite capacity for work. But work at what? Just one idea can pay off.

After dinner, when Lindsay Brent had gone up to his room to work on his book, George and Eleanor sat by the newly built brick hearth, where a wood fire burned. George was thin, brown, with two deep folds from nose to chin, a large nose, pronounced chin, bright blue eyes and a farmer's hump that went with his farmer's trudge. He had taken off his jackboots for slippers and had put on a clean pair of overalls, but otherwise wore his working clothes, a white singlet and blue and white sweater. A big accounts book lay on the table beside him and he had a sheaf of papers in a pocket. He stretched his long legs over the hearth rug, and looked dreamily into the fire. After a while he smiled, and asked Eleanor if she really meant what she had said at dinner—that she would do the farm accounts for him. "It looks as if you are settling in." His farm was run on strict business lines; as well, he read, studied and was trying to plan a small experimental section. The paperwork was too much for him. Eleanor held in her lap a book she had taken from his library entitled *Three Years on a Farm.* She had a business purpose in taking it, too: she hoped to be able to plan her own book.

"Do you really want to do my paperwork?" asked George. "Won't it interfere with your own work?"

"It's a daily splendid temptation here, the house and farm both, and just sheer lovely idleness," said Eleanor, "but those who work are those who find most time for work, and so I'd rather take over your accounts where your Marge left off. I know the farm has to pay its way, and I made our house in London pay too—it paid Daddy Charles jolly well."

A quaint bright smile ran down his folded cheeks. "Did you see my Marge today?"

"Yes, bless her, what a dear little busy housewife she is. She can put her hand to anything and make a success of it."

"That's true," he said soberly. "She can make a success of any man, too. What did you talk about?"

"Oh, mostly feminine chatter that wouldn't interest you. She gave me the recipe for her wonderful cake and I'll make it for you if you miss it. She said it can't fail. She showed me over the house, her cupboards, larder, library, kitchen, bedrooms, a guest room for the unpredictable guest. It's a dream cottage, Mayfield. But surely you've seen it, George?"

"Oh, yes, I went there acourting!"

"Since the—what shall I say—amiable disagreement?"

As George said nothing, she continued, "Marge is a heavenly housekeeper, you know better than I do. I envy her guests of tomorrow night. A Dr. Waterhouse and his wife—old friends, I believe."

George said they were. Eleanor said with a gracious smile, leaning forward and patting his leg: "And so you've kept up the whole circle, you're all friends. But this is a very broad-minded village, surely! Of course, I know the neighboring town is considered very radical, but I didn't know it had seeped into the villages. I suppose they are accustomed to a certain laxity, or go-as-you-please in the country. I suppose it is really true about the neat-handed Phyllis and her swains. How lovely to be able to lead one's own life, George. I'm afraid we're not so close to nature in London. I'm afraid you would not find your friends approved so easily. But then, it is, isn't it, a very personal thing. There are natures that can carry it off and Marge must be one of them; and you, George—I never guessed you had it in you. Such fairness, such open-minded-ness, such philosophy. I do think you've both been wonderful—I admire you both. But," she said, bowed over her knees and looking with a twinkle into his eyes, "Marge does get the good end of the stick, doesn't she? And can you really be so above this world as not to feel the arrangement a little bit unfair?"

George said, "I don't ask myself that. And neither would you, Eleanor, if you were me. Perhaps you would do the same. You're a good girl; you never put yourself first."

Tears came into Eleanor's eyes. "I'm afraid it is a bad policy. Fairness is not met with fairness: people take it for a sign of weakness, of suckerdom! You've suffered, George, I know it. I've suffered, too. We haven't managed very well, you and I!"

"Is there something wrong between you and Henry, dear? I know you always deny it, but I can see you're restless and you don't read his letters at the table."

"Oh, he makes me so impatient! It's like a child—if I have to damn and blast, I want to do it upstairs. He's willful and a show-off, and he tries out every kind of trick to worry me."

"That's more like a child than a man. Would you like to show me his letters? Would you like my opinion?"

A weight rolled off Eleanor's mind—she breathed freely. "Yes, I do want you to see." Suddenly she became angry. "You will see—he goes to any lengths; he treats me like a long-suffering sister."

While George read the letters his face lengthened. Meanwhile, Eleanor as she pushed the letters forward to him said, "Now you will see!—do you see?—this one is the bloody absolute limit! Here he complains he had no joy with me! Here I can't keep house! You know yourself how efficient I am! And look at this for crust! Not a word about the children for weeks and then he's worrying about some orphan brat!" She raved sulkily on, her lips trembled. Suddenly she put her arms on her lap and began to cry like a girl. "Oh, it isn't fair! I don't want to be a grass widow! I want my home, and everything that goes with it. Now he makes me look as if I were guilty, an adulteress, an enemy, or as if he'd left me. I'm pretty brave, George, but I find it so hard to keep a bright face and jolly the children along and answer Marge's hints and pretend not to hear and see. Did you ever, George, did you ever encounter such an irresponsibly silly spoiled man? Because you see," she said, lifting her head earnestly, "it is all an act, just a song-and-dance act, just the male bird dancing about to attract the female. But, oh, I was caught long ago, I fell in love with him and married him. This is perversion, to keep up courtship so long after marriage. I know he loves me, George," she said very earnestly. "I feel it deep down, a wife knows these things. But he is wearing me out; I can't sleep. I'd like to shake him. Oh, he's such a queer, tormenting, wearing, boring lover; he bores me stiff." She began to cry again. "I'm so unhappy, George. Tell me what I ought to do. You're a man. Tell me what to say to bring him to his senses."

George shuffled the letters and stacked them, handing them back. He said, his kind frank eyes looking at her soberly, "Well, Ell, I don't see what you see and I may be wrong, but I think he's in earnest—he wants a divorce."

Eleanor grumbled that he couldn't, it didn't make sense, their lives didn't make sense if he without any reason proposed to desert her and the children. "It just doesn't happen like that; you simply don't know the man as I do. A man leaves a woman for some fault, something she's done. But I've done nothing." She began to cry again. "I won't believe it, I refuse to accept it," she said through her tears. "He's got to come to his senses. He'll find I'm hard, hard as nails, true as steel. He'll never get away from me, because I'm right. I've given my entire life and time up to his home. You won't get away, Henry: make no mistake. This is for life."

George only said that he did not know Henry and that she might be right. She was right to hold on and if the marriage endured she was proved right. Afterwards, they settled down to the account books and laughed together over the eccentric though efficient way Marge had kept them and her comments. "Dear Marge, why isn't she here with us?" said Eleanor. "Perhaps these clouds will blow away, George, and a year from now you and Marge and Henry and I will be sitting cheerfully together talking about the children's future or the farm."

Later she said, "By the way, I passed one of your comrades in Market Square."

"Who was that?"

"Just a girl, getting signatures for or against—against, I suppose." She laughed delightfully. "Imagine such a grassy little Essex hamlet being so energetic. We do have true freedom in this country, don't we, when Communists are allowed to agitate publicly. I think that's the outside limit of toleration."

"Do you really think they ought to be jailed for having ideas different from ours?"

"Oh, goodness, no," cried Eleanor, shocked. "Free speech is surely one of our fundamental liberties. But do they tolerate us? Is it because we're so sure of our system that we're so tolerant? Or is it just laissez-faire; or are we really good as a nation? We go abroad and raise the living level of primitive peoples; we are always intervening without taking sides, to make peace or fair settlements. But don't you think toleration can go too far? Like you and me, George. Don't you think England, too, will have trouble from ungrateful frivolous partners? Not to say worse," she cried sullenly, "much worse, criminal, fiendish partners? Ingratitude, thou marble-hearted fiend!" And she wailed as she had never done before, "Oh, George, George, George, who can help me? He is trying to leave me. I know it! George," she said, pouting rebelliously, "we are both on the rubbish heap! Our family's not lucky in love."

"No," said George.

*   *   *

But upstairs, in bed again, she began to turn things over, worry and plot her next moves. She was straightforward, used to her own way, not good at intrigue, and yet intrigue rushed into her head, giving her neuralgia.

Henry wrote that he was in love with someone in his office, who was married but unhappy—"She makes beautiful embroidered collars." Her name was Barney. He went to great lengths in describing how natural and inevitable their affection was. He even sent Eleanor one of Barney's love letters to him: "You and I are made for each other, I saw it the first evening in the bar; it's chemical affinities, it's meant to be, it's fate." Wrathfully, Eleanor showed this letter to her brother, and then put it away in the fat file in which she now kept everything relating to her married life. She wrote to him in strong bitter terms.

Some months later he was in a good mood. He had seen a house at Harrow that he liked very much; they would be happy, the air was good and Russell could go to Harrow later on. Henry had made very good connections; all his work with the Society was an asset and he had very bright prospects, though at present he could not say what they were. In the expected situation "a wife and children are a moral guarantee, and I think you will find I am grateful for your cooperation."

Eleanor, looking at the farmhouse from a distance, eyed the window of her room: in it were goblins of torment—were her worries largely of her own invention? "He does need me! He's come to his senses! Oh, wouldn't I like to shake the life out of him for frightening me uselessly! I must hide my feelings, now it's come right. But I'm a good forgetter when I must."

But Henry's next letter said the "house in Harrow had fallen through" and he was too busy in a new job as public relations manager to even think of distant suburban residence, "Unless I kept on the service flat in town and joined you in the weekends only. But perhaps it is simply better to postpone our plans till we are clear about the situation abroad." Eleanor had not even Henry's private address. He could not give it, he said, for special reasons; she was to write to a box number. Eleanor read this with horror: he must be living with another woman. George said, No, he would not do that, it must be that his job requires it.

"You don't know his divine simplicity," cried Eleanor. She wrote asking Henry for an interview, "in which all our little deadends and mysteries must be thrashed out," but Henry was away in Scotland for weeks.

One afternoon she called upon Marge with a message about a Red Cross class, found the door locked and went round the side passage to the kitchen door, almost always on the latch. In the kitchen, at the table, in the afternoon sunshine, she found a yellowheaded young man dressed in dark blue airman's overalls. A workman taking it easy, she thought.

He said, "Hello, Marge," and "I just made tea—look over there, there's something for you," and peeped smiling over the top of his newspaper. Then he lowered the paper, holding it to the table in his long nicotine-yellow fingers and smiled agreeably. "You want Marge?"

"I'm Eleanor, Marge's sister-in-law," said Eleanor, thinking it a quaint, sharp thing to say. "Are you Andrew?" She felt sure it was. He had a bony long face with exaggerated coloring like a portrait, very large blue eyes that stared and were bloodshot. They had tea, Andrew allowing her to serve him; they sat there for some time, Andrew chatting fluently about his experiences on the airfield. "I could eat in the officers' mess, but I never go there. I go into the men's mess . . . I sent the man for some cotton-waste and he never returned . . ." Strange little anecdotes, flavored with little involuntary laughs and the sententiousness of a humane country wiseacre. "I have my gang and he has his gang; and his gang were following me round gibing at me; it was all because of a girl . . ."

Getting rosier and more eager, he began to talk about women lecherously, though in decent, poetic language—a girl in London, a girl in York; he drew slightly closer, putting his face forward, looking into her face like an infant, dribbling smiles and infatuation and giving out a feeling of sweetness. Eleanor's heart began to struggle, she felt irritated beyond endurance; she had never supposed he had any "morals"; she leaned forward and expected a kiss. He got up, brought his chair round to hers, and sitting up soberly, said, looking at her mildly, that he expected she understood men; a beautiful girl like she was must have had a lovely past —he could always tell by a woman's voice, she had such a sweet voice; and he began complaining about himself. He wanted women but women didn't care much for him. He kept on flirting, tempting her, till she did exactly what Marge had described—she seized his head and put it on her breast.

"I'm afraid we're being naughty, not loyal to Marge," she said with enjoyment.

"We're not naughty, we're natural," he said in a deep voice.

After a while she left; he strolled to the gate after her, laughing childishly, and leaned on the gate while she went up the street with her bounding stride; she turned to look back, waved her arm elegantly. He laughed. She was disturbed, a giddy smile kept appearing, she rushed along. During dinner she hardly heard what was said, and afterwards, she could not help talking about it to her father and brother; but to put a decent face on it, she condemned Andrew.

"I met Andrew at last, but he seems to me hardly worthy of our Marge. He's a vapid, empty-faced sort, I don't see what he contributes—what do you think, George?"

George said he didn't see how he could discuss it; her father was silent. Pouting, Eleanor said, "Well, he isn't worthy of her: he tried to make love to me, I can tell you. I just think he's Lovelace Wholesale, I think it's a bloody shame."

She went upstairs later and began, grinning to herself, thinking, I could cut Marge out in just ten minutes; she danced, looked at herself in the mirror, said, "The old Eve isn't dead yet," and then became excited, sat down and wrote a spiteful letter to Henry. She described the village activities; married women and bachelor maids, "the lady of the Hall" and the humdrum little back-street housewife, the soul of village suburbia. She "retailed some of the tattle going round, all well-intentioned and in merry mood": Miss Peach, the retired postmistress—she was tart and stiff-necked, she had kept her family home empty of people, but now she wondered if she wouldn't let her rooms to young men after the war. "Do you think I might have a good time?" Miss Peach asked. The snow of age had fallen suddenly and heavily, a thick layer, upon black hair; and that was like her life.

There was talk of "a black market in men," some scandal Eleanor had not followed up. She told Henry also, she had always taken care not to meet Andrew, thinking it "injudicious, not wishing to put the seal of family approval on the little affair"; but one day, by the purest accident, she had found Andrew in the house alone and had had a long talk with him, asking him what his plans were: "Someone in the family must be less quixotic."

She had found him a quite innocuous young man, not so very passionately fond of Marge, as far as she could see; she thought he was merely the kind who yielded to a stronger nature—a filial compulsion. She thought the thing might easily break up any day. "I should be glad, for I am very fond of my sister-in-law." George was liked well enough in the village, though they called him an extremist. "What a very temperate, balanced country we live in that in the midst of these doubtful times, George and others go unmolested; surely it is the outside limit of toleration. However, I do not stop the talk when the children are there, as I think they should learn to discriminate; I have good solid chats with them afterwards. They do hear Dad and George jawing away at Darwinism and land values at a terrific rate; it opens their minds, I'm sure. I have been terribly careful, Henry, about Marge's little problem, as I want them to grow up with the feeling of a complete, sure, happy home background."

Henry, in reply, said he was instituting a legal process to take the children from her: she was unfit to be their guardian. But as usual, his work, which often took him abroad, seemed to drive out this idea of his, and the family went on as before. Indeed, Eleanor heard nothing from her husband for some time.

George was more anxious than she was. "I'm afraid you have been too long apart," he said. "It isn't healthy in a marriage." She answered bluffly, "I don't mind it; it may mend mine. Let him have his bit of fun if he wants it. As long as he tells me about it. He can't keep anything from me; it's like a small boy. As long as he doesn't bring any sickness home to me and the children; I'd rather the women abroad get whatever he catches. But they manage these things better, don't they? English women are innocent about such things. I'd rather he didn't come back till he's sown his wild oats. A few disappointments and he'll be too old for lechery. It's the European coming out in him. It's the price I have to pay. Age will cool him down." She was receiving more money; she banked it; she kept her own expenses down; she was beginning to feel quite secure. When he returned, she would have a thumping big sum to show Henry; this would have a certain charm, and again, the children's early troubles would be over. He would be grateful for that. She now referred openly to "Henry's awkward age."

It was the dark of winter. They were cold, tired, down. At night she would sit by the fire with George and in anxious quiet conversations discuss their troubles—national and personal troubles were all one—and George allowed her to bring up the question of Marge and himself over and over again, because she would say, "It's not just one of us that's alone, but both of us, and in fact, we are all dreadfully alone." Once she sang,

> *"She weepeth sore in the night,*
> *And her tears are on her cheeks."*

She said wildly, "Oh, George, oh, George! Where did I go wrong? Did I marry the wrong man? I couldn't have—we planned it all!" She would look at her brother with large troubled eyes. "It's as if there's something I don't understand, but I do understand. I face all my problems squarely." She would put her chin out, while her lips trembled.

She enjoyed the village gossip and scandal; they kept her alive. She sparkled when she was up to mild mischief, tattling, trying to get at the truth of relations. She felt ashamed, "I never did that as a girl," and came to the conclusion that she was lonely. "I'm on the outside of everything; it's because I have no husband. But there must be thousands, millions of us! It's our duty to struggle on alone."

She followed, in the minds and mouths of others, the nation's history, and once or twice, after political defeats, she felt herself in a blind end: "What if we go down? If it's all been for nothing? If we've all been wrong? Can I live in a world where the British Empire does not live?" Sometimes this breathless terror took her at night when it was very dark; but it was just as bad in the daytime, when she could look over the wren-colored country —black, blue, green, yellow, the summer fields, smooth and plump, the woods and thickets—and think, This might be nothing but a wasteland! This thought would obsess her for days even when she listened to the village women. "What will we do? What will I do? Is life a waste? Would my children grow up and become accustomed to a beaten country?" She had perhaps had her children too late; she did not feel that they were enough for her. She listened kindly, but without much faith, to their plans and enthusiasms. She did not believe they would come to much. She did what she could for them—encouraged them to visit rich friends for the use of it and poor friends to soften their hearts; in the weekends she went for walks, chattered lovingly with them, teased out their school problems, helped them with their work, did their mending, washing, ironing and baked for them, but she only felt close to them and really alive when she was discussing her own problems with them, reading bits of their father's letters and speaking sentences beginning with "Mummy wants you to listen carefully, though this is a problem too big for even wise little heads," or like words. In the week, she would plan such conversations with them.

With others she had to act a part and could ask no worthwhile counsel. She could see she worried and bored the children too; they were silent, they sulked or even repeated their father's remarks. I must keep my problems to myself, she would think, and then irritably, "But why should I? Why should they grow up in perfect bliss while I sweat it out?"

She struggled along, keeping a good face on it and smiling in a good-natured, superior way at troubles great and small. She grew into the habit of blocking every question, always putting forward the commonsense view, throwing cold water on enthusiasm, discouraging fancies. "Our only problem is the job in hand," she would say. "I think we can leave it to our government to make wise decisions; they have all the information; our job is to get on with what's nearest to hand . . . I'm quite sure our journalists are directed and telling us what's best for us to know: they are given information we don't get . . . Why listen to the radio at all if we're not going to believe what we hear? . . . Whatever it is, I think as a nation we can take it." The worse the news got, the more she felt it right to resist evidence, to hold the line to disbelieve "scare stories," to talk "pure common sense." At the same time, she did not hold with "bogey" talk of fascism renascent. "Fascism is not people. I have been in Germany and met the real people; they are sweet, gentle, home-loving people like ourselves. We were on the other side; we were fighting for two opposite principles, but they are principles. We must be careful of listening to stories spread for a purpose. After all, who were the people in those camps? Communists and such fomenters of disorder and gypsies and such who are outsiders anywhere. It cannot be all black on one side and all white on another. You see, my dear, I *know:* I have seen the German people themselves." She would smile sagely, place her forefinger gently but firmly on the table, shake her head and go on with her sewing or whatever she was doing. She talked to the others as if they were her children.

But one night she said, "George, do you think it's possible for us to lose in another war?"

"Yes, it's possible."

"But what would we do? They wouldn't dare to overrun us —they'd make some treaty." He always knew better than the newspapers; she hoped for some way out from him.

"I wouldn't lay down my spade; and I'd join the Resistance."

"Oh, George, English people wouldn't form a resistance!"

"They would."

"I don't believe it," she cried, bursting with an intolerable feeling. "The proper thing would be to do your work and say nothing. It couldn't last long."

"And suppose it did? Suppose we ended as a servile nation?"

"Your Communists are defeatists; they've made you a defeatist. We couldn't swallow it."

"Then you'd resist?"

After a while she laughed and said sweetly, "I suppose I'm entangled in your logical contradictions. Believe me, George, history and humanity aren't run that way. I would be a nurse: help and keep the peace. It would recede. History would return to normal."

George called her authorities in history "apologists of Empire" and "ratifiers of the unrecallable."

"But we are the first nation in the world, surely you agree to that, George? Why I never heard anything else at school; that's surely one of the thirty-nine articles."

"You had a long sunny morning, but now it is afternoon," said George. He looked very tired. The work was too much for him; he worried about decline of the economy, "It is not all so certain as you hope"; and Marge was ill—she and Andrew were driving around the country consulting doctors, healers, wise women.

Eleanor gradually got into the habit of resisting every word and allusion that did not lead to Britain's being champion. She never recovered from those days, she never recovered her self-possession. She smiled, gestured, walked straight and stately, made eyes at men and was sweet to women, but she was never sincere. Every day and minute by minute she suffered from instability; it rotted her whole life, it spread and spread like an incurable disease which she was always concealing. Her voice and gestures were higher: she was sometimes almost light-headed; and she floated lightly over every suggestion of breakup in Henry's letters, answering with anecdotes and village scandal, a humdrum chronicle, which really meant spiritual exhaustion. Sometimes she thought of the faithful servant who had bound his heart with three iron bands.

But it was not long after this dark moment that her life began again. Her father had asked her to read a manuscript. He brought it and she saw that it was not *The Republic of England,* a subject she dreaded in these days, but a novel entitled *Brief Candle.* With the usual touchy modesty, her father said he wanted her honest opinion. "Fix it up if you can and give it away for wastepaper if you can't."

The story surprised her. It was the tale of a sick woman coming from London to "Easton Minor," a village like Market Square. "Sabrina" was a blonde of a coppery-rose complexion, kind and inveigling—to Eleanor a detestable creature, capricious, mean, a bag of tricks. Sabrina was dying of consumption (her father wrote in his old-fashioned way) and in the care of a family servant. She threw a spell over the men left in the village. "The red roofs of Easton Minor under the tall trees in the hollow looked from Sabrina's cottage on the hill like painted eggshells thrown into the bushes; and under each roof hearts throbbed feverishly because of her, a man who loved her, a woman who feared and hated her." There was a man who left his wife without a hope of winning Sabrina, a soldier had been court-martialed, an old man came to the house every day ruining himself with presents, looking ever more haggard because he was starving. When she died, men walked through the village behind the coffin weeping; pale-faced women stood behind the curtains.

With robust irritation, Eleanor laughed. "Who would have thought the old man had so much blood in him?"

The story was tender, forgiving, like a man writing about his daughter. She took it to her father and told him it was quite good in parts, it would sell; it only needed the few professional touches any editor could give it; the female psychology was not quite right but that could be "written in"; and there should be a "few more concessions to popular morality."

"And who can do that but you?" her father asked.

Eleanor began to work at it and found she could work. She fixed her work hours; she rewrote, polished and interpolated, and within a year it was done. Her father and she argued somewhat about the "female psychology," but she would smile him down. "Who is the woman here, you or me?"

About Sabrina he would say, "But surely she wouldn't say that, Ell?"

"But I know, I'm a woman. How can you know a woman's drive, Daddy?"

"Ah, I don't know, I'm not sure—every man has something feminine in him I daresay, and the better for him."

She would be struck by such remarks, and copy them into the MS.

The book, bearing their two names, Eleanor Herbert and Lindsay Brent, went the rounds for some time. Then they received an advance on it and divided the money equally. This was followed by a good deal of rewriting based on editorial advice. In the publishing house there was disagreement about the manuscript. One editor attacked it bitterly; two others thought it would sell. Eleanor was aware of the conflict and came to detest the first editor, a man named Waterman.

As she worked over her book, which she now called "Our Litel Boke," she would come across one of Waterman's corrections or sarcastic comments written neatly in the margin, and would stiffen with rage. Waterman seemed to her her bitter, reasonless, talentless enemy; she could never say his name without insult, "that stupid ignorant man." She would lie in bed at night in a spasm of hate, thinking over what he had said. He corrected her

English; he did not understand her allusions; he objected to her dialogue; he said the book was valueless. To beat him she worked over every word, gratefully took all the advice of the other two editors. Suddenly her father objected: this dialogue was not what he wanted, it could never have taken place. Somehow, he convinced her, and she worked it over again to please him. Once more she ran into "that loathsome Waterman"; and even the other two editors were against her. They now gave her mild lectures on the author's duty toward his readers. "You must have reader identification, you must use common coin; nowadays we can't take the risks we used to take."

She cherished all this knowledge and reasoning; it was intensely satisfying. She felt she was at last learning the business she had struggled in for so many years; and she repeated every one of their phrases to her father, "I'm willing to take your word that that was, or at least could have been said, darling, but you've got to convince the reader in terms he can accept! You must use the common coin."

At last it was published, not much noticed but well sold; it was reissued and for some years kept making money for the authors.

Eleanor had sent a copy of *Brief Candle* to her husband, and in return received a letter saying, in part, "You must have known that I would disapprove of this scurrilous, pornographic writing or you would not have called yourself 'Herbert' . . . this is the result of your salacious interest in local scandal and your unseemly acquaintances . . . I am starting proceedings to take the children from you, they must be protected from you . . ."

But the inconsequent man, in the next post, sent a long letter, from which there dropped out, as Eleanor opened it, a postcard-sized photograph of a woman and young child. With this photograph was a fatuously romantic letter and the remark: "Once you see them, I know you will look at it in a different light: you believe in respectability, you would want the woman I love and my child to enjoy what you enjoy, to be part of society. I remember that once when Deborah was first ours, you said, 'I see now that mothers and children are part of society. As soon as a child is born, it draws you into society.' "

Eleanor wrote to him at once, "Please remember if you can that I have two children by you and I don't intend to have them outlawed. It would be very hard if after we've all three been through your difficult years, we were not to benefit by them. It's not fair. I can't help laughing at your unworldliness, sending me this woman's photo. Do you suppose that I believe for a minute, that that is her baby, or that she even had a baby? Or, if she did have one, that it's by you? No, the chain of coincidences is too remarkable, and I didn't think there was anyone so unworldly as to believe that old East Lynne story: 'My chee-ild, kind sir!' Really, Henry, you do need me to look after you! It's possible that you're trying to pull the wool over my eyes, for this is just the sort of gimcrack trick you might pull, as you're quite incapable of real plotting and always give yourself away. And if that's so, it just didn't work, too bad. I'm not even angry; I just am taking no notice at all. And if the woman has fooled you, I'm not only within my rights, but it's my duty to you not to be taken in by a barefaced trick. Cheer up, Henry, let us come to our senses and settle down. And then, we'll see how you feel. I wouldn't keep you for worlds if you didn't value our relationship, and I wouldn't tie you to the children if you're incapable of loving them—then, they'd be better off with their family here, or even with a stepfather, than with you. But something tells me that this is just one of those trial periods that marriages go through. I believe in you and us still, and I know that when we are reunited, you and I and *them*, we'll be happier because we will know exactly why we're together."

Henry seemed discouraged. When next he wrote he said that the baby had died and the girl did not want him any more. He was very unhappy and could not help thinking of the harm he had done to people who had loved and trusted him. "Some men seem to know where they are going, I don't. I don't. I seem to be sailing under sealed orders: when I open the envelope, there are no orders in it—just blank paper. And when I look at the cargo, it's all sealed up—I don't know what I have to deliver." Never had Henry been so plain-spoken and so blue. Eleanor felt she had been vindicated; but the feeling of triumph had left her, and in its place was anxiety. Would Henry, in his weak crafty way, try to elude her again? She needed a breathing space. She did not believe that any woman wanted Henry very badly. She was tired of the struggle and thought that, "on the rebound," he would be coming over to join them. A period of peace, without conflict, would be best.

Presently, Henry was writing to her asking for some of her money. "I have many burdens, you have money." When she refused, saying she expected him to give them a home very soon and that she would not give up the money she had earned and which was for a rainy day, Henry told her he proposed to sue her for it: it was all his. But a little later he wrote and told her that he had seen a suitable house and if she would put the money into it, he would give her and the children a home. He came out to the farm to see them and was friendly, sympathetic, and had presents for the children. He talked for a long time with George asking about the farm and his "commonwealth" ideas and the prospects for England in Europe now.

George, her father and the children seemed quite satisfied with him; and when she said to him, "Is this affair with this woman and her abominably bogus child over?" he answered, "Oh, all that is settled; it is in the past. The child is dead."

Eleanor laughed at this; "How convenient that is!"

The next week, she handed over to him most of the money she had saved, and shortly heard that he had bought a house in one of the suburbs, near a good school. The houses thereabout were abandoned, suffering from years of neglect, but handsome. Henceforward Eleanor's thoughts were turned gaily toward the new home, the next stage of life. It seemed marvelous to her that she and Henry with an adolescent family would begin again at a much higher level. But she also knew that her days of independence were coming to an end. Now, once more she could not have a "working day," but would have to see to all a wife's chores, and satisfy a man's whims. How happy she had been in the country! Almost a girl again. And there had been "lovely episodes," dancing, chatting, even kisses and hugs, though she had "always remembered her marriage lines," as she said mock-quaintly. Now for real life, solid work.

She received a letter saying that the house was ready for her; and in return Henry wanted a divorce. He had met a woman who suited him exactly—companion, wife, friend, a half-German girl who had been working in his service. He wanted to take Cora to Germany where he had a chance of a high post under American patronage. He and Cora had had a flat in London for some time and he gave her the address. "Cora and I are quite settled on our future and I hope you will receive our decision with equanimity, as it cannot be a surprise to you."

Eleanor went in to town the next day, and called at the address given. It was in an old-fashioned block of mansion flats, on the second floor, with two entrances, one of which was locked; but one moved slightly when Eleanor pushed it. She heaved twice, felt it giving, took a couple of steps back and ran into it; the door opened and there was a crash. The door had been concealed by a curtain and some shelves holding ornaments and books. Facing her was the debris on a blue carpet, some chairs in striped satin standing by windows which overlooked the building's strip of back garden. It was a sort of bedroom out of which opened a small dressing room with a little window which looked over the entrance lobby. The bedroom led into the lobby and also into a long hall, where the first few rooms were a kitchen, an empty room and a drawing room partly furnished as an office. Evidently the occupants had only just moved in; there was a long Persian carpet rolled up, a ladder, and a valance lying on a bench. Standing in the bow window was an old style roll-top desk with drawers underneath; it was not locked. Against the wall were two large steel filing cabinets. Over them was an oil painting of a dark-haired woman of about thirty, sitting against red, blue and yellow cushions on a sofa. This same sofa with the cushions was at one end of the room. The woman had oval eyes, a pointed chin, a strong neck: a self-sufficient kind that Eleanor disliked and found without charm.

As quickly as she could, Eleanor went through the drawers looking for personal papers, and found quantities—letters from herself and other women, all classified in folders: Eleanor, Barney, Natalie (the girl with the child); a file headed "Various." There were two or three from a young married woman who signed herself "Bona"; she had pressed her lipsticked mouth three or four times against the paper and written *"Kiss here."* The letter said:

> I am being a very good girl, I have to be: I went to ask the doctor what was the matter with me and what do you think? You know the joke? Scotch is the juice of the barley, wine is the juice of the grape, baby's the juice of a pear. While you were in Ottawa exercising that bright roving eye of yours, we took care of poor Barney, she is looking over my shoulder while I write this and now listen to a duet: Please hurry home!

One was signed, "Your Little Polish Friend, Telimena."

> You scold me because I do not write to you. See, here is my first letter, but do not think you have convinced me. I am an introvert you say and afraid to trust anyone. Yes, I am afraid to trust you. There is not so much work to do now that you are not here and do not come in all the time to check something up in the files. You are so clever and had such a bad memory, you always had to check something up; it was so funny—we used to laugh at you. But I do not really laugh at you; I know you know how to kiss, and that is why I do not trust you. How did you learn? Well, no more for now. Perhaps I will be there when you come back, but I will be just as careful as before. I know you are not wasting your time when you are away. Well, I don't tell you what I am doing, either.

She tore open drawers, a blotting pad, files and envelopes tied with tape, scattering the letters she didn't want on the floor, thrusting others into the paper basket. A package of letters were from Barney. She sat down and read every one of these, ravaging them for mention of herself; her name occurred frequently. Barney had a trick of her own, she wrote the same letter again and again, only slightly altered. The letters began to dance before Eleanor's eyes, she felt that Barney had a strange power. She did not notice at the time that Barney scarcely varied her wording, and that she might have written this same letter to another man, or ten others. Without threatening, there was a threat in them:

Remember, my darling, that you are mine and no one else's, you are all mine, spiritually and materially and for life, we have given each other everything, nothing has been kept back, there is nothing left for anyone else. Remember, my darling, every one of your words is precious to me, I treasure them and will never forget them: let me have your letters, I watch for them and I treasure them. I have every one of them, I cannot forget, everything you said and wrote is burned on my memory, as if with fire. I can never forget the impression you made on me, and the impression I made on you too. Spiritually and materially, I am all yours and you are all mine. Remember what you said, that I gave you complete release, complete understanding of the physical, that I gave you the love you never had. I remember, oh, so well, how you said that Eleanor lacked all physical understanding that you had never had one minute's connubial bliss with her, that it was a case of total physical incompatibility. Remember, my darling, that you and I enjoy complete compatibility, what a rare combination, the one in a thousand chance. I treasure every moment of our life together, so intimate, so rich, so meaningful; remember, my darling, you are mine and I am yours; we fit together, I see us together—where does Eleanor come into our picture? Do not look backwards to that dull, loveless life, which was a complete wash-out, which neutralized all your energy; look forward to the rest of our lives, you and I together. Remember, my darling, I can understand how she destroyed all your self-confidence and joy in life, until you said to yourself: What am I living for? I understand every bit of it. Write to me, my darling, and tell me you are mine forever, in every way.

Barney

"I must think," Eleanor muttered to herself. She got up and paced about, she caught sight of herself in a mirror and stood looking at herself. At present she had a carnation flush, her eyes sparkled boldly, her finely cut lips curving with contempt and anger were dark red. Her hair had not a trace of gray, her skin was spotless; her long sturdy legs in new stockings looked elegant and made to attract men. "It's a mystery to me," she said aloud. "Oh, Henry, you fool! Don't tell me Barney and Cora and all the other sticky drabs you have got together, you idiot, are worth my little finger."

Spiritually and materially, she thought to herself, he can find nothing wrong with me. And what about the children? She walked about the place, closed the door she had burst in and pushed the shelves against it. I'll wreck his home if he wrecks mine, she thought, angrily pushing some bits of pottery aside with her foot, and stamping on the small china head of a woman.

She had with her a big handbag useful for carrying notebooks and groceries and another shopping bag she had brought to town. Into these she began stuffing letters and other papers, a memorandum book and a diary of Henry's, with entries such as this: "I bought two diamond rings from M. which I *intend to keep;* but I will show them to every woman and ask them to choose. It is perfectly true that a diamond makes a woman's eyes sparkle. Mrs. Whiffle left her glove here—was that intentional or not? What does it matter? I dreamed of a glove."

"Henry Charles, you'll pay me for all this!" she said aloud, filling her bags with anything within reach. She threw his desk furniture on the floor and kicked it out of her way. In spite of everything, she had never taken him seriously. When, years later, she declared it had all come as a great surprise and shock to her, she did not mean to lie. All this time she had really thought of Henry and herself as one. She was not greedy, but Henry was hers. Imagine buying two diamond rings! What an absurd thing! Mischievous! I suppose I've been naïve. She stared out of the window, brought herself back to the moment with a start. "But this is too real. I must do something, I can't let this pass. I must act."

The awful treachery of what he had been doing, saying, writing, the idea that he had talked about her and denigrated her to these women, the lies he had told—this was more than she could stand. One woman after another! She thought of her chaste, hardworking life. "Why, Heinz is a Bluebeard," she muttered. Could she have been mistaken in him? Oh, the devil, she thought. "They say there's safety in numbers," she muttered; then she jumped up and stood looking furiously at the oil painting. "Oh, no, no, you won't get away with it," she said between her teeth. "I'll ruin him: he won't get to Germany! He'll need his two diamond rings to eat! He'll come back to me on his knees!" She telephoned for a taxi and made a big parcel of files and odd papers while waiting.

The keys to the file were lying on top of the filing cases. She opened one drawer after another, reading all the titles. She looked quickly through for letters from women, but gradually she became absorbed in her detective work. There were drawers full of material in foreign languages which she could not deal with, but in a drawer labeled *Reports* she found a file called *Sunnytop Farm Reports,* another called *Farm Reports (Eleanor).* There she found retyped and annotated extracts from her own letters, many careless, "piquant, gay," that is, scandalous little stories retold by herself. Within were special sheets devoted to Oenone, a Women's Institute leader she flattered; a "Whig"; George; Marge; Andrew; the postal clerk, Miss Peach. "Officialdom hath made him mad," she said with a laugh, then fell into a brown study: the thing had an official look—was he a spy, a detective, an informer?

She looked elsewhere; he had reports on dozens of people of all sorts. She became enthralled. "What material for a writer!" She had only to rewrite some of this, change the names and there was a book ready-made. Courage and hope gushed up, for she had begun to worry about her next book, which must be done all by herself: "My Bigge Boke," she called it at home. She was honest with herself; she knew her father had supplied the plot, story and character for their "Litel Boke." With a flushed wolfish smile she tore through pages, looking for material; and some of these too she crammed into her case. A wall telephone rang: "Did you ask for a taxi, madam?"

"Yes, for Mrs. Charles."

"Yes, madam!" but the porter seemed dissatisfied.

"Ask him to wait! I'm expecting my husband."

She had struck a file dealing with stories told by workers in Henry's own office. She heard a sound at the door, turned round with her hands dipped in the files, a key turned and Henry appeared in the door. He was smartly dressed and carrying a satchel.

"Hello, Heinz!" she called. She noticed that he was fatter, had taken to glasses and a different mustache.

"Who's that?" he cried nervously.

"You're a worm," she said, "just about the lowest man in the world!" She shook some papers at him. He ran forward saying, "How dare you! How dare you! I'll send for the police! I'll have you arrested!"

"What!" shouted Eleanor, rushing over to him. "I know all I need to know, you utter beast, you wretched little shrimp!" She was taller, broader, stronger than Henry—she cuffed him on the ear while he protected his eyes. She snatched his satchel from him, throwing it away, beat him and kicked him in the calves. He trod on his glasses and turned away when she kicked him in the sleek seat of his trousers. He stumbled and fell sprawling. She bent over and beat him, shouting, "I'm here to put a stop to your little games, my little friend—you won't get away with it," until she became scarlet and the blood roared in her head. She stood up, said, "Ugh, how loathsome! You have just gone down and down," picked up his satchel with some idea of a trophy, shouted, "Don't you get up till I've gone, or I'll give you the hiding of your life," and hurried downstairs with all her loot.

Eleanor returned to Commonwealth Farm that night and at once told her father and brother what had happened. She was full of fight and quite resolved to punish Henry to the full, to show him up publicly and get a divorce with all the rights and a good allowance. It was not the money she was after. She said, at one moment, "His money would disgust me; it isn't his money I want—it's to put 'paid in full' to our long account." She was hungry and ate something, but she could not rest or sleep. At first she hurriedly read through all the letters she had taken, exclaiming, getting up, sitting down, bringing down her clenched fist on the lewd and cruel letters, setting her teeth, biting her lip. She put her cheek down on the scattered pages, with both fists clenched and her arms at an angle, her thick hair loosened on the table and she cried bitterly for herself, the hard world, and her suddenly empty future. "I can never, never take him back," she murmured. It seemed to her that in a rascally way he had concealed his true nature from her. "That isn't the Heinz I loved, that isn't my Heinz." It seemed to her that she had awakened suddenly from a dream of complete happiness and love, that beautiful, good, sane things had been torn away from her by Henry's unspeakable behavior. She slept a little in the afternoon and worked all the next night cataloguing and rearranging Henry's disorderly files. "What a mess! He could have got me a job as his secretary."

She laid aside in a special file all letters from those she named to herself "the guilty parties" and read these letters over and over, and in her anger showed them to her father and brother. Henry had described his "unhappiness" fully to Eva, one girl, and in the most painfully intimate details. He said he and Eleanor had never been in agreement in anything, had never understood each other and had given each other no happiness of any kind; they had never loved each other; and many other things which seemed senseless lies to Eleanor.

"But how can he, how dare he, when we married for love and were settled for life? As for bedroom happiness, he never gave any," she said, flushing with rage. "Our marriage was cold as a frog pond. I am getting up a file, and when it is complete, I am going to let you have it to study: you will see the raw truth of what I have faced without a whimper. I was mother, wife, housekeeper, landlady, domestic accountant, earner, and trying to follow my own profession of writing, too. I did much more than Heinz ever did."

The next morning she received the first of her letters from Henry about this affair. The letter made many accusations but promised to hush it all up if she would go quietly with the children to the home he had provided. Later he wrote that he felt a divorce was inevitable, because of her lovelessness and desertion. He wrote: "It disturbed me that you insisted on going to your brother George's social experiment Farm and taking the children with you, but you made the decision and felt you had to side with your father and your family. I put in my plea but you felt strong ties there. I was always anxious to have you here with me to make a home for me and the children whom I love, and during the war I did all I could to get you back with me and this has been a great worry and upset to me all the time, while I have been also harassed by professional duties. But I am afraid that your own family, your personal velleities and your concern for your own ambitions came first and I did not come anywhere near first with you. Now I am anxious to have you all with me again . . ." This letter went on in the same tone.

Eleanor read and reread this letter with rage, and then found it plaintive. "He has come to his senses," she said to her father and brother. "He foresees he will be ruined with the expense of a divorce and two homes. Should I push him further, to give him a good scare, or go and have a down-to-earth talk with him?"

She went into town to find him, and traced him from floor to floor and office to office in a large building till she reached a large office with an ambiguous nameplate where she entered an outer office and wrote on the form she was given: "To see Mr. Henry Charles—on personal matters. Mrs. H. Charles." She walked into his office, saying, "Hello, Heinz, I unearthed you at last, I've walked miles—"

Henry was standing up behind his large polished desk, his eyes bright, his face agitated. He placed a chair for her, shut the door and went back behind his desk. Then he said, "You did this on purpose to ruin me!" He opened a drawer in the desk and pulled a switch.

She called in her high-toned elegant way, "Heinz, don't be a bloody fool. I came to ask you when we can have a thoroughly good talk about what you said in your letter, us and the children, our future. Far from ruining you, I want to be generous, I believe I can. I want our happiness. Until the children are grown up, I'm going to forget the rest."

"I want you to leave this office at once. If I have anything to say to you, I'll write it to you. This is blackmail; I'm not taken in by words." He declared that no personal visits were allowed; if she did not go, he would have her removed.

"I'll go kicking and screaming. You know me, Heinzl," she said. "You make an appointment here and now, or it'll be the worse for you. Why can't a wife see her husband?"

His confused face enlightened her: she was not known to be his wife and the shame of her position overcame her. She got up with tears in her eyes saying she only came to make peace. "Then your letter was just a legal letter, pretending to call me home. Oh, dear me, I'm beaten at every turn. Heinz, you can have your divorce; I wouldn't try to keep you."

"Do you want me again?" said the confused man, with hesitation.

"I wouldn't take you back if you were the last man on earth," she called out. She hurried straight from him to her family's solicitors, Allcomes, Barnett and Oldthame, whom she had been consulting. Her solicitor was Hazlitt Allcomes, a pleasant fair-haired man, a genteel suburban Christian of conservative views, who played tennis, taught in Sunday School and acted in amateur repertory. Eleanor and he found each other agreeable, attractive, restfully charming.

"I had to be in town to see my publisher," said Eleanor, "and I thought I would see my husband, who wrote me a very plaintive letter, as I saw he wanted to crawl back into my good graces because I had found him out so thoroughly. It was a letter of reconciliation and I know you would rather not have us divorce," she said gently, looking into his face. "I thought I would strike while the iron was hot and seal up my own indignation and hurt completely. I hoped I would be able to tell that we had written *Finis* to the whole tragicomedy of our misunderstandings and war tensions. And now, oh, Hazlitt, I am afraid that what he writes has nothing to do with what he wants. He just won't put himself in the wrong; *I* have to be in the wrong. He really ought to be confined to barracks: there should be some treatment for a man with no will of his own. This letter," she said with sparkling eyes, tapping the letter on the desk, "is the latest thing in husband's come-hither, and do you know, he all but had me thrown out of his office."

Mr. Allcomes read the letter through carefully, put it down in front of him, and taking off his glasses, said, "You had better let me keep this. I want to study it and think what you are to say. My impression is that here he is letting you know upon what he is basing his application for divorce. I don't know him; he may be wavering; but I doubt it. May I ask exactly why you left him?"

Eleanor was so startled that it seemed for a moment she had lost contact with the earth. "I never left him! We had no home and I was saving every penny for a home."

Later on, in the letter, Henry accused her of having abandoned his name. "You called yourself Miss Herbert in public and private, trying to pass yourself off as an unmarried woman."

Eleanor at first remained obstinately unbelieving while her solicitor explained how the letter appeared to him—"It is disingenuous"; and beginning to feel cold, she said at last, bowing her head a little and in a more acquiescent manner, "You have made me see how this letter of reconciliation might look to the cold eye of an outsider—Heinz or Henry has the unfortunate gift of alienating people who have never even met him and always saying the unlucky thing—but I know the man. He means he wants us."

She copied out a letter dictated to her by Hazlitt Allcomes and decided to await developments. They had a few minutes of delightful talk about family duties, the religious upbringing of children, what flowers were out in the suburbs; and she promised to follow his advice.

"I am putting my future life in your hands, strange as it seems," she said rather mournfully, "for if I divorce, I could not marry again. I am not really a career woman, I want just my home and children. It will be rather lonely for me, won't it? But there is no other way, if Henry is unrepentant."

From then on in all outside matters like the routine of the suburban home, domestic entertainments, expenses, religion, she imitated Mr. Allcomes, leaned forward to reach his thought and express it with gentility, to earn his admiration. She felt lonely; he was her guide. She could see he did admire her. He was, though able, of a simple, sincere, unquestioning nature. He preferred not to handle crime, divorce or any complex matters. He stuck to his categories of the "simple, sincere" and the "very crafty, disingenuous, in fact, very shocking." Eleanor saw herself more and more in the primary colors of the world of light. Soon, her opinion of herself and her past agreed closely with the views held by Mr. Allcomes. A new woman was built up by Mr. Allcomes—clear-eyed, affectionate, clever, loyal, unconscious of the darker side of man's nature, innocently but firmly believing that the good and true would win. This English lady of fine character and decent upbringing had had the hard luck to meet a man of "Continental morals." She had not seen what women of more morbid, suspicious temperaments would have seen; she was essentially wholesome, pure in heart and faith, loving even where love was undeserved. With Mr. Allcomes, Eleanor now sometimes discussed intricate problems of Anglicanism, and when she left him she would go to the public library and read up on the question.

Next time, with genteel hesitation, modest affirmation, she would attack another morsel of the same problem. He told her little matters of parish and domestic interest. They felt warm and true: Eleanor said she had "a very nice wholesome relation with her solicitor, who is a good family man and an excellent but unassuming Christian."

During the two and a half years it took to divorce Henry she worked for the project of divorce just as if she had been under a kind sympathetic teacher. When she got her interlocutory decree, she was as fit as she had ever been. The sorrows and doubts of the past were gone: she was a new woman, honest, supple in mind, energetic, vindicated. It was a quiet triumph. Henry was to pay for the whole thing and to support her and the children for the rest of his life.

"Though that is not fair and something I cannot take," she told Mr. Allcomes. "The children he may, he must, support; but the sooner I can become independent the better pleased I shall be. I am willing and able. I feel ashamed to force money out of a man I'm not living with. Household money, a wife's money, is for child care and for cohabitation, isn't it? I could not take money from a man I wasn't doing my wifely duty by." She would say such things merrily, laugh and flush, and peer "enchah-ntingly" into her solicitor's chubby face.

He would clear his throat, "Er—eh, well, I don't think we should place it quite in that light. According to the law—"

Dear, dear Hazlitt! At certain moments she thought they would make a good pair; but, of course, he would never divorce and she could never endure to struggle through another divorce, "even from the sidelines!" No, no, she thought; I'm for a bigger man. I'll use my experience, but I must begin at once. For the next six months, I'm the coy fiancée of the King's Proctor; but when I get my final decree, then, eligible bachelors, watch out!

She still, at forty-five, had not a wrinkle that need count, the rich almond-shaped eyelids were a little darker, her eyes not so wide open—from all her reading—but she had not a single gray hair and the blood still burned in her dark lips. She had real health. She was thick-waisted, broad-backed, deep-bosomed and moved with a light powerful step, but swimmingly. When she was noticed, she would walk past self-absorbed, only glancing once aside with a sparkling look beneath her lowered lashes, but no smile; and if a man did not look, she would involuntarily do a "Hem-hem" as she passed rapidly by. She wore furs when she could, for they suited her. As she went along the street she tried to see herself in the shop windows; for the most part, she saw only a shape or a face that startled her. Her sight was poor, but of course she would not wear spectacles. She would stand in front of a window where there were mirrors, peering at herself, waiting till some man came near, then walk on, and board a bus. She liked the quiet teasing; she was safe in the shadow of the King's Proctor. She would think, "Oh, dear me, if the King's Proctor knew what very physical thoughts I have!" The King's Proctor became her teasing, tantalizing, invisible but all-present lover, a threatening shield over her.

Her interviews with Mr. Allcomes were no longer quite so sweet, for once he had got the divorce for her, that is, against his own principles and convictions, won freedom for a "very brave and sweet woman," his knightly act was finished. Now they had the irritating business of Henry's letters, his challenges, insults, complaints. No matter what happened, he sent a challenging letter, confused, but dangerous. Because of the children and the money she was taking she was still very much in his power. He hunted her from address to address: one place was too small, another too expensive, one in a district full of foreigners, another too far from a good school. He complained about everything they did, ate, said. He was pressed for money. He had lost his position and not got another; he became ill. As it was, Eleanor had not won a very large sum for maintenance, for Henry had represented her as coming from a well-to-do family and having savings and earnings of her own. She meanwhile had fought bitterly over the division of their household goods; she could not afford to furnish anew. She had now adopted hundreds of Hazlitt's legal phrases and neat little suburban expressions, as well as some curious ones of her own. She often called Henry merely "the children's father" or "that little wretch," or "my late husband." She began telling people she was a widow and forbade the children to say that their father was alive. "He is dead to us, he has left you, do you understand, he doesn't love you; he's sent us back to the warehouse, he doesn't want us!"

At the same time, she mentioned him more and more, for the shoals of embarrassing, nagging, threatening letters he sent all had to be read, sent to Mr. Allcomes, discussed, answered. It enraged her when Hazlitt found that Henry had some good legal point. The blood rose in her throat. "But what did I get a divorce for if I'm to be nagged at every day and browbeaten? If I were really rich as he lyingly says, I'd take a boat and forget all about him, never touch a cent of his slimy money!"

There were several years of bitter but courageous struggle with poverty while she tried to manage with Henry's check, but she was obliged gradually to draw on and extinguish her own savings; and then one week Henry's check did not arrive, and presently Mr. Allcomes ascertained that Henry had left the country. His parents answered her from Switzerland saying that Henry's health had broken down as a result of family worries, anxiety about money and disappointment, and that they had sent him into a sanatorium. They enclosed a small check, but could not promise regular help. She had better find work; they would be glad to have the children with them in Switzerland in the summer holidays if she would find the money for the tickets. The children were not to be sent to a common school. If Henry recovered and made money, he would have them sent to school in Switzerland to be near them. "We should be very glad to see you during the summer holidays."

She borrowed from her family, moved into cheaper lodgings and went out to find a job. Although she was strained, nervous and not looking her best because she was undernourished, she had confidence that she would get a job at once. Mr. Allcomes could suggest nothing at first, except the inevitable. "Why not go back to Fleet Street? They'd be glad of a real writer as a journalist, I should think."

"That is out. But I have my own little idea," she said, and put an advertisement in the personal column of *The Times,* as follows:

> Established writer, M.A., experienced
> Fleet Street journalist will undertake
> revision and rewriting of MSS. Fees and
> particulars upon application to Box No.——"

She inserted a similar announcement in a weekly for intellectuals. She received a long, pathetic and somewhat menacing letter from a woman who "had been a famous writer twenty years ago," and who enclosed a smeared, tattered old magazine cover with her name on it. "I cannot pay your fees unless you guarantee success, I know how to write," said this author. Another was from a man who said he had the outline of a musical comedy, but he would only let her see it when he had her *bona fides,* it could easily be "filched or manipulated." She received one serious letter from a girl of twenty who had planned a three-novel history of her family. She wrote to all three, being in good faith. The first two were unsatisfactory; the last kept sending her fluently written chapters of her family novel, with unusual descriptions of places Eleanor had never seen, with family documents and fresh characters, a style so debonair that Eleanor was baffled. She merely recommended a publisher. The lively young writer sent her a check for five pounds (10 percent of her advance), and this Eleanor accepted. It occurred to her that "she might develop into an agency." What could be easier? They did the writing, she did the selling. In the meantime, she had no money at all, nothing to pay for paper, typewriter ribbons, postage, shoes, sandwiches, or even rent. She could not wait.

4

·

The Guinea Pig

"LIFE MUST BEGIN again and I am ready to begin," Eleanor said with a light laugh to her children while getting them ready for the final trip to town. "I am a free woman! And now I appreciate freedom: your father, who has been so cruel and treacherous to Mummy, has taught me that—there is some good in everything, even in a dishonest man."

Russell, though he was thirteen, looked down and away. She laid her hand on his arm and shook him slightly. "You must grow up, Russ—you are too dependent, like your father. You want everyone to love you and lick your face like a dog. Life is not a dog and people are not kind; people are savages and brutes. We must set our teeth and put our shoulders to the wheel."

Deborah had a sulky look on her face. She was developing in a way Eleanor could not understand. Now she scolded her to "shake her awake." "I found your torn gloves in a corner of the drawer, Deb, and the other day you borrowed my gloves saying you had lost yours. Why do you lie? There's no need to lie. And you like dirty friends. I heard what you were allowing those boys to say when I was down in the street the other day. Don't you care how you dress? No boy's going to look at you with a creased dirty dress. It's bad enough to have that rash on your forehead. We must get a cream for it." Deborah answered impatiently and Eleanor scolded her. "You have got to help your mother now that Daddy has let her down: we're three orphans fighting for life."

Eleanor could not understand that the children did not see Henry's faults as clearly as she did. They had been through it all, fought every step of the way with her. She had read all his letters to them so that they would not feel they were in the dark; and she had impressed upon them all the time how spiteful and two-faced Henry's letters were. It will be a good object lesson in morals and in personality, she thought to herself.

At first they were puzzled and asked stupid questions. Later, they took sides with her, and Deborah especially began to hate her father. Eleanor was proud then and felt her motherhood. But it had a sad effect on Russell. He had been a loving, devoted little boy. He had gone to school willingly and liked it from the first. But about a year after her trouble with Henry started, he began to look at her and at other women too in a strange way, or, rather, he never looked in their faces, only suddenly to raise his head to steal a glance, as if at a forbidden idol, when they glanced away. He could never be enticed to their laps or arms any more and avoided his mother's kisses. When his father's name came up, he would begin to tremble or even rub his eyes, and one day when Eleanor was looking for an old notebook in the middle drawer of the sideboard where they kept the table linen and all kinds of things, she found a little glass filled with silver coins and then silver coins and pennies in every corner. She never went to this drawer. The children looked after the table, washed the dishes, cleaned the rooms. They were good children, real citizens and helpers, and she herself had the knack of sensing their protest and revolt and avoiding it. The money startled her; but it did not come from her purse, and when Russell returned from the street, he admitted that it was his own.

He had saved all the money his father and friends had given him for over a year; he had nearly three pounds. Now, Eleanor had always feared and hated the pocket money Henry could hand out and she could not afford; and whenever they saw their father, as well as at other times, she said bitter things in coarse language about him and the poverty he had flung them into. If he himself was having a struggle it was his own fault: he could have given them a tranquil lovely home, but the spirit of mischief was in him. He did not even want children: he had had them and cast them off. Russell said, "I'm saving the money so that when your money is gone, we won't be hungry."

Eleanor heard this with fierce joy; she hugged it to her heart. She knew now that the children were listening to her, and were on her side; he had not pulled the wool over their eyes with his trips and cinemas, ice creams, silver coins and birthday overcoats. Russell was growing up, having a man's thoughts, looking to the future, he would stand by her and protect her: later on, she could lean on him. Her great terror, which she had often expressed to the children, was that their father would run away, "vanish into blue beyond," "go up like smoke," and they see and hear no more of him. "I know Daddy—out of sight, out of mind. If he makes up his mind to stay abroad, we won't get another penny from him." She said this to all her friends, and they agreed with her.

"I suppose I shall have to go to work early and do without an education," grumbled Deborah.

"Daddy wouldn't care if you dropped your aitches and had a Cockney whine; his principal idea is not to be out of pocket over the children he finds a nuisance," Eleanor replied.

When Eleanor saw that the children and her friends were on her side, she became fiercer than before and used bitter language; and the true story of her marriage, of life at Commonwealth Farm and of the divorce became mixed up with many sentimental versions and the case Mr. Allcomes had presented. She began to find it hard to understand what had happened to her, although at first it had been quite clear. She was not so happy now, either, as when the divorce had been going on. Then she had been fresh, gay, active; now her skin had darkened, the first hair-thin wrinkles had appeared around her eyes and once, looking at her face in the bright sun, she saw faint lines on her chin that had never been there. The skin was dark, too, around her eye sockets, and though she was eating so little, she was too heavy. But she had no gray hair and still had magnificent arms and legs and a proud motion in walking. Her lips were still red, her voice could be cool, tender, refined; and in general, anyone could see, in a glance, that she had been a real beauty and had much beauty left, and it was not a cold style of beauty, either—it had "a come-hither sparkle." When thinking about her future she said to herself, "If you look, you find," for she did not intend to spend the rest of her life in loneliness; and her good looks when she was dressed for town or when half undressed made her regretful, glad, and stimulated her desires: I have simply got to get me a man.

She had scarcely any time for love affairs. Henry had begun to send checks irregularly from abroad, but with them insisted upon every comfort for his children. In spite of the grim housing shortage, Eleanor was able to find homes for them because she was strong enough to keep on searching. She looked in the papers, went to agents and took buses to likely neighborhoods, where she read the notices in all the stationers'; she crossed the street every time she saw a notice pinned to a gate or window.

First of all, she found a fine flat in Belsize Park near the station. Right inside the front door there was a large sitting room with sliding doors to a large bedroom, then a kitchen and bathroom-laundry, all spacious and airy, with old-fashioned cupboards, a boiler and a cellar. It cost her four pounds ten; but rent, within reason, Henry would pay. The place was furnished with splendid Edwardian furniture now out-of-date and which could only be fitted into big rooms for letting; but the beds and stove were like war salvage, and the walls to a height of seven feet or so were quite dark with years of damp and cold. Yet there was a garden-back-yard the children could run in and which she could use for washing. There was plenty of space, the place was clean, and the land-lords named Bonar were "darlings." She at once made friends with Mrs. Bonar, a pink-cheeked woman with pretty hair dyed golden, and with three talented children. The Bonars had a house down the street, architecturally identical with the one they let in rooms and flats. Their double sitting room in front, with sliding doors, was very pretty in the gilded birdcage style, with fine china, family mementos, photographs, and pieces of lace, as well as velvet cur-tains. She felt deliciously at home here and soon began to go down the street once or twice a week for tea, to talk over the children. Mrs. Bonar was devoted to her family, and the two women made storms of talk about ill-treated children, unworthy parents, educa-tion and the like; the two women agreed upon nearly every point, except that Eleanor was more modern. Mrs. Bonar regarded work-ingmen's families as selfish and cruel to children: they did not educate them. Eleanor held out that poverty was the excuse, and she mentioned her own experience in the lodging house long ago, in Camden Town.

Her children were now going to a Church of England school in the neighborhood, not very expensive, and where Henry hoped they would get the graces of the refined middle class.

"But you are just shoving them into a niche in a country that is rotted away with class," suddenly exclaimed Eleanor, in a letter to Henry, annoyed at the idea that he did not rely on her to give them the right airs.

"Everyone must climb, and the higher his first step, the higher he climbs," wrote Henry.

Although Eleanor loved to hear the children's dainty chiming voices and was proud when they mimicked their teachers' refine-ments, she felt that Henry only showed the soul of a "sneak and a flunkey." All these things gave her hours of discussion with Mrs. Bonar.

But this beginning of happiness was interrupted by Henry. The children had begun it by complaining about Marcus, the ugly four-year-old in the backyard. He had been injured in car accident;

but no pity or sympathy could overcome the revulsion felt at his appearance—he was also stupidly mischievous and babyishly indecent. "He lives in the next house with the Indians." The Indian students had the use of the same backyard as Deborah and Russell. Upstairs in their own house were two students from Israel, one in medicine, one in music. This was enough to bring a short threatening letter from Henry: he would take the children from Eleanor's care if she allowed them "to grow up in a disorderly neighborhood full of foreigners, Jews, people of color and bohemians."

After a souring quarrel Eleanor had to move. She found another place at about the same rent, but was driven from this one, and was only allowed to settle down in a third, where she had a top floor in the house of a woman "whose cousin was a baronet." The rent was cheaper, the situation much better for the children, and Henry knew nothing of the behavior of Annette, the baronet's cousin. Annette also became Eleanor's friend and once more the tea parties and long, warm-hearted discussions began, although they had a different tone now. Annette had done a good job in the war, organizing theaters, dances, shows, and although a few years younger than Eleanor, she had had a long, active life, had been busy in a dozen directions, had been on the stage, tried painting and sculpture, given an exhibition, belonged to a women's movement and the Labour Party, had had three or four husbands and now a number of lovers, young and middle-aged. She was good to the children, helped with all their parties, and sometimes lent Eleanor money.

Eleanor might look charming in her furs and silk stockings, but her ordinary clothing was so poor, plain and unsuitable now that at parties she had begun to take a back seat and adopt a motherly air.

Eleanor explained to Annette, "Henry seems to have the spirit of a bantam rooster; he crows, attacks, struts; in fact he quarrels with everyone. People are at first attracted by his charming air, good clothes, mincing affability. He is contentious and impudent. He got several jobs in excellent firms and at once lost them, by his vanity and pride. When he lost them, he made things worse by writing insulting letters to his former friends. Since his divorce he has got chicane in his system like a disease, and like a man trying to fight the whole world, started suits in all directions. Perhaps he, too, doesn't know what has happened to the world and him and us; perhaps he regrets the quiet lovely life we had before."

After a year or so, Annette gave Eleanor notice: she needed the upstairs flat for a grown son. Later, she found that this "grown son" was a lover. In the meantime she and Annette had quarreled over a young man, whom Eleanor had met in Annette's flat and had afterwards invited to visit her. He was Martin Hall, one of the ageless small fair men who attracted Eleanor, a member of small Chelsea circles, pert, confident, with a neat opinion on everything. There was something about him Eleanor did not understand; she found it alluring. They became fast friends; he even stayed overnight several times when Annette and the children were away in the summer. He loved scandal, gossip and smutty talk—which Eleanor found delightfully funny in so frail a creature; and he could pass hours tearing people to pieces or analyzing, speculating, laying down the law, or what Eleanor called "mutual introspection." She was very happy with him and puzzled at his chastity. Though he slept in her flat and lounged about it in pajamas, though they drank, smoked, yarned together, and came to the same opinions about people and books, though she told him all of her misfortunes with Henry, he never so much as kissed her. Night and morning, dressed or undressed, he behaved like a young brother. Only once or twice did she fancy she saw a satiric or intimate look. She would have been satisfied to have had an affair with him; she was at ease with him, and walked about carelessly dressed, or lay at full length, rolling her hips and arms and eyes, while they were together. She often thought about his modesty, which she admired, and was all the more ready to take on his views. He was a broad-minded man, called himself a Communist and appeared to visit Communist circles everywhere; but he was, she was glad to see, a free-spoken, "unshackled Communist." He criticized all the Russians, the Eastern democracies and the local Communists, much as she would have herself, and as Henry would have if he had been man of the world enough.

When Martin saw that Annette was jealous, he visited Eleanor secretly, and it was pleasant for her to laugh with him over Annette's baseless jealousy. When Eleanor had to move, she was afraid she would lose him. The new place she eventually took unfurnished had two extra rooms in the attic, "my workroom and library," she told people; one of these rooms was intended for Martin when he needed "a flop," and so, with a merry look, she told him. But Martin never made use of the flop; he merely left his luggage there with his books while he made a prolonged tour of the Eastern countries and then emigrated to the United States, where, he told her frankly, he expected to make plenty of money by exposures of these countries and of all the Liberals, Labourites and Communists as well as literary figures he had met.

"There's a lucrative career in it. But if I don't make it there, I'll be flying home to you," he told her.

Eleanor locked up his trunks, after going through them and fingering each rolled pair of socks and each book tenderly. He was very tidy, every piece of clothing was mended, clean and neatly packed. Year after year, his luggage waited in the attic, but gradually other things came to stand beside them, for instance, Eleanor's files. Since her divorce she had kept "every scrap of paper."

As soon as she got her final decree, Eleanor sought out all her old friends, women who had expressed their distrust of Heinrich Charles in the first place; or that "unsuitable acquaintance" as he said, of bachelor women living through hard lives and nameless love affairs. Vina de Saiter, the woman lamed by infantile paralysis, more determined than before, with a guiltless shine that came from self-satisfaction and success, had broken up a marriage and was not only a wife, but had got a job in UNESCO, lost her job there and become a cause célèbre (as she freely explained) and was now a

political organizer. Paula, who had been in love with the physiotherapist, had joined a love sect. Marky, whom Eleanor supposed
long separated from her foreign journalist, had gone to Belgrade
with him. Mary Bird, who, they had said, "would never get away
from her mother," had gone to Canada, married a French
Canadian and had four children. There was also Angela Fareforth
who had been in "a famous scandal" with a married professor; and
Janet Jackson; and Dr. Linda Mack.

But Eleanor imagined them all as they had been, more or less
unattached girls, and she was comforted by the idea of joining the
group again, once more one of the staunch women, singing and
swinging along, fronting life's problems, living their physical lives
frankly. She had adapted herself to marriage, but it had been, with
Henry, life in a cupboard. She wrote almost the same letter to each
one, with different allusions, quaint, sympathetic and sly, to their
buried pasts.

My dear,

I am my own woman again; that is to say, I have divorced
Henry and am free to look for a job to save us from semistar-
vation! I don't know if you knew I had two children, Deborah
who's seventeen—a nice child, still at the awkward age but has
a sort of gawky prettiness that promises a real bloom when she
has got rid of her brusqueness and angularity; and my son
Russell, just over fourteen, who is a dear, affectionate boy with
enchanting ways who is a staunch supporter of his mother in
all her doings. I am sorry you are so far away, Angela: I
wanted you to see them—and me. Life is going to be a bit
difficult for a few years, but I'm not afraid of work and I'm
putting in what I hope is the spadework of a real career at last.
At fifty I look like forty, and I'm going to remain permanently
forty; please take note! Do you want to write to me? Write to
me, dear, and let me know all about you . . . I have some letters
from Henry (to me) that would amuse you, I think, and I am

longing to show them to you and tell you all our news . . .

Affectionately, Eleanor Herbert

P.S. I am adopting the name Herbert, one of our family names, and throwing in the limbo of things best forgotten the name of *Charles*. I know you never liked Henry, so my news will not upset you. Blessings on you! The children send their love.

In return, she learned that their lives had run on, that they had married, had dependents. These letters contained unpleasant shocks for her. But she was comforted at length by a second letter from Mary Bird which told that she was separating from her husband and coming home, and a letter from Angela Fareforth complaining of her spoiled life. Eleanor took heart: a smooth wall of domestic happiness was not standing between her and her friends; she began to reason it all away. She persuaded herself that in any case the sexual life must be nearly finished for all her friends, so that, even if married, they would be living chaste lives. She was concerned over it. It already seemed to her that her life was entirely normal, and the idea of sexual relations between men and women of her own age began to offend her—she could not imagine how they could take place. Routine, age, domestic ennui, she had read so many times, separated couples at this age: she expected to hear of other divorces besides her own, or of philandering husbands. It already seemed to her that her divorce had come by a law of nature, and therefore, was no longer a disgrace or misfortune. She was happy womanhood liberated from the drear time of necessary bondage.

"But I am not becoming a nun," she wrote. When she visited her old friends who were married, strange little scenes took place. She would hurry into the bedroom, ask, "Do you still sleep together? No one has double beds nowadays, it's gone out"; or tear up the corner of the bed to examine the mattress, the sheets and blankets, throw herself on the bed itself and say, "Oh, just let me luxuriate a little, this is delicious; is this where you sleep or Bob?" and a twinkle would come into her face. She might catch her friend around the waist and say, "How is it? Are you still going strong?" She was very friendly with the husbands too, looking upon them as brothers and with a mischievous smile too, as if she knew a little secret about them; she hugged them and kissed them, threw herself into their arms and hung around their necks. She would tease the women. She would suddenly cry, "Ah, I know all about you, Diana. There's nothing you can conceal past, or present!" or, smothering a laugh, "Oh, it makes me laugh to see you doing that roast—you aren't the housewife type a bit, my pet"; and it seemed to her that all of those men were ready for her affections, and that once they had tried her, they would have a very sweet surprise, they would find out how humdrum their wives were. So she would be at first, prancing, preening, laughing deliciously; and she would like to stay overnight to listen to the "little noises of the settling birds," as she put it, or she would hurry over on a Sunday morning or Sunday afternoon to surprise them in their intimacy. It seemed a friendly act to her, it proved how friendly they all were; and if it was hinted to her that she was indiscreet, she would frown, her forehead and lips pucker and she would make a visit just the same, impudently, inquisitively, thinking to herself, But what can they have to hide from me? They're an old married couple. In fact, as she grew farther away from her marriage, marriage itself became a kind of mystery to her, just as if she had still been a young girl.

When she was in town, shopping for the children, or visiting Mr. Allcomes, she sometimes visited Dr. Linda Mack in her office. Linda looked much older. She was thin, parched, her hair was white, her strange blue and white eyes stood out in her tanned face. She dressed always in the same sort of frock, all white silk or all brown linen or all natural wool; she had a lambskin coat and a goatskin coat, no hat summer or winter, and horn-rimmed spectacles. She had developed a more gentle, caressing note when she spoke of a patient; but at other times, when she gave Eleanor advice, she had a brisker, sharper, even menacing tone. She laid down the moral law without hesitation. Eleanor would go and gossip to her, just for fun, telling her all her friends' sins and peccadilloes, and she would listen, with delectation, to Linda's bitter denunciations.

"I must say, Linda, that I don't see how our dear little Vina quite brings her conscience into line, but of course she is capable, our Vina, of bringing almost anyone and anything into line; 'a born agitator,' she calls herself, and I suppose born agitators are born without conscience. Yet Vina is a Christian woman and was considered almost a spiritual leader at the university. I suppose she knows the wiggles and quibbles better than we do. But it isn't like Vina, or, rather, like my idea of Vina, to break up a home and take another woman's man. I should never have thought it of her. Weren't you very surprised? Or did you, with your clear-eyed vision, see that Vina's firmness of character was just a part of her egotism?"

"As soon as I heard what Vina had done, I wrote her a short letter, telling her that I could not care for her any more; but I, of course, gave her the name of a colleague," said Dr. Mack.

"And that is a very serious thing for a doctor to do, isn't it, Linda? I mean it is almost a breach of the Hippocratic oath, isn't it? But I know that your views of morals are irreducible. We were a band of like-minded people, weren't we? We all seemed to believe the same things, we had very clear-cut moral ideas I remember, Linda. And look at Angela Fareforth and Janet Jackson, though of course she was always, shall we say, unfortunate? And I suppose the miserable thing is they have a right to snatch any bit of happiness that comes their way, any ray, however filtered, in the rain? Yes, poor dears. But what accounts, I wonder, for these crumbling moralities? Is the personal factor explanation enough? I have been disturbed, deeply upset, you see, by a very unpleasant scene I had this week with Diana Cruse. Naturally, she has never lived with Thomas, but she keeps up the old flavor of an affair and we had high words. For Thomas, my dear, is married; but he sleeps over at Diana's home whenever he's in town. And Diana says she will marry him in the end. I gently put my view of interlopers in a marriage and I'm afraid it hurt!"

"It is a lack of discipline," said Dr. Mack. "This lack of discipline leads to mental and physical illness. As a doctor, I always preach severe regimens, rigorous self-discipline; it is a simple cure. When you were all girls you were like puppies, you needed training; you all had some moral ailment, I thought, but I thought in our little band we could strengthen and re-create ourselves. Now I know that salvation is personal, and the more personal the more impersonal, until one is part of all impersonality, where there is sureness, meditation, and tranquillity . . . I still haven't achieved my aims," she said in a lower, more affectionate voice. "I have the illusion—perhaps it's an illusion—that in the center or on the other side of one of the great deserts, or beyond many hills, there is the solution to some secret. It's a mystic idea and I don't approve of it, but I do believe it's there. And each one of my holidays I go looking for the answer to the riddle."

"But what is the riddle, Linda darling? Is it happiness? Yes, I suppose so."

"Not happiness: certainty, pure light."

Eleanor came away from Linda's refreshed. They had talked a little over youthful days; she could privately sport over Linda's notions and yet she felt uplifted by them; she also felt solutions in long walks, and then she had brought her problems out into the light, and Linda had given her a moral rule.

"I dropped in at Linda's office the other day to see the poor pet—Linda is looking a little dried up, but the same old Linda, starched and uplifted—and she gave me a look-over, and also lent me a little money. Linda is the perfect friend," she would say to Angela Fareforth. Angela Fareforth, energetic, comely, well-dressed, at fifty, was a woman she admired; she was editor in an artistic publishing house.

"Yes, I must drop in on good old Linda one of these days."

"Have you heard from Linda recently?"

"No."

"Then, I'm afraid, my pet, you might get an unpleasant surprise. Linda does not particularly care for your way of life," Eleanor said.

"My way of life? Linda's a fine woman, she has a great character. You mean about Geoffrey? What should she care? Sex means nothing to her."

"That is just why, my pet—I'm sorry to say so, but she happened to mention your name—that's why she doesn't understand your lack of discipline."

In this way Eleanor gradually mastered her environment and felt equal again to her equals. At first she had given to her rediscovered friends Mr. Allcomes' version of her marriage and divorce, and then, when she had set up her new society, she announced that she would now pass as a widow—"Heinrich is dead to me, the children don't want to mention his name"—and at the same time, she began to use the name Miss Herbert. "It is much better that way—and the children, too, are anxious to be rid of the name Charles, and when they are one-and-twenty, I expect they will come to a decision."

The last flat she had moved into had been a maisonette, that is, two floors of a house—a small house it was—in Willesden Green, an area with thousands of small terrace houses exactly the same. The house was so thinly built that you could hear a mouse scratching in the flat below; on still nights, the family next door could be heard coughing, sneezing, talking, and a visitor on their stair seemed to be walking into Eleanor's flat. It had the usual fault of English houses: it was a draft-catcher, with a number of rooms built on several levels around an open staircase, so that each room was as cold as possible, and there were through drafts everywhere. Yet it had plenty of rooms, stairclosets and built-in cupboards, and a view from the high back steps over many little backyards and old trees. Eleanor told Henry that by great good luck she had got it for only a hundred and fifty pounds a year; but she had secretly paid a premium of two hundred and fifty pounds that she had recently borrowed from her brother to the former tenants, to get the flat. She furnished the flat very sparingly at first and did the decorations herself.

In this new home in Terrace Avenue, Willesden Green, Eleanor really began her new life. The boy was going to a nearby private college; Deb had started at a business college. In the weekends they worked at the flat which was in disrepair, and needed paint. There was a front attic room with a half-window under a gable, a pretty place which Eleanor at first reserved for Martin Hall, and a square room next to it, for Eleanor's workroom. Underneath were bedrooms and bath and a long kitchen which could be divided. On the front door Eleanor added a new little plate—*Brent-Herbert;* and when tradesmen called her Mrs. Herbert, or Brent-Herbert, she was pleased.

A few months after she had moved in, just as winter was beginning, Henry's promised check was not in the post. The next day Eleanor telephoned her lawyers, and the following day learned that Henry's parents did not know his whereabouts. For some months he had been hard up, doing many mean temporary jobs for a living. "Now it seems he's become an alimony-skipper," said Eleanor. Fortunately, she had had to pay the rent six months in advance when entering and taking possession, and she had a hundred pounds left in her account which had been left for a rainy day. The lawyers might hunt for Henry, but the children had to eat and be clothed today. It was raining and windy outside, and on days like this the attic was uninhabitable. Eleanor had not yet spent money on lining the walls, or on extra heating appliances—she was glad of it now. After spending a week in her rooms with the heat off, working in her jacket and fur coat or a blanket, and still without news of Henry, Eleanor decided that she must go and get a job.

She had put it off because she had hoped to get another story or book written, but she had got nowhere—she had only a few scraps of writing. Even if any of it was salable, it would take months for her to get payment.

She had never been afraid of work and had always consoled

herself with this idea: "If the worst comes to the worst I can get a man or go out washing floors." What looked to her like good salaries were now being paid for bus-conductors, station clerks, ticket collectors—they were getting eight or nine pounds a week; canteen workers got six guineas and more, and shop assistants in milk shops—all housewives—got four and five pounds. As she considered the possibilities, she wondered at herself: she could have been earning a lot of extra money for years if she had not had the notion about writing; why hadn't the war taught her? She had just let herself go and had been happy in the little community in Market Square. "But now reality calls."

Eleanor telephoned the editor she knew at her publisher's and asked for an interview. Mr. Carrol Humphreys was the sort of man she liked to dance with—tall, broad-shouldered, lithe. He was a man of fifty, partly bald with a big dome and big blue eyes glazed in alcohol. He was genial, imposing and belonged to a celebrated family. They called each other "Eleanor" and "Carrol" and liked each other.

On the way into town, the bus passed some demolished houses, among which was the house she had stayed in with Henry the night of their marriage. That is like my marriage, she thought. Blasted. There were vines about and a thin little tree was growing in the middle of what had been their bed/sitting room. Soon it will be rooted up and forgotten; they will rebuild and new people will come, like a new house on an old grave. Yes, it was all lost, except for the children. I was ignorant and married the wrong man. I was confiding, romantic, trustful. It doesn't do. The trouble is I am romantic and want to be happy. But haven't we a right to be happy? Isn't that one of the inalienable human rights? How could I have guessed?

Rustling, furry, with a bright smile, she went through the large outer office and was taken into Mr. Humphreys' private office, a well-lighted small room, with manuscripts on the desk and glossy new books in shelves. Carrol himself came in a moment later, saying immediately, "What are you doing? Have you got a novel for me?"

"I'm on the other side at present, or want to be," she said very nicely. "I need a job and I wondered if you would fit me in here."

"What do you think you could do?" said Carrol lightly. He was standing at the desk, one foot on the desk, one elbow on his knee; he used his big blue eyes on her half smiling.

Eleanor settled her gloves and bag and spoke the piece she had thought out: "I feel I have more creative ability in union with others than by myself. In short, I have the editorial angle; and I feel I'd be a success reading manuscripts. I've done plenty of it and done a lot of rewriting. As I told you, I worked for Beresford Banes for years on and off, and I know the seamy and the glossy side, I know what the market wants. I've given a lot of time and thought to the marketing of ideas, and I'm sure I can pick a winner, and weed out the wheat from the chaff. I've got a good general background and plenty of sympathy with the author; I like to help; I can pick a sprig of genius out of the wild weeds it generally goes with and cultivate it for our good and for his, the writer's."

"But editors never grow to be writers, I'm sorry to say. We all try, but we mostly haven't the time, or we lose confidence when we see all the manuscripts we reject, or something of the sort," he said, a firm, rich regretful tone in his voice. "Now you're a writer and a darn good one, and you ought to write. I for one, Eleanor, would never help you to get an office job; your job in life is to write. One of these days we'll get to the point where there are more editors than writers if all you writers want to start editing."

"But I need a job, and with those fine feelings I can starve," she said, laughing.

"You won't starve," he said heavily. "Why don't you just sit down and put your mind to it?"

"I have children, you know, and their father seems to have forgotten their existence. I need money for them and I need it now. You can ask a writer to starve but not children."

"Well," he said gaily, "I'm not against writers starving, it's good for them. I think they should support literature entirely, they should even pay for publication—it would be excellent medicine for us all. So for you I wouldn't do anything." He gave her a radiant laugh, took her by the elbow. "Come on, let's go to lunch and we'll see what we can do for the children. But why don't you do something to that son of a bitch—light a fire under his tail. You're not a recessive character."

"I'm getting after him, but he hasn't got it."

"What's the matter with him? Everyone's got a job now. Come on, let's eat somewhere nice."

Carrol was very fond of the restaurant *"À l'Écu de France,"* and that is where they lunched. Eleanor persisted and told her plan: she wanted the firm to let her do a few weeks' work in each department, and then settle down on the editorial or merely the reading side; "then I could size up a manuscript from every publishing angle." She knew some firms had permanent readers and others had outside readers with fairly regular employment. "That would do me," she said. "I enjoy it; and whatever you may say, I still think reading and editing is creative and actually helps the writer."

When they returned to the office, Eleanor stopped to admire some of their new publications, especially a two-volume *Treasury of Literature,* and when Carrol said, "Would you like it?" she promptly said yes, to his discomfiture, she thought. I'll get something out of them, she thought angrily.

In his office Carrol said he would give her a letter to the celebrated firm of Rainshelter, Ltd., of which the managing director was a multimillionaire, Lord Parashok. This firm had taken under its great wing many small firms.

"I don't know Lord Parashok, but I did Sir Jones ap Jones a favor some time ago and he is a close friend of an M.P. who can do something for you, I should think; I'll write to Carton McMurdoch, who's a friend of mine, he plays golf with the M.P. I mentioned. Now, I'll say you're an M.A. and the author of a successful book, with Fleet Street experience and reading experience; is that all? I don't know what your political views are, or even whether you have any, but I'm sure whatever they are, you don't bring them into the serious business of fiction."

"I'm almost impartial, with a fondness for stability," said Eleanor sweetly. "I like natural change, if any—I'm not a stick-in-the-mud, but an evolutionist."

Carrol smiled. "Well, I wouldn't say even that, if I may take the words out of your mouth. Rainshelter's hardly know what they're publishing, there's so much of them—they might even like a radical author sometimes."

"Oh, I'm quite in sympathy with radicalism, and my father even believed in a republic, poor dear—he died last year—but I can keep my views out of my work. I'm above all a realist."

The talk ended agreeably, Carrol Humphreys saying, "But I hope you give up this whole idea and go back to writing: that's your best bet."

Eleanor went out looking radiant and composed; she felt humiliated. Carrol had treated her like an employer and the comradely feeling was gone. However, when she reached home she got out her old manuscripts and the next morning telephoned Humphreys to say very sweetly that she thought his advice was good. For a few minutes they had a pleasant murmuring chat on the old lines.

That same morning she received a check from Henry, but only two-thirds of what she had expected.

A few days later, Eleanor received a letter from a Miss Saucing on the Rainshelter letterhead, asking her to telephone for an interview. Eleanor telephoned at once, but her inquiry was received with extreme caution. The switchboard girl asked which of several secretaries she wished to see, but eventually she found a Mrs. Werner, who said, "I have instructions here to make an appointment with Miss Herbert. Miss Saucing is a very busy person, and if she is free she will see you at eleven o'clock on Tuesday, Thursday or Friday of next week or the following week. If she is engaged,

Mrs. Werner will see you." This protocol and complexity looked like business to Eleanor.

Six days later, the nearest possible date, Eleanor put on her best clothes, gloves, "a jaunty little hat, a dash of perfume," as she described it to herself, "and earrings adding interest" and took the bus into town to Pennycoin Street, a sort of courtyard leading to an immense square, in which Rainshelter's had a Palladian palace as large as the Admiralty. Though gray from the war, it was a splendid building. A fine old soldier behind a polished counter covered with the newest catalogues from Rainshelter and its protectorates telephoned to know if she was expected and then she was admitted to a waiting room which had once been a small ballroom in which were full-length oils of great men. Eleanor sat at a heavy polished table in a carved and polished armchair and waited.

On the floor Eastern rugs were strewn. Presently a door opened and a middle-aged girl with loose hair and a homemade dress of washed-out blue, with down-at-heel shoes and anklet socks wandered with quick nervous movements into the center of the room, came toward Eleanor, asked her if she was waiting for Miss Saucing and then asked her if she knew where the ladies' room was. "I have been waiting half an hour and I am so nervous." She had a pale, dirty fair face and uncertain eyes. Presently she darted into the gloom of the giant walls and curtains, trying various doors; she disappeared. She won't get back in time, thought Eleanor. Out of an inner room came a small ruddy man with a peardrop face, bony, countrified, with rich hazel hair. He was dressed shoddily in checked jacket and gray pants. His spare beard had been cut with scissors; his worn shoes were runover. He held three new books under his arm. In an armchair sat a fat middle-aged woman, with black and white hair under a Robin Hood hat. Oh, the run-to-seed Chelsea intellectuals, thought Eleanor with a satisfied inward grin. She was glad that she was so opulently, conservatively dressed.

When she had waited forty minutes feeling more and more contented, a side door opened, showing a lofty small room full of desks and clerks. A small woman hurried through the door with papers in her hands and looked at all present.

"Mrs. Werner?" said Eleanor, thinking that one in "tatty hand-me-downs," like this one, could not be the great Miss Saucing.

"Yes," said the lady. "Miss Herbert?"

She came and sat down in a little chair by Eleanor, holding a file open in her hand. "I have here a letter from Sir Halberd Pike to Lord Rainshelter, and also one from Mr. Carton McMurdoch to Mr. Wallace Purfoy, who is now with us. They recommend you for a readership. I understand from these letters that you are acquainted with French and German, have a university degree and know the American market."

"No," said Eleanor, "some German and *no* French."

"I am glad to hear you read German," said Mrs. Werner. "Many of our readers read French and very few German." She made a note, *Reads German*. She continued in her quick, harsh but friendly voice, "Have you any experience as a reader?"

"Well," said Eleanor, smiling (and she could not help a note of patronage), "I am a writer myself. I brought out *Brief Candle* a year or two ago. Published by Abbess and Prior, Ltd."

Mrs. Werner, unfortunately, looked quite blank, so Eleanor continued, "It did rather well; but that apart, I am an insatiable reader."

"Um, but have you read for any publishers? This is a special profession, one might say—you have to be able to get the publisher's viewpoint. However, since Sir Halbert and Mr. McMurdoch have written about you"—she looked at Eleanor thoughtfully—"we should like to give you some books, if it can be managed. We have a lot of readers. We might begin with this little book in Spanish."

"Oh," cried Eleanor, "but I can't read Spanish."

"That's a pity," said Mrs. Werner, musing. However, she continued after a moment, "We might get a little farther if you told me your special interests—that is always worth knowing with readers."

"I have children, of course," said Eleanor. "I feel I can adjust myself to their level. I have views, like all parents, on education and sat on an education committee during the war. I am not interested in politics or science, but history, philosophy and, of course, literature are my long suits," she went on talking, smiling; her cheeks grew redder and her red lips pouted as she thought what to say.

Mrs. Werner meantime was consulting her papers, "Well, would you have any objection to reading plays, detective fiction, educational books, plain novels?"

"None at all," said Eleanor. "I read for the pleasure of it: anything's grist to my mill."

"That's very good," said Mrs. Werner. "So many of our readers won't read one or other of these things."

"And I am interested in modern agriculture and orchard-work," put in Eleanor hastily.

Mrs. Werner looked straight in her eyes, with surprise. "That is very interesting, very interesting," she murmured, making a note, *Agriculture, orchards.*

"I love gardens of course, though unfortunately at the moment I have no garden of my own, and then there is architecture, and I am most interested in old silver and good furniture: I thought of taking it up as a hobby, but—money lacked, and one can't do anything."

"No, of course not," said Mrs. Werner and noted, *Gardening, architecture, old silver, furniture.*

"And I have some stage experience," continued Eleanor.

"All this is very interesting. And how long will you take?"

Eleanor hesitated.

"We don't care for readers to take more than ten or twelve days at the outside."

Eleanor laughed with relief.

"And now let me show you how we like it done. Half a page at most for almost any book. We have had one report on this Spanish book from one of our best readers. He has been with us for three or four years. He gave it a page and a quarter: that is why we wanted another report. But never mind, I'll probably send you some book next week. I have your address, your telephone number, haven't I? Is it B.A. or M.A.?" She corrected her notes, and closing her file, said earnestly to Eleanor, "We pay fifteen shillings a book for English manuscripts, one guinea for nonfiction, and two guineas for foreign. Does that suit you?"

"Yes," said Eleanor.

She strode away from the great gray palace and walked a long way along Oxford Street, looking at new shoes, blankets, clothes. She would have liked to have tea and a bun to celebrate, but she was "budgeted to the bone." The main thing was attained: she had her foot in the door, she would work as she knew how and begin to liberate herself. What a sunny day the day when she was no longer dependent on Henry's whims, illnesses, jealousies!

Three weeks later she received a bundle of three separate manuscripts, two small and one very large novel, in three parts, each part as long as an ordinary book. "I'll get them all in within a week," said Eleanor, "and just show them." She began to work from daylight to midnight, with an instinctive urge and joy. "Work that will be paid for!" It was now that the burden fell on the children. They had to get the meals, clean the house, do the shopping, wash and iron their clothes.

"If it's going to be like this, we'll have to become time-saving experts," she said to Deborah and Russell, "and that means more work for all of us. But I was always good at organizing, and as time goes on and I get paid, we'll get labor-saving gadgets. In the meantime you must buckle to; your father deserted you as well as me, remember."

She drew up a timetable of work for them, and when they groaned, she said with a severe smile, "That's your way of earning your living at present, and I don't ask any more of you just now. Later you must put your shoulder to the wheel and help your mother. And now, darlings, Mother's going to plunge in. I'll give Deb what housekeeping money I can spare for the week, and she must learn to be a little economist, like Mother; and Russell must try and be as good in the house as another daughter."

Russell smiled happily. "I will try," he answered eagerly. "Perhaps I'll be as good as a daughter."

"But your schoolwork mustn't suffer," said Eleanor. "Remember that if you want to go to the university you have to win scholarships, and anyhow we want to show Daddy, don't we? We want to show him! He left us because he's selfish; but we're unselfish and we can get on without him."

She knew their difficulties but turned a blind eye to them: the children must not let her down. At times she gave them pep talks, which always included spiteful remarks about their father. They were probably on her side against their father, yet Deborah often wore a gloomy, obstinate expression, lied to her mother and had inexplicable up-and-down moods; and with childish inconsistency, in spite of their ages, they dreamed of invitations and presents from their father's parents. Once they had accepted joyfully an invitation to Lausanne to see their father. Eleanor set her teeth and tried to endure this without reproaching them. When they returned, she made them give a complete account of their stay and vivaciously pointed out their father's ignoble motives, poor taste, light-mindedness and egotism. She was glad to see that Deborah was witty at her father's expense—but how could she "turn down a new overcoat when it was offered?" Yet she took the overcoat and showed it to her mother with exactly the remarks Eleanor herself would have made, and Eleanor blushed with a warm, youthful happiness —she had won.

"We'll soon be making all our own livings and won't need his handouts," she said.

"Yes, and I told him so," Deborah responded.

Deborah at sixteen, though she still had a rash on her forehead, seemed to her mother a long-faced, pale beanpole of a girl with draggled locks of black hair and large oval dark eyes which seemed larger because of her nervous looks and pallor. She had slim hands and feet which "at least showed she had some breeding," Eleanor said. But she had a strange taste in dress. She preferred black and red, black and russet. "Black is not for young girls," said Eleanor, fussing round and trying to fix up something pink or blue for her. Deborah had always been popular with boys and now went out dancing and to all sorts of gatherings, concerts, lectures, always with a different boy.

"Where is Melville? I like him," Eleanor said kindly.

Deborah nervously replied, looking her straight in the eyes and with her turned-down rainwater look, "I don't know what's the matter with me! I get them and then I can't stand them. Sometimes I'd rather bring them home and leave them here with you."

"With me," cried Eleanor. "Don't you think I'm a self-starter?"

"Oh, Mother, why don't you get married again before it's too late? You're still nice-looking. Why do you hang round Father still?"

"Hang round Father is just what I don't do, my dear. What have I been trying to get into your thick head all these years?— that we must be independent of Father. Henry cheated me of my whole young life; he lied to us all in effect and I have told plenty of people I am a widow."

"But you talk about him all the time. That isn't being free," cried Deborah. "I don't like him either, but I don't talk about him —I forget him. You're involved with him. Your whole life is tied up with him. You ought to get out of it. Russ and I wouldn't mind if you married again; we've often talked it over."

This was unpleasant news. "But I loved your father," said Eleanor in a low humming tone, "and I would have loved him always, with no other thought, if he had not cheated."

"But if you lived away from him for years, what could you expect?" said Deborah in her bold rancorous style; her face and nervous hands expressed weary experience and suffering. Eleanor became angry; she was not understood by this child, and yet this child was a woman.

"If it had been merely a need, as you say," she said in a harsh tone, "I would have forgiven it. A man has to eat in a tea shop, he can't always eat at home; he has to go to the W.C., he can't always use it at home."

"Ugh!" groaned Deborah.

Eleanor laughed in a bold haughty manner. "But why couldn't he have had his little bit of fun on the side? The real reason for these breakups is a man has got tired of his responsibilities: he doesn't want to support his wife and children."

"But one of the girls had a child," protested Deborah.

"He would have left her—and promptly," Eleanor declared.

The big girl turned away. Eleanor said, "I don't want to foist my troubles on you, though you've got broad shoulders enough," and Eleanor glanced at a physical feature of Deborah that she disliked: Deborah's upper body was a long elegant triangle. "You're such a gawky unhappy sort of thing as it is, like a long rag of seaweed. What is the matter with you, you've got youth and no troubles. All your troubles have yet to come. Why do you always wear black? You're not in mourning! Or are you? It makes you look as if you've got a taste of the tarbrush. You look like a half-breed!" She used another coarse word. "You've got none of the Brent in you! I'm tired of seeing you grizzling and drizzling around me: what troubles have you had? Look, I'll show you my grounds for divorce now. I was going to wait, but it seems to me you're well able to understand. You've got ideas about your father still. I'll show you," said Eleanor spitefully. "It's time you understood."

"I don't want to see anything," said Deborah slowly. "I'm on your side, Mumsy. You oughtn't to show me those things, I don't care about them."

"You don't care about them?" cried Eleanor. "You *must* care about them! I'm killing myself with work for you."

She went up to the attic room reserved for her work and in a moment found the papers in her well-stocked and well-arranged filing cabinet. It was a large envelope marked "For my daughter Deborah and son Russell on Deborah's twenty-first birthday." She tore open the envelope and hastily pulled out the contents, letters, photographs, depositions and the like. She looked through them; her eyes sparkled, her flush rose, an angry smile came. Triumphantly she ran downstairs and put the things in Deborah's hands. "Read that, read everything; it's time for you to know." Then feeling a slight shame, she added, "It will help you perhaps and you'll understand your mother better. I've often felt you were standing off, impartial: you just can't be impartial in crimes and horrors. You can't be a bystander, Deb."

"I don't want this, I won't read it," said Deb. She put the packet down on the sideboard.

"Deb, for my sake, I want you to understand what it was like. I've never asked for sympathy. I've kept a stiff upper lip. You children didn't know what was going on under your innocent little noses. I wanted you to have a happy childhood." While she explained this, it seemed to Eleanor that she had never breathed a word to them and had always painted their father to them in agreeable colors. But Deborah silently put the packet into her mother's hands.

"Well now, to work, to work, said the caterpillar tractor," cried Eleanor, quite relieved. "I leave the house in your hands, Deb darling. Mother is a working stiff."

As she read her manuscripts she wrote down the names of the characters and the incidents on a piece of paper, noted defects in style and spelling and rewrote her opinion three or four times, reducing it "to a clear crystal of criticism." Two of the novels belonged to the types she had often seen in magazines: the Cornish summer holiday romance and the village-and-manor-romance, with rector, city visitors and the deserted lodge. The three-volume work was on the old theme of elective affinities through the ages, the naïve magnum opus of a young married woman who saw history in primary colors and in terms of beanfeasts and slave girls, lions and Christians, Borgia poison rings, and troubadours. Eleanor recommended one and turned down two, on principle, and counted that the Elective Affinities, being in three books, would bring her in forty-five shillings. At Rainshelter's she gave her work to Mr. Steward, the uniformed attendant, and collected a handful of catalogues.

"If I am going to read for Rainshelter's I must know the requirements of all their subsidiaries." She had budgeted, this day, for tea and a bun: "a rare splurge to celebrate my first completed job." While having her tea, she wrote in a little memorandum book:

Rainshelter: 5 MSS. six days' work/Receivable: 45/— (or
                                                75/—?)
                              Expenses: Fares: 10d.
                                          Tea: 9d.

Of course, she had worked eighteen hours on some days, including visits to the library to check on some of the history in the long novel. "But my time's my own, they didn't ask me to stay up all night. Then, though, there is wear and tear on the machine, ribbons. But after all, I don't cast that up against my friendships, do I, when I write letters?"

The next week she again received two MSS. and a note from Mrs. Werner: "I hope you can do them soon." It was mounting up. She had only been going two weeks and would have earned 75/— (or 105/—) by the end of this month. She "bashed into them with zeal." At night she thought about the plots and style and other things. The manuscripts were all numbered, and the present two bore the astounding numbers 194—/CD1071 and CD 1073. "She must be satisfied, or she wouldn't send me these," Eleanor explained to her children at breakfast. "I'm going to get it down to a fine art, speed, competence, a nugget of opinion, fair to author and publisher and plenty of market sense." She polished these two off in the same way, and the month having ended, waited for her check. The first week of the next month she received two MSS. CD1110 and MD 2714, the latter not fiction. Eleanor prided herself on her business attitude, and after examining the second said, "One guinea: a nonfiction tear-jerker." It was a book by a mother about her infant son who had died of a rare disease; she had collected funds for the study of this disease.

Eleanor was obliged to recommend both these books, but felt uneasy about it. When the eighth of the month came she received a check from Rainshelter's for 45/— and when she complained she received a sharp letter from Mrs. Werner: "The manuscripts are paid for according to the month they are sent out in. And manuscript of whatever length is paid at the rates agreed upon: it makes no difference how many parts the author sees fit to divide them into. You are expected to send me a bill for the work done, so that I may check on what is owing to you. Please do this in future. We will take note that you received a nonfiction title."

"Well," said Eleanor, after reading this letter to her children at breakfast, "my dear chicks, Mother will just have to get more work. Once they see I'm a slogger and can polish them off competently at the rate of three or four a week, I'll have a small regular wage. Just the same, at this rate, at forty-five or sixty shillings a week, or a bit more with nonfiction, working full time and enslaving you, my dearests, that is to say, sixty shillings full time for me and half time for you, we are not in the higher income brackets. In fact, we're damn badly paid, sweated labor. I could actually earn more going out charring, six half-days a week. But I like the work and I'm going to build up a career." She then told them what she had been thinking out "in the lonely reaches of the night." If Rainshelter's received 1,100 MSS. fiction and 2,714 nonfiction, not to mention other sorts, in one year, and of course it must be one year, and if their other branches, departments or subsidiaries received a considerable number, and if all the publishers in the city received a considerable number, and if all the publishers in the city received their own share of MSS. during the year, and all sent them around to readers, wouldn't it pay her to set up a readers' agency, from which "competent, judicious, impartial opinions with an eye to the various markets," could be sent out and paid for at a reasonable fee? Eleanor could employ plenty of well but vaguely educated girls wanting to work at home, and men too, who could do spare-time reading—what could be easier?—and make a rake-off which would be enough for office expenses and a little for herself. But further, she had noticed that two of the Rainshelter manuscripts already had come from country typewriting agencies which also acted as agents for the authors who gave them work. "Get a name, a staff and I'm in business," she explained to them. And she thought that Deborah could leave classes now and get a job. "In the meantime, if things work out, I'll employ temporary helpers."

Work from Rainshelter's in the succeeding months was spaced so as to total not more than four pounds a month, and when she asked for more work Mrs. Werner told her that they had many readers and "must be fair about distributing the work."

"But I've got my teeth into it and I won't give up," said Eleanor.

Things were serious, in fact. Russell's school fees were two quarters in arrears; they were all going hungry and Eleanor had to ask her friends for clothes to make over. She covered all this with a grand manner of beggary, thanking her friends in a fine high tone and dragging the children before them to show off the made-over clothes and saying, "We are all very grateful, I can assure you, darling—we know what it is to be without and we have no false pride. The children don't mind at all; on the contrary, having a father whose generosity went no farther than a grand gesture when his pocket's full and who has now skipped into the blue beyond, like me they are doubly and sincerely grateful to friends like you who are there all the time with help and sympathy and good old clothes. We are not ashamed; if we were working-class we wouldn't be able to find good old clothes, but being middle-class people our friends at least buy things of good cut and good material, good even when they're old and that is where we come in, my dear."

She was carried away by conflicting instincts. She did not mean to humiliate her children; and in spite of their pride, they knew it.

Eleanor took odd jobs. At Christmas time she worked for three weeks in a large department store; for some time she helped in a dairy shop, selling milk, cheese and groceries. She received no work from Rainshelter's over Christmas when the readers had a "holiday"; but the same week she started work in the dairy she received an offer of work from a publishing firm, smaller but with a much higher literary reputation than Rainshelter's. Work is never "offered," really: this came about through a connection recently made.

On the strength of her book *Brief Candle* Eleanor had been put up for the international United Artists Club and went to all its local meetings to look for business, and for the same reason to the meetings of a small London Artists' Club recently founded. The second one had a man of title for its president and was commercial in viewpoint: it "screened" its members' politics and otherwise was a cozy little group consisting almost entirely of commercial writers and poor devils like Eleanor, but they were cheerful, talked as if literature belonged to them, schemed against each other and also for each other. Eleanor went to all these meetings "frankly with business in view," as she told everyone. Her frankness was appreciated, for these small business people were uneasy with anyone who did not write for money.

At a publishers' cocktail party she met "Jaffa" Tomkins, a big soft blonde dressed in pink and maudlin-drunk, kissing and hugging men and women alike and saying, "I love you." She was a reader in a very large publishing house and promised to help Eleanor to a job. Eleanor wrote to her the next day, and was invited by her to lunch at a coffee restaurant in Soho, a sort of Rialto, where the poor workers dependent upon publishers, the weekly intellectual press and the B.B.C. gathered for lunch. "Jaffa" was there first—well kept, plump, boldly pretty—trying to pick acquaintance with a gypsyish girl at the next table, who looked as if she had just tumbled out of bed, "unscrubbed," with thick blue and red make-up, very young, with dirty elfin hair and dark circles around her eyes. She sat between two nervous clever men, one of whom looked at Jaffa with detestation while the other acted indifference. "Do you like her or hate her?" said Jaffa to Eleanor in a rich gruff voice; she blew blue smoke rings toward the girl.

Eleanor was not sure the question was for her. She took off her gloves, and putting on her spectacles to read the menu, ordered some tea and beans on toast. "I simply must indulge just once, the atmosphere of this place is so perfect, dingy but authentic, that I am too tempted, I must just have an excuse for sitting here and enjoying it," she said with meek charm, attempting to get the right note. "A sort of *Mermaid Tavern,* for there is a definite aroma of poetry here," and she flicked her eyes toward the young man she preferred.

The restaurant filled up rapidly; people came to their table. Jaffa did not attempt to answer her, but with good-natured casualness introduced her to Henry Denmark, a novelist and poet who worked for the B.B.C., did translations and "barely made his rent"; and a sympathetic man called Shackbolt who said, "Can you translate?" She could not. "A pity. For though it's not well paid and you're plundered, you get six or eight months' work straight off. You have to keep yourself meanwhile, of course, but you get work, especially if you're willing to do cut-rate work. I'm not, but I know there's work about."

"But I suppose," said Eleanor nicely, "they really cannot pay too much, as it is all added to the cost of the book—it more than doubles it."

"No, they know none of us would do it if we could make a living some other way," said Jaffa. "Don't waste time philosophizing, Henry. This woman wants a job. Is there a readership going anywhere in town? She's working for Rainshelter's and so she needs it. Not that I mind Rainshelter's. I worked for them once. I was grateful for the bread and butter."

"I work damn hard for Rainshelter's," said Eleanor in a businesslike tone, "but I want more contacts. I like the work and I feel I've something to contribute to the general scheme of things. I have a feeling for it. I can size up and reshape a manuscript rough-hewn from the hands of the raw writer and make it fit to print."

They sat around, pleasant and frank, in the sunlight that fell through the dusty window and lace curtains, giving her advice, mentioning names. There was nothing at all noticeable of jealousy, suspicion, fears and poison in this society. They were rather modest and self-deprecating.

"And the poor sod's trying to write novels, too," said Jaffa, referring to Henry Denmark.

"I'm afraid my boats have all reached harbor already, or else they've not set sail. I suppose that means my talent comes second and that means I hadn't much to begin with. I work eight to eighteen hours a day during the week and most weekends; and all I do is scrape together a bare living for myself and my wife and we can't afford children," he replied.

"I have two children," said Eleanor.

"We'll get together and help you, we've got to," said Shackbolt, and he mentioned a couple of small publishers who might employ a reader, "though at present they're doing all the reading themselves. One's trying to climb out of the one-room publishing business by publishing sex science, the other's trying the paper-novel business, but the competition's deadly. Those two are just as badly off as we are, but you can try."

"My God, there's your man," cried Jaffa. "Here comes the guinea pig." Denmark made a place between himself and Eleanor and said, "Yes, you must know him: he's the man. He combs the town. You may not like him. Or you may."

When he got near enough, Eleanor saw an unforgettable personage, confidently smiling, and precisely the kind of man who attracted her violently.

"Cope Pigsney!" said Denmark. "Cope Pigsney," said Jaffa, "the guinea pig!"

He seated himself stiffly, looking Eleanor straight in the eye, his face raised. He was very short in stature.

"Have you seen *John Bull?*" he asked Denmark, handing him the issue, and turned from him. "I've just spent two and half hours looking for boots," he told Shackbolt. He turned to Eleanor and began to explain about boots. "You can't get along without good boots. To make good boots is a fine art. Our feet are tender and they get tenderer the more we walk. Your feet never stay the same size; and you don't walk the same way in the country as in the city. Try and walk with a city walk down a rutted country hill road with stones on it! You'll fall on your face! A country man shambling along in the city as if he were jumping ruts in his jackboots is a ridiculous sight. You can't get boots for all purposes; at the same time, it's hardly any use having them handmade. They never fit. There's so much trouble in a handmade boot that you'd do better to buy the cheapest; and you're stuck with them for ten years. Doctors ascribe foot troubles to smoking or occupational causes—what about waiters, or pharmacists, or teachers? But the whole cause is bad boots. There's not only the question of leather, that's quite secondary. I believe that leather is not the best thing for boots and shoes. My father, who was quite an expert, used to say that he was sorry there was only leather to work with. And rubber isn't the answer either. What you need is a good rawhide sandal soaked in running water and tanned by hand with the use of dog's dung as they used to do in London, and put together by hand, and all those imperfections give it a suppleness you'll never get in a city boot. However, today I found a place in Old Jewry where I think they make a pretty good boot."

There was a pause. Jaffa had gone to the ladies' room following the gypsylike girl. Cope Pigsney turned to Eleanor, and addressing her, began to denounce, firm by firm, the people who made boots in London. He called them tradesmen. He talked about Italian and French shoes; he denounced Czech and Russian shoes; he mentioned the ballet styles in a shop down the street. He constantly referred to his father and with a rustic swagger which convinced Eleanor that he was the son of a boot-mender. "My father, when it came to the mending of boots—" Eleanor with a smile leaned on her elbow and looked into his face.

He was the kind of blond who looks as if just come molten from a furnace, red-faced with a tussock of burning yellow hair.

This hair was heavily waved by nature, and so thick that it had to be held down with lotion. It grew low on the forehead and tried to spread down the temples and sides, where there was a fair down, seen best in the light they were now sitting in by the window, with the high afternoon sun of late January. This fair down joined the coarse yellow eyebrows. His thick eyelashes were yellow too. His face was red as paint and he had slender red lips neatly turned, but compressed often into a set line. This went with red ears that stuck out and a noticeable Adam's apple, a piping voice that suddenly became baritone, and a hawk nose, also flushed.

Cope Pigsney smiled questioningly at Eleanor. She muttered, "Oh, you are right," and she had a feeling that she had seen him before, although she had not. He had a pleasant London accent, the sort of "gentleman's accent" which genteel middle-class workers have, but his voice would suddenly soar into a country twang which she could not place. But he instantly told her. He was from Doncaster.

"And I expect you can still hear the Doric," he remarked. "I've tried to get rid of it, but it sticks. My brother never tried to get rid of it and with it he cuts great swaths in Fleet Street, so he says. I expect he does. No one can understand a blessed word, and they think they may be missing something." He talked for some time about his brother, named William. William was making twenty-five guineas a week and his wife seventeen. "Literature is low, as has been said," remarked Pigsney. "When Thackeray was running the *Cornhill Magazine,* he got two thousand guineas a year. The rates of pay have been going down every year, and the cost of living going up. A writer has to be presentable and his wife too, nowadays: gone are the days of rags and grisettes. Potboiling is a thing of the past; we need cars and washing machines. I have a whole floor which I need for my wife and child and we have to pay eight guineas a week for that. I need thirty guineas a week for expenses, without saving anything. How can I make it? I write for *John Bull,* the *Times Literary Supplement, Pick, Flick, Slick,* and

I had a story accepted for the B.B.C.—I mean, I never stop working, but there are weeks when I earn only twenty-five guineas. What do they pay you at Rainshelter's?"

Eleanor told him, and he glistened attentively. "One guinea for nonfiction, two guineas for foreign languages—that's low. Dodson's you say? Dodson's, I know for certain, pay two guineas for English, fiction or nonfiction, and three guineas for foreign languages, even more if it's a rare language. But you can get outside reading for four or five guineas; sometimes a firm sends a book to a specialist—though I must warn you that if you ever get one of those outside fees, four or five guineas, it's as good as telling you, 'You won't hear from us for a year or more—perhaps never.' But if you can get a story of a page, say, in *John Bull*..." He continued in this strain without stopping, eager, intent, and to Eleanor it was sparkling water to a thirsty man. She forgot no word of his. They exchanged addresses.

Early next morning Cope Pigsney was on the telephone. "Eleanor! If you've got any short stories, why don't you send them to the B.B.C.? You can easily get forty guineas for a story, twenty-five at least. Do you want to review for the *Times Literary Supplement?* I know someone, Hay Goff—a woman it is—on the *London Weekly Letter;* write her a letter and say I recommended you. Have you got a pencil? Take it down. Why don't you write for *John o'London?* They pay ten to fifteen guineas for a short article. I don't suppose you have any connections with the *Reader's Digest,* have you? I want to get in there; they pay well. Do you know anything about county place-names? I've been offered an article on that, for twenty-five guineas, and I don't know much about it. If you know anything, just send me a line . . . There's a new little magazine starting on current events, theater, film, books; there's a promotion group behind it, all young fellows, Denmark is one—it's really to boost books. You ought to get your name into that, you might only get a guinea or as low as half a guinea, but it's a starter . . . I want you to come and meet Bronwyn, my wife—she isn't Welsh, just a romantic mother. Bronwyn can tell you a lot. She makes about ten guineas a week herself and it helps, by golly. When you think there are big greasy Continentals and spivs"—here he proceeded to insult such of his neighbors as were richer than he was—"while you and I have our work cut out to scrape together the rent. Why shouldn't we have cars and a weekend cottage? Why shouldn't my wife have two fur coats? I need a bigger television for the child; we've simply got to pay for a washing machine and an all-day maid if my wife, Bronwyn, is to get out her work and do the work she does for me; and it seems to me we're pinched between two sets of new rich—the working people and these refugee spivs."

Eleanor listened, dripping joyous little laughs, her eyes glistening; her voice rang out as she said her joke: "Oh, but we can't keep up with the Cohens, you know, Cope." Cope was like herself, a forty-minute telephoner. When they had at last satisfied their appetite and she rang off, Eleanor cried aloud, "Now, that has put me in the mood for working!" and she got out all her manuscripts once more to see if there was something she could send in to reap the guineas.

This friendship, begun so suddenly, lasted. She and Cope telephoned each other four or five times a week; they were intensely interested in the same gossip, books, news, rates of pay. Cope was wonderfully good to her—perhaps he was generous to everyone, but she felt it was real liking too. She found it was quite easy to write for papers with a world reputation. The pay was small and slow to come; you might wait six months for four guineas, and through these literary papers were sifted all the struggling writers. Those who could stay the course were those who had a paying job, were university professors and the like. But for Eleanor, brought up to look upon literary London as Parnassus, to write for such papers was bliss. Though they might not publish her name, nor all she wrote, and though they paid her such small money, it was a great reward: alongside her, unknown to her, were some others working not for money but "for glory."

She never forgot the first evening she spent with Cope and Bronwyn, the real beginning of their great friendship. Somehow

Cope's enthusiasm for herself had given her the idea that Bronwyn was a dowdy, porridge-faced woman. No. She was very fetching, with a flair for dress and cooking, capable of originating her own dishes; she was well educated, had an uncle teaching science at Cambridge, knew people in the counties, was "a dear." They had a small daughter. She made clothes for the child and herself, ran the house and worked six hours a day for Cope, and often in the evening. She was his typist when typists failed; if he had a press of work he outlined his idea to her and she wrote it up. Cope very soon suggested some ideas to Eleanor, also—he would halve his guineas with her—but after a good deal of trying, Eleanor realized that she could not work with other people's ideas.

Eleanor arrived for high tea at six, after a day's work. It was a pretentious brick house in a long road of similar houses standing in their own grounds; a corridor ran between rooms to the kitchen, but the rooms were large and lofty. Bronwyn, in an apron, let her in with a subdued but kind manner, and said nervously that she did not know if Cope was ready yet—he was still at his desk. However, Eleanor was sent right in, while the wife hurried back to the kitchen, and Cope rose from his desk with a gay, inviting smile. His desk was by a fine big window overlooking damp overgrown gardens. The room was comfortably arranged and Cope seemed to glow in it. He found easy chairs for them, saying, "Bron will be in later, and she prefers a straight chair," and got out a bottle of wine. Bronwyn very soon appeared in a fresh blouse and a colored circular skirt which did not suit her but which Cope had just bought her. "She typed for me for a whole week last month."

She ran backwards and forwards bringing in several large plates with hot bacon and egg tartlets and hot tartlets of various shapes containing red caviar, shrimps and mayonnaise, and salad eggs. Afterwards in the dining room, which had the remains of an old range in it, they ate roast meat and stewed fruit, with more wine. Bronwyn was a nervous hostess, eating only a few forkfuls and then hurrying to the kitchen for her service. When Eleanor, graceful and sisterly, moved into the kitchen, Bronwyn kept turning her back as if she had something to hide in her cupboards, cabinets and pots; she talked over her shoulder, explaining things in a rush, never facing her visitor. Yet she was decisive and competent.

"Cope insists on having the dishes washed at once, and of course Mrs. Meggy may not stroll in till half past ten tomorrow; but I prefer to do them alone and I know Cope wants to talk to you," said Bronwyn.

"But I know we are going to be good friends. I'd love to help," Eleanor said, finding a towel.

Bronwyn turned toward her with a warm face. "I was afraid to meet you," she said. "I've never got used to meeting Cope's authors, though goodness knows I should have."

"But you're a writer yourself!"

"Oh, not that sort. Just a hack. I live at the bottom of Grub Street. I hate Grub Street," she said suddenly, putting her head down toward the sink with a mourning air. She had a long neck and chin line, was graceful, soft and carnal, but spoke turbulently.

"Grub Street?"

"Grub Street—where you grub in the garbage of literature for a living. Cope is happy at it, though Cope's a good writer. I'm not, though I'm not a good writer. I'm trying to work up pieces on history and science; it's grubbing too, I know. When I'm cooking I use good materials—why should I use rubbish when I'm writing?"

Eleanor did not answer. She had never heard of Grub Street and did not care for the expression. After she had thought it over, she said sourly, "Yes, I am eating my bread in Grub Street too, but if I were at the top I wouldn't mind at all. Yes, I'd like it."

"But the population of Grub Street are mostly wasters," said Bronwyn, "nothing but *lazzaroni*. Do you know, some of them just wait for work to fall into their laps; if they have nothing they'll go and sit on Hampstead Heath, dirty and hungry. I can't like them. They think it's a lark to say anything, write anything, do anything. They join any party for a lark and go to any party for a lark. I think they're lazy. Give them sixpence and they'll sing. And Cope is like that, too. Of course he works like a horse and earns every penny in his and my sweat, but the principle's the same. If you write garbage and sneer at other people for reading it, you're just one of the *lazzaroni*. I'm ashamed of our work; there's nothing worse."

"Well, I'm not ashamed of my work," answered Eleanor. "The laborer is worthy of his hire—or, rather, when he gets paid his hire, if you're talking about Grub Street. I'm looking to it to support my children and me and I'm making it my career."

Bronwyn began to complain about her char, Mrs. Meggy: "All people like us are in a cleft stick, between two classes with regular incomes. Mrs. Meggy lives in a bigger flat than this and bought herself a fur coat last winter. When you think what's paid to educated people like us, we never can get anywhere because we haven't enough degrees or experience or something like that, and we have to eat dirt for our money, run with our hands out to editors and kowtow to disreputable bohemians—and people like busmen with nothing to do but stand in a warm bus and collect tickets want more money than we earn. I'm cold here all day long—we can only afford to keep a big fire in one room and of course Cope has to have it."

Eleanor meanwhile was thinking about the expression "Grub Street." Sometimes after three days' work, she had only made fifteen shillings or five shillings a day with Rainshelter's. Those nights, when hungry and exhausted she had got into her cold bed and covered her head to get warm, a horrible taste had flowed into her mouth, a taste of human excrement, and she had cried to herself at the work she had to do. She was not one of the *lazzaroni;* she did her work well, but she was as poor as they. Her life was going each day in wretchedness. This had been the worst year of her life: "the ugly year," she called it. The Charleses were sending her a pittance; Henry was beyond reach. Poor Henry. No one understood him as she did; she had seen him in his hopefulness. Poor Henry: the little muddling devil.

"My father was a country doctor and I was brought up

strictly; I thought writers and scientists were honest. I can't swallow it that they're not," Bronwyn was saying.

"All work is honest, surely," replied Eleanor, hanging up the towels.

"You'll see, Cope will be annoyed at my keeping you out here," Bronwyn said.

"I won't tell him a word we said," Eleanor assured her.

"Oh, let him know, he won't care!"

Bronwyn sat on one leg on the cretonne couch while they jawed and jawed. Once or twice she put in a word suddenly. Cope mentioned Harry Green and Eleanor had never heard of him. "Thank God for someone who has never heard of him," said Bronwyn. "They sit here all night and chew those names dry."

Cope laughed dryly, and with his bright spaniel look went on eagerly talking to Eleanor. What an evening! Eleanor had never had such proud pleasure. Dylan Thomas, T.S. Eliot, and fifty others, all the successes, they just touched on in passing, swimming casually in this rich life, with a stroke here, a stroke there, wheeling and floating just as they pleased, but spending most of their time examining the serious affair of earning the guineas. Bronwyn interrupted once or twice, tried to draw them to shore, as it were; but once Cope told her to refill the stove which was cold, and another time, something she said—"Isn't he a homosexual?"—made Cope tell three or four long, filthy Cockney jokes, at which Eleanor laughed uproariously. The evening was a complete release for her. She had been stumbling about, trying to understand her craft, and here was a past master who enjoyed teaching her and liked her company. Cope was gay, spiteful, confident, helpful, a scandal-monger and backbiter. How many years had Eleanor had to watch her tongue, hide her thoughts, sham the lady, live a double life with double tongue! Here she did not have to be a hypocrite: she could say what she liked. They both laughed and "bit backs," as she said, almost out of breath with laughing. "Oh, it is so good to sit down and talk scandal about your nearest and dearest, it is a real purge. I feel twice the woman," said Eleanor. But Cope restrained her; he respected those who could help him. When she asked if So-and-so was not a homosexual, he looked pained; So-and-so had been very kind to him and helped all literary people.

"Oh, I don't mind," Eleanor sang out. "I don't mind their bedroom habits! I'd like to meet him. I've never met one that I know of."

"I thought you were a friend of Martin Hall?"

"Yes; why?"

"I see," said Cope.

"Surely you know he's one," cried Bronwyn, "the sandy little shrimp. If you don't, you're the only person in London who doesn't."

No, Eleanor couldn't believe it!

The evening was full of such exciting moments. "Oh, Cope, you're as full of knowledgeability as a Christmas pudding of goodies." But it was very late; the fire had gone out a second time and now Bronwyn made no move to relight it. They began to shiver. What could Eleanor do? It was two o'clock. She could walk. Her home was near the station, only a few stations farther up. But now Cope said he would go with her. He had been in all day, working, and he liked the walk.

There was a slanting moonlight, it was cool and still; and they walked along the terraced streets and broad avenues leading to her home, talking, talking, with Cope's voice jingling guineas, guineas, and Eleanor still alert and happy. They might have been lovers, but they were better than that: they had found each other, they had no agonizing doubts or fears, they were at one.

Eleanor never tried to supplant Bronwyn; she only thought of it very idly. She and Bronwyn were friends. The wife soon became quite cheerful with her and told her all her troubles and revolts. Cope had nearly let the child drown in one of the Hampstead ponds. She had had a miscarriage in a cab. She would have left Cope three years ago if not for the child. Cope knew she was unhappy and wanted her to have another child to pin her down. She detested London and London's climate and wanted to emigrate, but Cope would only go to the U.S.A. and he had no chance there because once he had written a couple of articles for the radical press. That had been when he first came to London and did not know with whom to throw in his lot. He had been rather red in those days and had written a good social novel, *Seeds of Time;* it had been brought out by a well-known publisher but had not done well, and this had cured him. They had had a very hard struggle and she had worked in an office to keep them both, until suddenly Cope began to find his way about. Now they made thirty guineas or more a week, but they needed more. "No one in this neighborhood," she cried angrily, "lives as poorly and shabbily as we do. Everyone has a car. Why should I have rheumatics in my bones at thirty? We need heating, a maid in, a typist." She bounded along the street when she walked, the men looked at her—her garments flowed on and by her in a wonderful way, she had large blue-gray eyes and waving chestnut hair. When they passed a man who looked at her, she turned pink and smiled.

"It's not only that," she said more cheerfully to Eleanor, "but other things too. For one thing, I'm going to kick over the traces one of these days if he doesn't do better by me. I'm going to buy me a gross of condoms and get to know what life is, and then—"

"You're not going to leave Cope, surely—don't leave him, Bron!"

"I don't know," Bronwyn said in a different tone, "there is something he does which I hate, I just can't swallow it. I wasn't told but I soon guessed. We began to live better, our real money troubles were over, and I wondered how it was. I too was making a bit of money, of course. First he was anxious and even thought of emigrating as I wished; then suddenly he was in the money—he said he had a job. But he didn't go to an office. What job? He wouldn't tell me. Well," she said biting her lip, "I had better not say any more. I oughtn't to. But there is something degrading being done and it will finish us, him and me; that's all."

Soon Cope and Eleanor had a regular morning call at about ten; and if Cope was out Eleanor would have a long chat with Bron and hear all the news, and she would tell all her worries and ideas. She had not had this kind of intimacy since her girlhood. She had been bottled up, and now she felt a return of youth. Cope had just read *Vanity Fair;* she had just read *Ulysses.* Cope had just received twenty-five guineas; she had just got ten pounds from Switzerland. Cope was in bed with a cold; so was she. Cope denounced the work of a radical writer; so did she. Cope wondered if the wife of a busy B.B.C. news-gatherer was not a secret Communist; she promised to find out. Cope had an appointment with a traveling correspondent of *Life* magazine—he had a scheme to interest them. Eleanor sighed, "All you bright young things are going to America." He was trying to do what he called "placer articles," which, once they appeared in some noted paper, were eligible for reprint in the *Reader's Digest,* "where you get not a few guineas but three or four or five hundred dollars." He had hopes still of going to the U.S.A. And Eleanor: "But isn't there anything to stop you? Haven't you a record?" She grinned to herself, but Cope replied, "I've washed that all out."

Cope also called upon her quite often, at least once a week. With a cup of coffee in front of him, one only, he would sit for hours while she went about her duties, while she ate her lunch, refusing food, "Bron's got lunch for me," or "I mustn't drink, I can't work." At last she would have to send him home, for he never came until his work was finished, but she always had work on hand. She did not mind when he talked guineas, for he was generous with literary tips, but now he often told her his ideas for articles and stories.

"I was just coming down your street when an idea came complete into my mind." He would tell it colorfully in detail, but nothing made Eleanor more impatient than these trivial fantasies. This was not work, but idling. Only printed and therefore in the form of a "receivable" could she understand and admire it. Cope would go home, write the story, polish it, have it printed in four or six or twenty-four months and at last Eleanor would be able to appreciate it. At these times she cut him short—she found him a nuisance.

When spring came, a new light came into her flesh and eyes and she began to coax and flutter around Cope with a different air. There was nothing to it, though; it was just the season and she was just as pleased to be alone.

"Long years of celibacy have made me something of a dreamer. I don't mind being alone and keeping my own counsel," she said to Cope once as a hint to him to be gone. He never took hints. She became more and more impatient, until she had to say, "Now you must go, my boy." Then she would accompany him downstairs and to the gate, where they would stand talking. What will people opposite think? she thought to herself. They'll think I have a lover. So much the better! I wish I had.

In the meantime in her home she had developed an interesting and harmless game. She was one of those women who feel at home with their flesh, love their bodies: she liked washing, dressing slowly; and whatever she wore round the house, she liked the feel of it on her skin. She liked rolling on her bed and waving her arms in the air, dragging her fingers through her hair as she mused. She would stroke her long beautiful thighs and think, What a pity! What donkeys they are! I'm wasted. The golden girl wasted.

A tree stood halfway between her window and three or four flats opposite, on the third floor, about thirty feet away. The morning sun shone directly into the window of Eleanor's bed/work room, and so far she had no curtains for the window. She had been able to afford one pair of curtains only, for the back room where the children slept. In midsummer the great tree was a screen; but in the early and late year Eleanor could distinguish people opposite, and she knew that there were numbers of students there, living in ones, twos and threes. She could not see them clearly, but knew that they were often at their windows working, reading, chatting; and until late at night they would lounge there. It was a wide shallow box window and she had installed a couch there. If anyone stayed over, one of her friends, they undressed in the dark; in the morning they got up giggling because of the men opposite, perhaps stationed at their uncurtained windows, and ran to the kitchen to dress. Or Eleanor might say, "Let them see our bare bums; it'll give them a thrill; I'm not ashamed of mine." This developed into a sport when she was alone. In summer she had no scruples. In spring and autumn when there was a light screen of leaves she would let the sun fall on her bare arms and shoulders, or her naked back; it fell on her and glided gently over her like loving touches. Surely I can sunbathe in my own home, she argued, one gets so little sun in town. It is not like the farm. She walked about nearly naked, or lolled on the couch in such a way that the students could see something of her but not all. If the doorbell rang, she would throw on a Japanese cotton wrap she kept handy, which veiled but did not conceal her splendid build. Indeed, she would try this kimono and a length of silk, an Indian sari she had, in a dozen ways and sigh, for she looked like a statue in them, while the shirt-blouse and tweed costume she wore made her look fat and aging. There were times when she would walk about the house singing to herself, dressed only in this cotton gown. She hummed, pulled things straight, went up and downstairs just for the pleasure of feeling one thigh rub against the other; and then she might go to her favorite seat and glance toward the boys opposite, whom she could not really see. Her short sight gave her a foolish feeling of modesty and safety, as if she could say, "Well, I was half hidden by my eyes." But nothing happened. What could have happened? Could a student have come across and asked her for love? Would she have admitted him? It all led to nothing but dreams; and in a sort of irritated affront at the boys opposite, she would go and wash herself, or even urinate almost in public. There was a floor-length window in the W.C. and a low broad window in the bathroom. The glass had been broken during the bombings and replaced with plain glass.

This was her love life throughout the time that Cope was visiting her; he seemed to forget she was a desirable woman. He seemed to find her mind interesting. There was very little Cope did not know about her. He had very soon asked her what was in her files and she had shown him everything—the divorce material which Deborah had given her back without a word, a few of Henry's personal files still with her and other files of correspondence with all her friends, bits of gossip she had written down, bits of manuscripts. "I just keep memoranda of everything, you never know when it will come in handy, and I have two projects," she told Cope. "One is a novel and one is a sort of companion to contemporary literature, don't you see? For there are not only those who have got there, but those who are getting there; and I am keeping tabs on them all. One of these days I'll have invaluable personal material, suitable for biographies; and I'll have letters and signatures for sale, as well. Providing for my old age, you see." Cope found this a treasury: encouraged her to keep it up. "I should love to look through if you'll let me."

"But you can't see the file on yourself, Cope, for how do we know that your signature won't be valuable one of these days? And that is the only profit I expect from our friendship."

Although from him she learned the meaning of many things, she could not help twitting him about his "red past."

"Perhaps I shall put in, too, that you were once a Stalinist," she said pertly.

"I don't mind what you put in: the chief thing is to have records and a diary, it's invaluable—and as long as you let me read over your shoulder."

She was pleased, but had to ask him how he had come to do such a thing. "How could the party have appealed to a common-sensical man like you?"

"I saw there was poverty and that the struggle was too much for some people and I wanted to find out why and to help; but I soon saw that the Communists were demoralizing the workers, or they would if the workers listened. The workers aren't worth worrying about in any case. Look at the stuff they read! I asked the news agents at several corners round here what the working sort of man bought—not one bought any magazine you or I would write for."

He was very hot on this subject; often and often he complained about the workers' stupidity and the money they spent on pools, radios, television, cheap cars, racecourses, on sending their children to private schools. "They don't appreciate government education—all snobs. As soon as they have a penny over, they equip their children in cap and coat and send them off to get a genteel twang."

At first, Eleanor had admired him for being a worker's, a boot-mender's, son, jacked up by his own bootstraps. He would always answer her questions about his past by talking about honest country life and the virtues of good shoes; but at last, in company, he was obliged to answer that he had been a lawyer's son, been sent to a gentleman's school and had given up the law after two years when he had decided to make a career in journalism. He had been "bitten by radical ideas" and had gone so far as to spend five months in the office of an ultra-left paper, where he severely edited articles on all subjects. This "red epoch" he did not hide, but brought it out in every political discussion. "I was there, I know. I saw the mistake. They wouldn't listen to me; I couldn't make them see and I got fed up. There isn't much can be done for them (the workers) because it's like teaching them reading and arithmetic and seeing them waste it on the pools. What needs to be done to make them useful to society is best done by the government which knows its needs, or the trades unions organized in the old-fashioned way, which know their needs, because they're run by men of capacity. That is, some of them are; though most of them, I wouldn't give you a penny a dozen. The Communist idea of having them do it for themselves—you might as well ask my youngster to run her own life; in fact, I'd rather ask her, she's such a damn bright kid. Besides, the Communist officials are what I call moral careerists, if they're not just plain careerists. You'll find anyone of talent in that puddle soon finds out he's made a mistake and skips out. They're people who live by their wits. There aren't many cranks, take my word for it; they're not starry-eyed. They're quite stable, but they're gamblers. They want to get into power the quick way. And they hold out impossible hopes—an easy life, safety from the cradle to the grave, no worries about children or old age, and all overnight by a strike or revolt—it's the lazy man's dream. Look at you and me: I've got to pay for a private school so my youngster can be properly taught; I've got to have a car to take her there; I've got to have a washing machine, a drying machine, a presser so that Bron can get through the housework; I've got to pay a typist because Bron can't do all my typing, I've got to furnish six or seven rooms, pay a charwoman because Bron's got her own work to do. If I have the charwoman all day it works out at four or five pounds a week."

"And do you know she lives better than we do? She has a fur coat and a bigger television set than we have," Bron would repeat her melancholy, pained cry.

"I may have to go charring yet," Eleanor said, cheerfully. "What would you say to me, with a monthly check from my late husband's parents, a widow's pension and some income from my only best seller? It looks well on paper. But I have to count the halfpennies."

"Oh, our char isn't like you," said Bron, with her strange wail. "All the money she gets from us she spends in the pubs and at the movies; she has no need to work, she does it out of greed."

Long, long talks they had at Cope's home. Bronwyn would sit with a colorful skirt spread out around her chair, her ankles just showing beneath; or in short velvet slacks, recline on the living-room divan she had herself covered in dark blue and rose, and always in some dark regretful mind; or after a restless moment, would start up, murmuring about housework or her child, and leave them together for long hours of literary gossip. Eleanor liked her, almost loved her; and if she found Bronwyn alone, she would kiss and embrace her, go with her to fetch the child, walk sprightly down the avenue from one shop to another, look over books in the library, and when they reached home, drink tea, loaf on the divan. But most eagerly of all, she would go with Bronwyn into the big front bedroom with the double bed, where she would lounge while Bronwyn, to relieve her agitation, brushed her hair, put on cosmetics, or sat down and got up from her chair every few minutes. Bronwyn would be distracted, abrupt, she might impatiently spill or break something, cry, "Oh, I don't know what I'm doing; what a damn fool I am!" She might at last sit down facing Eleanor with her clear pale cheeks and large eyes, her thick chestnut hair falling around her jawbone and neck and start to talk about her daughter, the household; and if Eleanor flattered her about the child, she might say loudly, "Oh, I wish I didn't know her name, but could start all over again." She was fifteen years younger than Cope, had met him while doing office work, been fascinated by his talk, gaiety, boldness, even his rash dressing and country airs. "He was a left-winger then and I thought he was a boot-mender's son and was self-educated. He seemed so fresh and worthwhile compared with my family. I simply adored him, I was afraid to lose him, I yearned and strained after him for years. I wasted years on him: it was one of those unhealthy young-girl obsessions. Some girls are lucky—the men they adore turn them down. Not Cope. He used to confide in me, tell me about all the other women. I expect there were some; I know there were."

"Still you're very lucky. Cope is a good man!"

"I sometimes think I'll scream if I hear another word about literary London. If I could I'd walk straight out of the house the next time I hear the words Newby, Hartley, Eliot—all the successes—because of course we only mention success names in this success house."

"But surely you love him. There must be compensations," Eleanor would press her. "Cope speaks of you so sweetly, he's devoted to you, surely."

"He doesn't want to lose my slave labor. He's proud of his daughter because she proves his manhood!"

Eleanor would rock with laughter. "Bron! How bitter!"

Then she would say in a pressing, wheedling tone, half grinning, anxious to get at the root of the matter, "Cope tells very full-blooded stories. He seems very loverlike to me!"

"He talks a good game! He drives me mad! I can't sit still! If it would only lead to something. One of these days I'm going to get fishnet underwear and go out on the town."

Eleanor would press her lips forward. "Dear Cope gave me another impression, but, of course, these things are a matter of—shall we say, counterpoint?"

But Bronwyn would feverishly throw off the discussion, and Eleanor would hear no more revelations for that day. It might be weeks again before she could satisfy her ardent curiosity. But to live so fully the life of another family was, besides the children and the swallowing down of amateurs' manuscripts, her delight. She felt like a kind aunt, a kind mother-in-law. When Cope was not in town she would telephone Bron at the usual hour, or Bron would telephone her. Bron's daughter was passing through all the stages Deb and Russ had gone through; the two women analyzed, Bron worried and Eleanor soothed, though Bron was too tense ever to be at peace for long. Eleanor liked to talk about marriage as a general topic; the mere mention of it irritated Bron like the sting of a horsefly.

"Oh, I can't talk about marriage! Let's drop it! It throws me into a fever; it's like a bed of nettles—you can walk through it and it will burn a little; if you rub on it, it will keep you awake all night."

"You don't get complete satisfaction out of marriage, do you, dear?"

"Oh, marriage is a bed of fire!"

Eleanor listened, later chuckled and even made notes: "B says, Marriage is a bed of fire! Very suggestive!" She replied, at the time, "And bachelorhood, too, my pet, is a bed of fire, if you think of it. Is it better to think of it and drive yourself to action—or better to let our instincts fall asleep?" She had told the Pigsneys as well as all her latter-day friends that she was a widow. "And so I am," she argued to herself and to her children. "Henry might as well be dead, he is dead to us; and I have buried him, but by request no flowers."

Cope excited her with his fever for guineas and his endless talk, to and fro humming like a hive, but only with a "guinea fever;" pondering over the open secret of Bron's married life threw her into pure sexual fever. She would, late at night, tear open some coarse, naïve erotic book that she kept hidden away, or recall some savagely suggestive phrase in one of the manuscripts—perhaps even a phrase she had at first quite misunderstood—and sit for hours in her armchair with the electric fire at her feet, or lie on her bed crudely, fiercely, thinking, picturing, but what came to mind was not anything that had happened to herself long ago. She had forgotten all that.

"I must, I must get me a man. I must start tomorrow morning." But in the morning she would merely have a telephone conversation with Bronwyn, hoping to stir her. "But I don't know whether, dear, I could really begin to look for a man. The children and I have such a satisfying life, good for work and good for health. I sleep like a navvy. We have shaped this life of ours; we are three such solid citizens. I wake up with the birds—I suppose I haven't got over the nursery years—and the trouble is, my pet, men don't like a woman to get up early, do they? Or have I forgotten? I wake and feel fit. I rise with the lark—the dear, good, solid day's work is ahead. I make myself a cuppa and get right down to it. I am never interrupted as I was in the old days with poor Henry; I do my groceries, chores and washing floors according to schedule. That's the point, my pet: there's the dilemma. Of course, I'm normal. I react to a healthy man's healthy desire; but is that a foundation firm enough for unsettling our nice, orderly life-plan? And at the same time, the other solution, the romantic interlude, is simply not feasible with sharp-eyed young ones in the house. They're so young yet, though Deb is seventeen and Russ fifteen; I simply daren't disturb their innocence."

"Taxicabs are convenient," Bronwyn might shoot out violently. "I've *got* to find a way."

"And what do you think Cope will say to that?" Eleanor would ask, very maternal. "My dear, it shows."

"My God, what am I to do? He'll never leave me—he says so."

"My dear, you don't mean that!"

A day with such a telephone conversation was a good one to Eleanor. When Cope himself came back to the routine, the next day or after, she had to tease him; her eyes twinkled. She had the tone of one on to rather a good thing, but keeping it to herself just for the lark of it. She teased Cope archly, offering him poisoned tidbits. Perhaps what was behind it was that although Cope was so clever as to make thirty-five or more guineas a week, on a yearly average, while she did not make more than four, she had had her "best seller," while Cope had earned nothing at all with his "prestige item." If she mentioned her book, it was modestly. "Of course, I had the immense advantage that my collaborator, Daddy, hadn't a clue, so we had beginner's luck."

Cope was jealous of Martin Hall, who had been accepted as an immigrant into the United States, and so she needled him.

"My friend Martin Hall, you remember him, don't you? He has managed rather well, and he seems to be a proof that those tales of persecution in the States are travelers' tales, rather, for he knows and is accepted by every genuine red group of our friends from Prague to Glasgow; he's not only in the States, as a desirable immigrant, but he's been interviewed by the *Reader's Digest* people and he is writing a series of articles for them on the parlor pinks in Europe. Of course, Martin is the kind of person welcomed everywhere with open arms. He had no difficulty whatever in Czechoslovakia and he's doing quite well already in New York."

Cope would refer to interviews he had had and the prices paid for articles in the States, three, four, ten times as much. "Of course everyone is trying to sell his stuff in the States. As Jaffa said, 'First editions are nothing: it's our first American editions we all want to collect.' "

Eleanor would murmur sympathetically, "But, of course, my dear, your record is rather smudged, isn't it? I'm afraid the Americans are rather unforgiving—you wrote for the wrong party, didn't you? They don't understand the higher motive, or the educative experience; they're rather naïve, they think you should have had the true faith from the beginning."

Once she saw she unnerved him with this sort of remark, she kept it up, merely by instinct. "And what about your novel *Seeds of Time*?" inquired Eleanor maliciously. "Do you regret having written it under Communist influence?"

"It wasn't done so," he cried testily, "and I still think that's my best book."

Eleanor went on teasing him: she hated this book for a reason obscure to her. She secretly felt and even hoped that in the end it would even ruin him. Whenever she spoke of Cope she would say, "But of course he made one bad mistake: that was when he wrote *Seeds of Time*. It's completely ruined by having a lot of political ideas pushed into it and it's bad as a book. Writing, I think—don't you—should belong to the great current of contemporary thought; it should explore, arouse questioning, but never give answers. To put politics into writing is to mix the eternal values with bits and pieces of topical ideas and temporary greeds." Although she had heard these words from Cope himself, she would repeat them to him to make him writhe. How could he ever have trifled with "reformism" (as he now called it)? She had been able to keep her skirts clear. But Cope (she admired him for it) would swallow this, clear his throat and continue with his ideas, all business ardor. He was generous, so fiery for his guineas that he could not help giving her all his ideas, spending hours and days on instructing her, pressing and arguing his system, his inventions. One of his principal discoveries was that a shortcut to literary success in the guinea world was to have a pet subject and stick to it: "Choose something, cultivate it, say it's yours and one of these days it will become your monopoly." For months one of the things they discussed was what was to be Eleanor's pet subject. At first she thought of the themes she had handled in Banes's Agency—baby care, topiary, street planning—but he scoffed at them: "Any hack can write them up, but only a gardener, a doctor, a town planner carries any weight." She then suggested modern history, English literature, economics: she had done those at the university. But though good for background, he held these were too large and she would meet genuine experts in all fields. What about county history of the Herbert counties? County prose and poetry? Did she know anything about amateur garden botany? Eleanor was humiliated that he dismissed all her learning without reflection: "It won't do, Ell." They almost settled, at one moment, for London's experimental and amateur stage, but this would mean, even with Cope's free tickets, much more expense than Eleanor could run to.

One day, after sitting with her for half an hour, Cope, with a face of a pleased pink, said, "How would you like, Ell, to collaborate with me on a diary of the London literary scene? Just gossip and effortless jottings! No legwork, just whatever comes our way. You keep a record, I keep mine; later we combine them. It ought to make a sensation—no libel, no scandal, but juicy stuff, suggestive; it'll be a record of the day. We don't need"—and he mentioned all the popular names—"we just need the people we meet. They'll all buy it. It's the kind of things the journalist will buy. We'll put the journalists in, treat them tenderly, then they'll give you a good write-up; and we'll put in country names. Because what you and I are up against, Ell, is that we're country people. Londoners consider London posts are for London men. We're as much out of it as if we came from Basutoland."

He made her begin at once and kept her at it. He would hear her comments over the telephone, and he came once or twice a week to read what she had. Everything went in. "We'll edit it later with a lawyer at each elbow," he said, "and no one but you and I are going to see this. Keep it safe, lock it up—this is going to be rich."

Stimulated and exhorted by him, glad to be on a "creative project" again, she yet found these notes taking up too much of her time, not to mention the hours Cope took up, riding his hobbies.

At this low sad period of her life when she was alone and her earnings were so miserable, the Pigsneys were her great consolation. She bent over them, puzzling out their lives, and took their attitudes about all things. She was deeply grateful for the help Cope gave her, and his energy poured into her veins. He was astonishing. Just at this moment when he started the diary of literary comment with her, she knew he was busy with the new job Bronwyn had mentioned, which required from him "a long working day." It was not an office job and he did not tell her what it was, so that she supposed he had become one of the anonymous leader-writers of one of the great dailies—the pay, at any rate, was enough to cover his increasing expenses; he was at last free from anxiety and did not depend for his rent and food upon the "shallow well of guineas," as he said. She sighed that he had got so far ahead of her; but he owed it to his unflagging energy. "I expected it for you, Cope dear—you leave no stone unturned. And now I suppose the Diary of Comment is to be shelved; you won't have time for that." But oh, dear, no—it was more important than ever.

"Now that I have less time, I want it more than ever. I think it's a terrific idea." Eleanor therefore continued with it, and her diary grew. At times she was half ashamed of the welter of material, some irrelevant and some base; at other times she was frightened at the prospect of collating and arranging. Wasn't she foolish to waste precious time on it? But Cope began to send her, quite frequently, half a guinea or a guinea, saying it was conscience money. "I used one of your ideas in a paragraph, and it's only fair I should pay." She never saw his columns, nor found one of her ideas in a newspaper, although she earnestly searched.

One day, Cope sent her an office filing case, as large as the one Henry had had in the flat she had burglariously entered. For warmth's sake, and because of the private matters in her papers, she now put in one room—which had a great wall cupboard, some shelves, which faced east and was relatively warm—her desk, tables and files, office furniture and her single bed. This room she kept clean and orderly. She had a beige rug, a dark-green bedcover; the walls were painted pale green, the wall cupboard was black. The decorations were her calendars, some photographs of the children, and there were also a pair of slippers, a dictionary, two wire baskets, a revolving office chair. There were two piles of manuscripts, the read and the unread; and behind the door hung her pink "candlewick" dressing gown, frayed, stained, ample; all her underclothes fitted into one small drawer and four hangers held all her blouses, coats and costumes. She did not mind wearing her clumsy, cheap old clothes; inwardly she mocked at people in the street who might think her a drab, pinched housewife.

Pigsney continued to coach her—she could find no reason for his devotion; and queerly enough, though to outsiders she defended him more than she defended her own children, she laughed privately at something absurd and outlandish in him. A certain Mrs. Blackstone had called him "the Jack of Hearts"; she called him that too. She was quite the equal of the Queen of Hearts, even if she reached her fifties. ("But remember I am forty-four, Cope. I'm going to be forty-four for the next fifteen years.")

It was odd that Cope, as he sat in Eleanor's secondhand chair with his favorite shoes, highly polished, on Eleanor's black sheepskin rug, should be dressed as he was: in a very loud sporting check, with a pale-blue tie and a yellow waistcoat. His thick sunburnt hair and face, his ringed hands made him look sporty, and he had a vulgar neighborly air. He boasted of his abstemiousness, his penury, in fact, and of his "flat belly." Arms akimbo, legs at an angle, he looked like the frog who went awooing. But it was not only all this; it was the fever he put her in. She would go to sleep with her head spinning, wake up eagerly full of plans for articles she never succeeded in completing.

The next day she would have a dreadful thirst for guineas. She tried to drown it in pots of tea, which stood on her work table and on which she endeavored to live through the workday.

Meantime they had decided to make Eleanor's speciality—her "monopoly"—East Anglia and its literature, for the simple reason that she herself came from East Anglia. She had gladly gone to work to "unearth the riches," and to read up on George Crabbe and Edward FitzGerald and others; and before long, Cope had got her her first book review on Roman antiquities in East Anglia. She did not sell the review books, as poor readers usually do for the few shillings they will bring when new, but kept them to found a Library of East Anglia to educate herself. The first review published, without question, because Cope had guaranteed her, the way was easy: she could now write to editors "Eleanor Herbert in books on general subjects, fiction: specializing in East Anglia."

Pigsney had been working at his new job of leader-writer (as Eleanor supposed) about six months when he was offered a visiting lectureship for one term in a college not far from London; he would merely have to stay overnight on each occasion. The fee was small, but with his usual all-round devotion to his career in letters he took it without hesitation. He would have a chance to meet students, he hoped to be invited to summer camps and he was laying the foundation for a lecture tour. As Bronwyn had South African relatives, Cope had made South African literature his "monopoly subject"; and it was on this that he was to lecture.

Shortly before he left for his first assignment, he called upon Eleanor for one of his lengthy chats. He followed Eleanor about the flat, into her bedroom-workshop and poked into her files. She hovered at a distance, anxious that he should not pull out the one incautiously named "Cope Pigsney." (In this file, in joking spirit, she had set down "converted to Communism by a Jewish fellow student and worked for the *Daily Worker*.") But he merely picked and shoved, and then said, as she had so little room, why not send her overspill to his house? He had plenty of room. A wave of temper rose behind her ears—she almost choked. Was he trying to take her work from her? She refused. He kept on trying to persuade her. When he left, she sat down with a frown and wondered at it.

She had become fond of her files. Set down with spite or devilment, greedily listened to with a rascally ear, she later found them precious, titillating, mysterious, an explanation. She had no means of combining one observation with another, but sad or salacious trivialities seemed to teach her something. Sometimes she would flush suddenly. This is prying! It's sneaking! But then writers must have material, mustn't they? And we are going to write it with a lawyer at each elbow. And as time went on she became penetrated with the piteous lives of some of these people. The Blackstones, two middle-aged writers, were living in a foul bed/sitting room in a side street of St. John's Wood, with a "bachelor's oven" in the fender. The bed was made with the landlady's coarse, patched and grimy bedclothes, thin, old blankets, yellow and gray. The couple translated from French and German, and read books in foreign languages for publishers. But they had dependents and were glad to have been able to find so cheap a room.

Denmark had a wife, Dawson had alimony, the Blackstones were Communists, X was starving wife and child and himself to write a thesis, Y was a political exile unable to write about England or to publish works about his native country, Z . . . , and so on. Cope held that even misfortune was a "rotten streak," but Eleanor, much nearer to destitution than he, often sat in racking pity and mortal terror before the files for her Diary of Comment.

When she got a small check perhaps, or on some anniversary, birthday or festive season, she would send them—the Blackstones, the X's, the Y's—the thing they needed most or a luxury, a piece of carpet, three pounds of French coffee, a patent grill that could be used on a gas ring. "I owe them something, I get my half-guinea from Cope!" she would say to her children. She enjoyed buying these expensive things which she never could afford for herself.

During this first lecture term of Cope's, Eleanor had a telephone call from Bronwyn Pigsney. "Come and see me, I can't talk over the phone." She found Bronwyn sitting in the large, bare, dark kitchen, with the blind half down on one side, the other window being shaded by heavy summer green. Bronwyn looked pale, stony. She seated Eleanor and herself stood stiffly in one corner, motionless, looking at her with large round eyes.

"A woman like you wouldn't understand it if I left Cope, would you?" She came out of her corner, gave Eleanor something to eat, and then in a soft friendly tone began to tell Eleanor her troubles. Cope, since his new job, was often away: he attended every blessed literary tea and meeting, and she didn't know what else. She didn't see him at bedtime once a week. She had headaches and felt depressed. Cope couldn't understand her at all and never had; he thought that if a woman was restless she needed a child. Surely she had enough to keep her busy, with the housework, his office work and her own "creative" work! If she told him what was the matter, he seemed not to hear. Worse, he would say, "Well, let's make an appointment, just as if we were lovers; I'll be your lover and call at three tomorrow, eh?" At lunchtime the next day she would be all fever and shame. Lunch would come and go. She'd hesitate, clear up; at half past two punctually, Cope would leave the house—"I need to walk to clear my brain," or, "I must call on Dr. Obernoke, I promised to talk over his book with him"—and off he'd go. "Every time, every time without fail! What's the meaning of it? So it's no use. I've spent ten years awake half the night. I can't do my work properly, and I'm ashamed, too. Another man loves me. I think he does. Once he said he'd take me with the child. He's unhappy. His wife sleeps with any man she likes; and then he says, 'It's infantile: she'll grow up someday.' And I know they suit each other because they're bohemians. I couldn't bear him sleeping with other women. Because—I know he's involved with three or four women. And I'm just one of them. So what am I to do?"

Eleanor couldn't help half smiling at this foolish story. "You'd better stay with Cope—he's very loyal. You'd soon find out what it was to be really unhappy."

"Perhaps you don't see it all," said Bronwyn. "I don't know what work you do with Cope. You do work with Cope, don't you?"

"In a minor way I do do a little collaboration," Eleanor agreed.

"Yes, yes—I don't know," said Bronwyn restlessly. "You may not understand it. It's hard to explain. Our money troubles are over. But I'm so restless, so anxious; I have such awful suspicions —no, I don't mean that. I don't want the food he brings. I'm eating it and suddenly as I put my tongue around it, I feel an absolute horror. But the child must eat. If I had the courage of my convictions I'd leave him. He wouldn't let the child suffer. He loves the child. He even loves me."

"You're in an awful state," Eleanor said. "It's you who need the change of scene and job."

"Can I go on like this, another year or five years, a lifetime? I suppose I must walk out, or accept it. I have no real principles; I can't betray my own husband! I expect he thinks that job is the right thing to do."

Eleanor scarcely listened to her, only feeling vaguely sorry for the young mother in her distress, but toward the end she heard Bronwyn say, "You oughtn't to help him, at least! I have no right to advise you, I suppose you have your own convictions; and you have your children to feed too. We have to feed the children! Why do we talk about the spivs? They're only feeding their families, giving them a decent life. But is every way of feeding your children so bad? Perhaps I'm hysterical. I ought to suspect myself."

Eleanor was puzzled. A few days later she saw Bronwyn in the library and hailed her; Bronwyn had tried to get out without being seen. She walked down the shopping district with her, as often before; Bronwyn was almost silent. It certainly seemed that in one department store they visited Bronwyn tried to lose sight of her. Eleanor bought some pretty things and shoved them laughing in Bronwyn's bag. Instead of her usual gay thanks, Bronwyn said nothing.

"I'll come and see you, Bron dear," she said at the street corner, "and give my love to the Blackstones when you see them."

"I don't see them; I'm not seeing any of those people any more," said Bronwyn, surly; she lifted her head and gave Eleanor a scornful, offended look. Eleanor was perplexed. She did not understand enmity. She telephoned Cope, who had returned, the next morning. Bronwyn said very coldly, "Your collaborator's here," and called him to the phone. Eleanor visited them after that, but never again did she get anything but a surly, cold word from her old friend. "She regrets what she told me."

Gradually she found she had a little less to do with Cope; and she knew, from Cope's outspoken complaints, that Bronwyn and he had had a quarrel—she had threatened to leave him and take the child to her mother's.

"Could it have been over me? Surely not!" And Cope had said vaguely that it was "political."

5

·

The Woman of Fifty

COPE TELEPHONED HER one morning at ten-fifteen, and in his lugubrious gossip voice, remarked, "The news is out that Wally Purfoy is out of Rainshelter's —he's your sponsor, isn't he? No one thought he'd last. Imagine Rainshelter's taking it into their heads to go in for literature! Don't they know they're wholesale pulp merchants, that they can imitate anything paper will imitate—handkerchiefs, picnic plates, boots, books—but not literature!"

"Well," Eleanor began, "they have published some good things, Cope. I myself recommended some good things."

"Yes, there's a saying round town for it, you know: Rainshelter's—every thousandth book a book."

Eleanor was nettled. "Surely, Cope, there is no positive harm in supplying the public taste in Westerns, stenographer romance and mysteries? I read them myself. And there are plenty of eclectics: Rainshelter's don't publish anything nasty or questionable; they do just as many good translations from the French and German and Italian as any of your arty firms; they do science and schoolbooks—that is, in one or other of their many branches, Cope! And I for one see the wisdom of this sort of production: it's all-embracing, highly specialized, it's technics applied to the gratification of an immense, diversified public need, and only a large combination with a foot in both camps—literary and commercial —could possibly take care of it; it needs organization. An arty concern like Fox and Vixen doesn't consider public taste, doesn't communicate, you might say; and an out-and-out vulgar set (I can't call them a house or firm) like Ambrose and Quaideson, is run like the gutter press—big print, sensation in whatever camp, no politics, near smut and the memoirs of mavericks."

Cope replied, "Well, you'd better watch your *p*'s and *q*'s. It's the usual thing, when a man loses his job and he represents a trend, to do a housecleaning; they want no stain nor smear of a bit of a liberal mistake. Wally Purfoy was a mistake for Rainshelter's, and you came in with him."

"Oh, butter won't melt in my mouth. I've always had printed on my heart, 'Strictly impartial,' and"—setting her teeth and in a hard voice—"I work so honestly and cheaply for them, I don't count the hours, they'd be mad to get rid of me. I've actually recommended three or four good sellers, and two of them were serialized after and one was made into a movie. Not that I get anything on that. We ought to have some sort of a contract. An agent does not do as much as I do: they're merely post offices, and spend their postage; they don't recommend. I recommend, I pay my own bus fares, I look up in the library and I get nothing, whereas the agent gets ten percent, and sometimes fifty. I've heard of a case where the agent got fifty percent on a movie."

"Still, I think you'd better be prepared for the worst," said Cope.

"Look, Cope, I'm cleverer than I look," she said sweetly. "The last two Christmases I haven't sent any Christmas cards, you know, but I've spent a couple of bob each time on a real arty card for Miss Saucing and Mrs. Werner."

Cope laughed. "Miss Saucing doesn't believe in Christmas cards. She says they have made Christmas commercial."

"So it was wasted? I sometimes feel nonconformists stand out as a peculiar people just to put us in the wrong, for a sort of exhibitionism, don't you? It puts us in such an awkward position."

Cope told one of his revolting Cockney stories. Meanwhile Eleanor was thinking of her situation; and her nervous heart, her sad knowledge of struggle had convinced her that in fact she had better look out. At the end of his story, she murmured abruptly, "Well, then I shall do what Millia Blackstone does or I'll clean the lavatories at tube stations with the black women. I won't starve. I won't starve for their tricksy maneuvers."

"Surely Millia Blackstone doesn't do that?"

"No. She gets up at six-thirty to get breakfast and go and clean a hospital, and she gets back at two-thirty to write reviews for the TLS. I can do the same."

"Of course, the Blackstones stand in their own light," he said. "They're extremists, terrorists, armchair terrorists, of course; otherwise, there'd be neither hospital nor TLS—"

"Are they Communists?" said Eleanor, licking her lips. "I thought there was some ideology behind what they said. It seems to me," she continued with a little laugh, "that Communism is a luxury for poor people, don't you? It's asking for the black hole and bread and water." She said sadly, "And they are so poor, very poor. Dear Ben Blackstone, he's a very gentle soul—you can't help liking him, he's winsome."

"It's certainly unhealthy to talk Communism when you're not sure of your income. I heard of a Blackstone who was in trouble in South Africa—I wonder if he's the same? Of course, they don't penalize you here; here it's the work that counts."

"Yes, we're terribly fair. I sometimes wonder if it's quite sensible," said Eleanor. "Opinion is free. There are Communists—Oxford and Cambridge men—on some of the committees I'm on. I've always thought it showed complete liberalism—on both sides! I can understand them, in a way. They want to reach beyond class." Then she added virtuously, "Still, you can hardly blame people, publishers and editors for not paying for unpopular minority opinions—that is," she added hastily, "for opinions they are in violent contradiction with; it wouldn't be human, and after all, they must think of reader opinion. Publishing is not concerned with experiment or lost causes, is it? Freedom of opinion is one thing, but to impose the beliefs of a sect and a fanatic sect on the general public would be a little too quixotic! Not that even Rainshelter's don't do a quixotic thing here and there. I don't think outsiders give publishers enough credit for being warmly and simply human—that is, when the cash is the same. Everyone I've ever met in Rainshelter's cares for culture and would rather publish a good book than a bad. A firm isn't bad because it's rich. In fact, just because of that it can afford to take chances: every book need not be a bread-and-butter proposition."

She found, to her surprise, that she was trembling; she could hardly control her voice.

There was a short silence, during which they both listened to the wires humming, but neither said, "Hello, hello! Are you there?" After a moment they began again. Cope ended by asking her why she didn't apply for a suitable job at the London Intellectual Survey, a government institution set up to place well-educated middle-class people. "It is just for your kind of person, looking for a job. I went there myself, I took offense when the clerk made some allusion to my provincial degree; but I was silly."

Eleanor was excited to hear of this free employment agency for qualified intellectuals; she asked the address and went there that afternoon. She felt confident: fifty pounds had come in from the Continent, an advance against a foreign edition of *Brief Candle.* "Money calls money," she said to herself cheerfully.

In Bloomsbury, among the many new monumental buildings she found the place she was looking for, near Euston Square: a large eight-story building occupying a whole block, made in red brick and white stone and with two large brass plates at the entrance and a porter in a glass office. After a searching but pleasant look, the porter gave her an application card to fill in, and with it she passed into a corridor and reached a sort of box office, where a woman clerk sat to take her card. She was directed to some wooden benches, where during three-quarters of an hour she had time to size up the others waiting—shabby gentry, modest, withdrawn, and all used to waiting. With her radiant looks, she felt sure of success and showed impatience. Presently she was called and given a double-sided card to fill in with particulars of her age, sex, condition, qualifications, record, languages, special gifts, and whether she was prepared to take up a job at home, in the provinces or anywhere abroad, and whether she needed notice or would go at once. She had something to put in every line and felt a little bashful as she handed the full card in. She was asked to take a seat and a clerk began to study her card. After some time and consultation, the clerk called Eleanor, and Eleanor, full of hope, thinking they must have already found her "a niche," tripped forward.

The clerk said severely, "You say you have written a book which has been published abroad?"

"Yes," and her heart began to beat, for she had counted on her special gift to get her an unusual job, one of those jobs that young men who advertise in *The Times* Personal are always hoping to get.

"Is there only one or are there several books?"

"Only one."

"You have not made that clear," the woman scolded. "And what were the dates of the translations?"

Eleanor filled it in, at the same time puzzling about the job that they had in mind for her. She would have to explain she could not translate.

The clerk studied her card again and then said: "You will receive a letter or even a telegram; and I hope you will be ready to come in as soon as you are asked for an interview, because we have a long waiting list and your interview might be deferred a month or even longer if you cannot keep it."

Eleanor promised that she would hold herself ready. She had

thought for some time about whether she would take a job abroad, but she had decided that she must take any job, and she had written in: "Yes, anywhere abroad." She now realized she would have to go home and at once make arrangements for the children, for subletting, for storing her few goods. She went home, and after that, scarcely dared to leave the house. She would hurry up to the nearest butcher's, not one she had dealt with before, and buy the rest of her goods in the various shops selling mixed goods, a stationer's, the candy store/post office, a Continental delicatessen that she had always been afraid of before. Meantime she was very active with the telephone. The Blackstones were paying by the week and could move in a week. She offered them her flat, plus the rent of any broken week, if they would move at once to her address to take care of her children while she went abroad. She invited them to tea, showed them the place, was pleased by their restrained joy, and then had a quiet, earnest talk with them about their political opinions. She hoped they would not express themselves in words the children could carry to their friends; children nowadays were so wide-awake and eager to get their teeth into something solid, it was not quite fair to make them take sides for or against, and she did not want her children to adopt in ignorance or innocence some "stigmata of a party." At their age children had the group feeling (their father, as a youth, had joined Mosley's Fascists)—best to leave them to solve the little dilemmas of social interplay; they were like puppies at shaping their brave new world. She had long sensible talks with her children, telling them how to behave now that harsh necessity was making adults of them too young; she looked over their clothing, took them to the dentist, wrote to their grandparents, trying to arrange holidays for them and asking to borrow some money against the salary she expected to get—"if I am to go abroad, I assume I will get a higher salary than at home."

While she was busy in this way and in finishing off her correspondence, she received a letter from Miss Saucing, saying that Rainshelter's had decided to employ a regular reader and that her services would be no longer required. Eleanor always answered letters, but she delayed the answer to this for a few days, hoping to be able to write triumphantly that she was taking a job abroad; and while she waited, she did receive an official envelope stamped "London Intellectual Survey." Inside was a printed form asking her to call two days later at two-thirty to be interviewed for a position by Miss Emerald Knight-Porter.

Eleanor dressed once more to suit her dead mother's idea of a lady, took a bus, and with a joyful trembling, entered the heavy stone doorway and trod down the polished corridor.

"Kenya, South Africa, Ireland or the South Seas," she said to herself. "Barkis is willin'. Where will I be, I wonder, three months from today?"

She was presently shown into a little green-curtained booth, bright with polish, plate glass and daylight, where a large milky golden-haired woman of about thirty-three sat. She was friendly, almost intimate, and yet businesslike; her tones were courteous.

"I have your application form here," said she, and she ran over a few of Eleanor's accomplishments. "Now, Terrace Street— you live at 36 Terrace Street? Where is that exactly? I believe I have been there myself but I can't exactly place it."

"N.W.2."

"Oh, not N.W.6? You forgot to fill that in, or rather it is unclear," said Miss Knight-Porter. "And is there another Terrace Street?"

"Not that I know of."

The interviewer looked rather suspiciously at Eleanor. "And is this your own telephone number? Yes? I see. Because we telephoned but we received no reply."

She listened noncommittally while Eleanor explained that she "had to leave the telephone alone" while she went for messages. She then seemed satisfied and leaned amiably toward Eleanor, saying, "I see! Well, the fact of the matter is, Mrs. Charles, that it is rather difficult for us to place a person like you, without any particular record or qualifications. You see, there is very little here to go on. Couldn't you give us a few more details?" She said it as if it caused her pain.

Eleanor reared with indignation but controlled herself, and realized it was impossible to explain, without looking foolish, that this was her whole life and that she had been proud of it. She thought of Cope Pigsney with his "provincial degree."

"There are no more details that would help me to a job," said Eleanor.

"My suggestion is, then, that you try journalism. I understand if you free-lance you can place articles and stories—and, of course, as you have a family, you wouldn't want a regular job?"

"Oh, I should," said Eleanor. "My family is trained to look after itself."

Miss Knight-Porter gave her rather a prim look. "Well, then, perhaps the best thing for you to do is to try to get some introductions to publishers or to Fleet Street editors. If you've been published, you must have some literary friends. However, here is another card you can fill in giving your literary experience; the information may be of use. You see, it is very difficult to place a person like yourself. Would you be prepared to take a position overseas?"

As Eleanor started but did not reply, she continued, "You see, it is just that the information might help. If something turns up we will write to you or telephone you. But in the meantime I suggest that you try to make contacts yourself, get introductions to editors and journalists. I understand editors employ people to read books for them. Anything like that would suit you."

Eleanor was about to say, "I do that now," when she thought that the London Intellectual Survey might recommend her to another publisher, so she said nothing.

A month later she was called again. She went in, and this time was interviewed by a Mr. Barlamb on the third floor. The third floor was divided into rooms by green curtains on rods and looked as if an amateur company were just going to play Shakespeare. A dark-eyed, athletic middle-aged man, looking badly put together, went in before her, and Eleanor heard him being directed to a job in the North. When she went in she found her interviewer, Mr. Barlamb, to be an unusually prepossessing tall young fellow with an engaging shy provincial manner. He looked at her with admiration and began a speech which filled her with hope; but she suddenly heard him saying, "This office is not really for people like you, not for people of quite your quality: what we do mainly is to find secretaries for high executives, mostly in commercial work, and a few science teachers; but we rarely have anyone asking for a lady with the qualifications that I see on your card. You would do well not to depend too much on us."

With some more deprecating and you-understand-me talk, he maneuvered her into ending the interview gracefully. For some minutes his charms lingered with her, and even he had ended with the remark that they would certainly telephone or write if anything came up.

A month had now gone by; Eleanor's fifty pounds was spent, she had no more guineas from Rainshelter's to give her the illusion of earnings. She had received ten pounds from her parents-in-law in Switzerland.

When she got outside the fine glass doors of the London Intellectual Survey, she glanced once into the side window where she could see Miss Knight-Porter's fine fair head and thought, How can she bear to fool work-hungry parents that way? and after taking a few steps up the avenue, came to a resolution, "I'm going to stump this town till I get a job, any job. I'm presentable; the trouble has been my passivity, that's all. I'll take anything. I have children to keep, I'm not proud."

It was not late, and she set off for the Women's Employment Exchange, which she had found out was near Regent Street. She had heard there might be a queue. But there was none and no one about, so that she wandered up and down the dusty narrow stair twice, noting the doors, "Hotel and Domestic Workers," "Office Workers," "Teachers." At first she entered a large room like a schoolroom, for clerical workers, and after getting her number she sat on a bench next to several young girls, who were pretty, fresh and smart, though one or two looked out of work. Compared to them she felt elderly and fussy. She heard herself rustling up to the table when her number was called, and she sat down trying to be as modest and small as she could. The careworn woman of forty or so said to her, "Do you want someone for an office?" and Eleanor could not help blushing to say, "No, I'm looking for a job myself. I'm a widow and have two children to keep, I need a job," and she told what her experience was, but she omitted to say that she was a writer not only because she was ashamed, but because she felt that somehow it would go against her, make her look amateurish.

The woman shook her head several times at the things Eleanor said, and said sympathetically but with sad resignation, "You can fill in a card and call in once a week; if you don't call in in a fortnight, we will assume you have a job and will take your name off the lists."

"But isn't there anywhere where I can get a job?" asked Eleanor, for she had thought that with full employment, nothing would be simpler.

"No," said the woman, sadly studying her face. "With the insurance schemes, you see, they don't want to pay the high rates that they have to pay for anyone above thirty; they prefer the girls who have just left school—the rate is very low."

"So," said Eleanor indignantly, "pension plans work against people like me."

"Yes, they do," the woman said in a quiet, worn way, not trying to make things smoother.

"Suppose I try domestic work," said Eleanor, rosy but determined.

"You can go upstairs," said the woman, "but even there they prefer younger women—you would find it hard to get a regular position above forty, and then you would usually have to sleep in. I suppose you can't do that."

Eleanor went upstairs, where she found another kind, resigned woman, much younger, with soft golden hair. But this woman did not so much as take her name: "We would not be able to get you anything."

When Eleanor returned to the pavement she felt shabby, and for the first time she saw herself as the rest of the people saw her: a more than middle-aged woman, an old woman, unemployable. She caught sight of herself, she looked for her face, in long panels of glass as she went reflectively along. She thought, Look at me— I look old-fashioned, fussy, a suburban wife and mother, but I've got somehow to get out of myself and get a job, in spite of age and looks. She walked on. I will not be downed, said she, looking in at a tourist agency's pictures of adolescents skiing in Switzerland. My children shall have all that too. I won't go so low as Millia Blackstone, I'm no defeatist. But her lips trembled. I'm just a normal woman. I am not cleverer than my neighbors—but surely, for that reason, they ought to give me a job. She stopped at Oxford Circus and looked in her little red notebook: she had there several other addresses. In for a penny, in for a pound, she thought, and she took the underground to Victoria, where there was a well-known agency for superior office and literary workers. She found it, situated above an army surplus store into which they were just carrying a great quantity of new umbrellas, suitcases and ladies' coats. If someone would stake me to a business, I could run it efficiently and to a profit, she thought.

In a cheerful mood she entered the little waiting room. She was no longer nervous; she had all her bland sweetness. Presently she was interviewed by a well-educated, self-respecting young woman of her own type, and as she filled in the blanks she thought, How can she be in, while I am out? She is no better than I am. The young woman was competent, pleasantly sophisticated and understanding. When she asked Eleanor if she could do shorthand, Eleanor could not resist "shaking her plumes" and saying, "So far I have employed a business secretary myself for my correspondence and articles, and in fact, you will find my name on your lists.

I have had several girls from your agency—and all but one was very satisfactory. I know your reputation and your girls quite justified it." For the moment she had forgotten that she was asking for a job. She suddenly smiled at the girl. "But now I am asking for a job; my circumstances have changed, I am a widow."

The girl meantime had been scanning the form she had filled in and said, "You might try the Red Cross—do you know anyone who could recommend you there? You might get work in the records or secretarial or almoners' divisions of hospitals. They also very often want half-day workers or temporary clerical staff. The best thing is for you to get some doctor who knows you personally to recommend you. Do you know anyone who is the head of a hospital and could get you in? The personal way is always the best."

Eleanor could not resist saying then, "But you are an employment agency. Can't you get me a job in the ordinary routine way like you got for the girls you sent me?"

"The trouble is," said the girl, after a slight hesitation, "that the kind of jobs you are suitable for are very much in demand, especially with the wives of half-pay officers, ladies who have come back from India and are having difficulties here, now that their circumstances have changed." She looked sympathetically at Eleanor and said in a lower voice, "They often come to us and they will do anything—of that sort. In fact, some of them are quite willing to do domestic work. They live in one room, sometimes with the husband. It's very difficult for people living on a pension." She resumed her official voice, which, however, was steady, pleasant and encouraging. "Would you be a telephone girl? You have the right type of voice."

Eleanor stretched her hand over the desk, took back the form and filled in the blank which said, "Telephone girl?" She wrote, "Yes: good voice; and patient, no experience." She handed it back. "Well, then," said Eleanor, "surely if I too am willing to do anything but domestic work—I have enough of that at home, looking after my little family—you could get me something?"

"We will try," said the girl, "and we will let you know if we hear of anything that suits you."

Eleanor came out into Victoria Street, walked slowly to Victoria Station, amusing herself by looking into the hundred little businesses that she passed. There were many things that she could do efficiently—run a lunch counter, a stocking shop, be a hostess, a manageress, run a tourist agency, a bookshop. She was hungry, but she took the underground home and telephoned the Pigsneys as soon as she had had a cup of tea. Cope was out—he had gone down to the TLS to get a book on psychology in which he was specializing then. He watched the publishers' lists and promptly asked for anything that was in his line.

Bronwyn Pigsney answered, and when she had heard about Eleanor's day, she said, "I have just heard from my next-door neighbor that they want a countergirl up at the dyeing and cleaning, the one near the station, do you know it? They pay four pounds or four pounds ten a week, something like that. Why don't you go down there?"

"I will go," said Eleanor, "though I hope they stick me behind among the dirty clothes—I don't mind admitting it will be embarrassing for me to be fingering the dirty clothes of my own butcher, baker and candlestick maker, and the mothers from the school. However, as long as they don't see me—for the children's sake."

But she waited two days, unable to nerve herself to the idea of handling the dirty clothes and of herself in such a place. She thought a great deal in those two days about her education, her past life, and why it was she found herself in this position. People were trying to help her. Her landlord sent her a clipping from *The Times* reading:

ARE YOU A LADY of literary talents who likes office work and has organizing ability? Would you like to help run a literary agency just starting out, with brilliant prospects? Readers wanted: languages an asset, but the chief thing is your personality. Write mentioning qualifications to——

"This seems as if it were created specially for you," wrote her landlord (a very nice Greek with silvery hair and a fine baritone), "it fits you like a glove! I hope it is not too late."

Eleanor applied for this, as she applied for all, with good faith and in hope. She received an answer, and on the day appointed, went to a street in Soho and entered a half-ruined courtyard in which a group of temporary offices had been erected, with wooden and glass partitions, in a warehouse. At the end of a deserted corridor filled with boxes and disjointed scaffolding she found the Anglo-British Book Agency, a modern, expensively installed set of offices with bookcases full of new bindings and staffed by two handsome young women with strong temperaments. A dark-eyed middle-aged woman came out of the inner office with bundles of manuscripts saying, "I'll file these and then go home." "All right, Mrs. Hersco." Eleanor was sent in to see Mrs. Jonovich, a dark young businesswoman, neatly and expensively dressed. The carpets were rich, there were no books and few papers on the glass-topped table; there were white and blue Venetian blinds, white curtains with a pale design. Mrs. Jonovich's friendly manner did not attempt to conceal the inquiring glances at Eleanor's face, hands, shoes, handbag; and the only strange thing in their interview was that the woman continued to give Eleanor these searching intelligent glances. Eleanor was used to making a good impression quickly, and so she assumed her best and weightiest style. She said, "I should really like to begin with a new firm and help to build it up from the ground floor." She answered questions. She was no playwright but considered she had good average taste; she knew what she liked, she knew what made for good entertainment, she could easily take charge of plays. As for children's stuff, she had learned to see things from their level—she had two children and had never imposed her own tastes; as for ordinary fiction, there she was quite at home, being a writer and a successful one—she read for large firms and did critical articles for leading literary papers. As she spoke she wondered how it was she was so poor. Her record was good. When it came down to questions of marketability, judgment, taste, she felt quite sure of herself; she even thought she knew what made a success.

"You mentioned your children," said Mrs. Jonovich, "but if you work for me, I hope your responsibilities at home won't interfere with your work here. I don't want an assistant who feels she has to hurry home to her husband and children, like Mrs. Hersco, or who worries about them at work. Mrs. Hersco is leaving me because she doesn't suit me, for that reason. I want someone who'll stay to ten or midnight, if there is work to be done, and who'll go home with us in the weekend, if need be."

While this was being said, Mrs. Hersco, a plump, lively woman, had come in to file something in the cases there, and had given them a hostile but curious glance. Eleanor said when the door closed, "Ah, yes, she is a displaced person, isn't she? We give them work, but we need work, too." She raised her voice, said in a fine clear tone, "My children are quite grown, fifteen and seventeen. They know their mother is a hard-working widow and that I have my working hours which must not be interfered with—their bread and butter depends on it."

The talk continued for some time in a more intimate tone. Eleanor always felt sure of her ground after saying something about aliens in the country, as if a fine silken bond had been tied and the differences of employer and employee were obliterated; and she said suddenly on a girlish impulse, "Oh, I like you very much, Mrs. Jonovich. I feel we should get on."

Mrs. Jonovich raked her with a glance, spied on her silk-covered legs, noted her size in shoes and sat back in her chair with a hard, sour, bright look. "Very well," she said at last, smoothly, "I'll let you know in a few days. I don't know when Mrs. Hersco will make her mind up that she must go. She has been very useful to me because she knows four languages."

"Oh, yes, foreigners are so good at languages. I suppose we are inferior to them in that way," said Eleanor against her will—her tongue acted—she felt it a mistake. "One day," she added hastily, "I *must* take up my German which I haven't touched since

[269]

I was in school. I was good at it then. Well"—she gathered her things and got up nimbly—"I think we have talked everything over thoroughly, haven't we? I'll be anxious to hear from you." And after a false exit (she went into a bare room), she went out. The wages mentioned had been ten pounds a week, and some share of commissions. Ten pounds a week! They would eat and save. That's something settled; and she felt as if she'd won in a tennis tournament.

On the way home, scraps of her conversation with Mrs. Jonovich forced themselves on her: "I love the prospect of ripping into a mountain of manuscripts and sending the bad ones to the right about and cutting the good ones about so that they'll get a real chance. Every author needs a guide, philosopher and friend, a censor and a literary stepmother, too." (A good laugh!) "The more energy required, the more I have; this combination of brawn and brain is just my meat. I look forward to long hours and a seven-day week—that's how I always work—if I have a job in front of me that I respect and enjoy. I am a widow, and except for a little money laid by for their education, and some money later on from their grandfather, I must depend on my own work to make ends meet; so I have an urge and drive the ordinary business girl has not. I have my children to work for."

In expressing what was really a part of her nature, she had felt happy and she felt she had met the kind of woman who would feel with her. She went home, told the children of her hopes and began to "plan ahead," a thing she loved. But she did not hear from the agency, and when after some days she telephoned, a nipping secretary voice told her that Mrs. Jonovich had filled the vacancy and "had not thought it necessary to notify all applicants." Eleanor was very angry and puzzled. "Probably the languages," she said at last.

On Saturday at lunchtime Eleanor sat down to table with the children, to the meal they had prepared, shepherd's pie from hash, then rhubarb and custard, and told the children all her difficulties. "I must find work. We must have money coming in every week, even this kind of food has to be paid for."

To her surprise, Deborah began to cry. "Don't criticize, I can't do any better."

"I wasn't criticizing."

"I'm leaving school tomorrow to get a job. It's all Daddy's fault that I have got to go out into the world without an education. But it's too late now. Things are spoiled. I've just got to go to work as if I came from a home in the slums. Well, all right, I don't care. I'll go and get a job next week. I'll just get through my exams, and finish. Good-bye. Oh, I've made a mess of everything. Daddy's made paupers of us and I'm just a mess myself. I'm like him, I think. But it's too bad, it's really too bad," she said, crying. The teachers at school had wanted her to go on to the university and become a language expert: she was so unusually good at languages.

"Mrs. Jonovich would have given you my job," said Eleanor, feeling very strange. "I suppose I just wasn't good enough."

Vina de Saiter wrote to her from Paris that one of Eleanor's old flames, Bob Standfast, was head of a sociological research unit in UNESCO; they had all been talking about Eleanor the other night and Bob had said he wondered Eleanor didn't get a job in UNESCO—it would be easy for a girl like her.

Bob Standfast was a man Eleanor had met just before her marriage and in a very unusual way. He had then been head of a press agency. One of his news gatherers had then been Janet Jackson, friend of Dr. Linda Mack. At that time Linda Mack had suddenly telephoned Eleanor, asking her to go to the emergency ward in a London hospital where Janet was dangerously ill after an accident which looked like suicide. The story Janet told was that she had been in love with Standfast, who had treated her fraternally, and then "like a friend but with a touch of passion." Suddenly he had married a very different sort of woman, "the cream puff sort," said Dr. Mack. "Would you like me to go and see him and bring him to see you?" Eleanor asked Janet. Although Janet had said no, Eleanor judged by her glance that she was not cured of the man, so she went the next day to see Standfast. She was very curious, too, half indignant, half despising a man Janet could love. She was surprised to see a hatchet-faced, dark-eyed, repellently attractive man with a jutting chin and a dimple. "Your friend is merely a neurotic," said Standfast. "I feel no responsibility." He smiled, his dark-red or almost black lips like a falcon's beak pouting. The thick brow hairs mixed, bristling, ran almost across the bridge of his nose. "She's a melancholic," he said placidly, settling his crossed knees, and then added pathetically, "I ought to know, I'm one myself; two melancholics don't mix and shouldn't try to. But I could get on with a fine optimistic woman like you. It would cheer me up."

Eleanor could not help feeling cheerful with this strange character; and the interview ended with an appointment for later in the week. He borrowed a friend's car to take her to a friend's flat, and there they satisfied their curiosity about each other. Eleanor would have been disappointed with the interview, however, if he had not done a curious thing at the end. He called a taxi, came to the taxi door with her, and there, with the man looking on, pressed some money into her hand. "That'll cover your expenses, I hope." He looked hard at her. She had laughed and laughed to herself on the way back home. He was a very queer bird: no wonder Janet could not make him out. Eleanor had often thought about him afterwards with an eager excitement—the thought put her into a teasing mood. What harm was there in him? He just needed to be taken for what he was. Later, when she saw Dr. Linda Mack and they talked about Janet, who had recovered and gone to the country, Eleanor said, "I saw Bob Standfast—do you know him?" Dr. Mack had met him and detested him. "Oh," said Eleanor archly, "he's just a twisted boy with a mustache—he told me his mother was very harsh with him and he can't help being harsh with others. He has his gentle side, Linda; it would be foolish of us to lay it all at his door." When Dr. Mack said that Janet could not forgive Bob Standfast, Eleanor said gently, "That is not quite worthy of her, is it?" But after some years Eleanor had forgotten this episode, and it came back to her now only in fragments. She remembered that she had gone on an errand of mercy. Somehow she had found herself having an understanding talk with Bob and she and Bob had gone to an apartment. Was Bob married or not?

Elated that her old admirer remembered her, she wrote to Bob Standfast at UNESCO. They exchanged letters, and in one Bob said, "I remember you promised to give me a call, but you stood me up. That's the way to get remembered. Yours, Bob." Then one afternoon he telephoned her from Paris.

"Hello, this is Bob, Eleanor! What do you want to get a job for? I suppose you want to live in Paris and have UNESCO pay your rent for you, is that it? Like the rest of us?"

"Oh, yes," she said, "but I don't know French, Bob."

"Oh, that's nothing," he said. "If you work in my division, I do—and I've two secretaries that do. The point is you know English. We don't talk French to each other, you know! Besides, a girl like you will pick it up in three months; I remember you, you see, gold medalist and all that! Besides, you're quite a person now, aren't you—best seller? Well, O.K., Eleanor, leave it to me. When will you be in Paris?"

Eleanor started a conversation, but he said he had a train to catch into the country and so they left it there. She said she would be in Paris by the end of the week, if he thought it would be all right. "Leave it to me," said he.

She borrowed money from her brother to go to Paris and stayed with Vina there. She had one interview with Bob, now a plump sparkling man in expensive Paris clothes, suede shoes, a hand-painted silk tie, and with two good-looking young women helping him in a suite of offices. They had books of type before them and were trying to decide what type to use for a quantity of reports from field workers in the depressed countries. They were laughing a good deal before Eleanor entered, but behaved courteously while she was there.

They exchanged a good many "Eleanor"s and "Bob"s and Bob said to her, "But why, Eleanor, should you waste your precious time, if you're a writer, doing this kind of hard work that any

[273]

dry-as-dust like me can do? The salary you get here won't pay your Paris expenses."

"Then why do you work at it?" Eleanor said gaily.

Bob and the two girls laughed, and he said, "Oh, I have a wife to support me." He said he could do nothing for her, but would arrange an interview with a Mr. Wolfering who was the last court of appeal—he hired and fired. "I'll tell Mr. Wolfering everything about you—all you have to do is to appear and shine," said Bob. When Eleanor left the suite, she once more heard the peals of laughter.

After writing several letters, she received an appointment with Mr. Wolfering, who had never heard of her, and told her that he might be able to employ a Persian who knew Persian, a Chinese who knew Chinese, or a Jew who knew Yiddish and Neo-Hebrew, but that he had so many "vaguely endowed English and Americans" that he was going to have to let them out. Mr. Wolfering looked very strange indeed: he had a broad white face, his hair standing on end seemed both dusty and sweaty; and his manner was both sarcastic and troubled. He did not rise from the desk when the interview was so bluffly ended. Eleanor stood and waited. At last he dragged himself from the desk and, step by step, glance by glance, dragged himself to the door. He at length held the door open and let Eleanor go out, with a good-day both insolent and hesitant, while he inspected her worn fur coat. It had been good once; and it was only now that Eleanor realized that "A good fur coat is always good," her mother's maxim, was not always true.

There was nothing for it but to return to London. From there she wrote several letters to Bob, got no reply, and at last wrote him a sharp letter, saying that he had done nothing for her with Mr. Wolfering. When this brought no reply she telephoned him. He was warm, friendly, casual. "Mr. Wolfering is a good man," said he, "but you must know him. Next time you're in Paris, drop in and we'll have a chat. Perhaps your approach was wrong."

Eleanor had wasted money, time; she was almost penniless.

Deborah was looking for a job; her Uncle George had sent money for her clothes but Eleanor had to find all expenses.

She found it eased her to talk her problems over with the children. They were no longer quite children; with one on each side of her she felt as if each was a staff, a warm friend helping her. They saw how she was struggling and had become patient, enduring, uncomplaining.

After bitterly telling the UNESCO story, and even crying in their presence—a thing she tried never to do—she became cheerful again and said, "Why shouldn't I simply put in my time, children, doing my own work? I've got to get down to writing some original stuff—regular hours, long hours, a workmanlike attack—that's the answer for this little family."

She put this into practice. She began a new book, which, oddly enough, was inspired by something the Blackstones had said— something about social medicine and something she had heard in the agency, getting a job in a hospital. She would get a job in a hospital and write about that most useful, most self-sacrificing of all public and private persons—the nurse. She knew that she herself, strong and patient and loving the sick and unfortunate more than the well and wealthy, would have made a good nurse, an excellent matron. She could see it forming in her mind—the hospital, the wards, the nurses, "Doctor said . . ." "Yes, Sister . . ." She wasted no time in daydreaming, but began to sketch out her book, *In the Wards,* and she was rejoiced while writing to think that "books about nurses always went." She put out her hand, dialed Pigsney's number and found Cope out once more, and Bronwyn very worried; tired and bored by an article on juvenile crime she was doing, Eleanor had a long, good heartfelt talk about nurses and hospitals. She heard what Bronwyn had to say about having her baby in hospital; and suddenly recalled that Vina de Saiter was a lifelong invalid, had had countless illnesses and narrow escapes from death—a heroine. But all would be heroes—a book about human heroism, the "little man" and the "ordinary woman": the sufferer, the doctor and the nurse; the relatives, too, of course; the woman who cleaned the wards, the sick people in the office—a wonderful calvary of heroism.

She was enraptured with the idea—a book of her own. Now her troubles began again: hours spent before a few notes on a page, a sentence or two, which at once seemed inept or hackneyed. "I have the idea, I have the desire, I have the strength, and I have written books and it can be done." She set herself squarely before her work and went at it with determination—so in the past she had got through her academic work and won prizes. She sat for set periods: "I won't get up for another hour, for two hours—I'll sit up till twelve, but a page must be done." She recognized in herself an inelasticity; she felt once she had broken it down she would be able to write freely. "I am simply out of training—the house and odd jobs have dissipated my power of concentration; nothing was ever too much for me before." She felt she was tired and disappointed, but she wouldn't be beaten. She wrote to one of her friends and made plans to go away on a walking tour of the southwest of England in the summer—three weeks, a pack on her back, sleeping in country inns, friends' homes, or even barns and haystacks, good serious woman's chat, opinions of life and the world. For she had fine women friends, all gifted, all battlers who had made their way and reached the middle of the road, the middle of life with serenity and common sense.

But she could not get beyond page two and a sterile summary. Cope asked why she did not take her summary with her and try to talk some editor into financing her project. He got on very well with Quaideson, the partner of Ambrose in the firm Ambrose & Quaideson that Eleanor had so often so bitterly attacked when she was working for Rainshelter's. "I hate them, I won't go near them, I wouldn't take their money," she cried out. "I will give you a letter to Ambrose," Cope said.

The publishing house was out in Earls Court in a large, light factory space divided by a few partitions and with light coming from glass slides in the roof. In the largest space sat a number of very poorly dressed girls just out of school, shifting papers, typing and looking in card catalogues. In smaller offices were men with desks, and the first room entered of the same size had a small desk with catalogues and newly printed books on it. Eleanor waited awhile and held her head high as she was led by an office girl in a short-sleeved blouse and a swirling taffeta skirt into the inmost office, the size of a pantry, in which the chief editor and an elderly male assistant sat. All through the interview this assistant, thick, soft and shabby, sat bowed over his desk. Eleanor saw only his back, and yet she sensed that he was listening with a desperate personal feeling. She made her voice clear and cool.

Mr. Ambrose was a youthful middle-aged man, tall, sandy, with a small potbelly. He leaned back in his chair, and though polite, threw distaste into his sharp-edged drawl: "I have here a letter from Mr. Pigsney saying that you can read for us, that you have some editorial experience."

Eleanor put her experience in the best light, mentioning Rainshelter's. "I know Rainshelter's, I was editor of one of their subsidiaries," he said, and his voice went flat, as if he knew the worst.

Eleanor blushed. "Of course I suppose my chief claim is that I myself am an author, and if I may say so, a relatively successful one."

"Oh," said he, looking at her. He found out about her books and then said, "H'm! Ah! Well, as a rule, we don't like to employ authors." After a pause he continued, "We prefer authors to write."

Eleanor thought, Oh, my God, is he going to take the bread out of my mouth because I am an author? She hastened to say, in a very sweet tone, "Oh, my work was done *in collaboration*—I simply softened and rewrote a little a manuscript left me by my father, and I am not sure that my critical faculties don't interfere with the naïve gush that I suppose is so necessary when one is spinning out of one's own guts," and she said the word "guts" with a grating sound to show she was no foolish touchy woman, but as good as a man. "What I really like," she insinuated, smiling slightly, "is to help others to see where they've gone wrong. My experience is that so many have just a touch of—something, something really good; but it is swamped by verbiage, overdone, and concealed by imitations and flowers of speech and such luggage not wanted on the voyage." After a slight laugh and a pause she said savagely, "I love to rip into manuscripts, tear them to pieces, rip out the flummery, show them the top-heavy stuff that simply has got to be jettisoned—show them where their own guts are, and tell them that writing is guts, nothing but guts." Her cheeks were hot, and seeing a more friendly smile on the editor's face, she continued more sweetly, "My aim is creative, but I never lose sight of the publisher's point of view. I consider a writer, once he has written something and offered it for publication, has formed a kind of unwritten pact with the publisher to conform to the rules."

"And have you written anything yourself lately?" said the editor. "Because you had these rather good sales, and of course, we'd like to see anything you have."

Eleanor had the outline of her hospital novel in her bag; but she had not made a move toward it when she thought, If I show it, he'll tell me to go back home and write it—and then, more hopeless struggle without food or fire. She made a pretty little grimace, and said daintily, "Art is long and the gas bill cometh; I want work now." There was a pause, and Eleanor saw the shoulders of the other man listening: his whole body—bowed, sagging, fat, dressed in the poorest clothes—was listening, his head hidden inside the bowed body; she felt he didn't want her, that both men were hostile to her.

Discourteously Mr. Ambrose said, "Well, we haven't much work here; here's a French book we want read."

"I don't read French."

"That's a pity: they send us a lot of French books." He paused and Eleanor's heart began to beat hard; he straightened his back and looked at her out of the corner of his blue eyes and said disagreeably, "Mr. Quaideson wants me to do something for you. I have a book here which was a success in the United States and which we've bought. It's for a certain public, a religious public. It needs rewriting. We have permission to rewrite. Will you rewrite it for four guineas and do it in eight or ten days?"

"Give it to me," said Eleanor. "I'll be glad to do it."

"If you could do it in a week or under—you can cut it, we have permission from the author—it would be convenient. You'll see what's needed: there are passages that won't appeal to English taste; they can be taken out. The principal thing is to cut it from a hundred and twenty thousand words to seventy thousand. I'll show you how to count the words." He began to turn the pages, counting, measuring, scoring through lines. "You can take out all these flashbacks—"

With pleasure Eleanor took it all in and could hardly wait to get the book into her hands. "This is right up my street," she told Mr. Ambrose. When she got up to say good-bye, the other man straightened and looked at her—a man of fifty, with a soft pale face and blue eyes, very fatigued. Mr. Ambrose introduced him, "Mr. Jeepy," who got up, his stringy tie hanging loose in his open collar. His baggy short trousers and cotton shirt were of the poorest materials. On his face was fear; he was the picture of desperate poverty. Eleanor realized that he was afraid she was a protégée of Quaideson, and by doing outside work, might take away his job. She made a slight acknowledgment, pretending to be what he feared.

Eleanor went home in the underground, holding some bags in her hands, but she managed to hug the book to her chest as she jubilated. I'll do such a bang-up job he'll have to give me more work. Four pounds for the job is miserable pay, but I'll surprise him and do it in under a week. I know Ambrose and Quaideson do plenty of this piracy-with-permission, the shameless authors agreeing to be cut up in order to sell. Perhaps I can get regular work at it. Perhaps that's Jeepy's department. Well, I'll put Jeepy out of business: it's him or me. My time's my own, I can put in all the work I like, no one to spy if I work eighteen hours a day—no husband to work for, my children self-sufficient, and I'm strong, willing and able—that's all to my advantage, my blessed advantage.

Nevertheless, it took her eight days, working day and night, without cooking meals or cleaning the house. Every time she cut or rewrote a passage she had to recount her "wordage," for the essential thing was not the sense, since the book made little sense; the essential thing was the number of words. She was aiming not at the expression of a thesis or the resolution of a problem or even the expression of the writer's ideas: she was aiming at seventy thousand words. She achieved this aim. "And a very neat, workmanlike job, too," she said to herself. "In fact, it's better than the original."

The work was done on the American printed book itself, and it was a curious sight when she took it in. She had rewritten in ink, pasted in typed passages, crossed out naïve and crass sentences, changed coarse expressions; but she was businesslike enough to see that one of the appeals of this book was its coarseness. The writer referred to humanity as "the herds of Heaven," and constantly referred to men and women, in all their relations, just as if they had been herds and flocks. Eleanor enjoyed this part of it herself, laughing uproariously when a man was called a steer, a buck, a ram or a bull and a woman a cow or a sow. This repulsively clever trick of the author enabled him to insult native races and minorities with sham innocence—he had white rams and black rams; and with it, he had put in as "facts and true adventures and sights" many suggestive symbols, such as "writhing nests of snakes" and native women wearing "nothing but a single garment," and strange "initiation rites." The book purported to be true adventures and "truly Christian."

Eleanor telephoned Mr. Ambrose and said she thought they ought to have a little conference. When she arrived full of spirits, Mr. Jeepy was sitting at the table, too, with a jacket on and looking better pleased. Eleanor put the scarred and bandaged book on the table and said, "I hope you'll like what I've done. I've been pitiless. In some places I've torn it to shreds and put it together again, better and clearer and more humane and perhaps more Christian. It will appeal here, at any rate, much more. At the same time, I've left the blood and sinew in it, it's very meaty, and has a direct appeal to the senses, as well as the religious feeling. It gives a feeling of crude poetry by forcing lilies out of the human-all-too-human blood and muck and sweat of the humbler sort of Christian; and it appeals to him, too, by not neglecting his animality. Its message is rather all manner of pigs may go to heaven, and I don't think we can quarrel with that, however much we may wish the author had been a little daintier in his language and less offensive to our nostrils. And it's seventy thousand words."

Ambrose, who had let her talk, took the book at this, said, "Good!" After he had looked through it, he said, "Well, I think this is going to be all right. I've talked it over with the accountant and we'll pay you five pounds for this job. You will be like the author and take care of the job up to publication for that sum." Eleanor gladly agreed. They had some discussion and Mr. Ambrose gave her another manuscript which needed rewriting, a very different kind of job; he merely wanted an opinion; the fee would be one guinea. They paid her the five pounds at once. Eleanor was pleased enough, but as she went away, she suddenly felt in her arms, legs, body, the weight of all the work she had done. Even with a regular connection, for it looked like that, how was she to live? She went into a teashop and while having her lunch, a cup of tea and a bun, she drafted, as she had done years before, a literary agent's advertisement, which was subsequently printed in *The Times* and a literary weekly.

Among the first four manuscripts was a good one by a young girl called Mary Darling. Eleanor took it in to Ambrose & Quaideson to sell it to them. Mr. Ambrose said they were not interested in developing writers; they had other business: "We do not want to keep on paying off writers." The accountant came in, a short, muscular, thick-skinned young man of forty with lustful berrylike eyes hidden under his black brows. Eleanor explained about the girl again, a "sure-fire success." When the two men did not show any interest, she asked if she could see Mr. Quaideson.

"Go and see him if he's a friend of yours," Mr. Ambrose said carelessly.

Mr. Quaideson received her in the lounge of a small flat furnished with chairs, rugs, divans and a good many bookcases in wood painted white. Putting down her bag and gloves, sitting upright in a tapestry chair, Eleanor got out the manuscript of *Smokeover Farm,* Mary Darling's novel, and asked if Mr. Quaideson wanted to read it—or would she read some of it to him? She had carefully prepared her speech for Mr. Quaideson.

She said, "I have a very simple suggestion, after speaking to Mr. Ambrose and your accountant, that you go in for young unpublished authors of promise; tie them up with a long contract, which they'll be glad to sign, at reasonably low terms, just in case your judgment has had a blind spot, and then just sit back and let your firm build up its own reputation and bank balance."

Eleanor intended this to be an up-to-date, no-nonsense sales talk. She went on talking and Mr. Quaideson sat back looking at her. Light was filtered through a modern skylight from a terrace above. The old hangings and rugs of the flat made a handsome setting for the fine-looking middle-aged woman. Mr. Quaideson, sitting some distance away, with his legs crossed and out from a polished desk, also looked well in that light. He was a tall, fleshy man wearing a silk shirt and scarf and a dark suit of fine material. He had the complexion of a yellow peach, and a rather ecclesiastical dignity; his hair was thick and pale. He had false teeth with an agate shine, handsome pale-red lips and bloodshot eyes in large eyesockets; the face was long with fine cheekbones.

"Don't read me the prose, Miss Herbert," he said when she had finished. "It may be everything you say, but to me, authors merely produce the raw material for my presses. I have always been sorry that we have not a sort of author-machine: press a button, put in a royalty and get out the kind of syrup you want. Does that shock you very much? I am afraid I think that the life of the palest shopgirl or the barber with the emptiest head is worth all the manuscripts ever written: I am afraid I am simply not interested in writers. I bought up a firm very cheap, just as I might have bought a paint-and-varnish shop. I'm rather sorry I didn't, as a matter of fact—I like paint and varnish. I like ironmongery too; do you? It's quite a passion of mine; and I don't know if you believe in cartomancy—I don't—but a woman wrote me a letter saying that a fortuneteller had said that she should eventually make a match of it with a man who liked ironmongery. I thanked the lady for the offer, but I turned it down. She was not an author—I happened to buy an old brass lantern clock from her. I am very much interested in antiques. I just acquired this old Bible box; picked it up in Woking."

Eleanor folded up the manuscript and put it in her bag. Mr. Quaideson, while chattering about his antiques, was watching her with interest; and then said, "What are you going to do now?"

Eleanor told him that she was going to offer the book to several other firms, and that she had decided (on the spur of the moment, but she did not say that) to offer her services with it, as a condition. If she was accepted, she would quit A. & Q's. She rose and went to the door before he could get up.

"My dear Miss Herbert," he said starting from his desk. "Come back! Come back!" She stood with her hand on the door, looking at him proudly; then she returned slowly. "What is the matter? Why do you take such an interest in this young author? It is Miss Herbert, isn't it? Or is it Mrs.? You're not an agent, are you? You're quite new to all of this, aren't you? You see, I am very little of a publisher, also. So sit down, take off your furs, I'll make some tea and we can talk about ourselves—that will be more interesting. I am quite serious when I say that your life or my life as we have lived it is worth more than ten thousand *Smokeover Farms* even if it's all you say it is. I've always had a tremendous craving for life and I'm always irritated with books, they are so far from it. And the only time I am not irritated," he said, with a charming flash of teeth, "is when I am working on my own manuscripts—for I have what is best of all, unpublished manuscripts of my own. That is why, I think, that published books irritate me so much: they are so confident, glossy, hard-faced, pushing. To me, all the juice of the book is in an unpublished manuscript, and the published book is like a dead tree—just good for cutting up and building your house with. Now tell me why you are so anxious to see this book published."

"I must live."

"Ah! You're a widow?"

For the first time in her life Eleanor broke down with a stranger. She suddenly put her hands to her face and with a sob said, "My husband left me. I never thought he would—he had no reason to."

Mr. Quaideson's face brightened and softened. He lost his teasing and callous expression. With a mocking smile, he offered to take *Smokeover Farm* if she wished him to, but said she would do better with a fiction house. "We like curiosities, topicalities—we are more like a newspaper than a book publisher's. It's quite a good idea, and always a paying idea. Authors are a nuisance to us. You peddle your authors elsewhere, my dear Miss Herbert; let us have the benefit of your help and advice, and let us remain friends, but I mean personal friends." He drew his chair beside hers, bathed her in the full light of his smile and glistening eyes and said, "But you yourself must have a story worth anything ever written; I can feel a special flavor in you; I know it would make a story. Did you yourself ever try to write it? For instance, how does it happen that a woman like yourself—a fine-looking and, I can tell, aware, sensually aware, woman, aware of the sensual values—is living alone? You are not the kind of woman who lives alone—your children, your children!" He leaned closer to her, his large face coming nearer to her large breasts. "A woman living with her children is indeed living alone!" When she got up he put a fleshy arm around her shoulders and "propelled" her toward another room. "Come with me, my dear Miss Herbert. I want to see how you react to some of my antiques. I have choice, curious things; I like age, but quality, and I prefer things with strange associations. Do you believe that an idol which has seen many sacrifices is impregnated with the smoke of the burning blood and just as much with the mystic adoration, the mental fumes, steeped in thousands of past lives in dead history? Do you believe you can tell by *feeling* that a rope has taken a man's life? I believe that blood has a voice; the worm has a voice that we can hear if we try, so Blake suggests; and the blood of torment has a voice. Otherwise sacrifice is aimless, the realists win and the rest of us may as well cut our throats."

He had now taken her into an inner room in which she expected to find a bed or divan. But there was none there. There were several cabinets, showcases, a prie-dieu, some masks on the wall (one of those being the mask of an ancient tribal god, so he said), in the drawers of the cabinet some spiced silks once worn by a mandarin who had been murdered, the wrappings from a mummy, poison rings, a photograph of the Paris executioner and his family; and such things. He remarked, "I can imagine many uses in the old days for this prie-dieu: the little maid in the cold garret is saying her ignorant foolish prayers, the master himself comes up to find out whether the maid shouldn't be warmer. Why should he take her away from her prayers?" Mr. Quaideson at first had to emphasize his theme and make his meanings clearer, for Eleanor found antiques distressingly dull, but soon she began to apprehend him, and she smiled in a warm, friendly and almost maternal way; and then she became a little excited.

She laughed and put her hand on his arm. "I see that here you have just the stage props for a book that is being written!"

"Oh, no," he said, "these give life to me. You've no idea how much truer that is. It's the life that's seeped into these things and dried into them that I can imbibe. The other side of dried-in cruelty is love. As a sour grape, dried, is sweeter than sugar."

Such talk, which had never before been addressed to her, enchanted Eleanor; and seeing she was so innocently charmed, Mr. Quaideson showed her a pillory in ivory, a full-size bloodstained whipping post for slaves, a silken swing from a brothel and a curious screen. And then he made her tea. He proposed to take *Smokeover Farm* into his firm to please her, but she at once drew up, faced him earnestly and said, No, she must do her best for her writers. She must find a sedate firm run on classic lines which was interested in starting young writers and keeping them till they were old.

Mr. Quaideson laughed negligently. "That does not sound like me." And they dropped the subject. Eleanor was disappointed. However, she sat through tea, making literary conversation, until Mr. Quaideson touched her on the arm and said, "Well, if that is the way you look at manuscripts, I think I might trust mine with you. Take this home and give me a report exactly as if I were one of your authors. Count me one of your authors. But I must warn you, as a publisher-author—that his bashfulness makes the most modest violet look like a brash peony—a publisher-author's skin is tenderer than any. Spare my feelings. Make it gentle. I'll believe every word you write." He confessed that he had thought of submitting his MS. to *Marco Marvel,* which published horror stories. "But I never had the courage of the most draggle-tailed typist writing her life out to get from behind the desk and be a Writer"; and with many more such remarks he whiled away the afternoon.

However, at the end of it, when a red and yellow sun-spoke shot through the rim of one of his windows, it fell like drops of hot water on the opened pages of his manuscript—a book entitled "The New Curiosity Shop." What Eleanor read there embarrassed her, brought her into a soft general state of excitement, and gave her the sort of alert admiration you have for someone who admires you.

"I have a house down in the country I'd like you to visit," said Mr. Quaideson. "Come soon, and you'll see the trees—I have flowering cherries and producing cherries and apples and plums; come later, you'll see the lilacs or the rhododendrons. I have an oddity for housekeeper. You'd like to see the very special section of my library where my whips hang. As I'm thin-skinned and cowardly, I'm very much interested in cruelty: I have a library of cruelty. Do you know how many ways death has been devised, and how they have schemed to have pain defeat time? No, of course not. But I think we liberal souls turn our eyes from the nasty and painful; I think we should steel ourselves to look it in the face. Where will it get us? That is another question . . . If you'd care to come sometime, I'll arrange it with my housekeeper. Perhaps you can help me too—to give life to old instruments."

Eleanor, without being able to listen to or comprehend all this, had her usual timid resistance and hastily said that she saw little of her children during the week; they expected their Mummy to be with them during the weekends. "I don't want to encourage them to look for love in other homes just yet." She described them— Deborah as a very nervous girl, handsome but distrustful, who went in and out of love affairs as if treading a complicated figure in a country dance. "She is irritable when she's in love and mournful when she's out, reaching a sort of desperation as time goes on which can only be solved one way, I'm afraid," she said; with a slight smile, murmuring, "That is by putting her arms round Mummy and asking Mummy if she knows what it feels like." She could not desert the children now—they had been "hurted" enough by life. Russell, between sixteen and seventeen, was a sweet, obedient, mild boy, absorbed in his friend "The Rev." Jonas, a boy with tirades on all subjects, and in his mother and sister. They had talked over ways and means and decided to make what sacrifices were necessary to give Russell a scientific training so that he could be at least a laboratory assistant—he would then be excused from military training. He was not particularly interested in science, but "The Rev." was, and that was enough for Russell.

Eleanor talked on and on about her children, foolishly maternal, in a warm, affected, oily voice; and she herself, in her elastic maternal roundness was full of sweet affectation, gestures and words worn to a dull luster by use. It seemed soft and natural. She began to talk freely as if to an old friend. Mr. Quaideson did not repeat then or at any other time the invitation to his orchard, but as they sat there in the dimly lighted, darkly furnished flat their two large masses took on supple outlines. They sat as the obese sat, firmly, but their outlines softened sensually toward each other. When Mr. Quaideson took her to the door, he passed his hand over her upper arms and broad back and said, "A real woman's back, what fine firm arms!"

"I need them," said Eleanor.

The story of "The New Curiosity Shop" was about a man who sat all day long among his curios and became enamored of a woman client, elegant, enigmatic, and perhaps dissipated. He courted her, fitting out an apartment for her with a prie-dieu and many other curious things Eleanor had seen. The woman never saw the flat, but in the shopkeeper's fantasy it was because she had died. Once, after she had "died," he saw her in the street. He then tried to lure her to the shop to kill her. The story had a lingering sensuality and sudden whiplashes of unseemly horror. It was not anything that Eleanor could deal with, but she bravely read through it and wrote a long report on it. Quaideson thanked her, but never mentioned it again and never paid her for it as he had promised.

Nevertheless they continued friends, and Eleanor continued to get work from A. & Q.'s. She went in with the work whenever it was ready or whenever she was summoned, and as a rule, paid one visit a week, in the afternoon, to Quaideson's rooms over the antiques shop in which he had a partnership. They had very soon become lovers of a strange sort, not of a sort she had ever known before; but this affair of "classic poses" and "love portraits" as he called them, were restful to her—she found them curious and amusing. She never quite understood "Geoff," and he was always able to interest and surprise her. She felt that for the first time she was beginning to understand "mature sex." She liked to stand exposing her smooth, powerful body in the quiet old rooms in some noble or perverse pose; she felt perfectly feminine. Mr. Quaideson had explained to her in the beginning that love and pleasure were best in the imagination: nothing can disguise the crudity of ordinary sexual love! "I found it offensive though at one time essential;

but I trained myself away from it and very soon was able to make it lovely through the obscure senses."

Eleanor's life was now tranquil; she was happy. A publisher had taken *Smokeover Farm,* and after its success her literary agency business had increased so much that she employed a secretary several days a week. She hoped soon to use one of her rooms in her flat for an office. Deborah at twenty was working in an office and earning so much money that she could pay her mother's rent and bank money as well. Poor Russell had turned out to be tubercular: there was no question of the army for him, and he had been invited by his grandparents to stay in Switzerland, where they would provide for him until he could provide for himself. Deborah was businesslike though somewhat reticent, and "with moods of rain and shine," which made Eleanor twitter a little asking, "Are you getting ready to leave me, my darling? Have you met the right man?" Deborah would reply firmly, "I'll never marry till you're married, Mother! I won't leave you alone. You're my responsibility." Sometimes, when Eleanor was praising Mr. Quaideson, repeating his opinions, with "Geoff told me," and "Geoff says," Deborah would say impatiently, "Oh, Mother, why don't you marry Mr. Quaideson and have done with it? I wouldn't mind. Don't you realize I can't marry till I've got you off?"

Eleanor would reply with false simplicity, "Geoff and I, dear, are just friends—very good, very dear, very sincere friends; but it's a middle-aged comfortable friendship with no future and no strings attached; and you must remember, my pet, that Mr. Quaideson is over seventy, and Mummy, though she is forty-five to the world, is, according to the registrar and to Father Time, really fifty-five. People simply don't marry at fifty-five. So you must go a-Maying, it's your age—and you must marry, pretty maid. Mother will be able to manage quite well: she has so far."

Eleanor kept up a busy, cheerful correspondence with all the authors who wrote to her or passed through her hands. She did them favors if she could, apart from her fees, offered them work, asked after their families (though authors don't care much for that), wrote long, kindly phrased criticisms of any manuscript, was playfully modest, deliberately humdrum, "for I never compete with my authors by *languaging,* when I am an editor." Some of these authors, after telling her all their troubles, misfortunes, the injustice done by others to them, proved ungrateful, restive beasts who got away from her and resented the fees they had to pay her; her quaint and kind remarks insulted them. One stopped answering her letters; another was enraged at her remarks about a coal-mining novel—"What do you know about it?" Another drew away because she advised him to take politics out of his novel, although she used exactly the terms she and Geoffrey used in conversation: "We ought not perhaps to make a cocktail of the ephemeral and the basic eternal: how dead old novels seem which concerned themselves with topicalities! And besides, it does set editors against you if they're not of your stripe—unfair of course, but human-all-too-human. We all have our pet corns."

One of her satisfactory authors was Mary Darling, who had sold her third novel and had just signed another good contract for seven more novels, with Rainshelter's, a most unusual affair, but which meant to Eleanor that her ten percents were safe for some time to come, and an easily earned ten percent, too—the author sold herself and made up for the "rough patches" and "disobedient ungrateful children." Another was Huie Dele Casterbridge, an author of several small books about landscape painting and aesthetic pilgrimages, with whom she had been in correspondence for nearly two years. He wished to write a "real novel." He had an income, lived on a small modern farm in Scotland. He sent her portions of a manuscript always conscientiously, painfully re-worked and retyped. They had written to each other about farming, and even about Mendel and Darwin. Eleanor knew little about the subject but could write glibly; and she knew the names of Huie's dogs, and pigs and pigeons ("Pigs are very intelligent, they know their names"), and that he had just installed a stove which heated the house centrally and an immersion heater. She knew how the big fireplace was arranged; he had sent her his mother's "old-fashioned recipe for giblet pie," and described his visit to the weekly market in the nearby town—"I'm sure you're an expert at picking up things in weekly markets."

She said of him in her report to Orchard's, a large fiction firm: "This novel is without beginning or end and with splotches of Walter Scott that must certainly come out; or at least, we must clean up the heavy old canvas; and yet he has a kind of intuition of genius and we must put our foot down firmly there, or it will ruin his talent. His characters do not quite come alive, but they retain our interest; but at the end of it we have, I am afraid, a lucubration, he lets himself go, very grand indeed, but which will simply have to come out. However, this author is a lamb, and that is a virtue for which I would trade in many more literary ones."

Huie was enchanted with all she did for him. He knew she worked very hard and was in poor circumstances—he invited her to take her holiday with Deborah at The Bents, his farm. Then they would work together on his novel, as she had suggested, but only if she wanted to. They had already a scheme, a plot, "a likable hero, boy meeting girl early in the day," and he had managed the heroine according to Eleanor's recipe, "someone the male reader at least wants to get into bed with." He had "tightened the writing, casting out superfluous adjectives."

This had been one of Eleanor's most pleasant jobs. She was still working very hard, for she spared herself nothing, reading far into the night, or sitting up all night preparing her correspondence for her secretary. She wrote to Huie, "I luxuriate in work. I glory in all my free time which is putting me so far ahead of the clock-watchers, and I don't regret the guts I put into my job. My agency is not a sub-post-office like most of them." Her coarseness toward Huie seemed to her salutary sternness, she had the fun of putting a man on his feet, leading him, giving him hope and joy. So they wrote and wrote, and a few months before Geoffrey Quaideson's retirement, Orchard's had accepted Huie's novel *Touchdown*, "now a competent job with recognizable people and the author has revealed a natural gift for communication." But Huie wrote to her,

"You are really my collaborator and your name is going to appear on the title page; you are not getting ten percent but fifty, for that is what I owe you and more."

Huie had written to her that as soon as he could leave the farm, he was coming to London to meet her, to celebrate and to "make their pen friendship flesh and blood." The editor signed the contract and sent him the money—only a small advance—because Orchard's were niggardly, but for Huie it was a "very great day." No sooner had he got the money than he telegraphed Eleanor that he was on his way to meet her. He booked at a hotel quite near her that she had recommended, and within a few days she "found him on her doorstep." He had driven down in his small car and was "bursting with plans, for both of us."

Eleanor had long ago given him some idea of how she lived. He took her to the theater, to dinner; he excused himself for not dancing—"I can only do the Highland fling!" He was sturdy, square-headed with black-gray wavy hair, about fifty, of a rosy-brown complexion with friendly dark eyes; he talked and smiled eagerly, gestured, had plenty to say and was lively—he would walk up and down thrusting his hands into his pockets, turning to her, thrusting with one shoulder. They seemed to be very old friends. He sat by Eleanor like a schoolboy as she explained things to him, showed him various letters and manuscripts; he saved her from answering a peculiar letter she had received which touched her but which he found "dangerous and filthy." The letter, addressed to her, said, in part:

Dear Miss Herbert: You are well off, you sit there
in comfort, enjoying your fame
and money and do not think that right near you, almost in the next street, perhaps, are people like myself who would be glad of only a little bit of what you have, the very smallest coin in your purse might mean for them something they need badly, and which is necessary for life itself. You cannot imagine such a condition; you are a lady, you have a fine home and rich

friends; how could I ever make you understand? (And so forth).

Eleanor had already started a letter to this beggar, explaining her poverty and asking for details of his troubles so that she could help "if it were, I mean this literally, possible." Huie, as she told Deborah, "tore up both letters and lectured me severely on answering begging letters."

She was very happy while Huie was in town and promised to think over the summer holiday.

"I want to be frank with you. I don't want you to come up there without knowing what is in my mind," he said. "My idea was, if we hit it off, that we might become real partners—" He looked at her with meaning, then added, "But it is not fair to ask you till you have seen my farm, my home, what other work I have done and so on. You've got a full life of your own here."

Eleanor thought it quaint that Huie should want her to go into farming with him, and she was a little curious about his way of speaking. He could not be thinking of—? She was not at all ready to quit London, which had been her whole life and where she had all her contacts. She told Huie they would wait for everything else till the summer. When she left him at the train, he kissed her. She turned away so that the queer flashing grin of joy disfiguring her face would not be seen by him. "He loves me!" For a few minutes she lived automatically, smiling and waving; she returned to normal, but in the evening and that night, for the first time for many years, perhaps, she felt a normal feeling of love for a man. It was not love, she knew: it was a physical answer. She saw to it that her letters showed no change.

At the end of June she received his formal invitation to the farm, "with Deborah and Russell, I want them too."

But by this time Geoffrey Quaideson had begun the long decline which ended in his death, and Eleanor spent much more time with him. She told Huie that she had promised to go on a walking tour with Mary Darling, and had to put it off for "private domestic reasons." She received an anxious letter from him and answered that "there was illness in the family." She might come later, she needed rest; she had been shocked by unpleasant news, the illness of someone dear to her. "Is it a man?" Huie wrote. She did not reply.

He telegraphed saying that he was making a quick trip to London and would call upon her. He called in one sunny afternoon about three. She was dressed in her old tweed suit, which had been sent to her by her mother-in-law and had already served five years. With it she wore a black-and-white striped blouse a cousin had given her, her walking shoes and some very cheap rayon stockings that had lain in her drawer for several years and that dated from the days she had meant to work as a charwoman. Her thick hair was brushed back into a low knob; she wore no make-up and she showed him no charm—she had wanted to work all the afternoon.

"Well, Huie, my dear, you're becoming a gadabout. I'll make some tea and then tell me your news and then I must get down to work. All I have is what I earn."

She felt Huie was intrusive. She had a pile of manuscripts two feet high on her desk and they called her; she still had an eager, almost lecherous interest in the next book, the next author. Besides, she wanted to think about Geoffrey and her life with him; many of the things he had said casually were precious to her, she repeated them to herself. He was the only man who had ever understood her, and appreciated her, "in every intimate nook and cranny of me, body and soul." Her life had sunk into a routine of hard work and the long languorous communion with Quaideson. She was sinking back easefully after the "years of the terrible Christmases," just before and when she first knew Quaideson.

She had been almost penniless, having only the money she had made during the Christmas rush, in a toy department or bookstore, and would have had no Christmas dinner but for the eggs and chickens sent by her brother. To these black Christmases she had invited the poorest of all the people she knew: the Blackstones, or another pair of struggling writers who belonged to Cope's team.

Everyone gave presents at these Christmases, and wine was drunk and cake eaten and the rooms were warm. But the rest of the cold season was spent facing fear of hunger and dispossession, and illness, in her freezing flat. Every year during these bad years she and the children were ill all through the winter, sometimes dangerously ill. No one, except Cope perhaps, had ever known about her misery, and Cope had done his best for her. When, the first year after she met Quaideson, A. & Q. gave her a contract, making her a kind of outside editor, she realized that she had a very tender feeling for "G.Q." even if she did not love him. A few months later, in the spring, one day when she came in with her hair freshly washed, pink-cheeked and happy, "when I felt very lovely, some boy and girl kisses were indulged in." Early the next morning the thought of those kisses between a man of seventy and a woman of fifty, made her spring from bed as fresh as a girl, pink, soft-eyed, with a curving smile, and she went hallooing down the house, rousing the children, driving them on to breakfast and work—"Oh, I am twice the woman I was, when I have a man." She drew closer to him during the year in respect and a tenderness that seemed to grow quite apart from their rendezvous in his little flat. After a time they had begun to go out to dinner and he would talk about his views, his own work, his hopes. He had, besides his manuscript, a mass of written stuff which referred to "very curious adventures of the human soul, mind, spirit, heart, call it what you like." They might do something with it together.

"I had an idea in collecting all this material," he told her. "I want to leave nothing behind me beside the not very proud name of A. & Q. What if a cheeky young bounder comes along and makes it into another Rainshelter's." They smiled with the same scorn and touched hands lightly. "But I would like to make my contribution to the *curiosa* of this life, a territory which burns with the heath fires, the pure fire of original creation, sacred to Pan and Priapus."

Eleanor sparkled and turned red and white at this academic talk: it was many years since any man had spoken to her of "the grand rites of paganism, and the mysterious fires of tabu."

This clear-voiced strange old man who held her living in his pocket enfolded her with an idea of happiness and safety. They could have married, and at one moment she thought he meant to marry her.

Though she still had phone talks with Cope almost every day when he was in town, she had become very critical, had almost freed herself from him. Once, when she was sitting with Geoff in one of his favorite "wine lodges," he said to her confidentially, "Do you think your friend Cope Pigsney would make a good editor?"

She concealed her mortal fright with a severe simper, played with the stem of her glass and at last said, "I should think he might be, and I suppose the only reason he hasn't been taken in is his radical past. He regrets it himself, but people feel they never can quite trust a man who has worn a red flag on his sleeve the way Cope did with *Seeds of Time*. A very bad novel, besides, but then works of propaganda must be."

"I thought," said Quaideson, teasing in a manner that made her sick with anxiety, "that Cope was a very good friend of yours —that is why I asked you."

"I'm afraid Cope and I never did get together on fundamentals."

Quaideson relieved her by saying, "Radicalism is a youthful sickness of many writers; they are all square pegs in round holes and love to rebel against something. One expects them to grow up as the sensual field and their sensuality develops; but the queer thing about writers is that most of them remain perpetually young. They remain outside life. It's very important for a writer to love something practical, to bring him into life, even if it's only his neighbor's wife, or cats or money, particularly money. It's just too bad if he falls in love with being misunderstood; it's just another way of putting your head in a handwoven noose, or art for art's sake. I think I am a little of a dabbler in the arts. I belong to them by impressionability, and in that I'm eternally young too. But it is really, for me, just another form of illness, which we'd be well rid of. I'd so like to be a husky, strong man with a thick skin and a good laugh that would make people turn in the streets. What do I look like, I ask myself: an intellectual. There's no mistaking the lineaments of unsatisfied desire. All writers look as if they had stepmothers. The artist always has an expression of unsatisfied desire," he said, spittling slightly, "no matter how many women he —" and here, with an odious expression of joy, he used a vile word.

Eleanor said, "He shacks up with."

"I'm afraid I haven't yet been able to use that quite revolting American expression."

To Eleanor all such conversations were a true delight. His phrases stuck in her memory, and smiling and wriggling she would use them afterwards in conferences and with literary people, very often acknowledging their origin by saying, "As Geoff says."

Geoffrey began to be very ill. She saw him for the first time in bed, although he detested bed and would sit up in a wing chair with gowns and blankets on, and tell her about himself. She was strong and tender, a natural nurse; and now her affection became deep, sincere, and her voice took on quite another tone when she spoke of him. She no longer thought about marrying him: her sentiment enfolded him like a soft blanket to keep off the chills and aches; her part was to enfold him.

To begin with, he was a poor sleeper and he had several times said, "I wake in the night, I get up, read, make myself tea (I don't like to drink by myself in the middle of the night), I fix the blankets and my pillows, I take a sleeping pill, rub salve into my aching neck and I use every device I've ever thought up for going to sleep. I remember conversations, try to remember the incidents of the *Three Sisters* or *War and Peace*—a pretty difficult feat, I can tell you—and if that fails, I know I'm in for it. Then, my dear, if only I had you to talk to, I would be well: an hour or two of your calming presence and I'd go to sleep. We must be opposite types, you have such a good effect on me. You restore the tonus. And then you know, apart from your being a charming woman and a sympathetic friend, what appeals to me, if I may say so, is your wonderful strength. You must have been an athlete; you remind me of an old picture I saw, for some reason I can't imagine, in a book of curiosities, 'The Spanish Beauty.' What power and grace . . ." As this was said in a quiet, thoughtful, dreamy tone, Eleanor was pleased and neither giggled nor felt coquettish—she knew she was admired for what was best, for her own sort of woman. He did not make her think but induced in her a purely physical dream, empty, healthy. In a dreamy and languid tone, he would go on to ask about her championships, the roles she had taken in amateur theater. He looked at her admiringly, would say, "I can just see you as Hippolyta, as Boadicea. If you'd been at the court of Louis the Fifteenth or Sixteenth you would have had your own sort of pleasures. I regret, too, I was not alive then." He would go on to tell her of the pleasures the courtiers had. They might dress up as stags and does and act the part at mating time. There were always two parts to their history. "If they played at milkmaids and farmhands, they also imitated the love life of the farm."

He began to take up too much of her night hours; but the next day she would swab up her desk with a "work, work, my dear."

Without having any feeling for Geoff's curious prints and books, she had now quite got the hang of them and had worked through his catalogue with him. He had many times said he would like her opinion on this and that. "This must be left to some intelligent, sympathetic editor," he had several times said. "Catalogue or no, I don't know what's in my files or these stacks of manuscripts: in the basement are at least four trunks of drawings, some of which are valuable. Someone must take care of them; and, of course, it is not the kind of thing one leaves to one's children —even if they are grown up and married. I shall never forget the fate of poor Richard Burton in the hands of Lady Burton; and of all the men, writers, statesmen and just plain individuals like myself with natural curiosity, when their estates got into the hands of their sons, daughters and lady wives."

"Surely it's utterly wrong to destroy a man's literary estate,"

Eleanor exclaimed, though she felt uneasy. "But of course, one can understand the position of those wives and daughters. What were they to do? Couple infamy with one's father's name; show that one's husband had a mistress or two?"

"Yes, indeed; that is why, though I except the word 'infamy'—"

"And I withdraw it—"

"That is why one needs a friend, not too involved, who can stand aside and see what has to be dealt with and doesn't want to lay his own hands on the collections . . ."

"It's a very delicate problem."

They both agreed that there was a strong case for the friendly editor. "Supposing a manuscript of the very highest literary value was left, an acquisition to the literature of the nation and this manuscript was marred by coarse sexual digressions or it advocated anarchism or communism, wouldn't we be perfectly right in editing out the excrescences?" Eleanor said. "I would do it without hesitation out of respect and reverence for the author's wrong-headed genius."

"Ah, yes, but here we have a quite acceptable thing, for the things that are tabu are always accepted as part of society, like the dark of the moon . . ."

In his house or in the office at quiet times they talked about his literary estate, and the part that Eleanor could play.

It was at this moment that Huie sent her a short letter.

Dear Eleanor: I didn't get any reply to my last
                letter, which I know is very unusual
with you; and I feel you must be too busy in some direction
to have time for me. Well, to be frank, I had hoped you would
have time for me always; by that I mean, I have been wanting
to ask you to be my wife; and what gave me the hope was, I
expect, that I love you and hoped that you might get to be
quite fond of me. We seemed to be such friends and I thought
more. Will you marry me? Perhaps you don't like the farm:

we might be able to arrange something, when the books begin to sell. My dear, dear Eleanor: how happy you can make me.

Huie Casterbridge.

Eleanor showed the letter to Quaideson, who said, "Why don't you accept him?"

Eleanor at once wrote saying that she was afraid her marrying days were over, that she still felt the responsibility of her little family, that recently she had had news of her former husband that had revived too many distressing memories and that, "perhaps it is that I am not in a marrying mood."

Quaideson never mentioned the matter again; but to Cope and others she explained that "a farmer had asked her to marry him, and she would have relished filling her lungs with good fresh air for a month, but that she could hardly give up her London days and nights and count sows' litters."

She dismissed the offer with scarcely a thought then, and some months later, when she realized that she might have been married, a wife, with a new domestic routine and a connubial life, she trembled as if before a horrid mystery—she felt as if she had escaped carrying a wearisome burden for the rest of her life.

One day she noticed that a remarkably horrible ivory had disappeared from Quaideson's wall—a reproduction of a French church monument, a corpse in the tomb with worms writhing on it. Quaideson at first sulkily and then insolently repeated that he had sold it: "Why leave it to the Boeotians to destroy or hide?" Other pieces were soon sold; and before he retired to his country house, all that was valuable was sold. He showed her his will. The "four trunks in the cellar" he left to a nephew, and the money he had recently acquired through these sales went to a seventeen-year-old niece, a foolish creature, so he had always said. Eleanor herself received nothing and had no interest in what was left of the "literary estate." Nevertheless she took it with a good grace, attributing his unkindness to his illness and his "incurable whimsy."

Two years after his retirement, he died. She wrote to some of her correspondents that she had just lost a dear, good friend, one who was very near to her; and then she was silent about him and "laid him away in rose-leaves with the greater and best part of my life." He had filled her life with a tranquil passion just when life was saddest.

Meantime Deborah had been living with her in the roomy flat and they had often discussed getting a lodger. Deborah was against it. "You've always given us a real home, Mummy, without strangers; we've always managed; and now I'm earning, we don't want someone tramping in all hours and listening to what we say. I want a real home to bring a boy to, when I bring him to meet my Mummy."

The question of the lodger was shelved—"until you marry, my pet, and Mother needs the lodger to keep her."

"Mother, why didn't you marry Huie or Geoffrey—well, Geoffrey's too ill—but why don't you marry someone?"

"When you're my age, darling, you'll understand that everything has a time and place and women my age are glad to have had their marriage and their children, and their happiness is in just being themselves, and, of course, seeing that their dear ones are happy. What better thing could I have than just looking at you, seeing you're in good healthy animal spirits, doing a good job and realize that somehow I've turned out an excellent daughter!"

But Deborah was not in good spirits, as she knew. For some time she had been nervous, "alternately purring and slinking darkly about," which indicated that "she had a man on her mind." Eleanor, irritated by some long silence at the dinner table, twitted her and told her to "come out with it. It won't improve with keeping, you know."

Deborah then told her simply and like a grown woman that she had met a man she was mad about but did not quite understand. "I think we're going to get married and yet he worries me. I don't know what's wrong: am I wrong or is he, or is it just that I've never been going to get married before? I don't feel that I'll be happy with him; but I don't want to miss this chance, if he is the right man. You had such bad luck with Daddy and it wasn't your fault—you just married the wrong man. I really want you to look at him, I suppose, and tell me what you think. And then, I suppose, I won't take your opinion. I don't want him to know he's being looked at, either."

The man, Paul Waters, was older than Deborah. He was thirty-five, while she was just over twenty-two. Presently Deborah invited her mother to a performance of *La Forza del Destino*. (For some reason Eleanor always called it *La Sforza del Destino*.) Some of Deborah's friends were music students, actors and radio performers; they were all going to see a young conductor who was one of theirs. Eleanor was wearing a dress she had made "for the occasion of being a possible mother-in-law," a beige material printed with small brown and golden twigs, which she thought went with her "smooth, golden skin and hair the color of chestnut buds." She looked at herself with gratification in the pier glass before she put the finishing touches to her make-up. She was excited at her new role; she thought her dress, "softly draped around bust and hips, with a side panel giving a floating movement," not only flattering, but exactly fitting to the occasion and her new position.

"I do look the understanding mother-in-law," she said to Deborah. "I make a decorative background. The foreground, my pet, belongs to you."

It was a warm autumn evening with delicate air; if not for the look of the leaves, one would have expected to see cherry blossoms out. They drove to the hall, an ample hall with glass walls, staircases and foyers and balconies over the river. They stood about near a large mirror, rather impatiently looking for friends who had not turned up—time was getting on; Paul Waters, too, was not there. Eleanor had brought her glasses to read the program, but she would not wear them yet; she wanted Mr. Waters to see her at her best. She was too excited, she knew she was being foolish, but she could not help making bright little remarks to Deborah's friends.

She knew some of them from Deb's schooldays, anyway, and had entertained them at "gay little bread-and-butter parties," which had cost her a great deal of effort, thought and more than she could afford, but which had been a great success. There they were now, grown up, like Deb; one girl was going to Oxford now, one was working in an orchestra. They were polite to her but they did not seem much interested in Paul Waters. Suddenly one said to her, "He's too old for Deb; he's thirty-five or six."

Just then, another said coldly, "There he is!" She saw a tall man swinging round toward them, his nose in the air, looking. His thick chestnut hair was a neat metallic crest, his bronze face was metallic too; he walked like those who spend an hour or two daily in gymnastics, he had a fine athletic bachelor air. He held his face upwards as if to catch the air, he walked so fast his coat opened and the dark red scarf around his throat flew out behind. Eleanor looked at him intently, though not knowing this was the man; all other things were still or faintly moving. It was like standing looking at a landscape when one still tree all at once moves—a branch and then all its limbs. This strange man whom she did not know yet to be Paul Waters came toward them and looked straight into Eleanor's eyes with the glance of a man who understands a woman wants him and who gives himself and means to take all, a dark look that existed long before language. Eleanor looked away, to hide it from the others. They were introduced and smiled like people who had been introduced years before and had flirted and were now hiding their acquaintance. Then they went up the steps of the hall to find their seats. Eleanor looked at his face with wonder, but she avoided his eyes. His face was of that harmony and regularity which gives lifelong beauty, and the eyes apart, had a great sweetness; and yet the sweetness seemed only part of the wonderful mask, for his eyes were not sweet, but dark, veiled, profound, disturbed. He stood up above them, looking round calmly, though he was in the aisle, holding people up. Then he sat down at the end of the row, next to her daughter and one place away from her. While he affected to look away and look at his program, she studied his profile, dark, rather fleshy. There was a swarthiness about him that she considered foreign; his beauty too, fleshy and proud, did not look English. Suddenly Waters looked straight at her and smiled: the smile of smiles! She gave him one of her society smirks and looked coquettishly away; but she did not feel like flirting. Her heart had begun a great circular thrumming, so it felt. Round and round it gadded, making larger swoops, and her head turned, making larger swoops, as if she were floating, with her large body, round the great dome. Her heart began pounding out hard and real thoughts, like pieces of metal, too; and she heard them, forceful, unanswerable: This is love and he knows it; it would be too strong for me, my life would be carried away into a whirlpool, round and round and down, in the center, lost and gone; I wouldn't want to get out of it, I would lose myself; I'd be swept away; I don't want that. I couldn't live, then all would mean nothing. I can't live like that; what of the past and future? There'd be no meaning to the world or time, but this hour and the future hours with him would break into everything, flooding everything, everything would be washed away: I couldn't stand it, I'm not strong enough, I'm too old to go in for it—

Meantime the people had settled, the music had begun and Eleanor, who was somewhat musical, began to be ordered by and drawn into the music. What a terrible, powerful beat the music had, threatening and promising sullenly, something tremendous, nothing good. In it was a life Eleanor had never known, and which frightened her, but now, for the first time, attracted her—a great potency, passion, which she had been always unconscious of; some great thing approached her and for the first time spoke to her, as if a new world came somewhere near her world and she felt its attraction and feared to be pulled away off the earth, out of life.

When the overture ceased, she looked round at the warm masks, turned toward the footlights. She smiled, tapped her daughter's hand to show all was quite normal, she nodded nicely to show she approved of Paul Waters. But she did not; she felt it was hopeless for Deborah to fall in love with such a man; it was all too great for Deborah—or could they love? A pain struck her full in the breast and she thought, Oh, save me from being jealous of a younger woman; I could not stand it, I'd take poison. I must never see him again, that's certain. I'll tell her I don't like him, I'll influence her as I know how. Then she'll see him in secret, they'll become lovers— Music and drama was going on before her; she took part in it, too, but while sometimes in the dark she smiled with intense joy, and clasped her hands at her success at such unexpected romance, at other times she heard nothing but her warning menacing heart, thudding out the news of her gloomy future.

I will not and I cannot, she said to herself.

During the interval, he went away with Deborah, but she ran into them by accident and stood gossiping merrily with him, quite forgetting the girl; when next they sat down, he sat next to her. Afterwards, while they ate and drank something, they took long looks at each other, drinking each other in, and there was something very bitter, cruel—almost detestation—in these glances. She saw in his eyes that he had appraised her, he could not help the attraction he felt but he was trying to repress it, by seeing her as she was—an aging belle, a faded animal; she felt her age, and dropped her eyes. Over his face all his thoughts passed like cloud shadows. Yet he turned his face up or away slightly so that she could still admire the powerful unlined throat and his traits; his eyes looked darker and larger. She could see he was trying to attract her.

When she got home with Deborah, she stood for a moment at the door, pretending to fumble with the key, feeling the great joy on her: I can love him, and he loves me. Then she went in with an ordinary suburban face and ordinary suburban remarks.

In the night, awake, she rose and fell, like a floating swimmer, on easygoing great waves of voluptuous joy, while thinking, Not for me, no, no, it's all nonsense; it's all past, not for me, no longer; how can it come now when it never came? It's an illusion.

She slept well, awakened early and had forgotten everything. She lay awake like a young healthy girl, happy, subdued, listening to the sound of birds outside; she heard the milkman; she was herself and suddenly remembered everything, jumped out of bed like a newly engaged girl, and ran from one thing to another, table to chair to filing case, hugging them—she hugged and kissed small things, she sat down at her desk in her nightgown, put her head in her arms and laughed for joy. Then she dressed to get to her work, and sat down to it, but when she heard Deborah call good-bye and go out to work, she hurried to Deborah's room, where she had installed a pretty dressing table with three mirrors, two of which, at the sides, could be turned all ways. How fresh she looked in the morning! She felt the little joyful waves begin again round her heart, leaping and beginning to swell round it, soon to drink it down in milk and honey. She smiled, looking downwards and picked up her daughter's hand mirror, peered in it, got her glasses and pored over her face and neck in the mirror.

It was a very long time since she had thought about these details. She was surprised to see that she had some small gray hairs; her skin was not so fine as she had imagined. The more she looked, the more disagreeable the looking became. Over the charming image she had carried with her from her girlhood of fine, smooth skin, rosy cheeks and smooth, shining hair, another coarse face had grown, heavy, but strong and real: herself in the present hour. Of course, he was already wishing he had never seen her, never given her that look, it was a ridiculous mistake; and they would meet next time with a cold, insulting play of manners. "Oh, the time will come when we'll laugh together over the whole business," she tried to say, in her old way.

The day went, she worked and forgot the incident. She had manuscripts to send in, and telephone calls to make. She went to bed quite tired and did not think of Waters at all.

In the morning she woke up with a dreamy smile, remembering the opera. She lay for a while going carefully over every moment of the evening, jumped out of bed, and going to the window, looked out at the little grassy field at the back. It had grown on some earth fallen off a little earthy bluff; grass hung over the head of the bluff, too. "Oh, world, oh, life, oh, time," she said, rejoicing. What poem was that? Where did it come from? She did not know what it was or when she had seen it. But soon she forbade the thought, thinking, more healthily now, with a pretty sad smile, How foolish, but how sweet! And so it was for a few days—she awoke each morning like a girl soon to be married and would lie feeling the sun on her arms and body, thinking, Soon not the sun but he—

During the week she began to feel tired, she was doing too much. She would sit at her desk with the work before her, doing nothing, merely annotating, reading, and her lifeblood beat fiercer and fiercer in her, till she found herself trembling, as if something stronger than herself had got inside, a turbine which had started out on a long voyage and was now well on its way churning up the shallow waters, satisfied in the deep waters. On the last day of the week she woke up feverish, after a feverish night, unable to think of anything but this miserable affair of her daughter's lover. She felt no love for her daughter, nor anyone; and hugged only one thought to her, that never, never again must she see this intruder, this man, this god, this tyrant, who had begun to squeeze the life out of her.

She got up slowly, trembling, hardly answered Deborah, who seemed to see nothing wrong with her, and when her daughter had gone, slowly put on her outdoor things, took her purse and went in to the city, each step, each stage seeming like an achievement. She would get to a bus stop and seem to rest; reach a well-known street, pause and feel at rest. Yet she was very anxious, very pressed. Dr. Mack's office was closed. The building was owned by a Greek restaurant-keeper, who was in his restaurant downstairs. He told her that Dr. Mack had gone away to northern India. She intended to "walk into Ladakh in Kashmir and beyond into Tibet; she may stay there. But I talked to her about Mount Athos and she is thinking of trying to get to the forbidden territory." He looked at Eleanor and said, "She has special clothing; it would not be easy to tell whether she is man or woman."

Eleanor went away. She felt she had no one to turn to. She

reached home and then something strange happened. It was just as if someone lifted the top off her head for a moment and let air in so that part of her brain blew cold. She lay down on a couch and was found asleep there some hours later by her daughter.

"I've been very, very cold, just as if I'd fallen into a c-c-crevasse in Tibet." She laughed a little. Deborah looked after her. She recovered, though she felt unwieldy, she who had been so limber. But she had her work to do and it was as if somehow she had made a wise decision: she was going to take things easier. A life full of work—good, good, she had accepted life. She could rest. She said to Deborah, "I kept to the rules, but the rules didn't keep me. But I hewed to the line; I cultivated my garden. So let us work, my pet. Soon I will have my pension and then I am going to write the story of my life; then I will really get down to it; and it will open some eyes."